The
Folding
Star

By the same author

Fiction
The Swimming-Pool Library

Translation
Racine: *Bajazet*

ALAN HOLLINGHURST

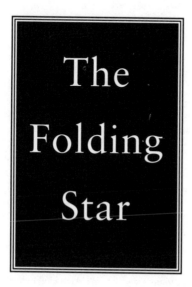

The
Folding
Star

PANTHEON BOOKS   NEW YORK

All rights reserved under International and Pan-American Copyright
Conventions. Published in the United States by Pantheon Books, a
division of Random House, Inc., New York. Originally published in
Great Britain by Chatto & Windus Limited, London.

Grateful acknowledgement is made to Warner / Chappell Music, Inc.,
for permission to reprint from "There's Nothing Like Marriage For
People" by Ira Gershwin and Arthur Schwartz, copyright © 1959,
1993 by Ira Gershwin Music and Arthur Schwartz Music. All rights on
behalf of Ira Gershwin Music administered by WB Music Corp.
All rights reserved. Used by permission.

Library of Congress Cataloging-in-Publication Data

Hollinghurst, Alan.
The folding star: a novel /Alan Hollinghurst.
p.   cm.
ISBN 0-679-43605-7
1. English teachers—Belgium—Flanders—Fiction.   2. British—
Belgium—Flanders—Fiction.   3. Gay men—Belgium—Flanders—
Fiction.   4. Gay men—England—Fiction.   I. Title.
PR6058.04467F65   1994
823'.914—dc20   94-5092
CIP

Manufactured in the United States of America
First American Edition

2 4 6 8 9 7 5 3 1

The author gratefully acknowledges the hospitality of the Djerassi Resident Artists Program, Woodside, California, where the early part of this novel was written.

Les grands vents venus d'outremer
Passent par la Ville, l'hiver,
Comme des étrangers amers.

Ils se concertent, graves et pâles,
Sur les places, et leurs sandales
Ensablent le marbre des dalles.

Comme des crosses à leurs mains fortes
Ils heurtent l'auvent et la porte
Derrière qui l'horloge est morte;

Et les adolescents amers
S'en vont avec eux vers la Mer!

Henri de Régnier

1
Museum
Days

1

A man was waiting already on the narrow island of the tram-stop, and I asked him falteringly about the routes. He explained politely, in detail, as if it were quite an interest of his; but I didn't take it in. I was charmed by his grey eyes and unnecessary smile, and the flecks of white paint on his nose and his dark-blond hair. I nodded and smiled back, and he fell into a nice pensiveness, hands in pockets, looking out down the empty street. I decided I would follow him.

The tram made its noiseless approach, headlamps on although the sky was still bright: the No 3, the Circular. We clambered up the steps together, I sought his help with the ticket-franking machine, which pinged as though I had won a prize. He swung into the seat behind me, and I felt his casual presence there as we trundled from stop to stop past churches and canals; when he whistled a little tune his breath stirred the hairs on the back of my neck. I thought, these are the evening routines which will soon be mine, the tug of an unknown suburb, or a bar, or a lover. I turned to ask him a further question I'd been nurturing, but it was just at the moment the tram seemed to lose its current and came to rest. A young woman was waiting, smoking, and gave a contented wave. My friend jumped off and trotted her away under his arm, whilst the doors folded to with a sigh.

I went on out, beyond the Stock Markets, hardly noticing, wondering what it was I had expected. For two or three stops I had the car to myself; I sensed the driver's puzzlement, and stared determinedly through the window at the featureless district we were passing through; then I panicked and rang the bell. When the tram moved off I found myself alone, and knew suddenly, as I had not done at the station or the hotel, that I had arrived in a strange city, in another country. Part of me shrank from the simple change of place.

There was no one else in the street that led up to the church, no one in the shabby square that its tower overhung. St Vaast: an ugly old hulk, with a porch tacked on, all curlicues and dropping yellow stucco, with a nest-littered pediment above. It was locked, of course: no last light glimmering from a vestry window – no choral society meeting after work to rehearse their director's own Te Deum or some minatory Flemish motets. I went on with a shiver.

From the further side of the square a lane led out to a still bleaker area. The street-lamps flickered into pink as I approached, but nothing else responded. The buildings were grandiose, like cinemas gone dark, the lower windows boarded up and plastered with posters for rock groups and the dud grins of politicians in the previous year's elections. The names of newspapers, printing works, engineering firms, in forward-looking Deco script, could still be read above the padlocked entrance grilles. There was a sense that cacophonous all-night business had been done here, and that the city, with a certain unflustered malevolence, had chosen its moment, and stilled it, and reasserted its own dead calm. At the street's end was the long vulgar front of a hotel, the Pilgrimage and Commercial, still with its brass entrance rail and the red and blue badges of motoring clubs. I climbed the steps, among the ghost-throng of arrivals, and peered through the splendid glass doors on to a shadowy half-acre of mud and rubble.

I was at a bar that was quite crowded, back in the middle of town. I'd had a few drinks, my sense of possibilities was bobbing up again, as well as a feeling of justified delay – I'd only just arrived, there was time for everything. I looked out through my cigarette-smoke and the coppery half-light at various strangers, some chatting, some embracing, others airily alone. It was called the Cassette. I had a presentiment of it in a month or two's time, when these first impressions of brass taps and bottle-glass windows and little varnished compartments would

4

be dulled, and I would take the manners of the two barmen, one taciturn, the other solicitous, for granted. I smiled at my own sense of anticipation, of being poised for change, ready to fall in love, and finding myself in the midst of this ordinary evening in the oddly mock-Tudor surroundings of the city's one gay bar.

I thought perhaps I should go and eat somewhere, but I ordered another beer first. They were quick and lightweight – you could have as many as you liked. I stretched and admitted how tired I was. I'd been up at dawn to leave, my mother speechlessly helping, unable to disguise her misery and anxiety as she drove me to the Dover train. I sympathised with her, and felt confirmed in the rightness of what I was doing. It was something I couldn't explain, although explanations were asked for. I had mumbled reluctantly about time running on, and about the job abroad being only temporary; but not about the darker sense of stepping already along the outward edge of youth, and looking back at those who were truly young with unwelcome eagerness and regret.

Just in front of me was a boy with thick fair hair and a long rather mouthy face – it must be a local type. I saw that the older man he was with couldn't quite believe his luck and was clinging to it with clumsy determination while it lasted, though the boy himself appeared relaxed by his frequent caresses. I caught the boy's eye from time to time, while he carried on talking as if he couldn't see me. I found myself idly imagining our life together.

A middle-aged man in a suit came and stood by me and started talking about his success in business; I was polite, as always, but he could probably tell I thought something wasn't right. He looked around a good deal and wanted seconding in his view of other people here; several times he backed into the pathway of kids who were going to the loo and then turned his apology into a hurried half-embrace. Sex was very firmly at the top of his agenda, but in some obscurely unflattering way he seemed not to regard me as a sexual possibility myself. He asked if I had any contact numbers. I said no, and then wondered what they would put you in contact with. I couldn't explain to him my odd sexual economy of the past few years, the fantasy-ridden continence, the sparse ration of intense and anonymous treats; I didn't know myself how it had come about. I wasn't sure I could expect much from my hotel, the Mykonos, which advertised in the English gay press. It had seemed the usual stuffy warren when I checked in, the tiny lounge sour and abandoned.

At the other end of the bar, near the door, a man smiled at me quickly and sceptically, looked away, looked back. I stopped off by him for one more drink, offered him one, puzzling for a moment over my fold of high-denomination notes, the unfamiliar portraits of the makers of Belgian history. There was a dangerous quality to him, square-jawed, handsome, offering some unspecified challenge, spittle at the corner of his mouth. He could have been an off-duty soldier, nervily alone, counting on the power of his build and his close-cropped head. I felt the hollow burn of attraction in my stomach, but he didn't give away what he felt. We stood close together, both of us also looking past each other, so that I saw him against the movement of the men beyond him, an arm around a waist, fingers that lightly touched a cheek. The surly barman, jowelled and braceleted, pulled the beers and muttered something to my friend, whom I watched pretending not to hear. The boy reached out his hand for the glass and I glimpsed tattooed letters on his four fingers: R, O, S, E.

He was quiet and tense, and didn't react with much interest to anything I said. I felt his attention searching for a focus in the crowd behind me; or he looked into his glass in the grip of some bitter memory. I asked if he was in the Navy, and he waved his marked hand dismissively, without saying yes or no. I began to wonder why I'd bothered with him. Then with a little smile that made me think it was all shyness, that the tenderness he sought involved some cost to his pride, he said, 'So tell me what you do.'

I told him I was a teacher, I'd come out here to teach some boys English.

This didn't thrill him, it only ever touched those who had liked being taught: I saw a kind of wariness in his eyes, as if he might have owed me an essay.

'Do you come from London then?'

6

'A bit south of there. You won't have heard of it. Well, it's called Rough Common.'

'Then why did you come here, for god's sake?'

I suppose I should have foreseen such casual and incurious asking of the hardest questions. I had the sense again of being guided deep down by motives too tenuous to explain. It was something to do with growing up in a singer's household, to the daily accompaniment of art, and with this little old city being famous for its music and pictures; I couldn't quite admit to myself the uncertainty I felt already at its deadness, its air of a locked museum, the recognition that what had happened had all been centuries ago. I said, 'Well, I wanted to use my Dutch – my mother's family was Dutch, I studied it at school. I think you learn these things, then you discover a use for them.' Over the past month of muttered revision I had imagined conversations that ran more smoothly, where the cheery exempla of the grammar book gave way to passionate declarations.

He started to refer to all the money I had, and I said, 'But that's everything I've got, I'm terribly poor!' I patted the pad of notes zipped in my jacket pocket and he looked at me with a friendly scepticism, that said he knew about the traveller's cheques folded among my shirts in the hotel cupboard, and my reliable background, how I could never fall through the net. And it was with a little bourgeois shock that I finally read the message of his eyes, the pupils shrunk to black pinpoints. I didn't know whether to mention it or not, wasn't totally sure I was right. Drugs frightened me and moved me to an impotent desire to help.

I bought both the following rounds – I couldn't pretend that they weren't within my means; he accepted them with a hint of irritation, as though to have thanked me would have been an admission of his dependency. I was the victim of a con, in a way, someone who didn't know him, a fresh fool, on the first night of my capricious little exile, drunk and hungry for contact. Sometimes he scratched at his chest with a thumbnail, and the tiny crackle of chest-hairs under the cotton of his polo-shirt filled me with a wondering sense of his whole body, as keen as if he'd been leaning by me naked.

7

I offered him a cigarette, but he shook his head contemptuously. 'I've got to get hold of some money,' he said, looking away from me, pretending to accept my plea of poverty. I saw it was all over, I hadn't worked out for him; he hadn't even told me his name. I thought of him simply as Rose. Rose of the Rose Tattoo! I suspected it wasn't worth explaining the literary joke. I muttered, 'What is it you're on?'

He was silent, I'd have thought rather vain if I hadn't felt his desperation. 'Bad stuff,' he said at last, firmly, but he wouldn't reveal what. Then, with unconvincing interest, 'So who are you going to be teaching English to?'

'A couple of boys, to start with.'

'Just two.'

'Rather difficult boys.' He nodded. 'They've been in some sort of trouble,' I assured him. 'The older one looks very sexy.'

Rose gave a little snort. 'I should have known that was your game.'

'No, no. I can show you if you like.' And it was true I had his papers on me, like a keepsake of a lover, of a contact, perhaps, whom I was yet to meet. I pulled the envelope from my inner pocket, and took out the folded sheet with the photo-booth image attached – Luc Altidore, 17, interests History, the Arts. It was spread on the damp counter, offered slightly anxiously to Rose, as though I were searching for this boy and thought he might recognise the picture and give me a lead. Surely no one could forget that pale mask, with the large dry lips and the hair falling forward and a mutinous blankness to the eyes in the camera's flash, as if dissenting from his own beauty. I recalled distantly having taught him already in dreams, I had lived through the slow-burning hours of tuition face to face with him.

I had become less likeable to my companion, as if I had already gained power over the kid through the corrupt persuasions of literature.

'I may have to do other work,' I said. 'I'll need the cash. Besides, I don't want to read books all day.' I stroked his forearm, which I felt actually vibrate with the mastered desire to withdraw it.

'Why not?'

I hesitated and said, 'Books are a load of crap.'

'You're really wrong,' he said fiercely. 'You're lucky. You're a teacher. Books are your life.' And he walked away from me, leaving me with nothing but the private and lonely satisfaction of my quotation, which perhaps proved his final point.

When I came back from the lav I saw him making for the exit, his arm round the shoulder of the suited bore I'd escaped from earlier, whose face was flushed and confused at his almost too sudden change of luck.

In the austere Town Museum I picked up Cherif, a Moroccan, but born in Paris and uncircumcised. I felt a little out of step among those chaste northern saints and inward-looking Virgins – there wasn't one of them that welcomed you or held your gaze as the dark-eyed Italian gods and holy men so often did. Absurd, but I wanted a greeting, even across five hundred years. Here everyone looked down or away, in gestures of reproachful purity. The pious, unflattering portraits, too, of capped and wimpled worthies, were proudly abstinent. They drew respectful crowds of Sunday couples in rustling waterproofs (the day had made an uncertain start).

They were not to Cherif's taste, however. He was mooching about, shaking his head and scratching his balls, in front of a hellish-paradisal Bosch. Later he told me he had cruised men there before: he didn't know much about painting, but he knew the deeper drift of museum days, the art compulsion of the single man, reflections in the glass that screens some dark old martyrdom, the licence to loiter and appraise, the tempo of pursuit from room to room . . . I came alongside and we pointed in turn at the viler mutations in the Garden of Delights: the pig-bottomed lady, the slug gentleman, the whore with lobster claws. My friend pushed back the staid tweed cap which gave his brown features and dull black curls a touching air of displacement and grinned at me in a manner unclouded by questions of art history.

We wandered on past the sour sermons of still-lifes (the fly on the lemon, the perishable plenty) and across the hall into the deserted galleries where later pictures hung: waxen historical tableaux, brown cottage scenes, dusks of phosphor and violet, the Sphinxes and Athenas of the local Symbolists. And one of these did extend a troubled greeting – a woman with disordered red hair, ruby ear-rings, one breast uncovered: I stooped to read the printed title: 'Edgard Orst: "Jadis Hérodias, quoi encore?"' To the badged butch lady-guard, who stepped from one room to the next to keep us in view, we must have seemed a couple tired of each other's company, killing time, hoping that art might help us through a rainy Sunday, but finding ourselves as bored by the pictures as she was. Cherif caught my eye and I swallowed at the secret certainty of our plan.

Even at the Mykonos, I thought, Cherif, in his brown leather jerkin and working-man's boots, might appear too rough and set on mischief to be admitted. But that was only British class pudeur – the receptionist nodded to him equally as the key was handed over. (And then I thought, perhaps Cherif had brought his custom here before; and wasn't there something shrewd and cold-blooded about the desk-clerk himself, doubling and trebling as barman and hooverer of the TV lounge?)

The moment I had locked the door he was on to me, chewing and stuffing my mouth and knocking my glasses up skew-whiff over the top of my head. He was an animal, that great thing for someone else to be. A second or two later he was grinding one hand up and down on my bum and with the other guiding me down to rub his cock where it stood out hard and at an angle in his loose old jeans.

On the way from the Museum we had crossed a bridge above swans and the putter of an empty bâteau-mouche, the commentary running on regardless, when he had suddenly held out in his palm a little packet with a rubber's squashed ring contour. I didn't mind the wordless confirmation, but I turned my head away, too full of feeling for this boy, who had only been my friend for twenty minutes, who felt nothing for me but was so unhesitatingly himself, a little overweight, his upper lip and chin roughened already with shadow. Now he was sitting in my lap, riding on me with a certain urgent disregard – I swept my hands across his sleek and trusting back, and reached up to shoulders where muscles powerful from work gathered and dispersed. I was glad he couldn't see me, gaping and heavy-hearted with praise for him.

We were on the end of the bed, and I hugged up close to look round his shoulder and into the full-length mirror. Our eyes met there, but he was a little bothered by that intimacy. Then, as I was climbing to the end, he got right off me and stood on the floor. I scrambled up too, confused for a moment by my own reflection in the glass, as if without my specs the image needed to be blinked back into focus, or as if a sixth sense revealed a face within my face, ghostly features caught in the very silvering of the mirror. Cherif took a half-step forward, and fell against the glass with flattened palms. A sequence of sounds emerged from it, or from a distance beyond it; and then for a couple of seconds we saw ourselves dematerialise and a perspective open up within – a shuttered room with stacks of chairs, lit from the side by an opening and closing door. Cherif was sighing and laughing quietly, and sat down again on the bed while I pulled on my trousers, hopping and treading on the legs.

I had been exploring the city rather fast and anxiously, referring on and off to a tourist map which omitted side-streets and alleys and showed the famous buildings in childishly out-of-scale drawings. Its poetic effect was to give me the shape of the town as a fifteenth-century engineer, expert in dikes and piles, might have shown it in plan to a ruling count: a mounted opal veined with waterways and suspended from the broad ribbon of the sea-canal. The industrial park, the post-war poor estates, the spent suburb of my first-night wanderings, were shown as fields, confirming the sense I had at every corner that the whole city aspired to be an artist's impression.

It wasn't a big town, and its great monuments, like the pinnacled elevations jostling on the map, were out of all proportion to the streets, courtyards and canals beneath them. The tapering, windowless monolith of the tower of St John's and the ugly green spirelets with which a turn-of-the-century surveyor

11

had capped the ancient tower of the Cathedral were mere satellites to the legendary altitudes of the Belfry. From far off, in Ostend, when we had cleared the cranes and the edge of town, these three appeared across the plain as a mysterious trinity, with the Belfry, growing epoch by epoch in battlemented stages towards its octagonal crown, the most doggedly heaven-storming of all.

Today the sky was low and the air fenlike and damp when I crossed the Grote Markt and saw the maestro of the famous carillon — a shovel-bearded young man in corduroy jacket and knee-breeches like a figure from some ingenious Flemish clock — unlock the gate and start to climb the two hundred stairs to his console in the clouds. Even in the Grote Markt, beneath the stepped gables of the best restaurants and the gilded angels who had paused on top of the Town Hall and raised their trumpets high over taxi-ranks and bus-stands, there was nothing happening. A few visitors wandered out of the glassed-in arcade of the Tourist Office, but the school holidays were almost over and the visitors were studious couples. A few women clambered with supermarket bags into one or other of the waiting buses that showed the names of outlying villages. Sometimes the silent tram came through. These were the days and weeks of a ceremonial square. And then the carillon banged out its lifeless rendering of a folksong or hymn.

It was the silence that followed that was most challenging. As I went round with my list of addresses the stillness of the town fused with my new suspicion of being watched, of something calculating in the mid-morning emptiness. I found myself coming back with relief to those two or three streets lined with ordinary shops, red flashes of special offers on sausage or coffee on the windows, outfitters and stationers cheerful with skirts, satchels and coloured pens for the *rentrée*. And among the red-nosed Brueghel boys with bicycles there were others who looked bored and stylish and desirable. I found myself marvelling that they lived here.

I saw five rooms in all, but chose without hesitation. The others were such vessels of loneliness, or else too pinned and stifled with rules and considerations for someone who had finally left home. I had a horror of lying there, forbidden to smoke, listening to the cistern filling overhead. It was usually a house-wife, garrulous and noncommittal, who would let me in and take me up, observing resentfully as I felt the bed or opened the hanging cupboard. In two of the houses other pallid lodgers were caught on their way between bedroom and lavatory and given a warning. I hardly saw Cherif as a welcome regular in such a place, or the romance of my new life unfurling under such surveillance.

The room I chose was so hidden away that it gave me the sensation of having entered, with dreamlike suddenness, into the secret inner life of the city. On the street it was a doctor's establishment, a bare white house with a brass plate polished almost flat. At the side a gated passage led through into a shallow courtyard: the doctor's residence backed on to a far older range of buildings — rough pink brick, steep roofs with the high-up doors and hoists of warehouse attics. Like a tiny Cambridge college, it had two stairways, one at either end, leading up to disused workshops, storerooms, and, on the second floor, two sets of rooms that were let. One had just been taken by some Spanish girls; the other, which was cheap but primitive, was mine; the old doctor (who still saw a few patients in his retirement) told me in French how pleased he was to have an Englishman there.

All down one side of the room ran unusually deep cupboards, each with an enamel number, and a door that shut with a boom. I could only occupy them all by putting underpants in one, shoes in two, jerseys in number three; when number four was opened my leather jacket was revealed like a historic vestment in a cathedral treasury, flanked by the monstrances of my special bottles and jars. Each shelf had been neatly lined with old newspaper, held in place by drawing-pins; I turned my head sideways to scan the time-silvered sports news and antique auto-tests. The facing wall was a wooden partition, rough with nail-holes and nail-heads hammered in, that made me wonder what had been stored here, what work had been done here, and when it had come to an end. It seemed an encouraging setting for my own projects, the bits of writing I was going to take up again. Behind the partition was the sleeping area, choked by a high iron bedstead in which three people could have slept

13

abreast. Outside, at the head of the stairs, was a little wash-room, with a sink and a fragment of mirror, and a rudimentary shower that dripped and left a rusty stain.

As soon as I was alone I set out my dictionaries, English, French and Dutch, and my notebooks and inks; I checked the crockery – two of everything, which seemed another good sign – and switched on the creaking electric plate. I'd persuaded myself it didn't matter there was no heating – only a little blower that roared and ate electricity. I bounced on the bed and set its loose finials jingling.

At the front of my main room a leaded dormer looked down into the courtyard and across to the shuttered upper floor of the doctor's house; but at the back there was a big sash-window. It looked westward, across to the mouldering apse of the church of St Narcissus; on the map the drawing of its singular brick tower and pointed lantern obliterated my house and the garden that lay between us. I heaved open the heavy frame and stared into the silence of the leafy space below. On the left was the ivy-covered height of the cinema's blank back wall and on the right a canal in which the rotting water-door and tall barred windows of some ancient institutional building were reflected. The garden itself was not a churchyard, although the church pre-sided over it and someone had chopped back the alder at its base and poisoned the creeper that still blackly covered its sunken outhouse or boiler-room. It was hard to imagine who – there seemed to be no door into the garden, and where the canal lay by the far wall of the church I could just make out fanned black spikes. The grass between the fruit trees had been scythed and left. Craning round I saw the blue ribbon of a toilet-roll thrown from a height and caught in the branches. And there was something I couldn't quite see, a little stone figure of some kind, herm or saint, satyr or cupid, sheltered by leaves and ankle-deep in hay. I wanted to get down there, and then a moment later felt I would rather leave it unvisited for ever. The beauty of it lay not so much in itself as in its solitude, like any high-walled place in the middle of a town – deaf old widow's garden or padlocked grave-ground of the Jews or Trinitarians.

Half-way down the stairs I stopped, hearing an earlier echo than Cambridge and my first independence. A church tower,

14

somewhere in Kent, its narrow door left open: there's a re-hearsal, part of a festival, and my father is singing in it. I'm a little boy, clambering up among the junk the verger and cleaners have stacked at the foot of the spiral ascent, mops and brooms, rolled-up banners, tumbled flower-tripods with their dry Oasis and bent cowls of chicken-wire. Dust and secrecy. I haven't been missed. I go up and up with my hands on the steps above, until there's the slit of a window. When I look out over the churchyard, our Humber drawn in by the lych-gate, the drop of the land beyond trees, I feel afraid, giddy, I have gone too far. And then the beautiful tenor sound starts up, high and untroubled, probably Bach, though maybe something lesser, I know nothing of all that, only the rise and fall of my father's sung line, which I have the illusion of seeing, like a gleaming trace across the shadows. Without knowing why I sit down with a bump and start to cry.

The bar Cherif had named was a good walk away, along the broad deserted quays of broad deserted canals, linked by rare stone bridges. The cloud had lifted in the afternoon and in the cool that followed there was a first hint of autumn. I passed a small park with empty benches and an odd dreamy restlessness in its trees. Then there were wide wooden boathouses, broken-down cottages and dogs and children playing who looked un-accustomed to strangers. I wondered for a minute if I had gone wrong, but there was Wanne's bar; there was a curtain inside the door, and beyond it a narrow brown room with men at the counter listening to a football match and abruptly shouting their disgust. The long-haired barman dealt with me neutrally, or it may have been with mild hostility.

I needed something to do, and rehearsed and updated my Flemish on a discarded newspaper, which slowly revealed itself as rancorously right-wing. I drank my beer too fast, and ordered another. I wanted to be with Cherif again, the whole day's search had been leading back to him, and flat anger settled in my stomach as he didn't turn up; and then amazement at myself and my baseless belief that my needs could for once have been so easily met. Whenever the door swung open I knew it would be him and swallowed my distress at the sight of his friendly face and everything it offered, and it was always some-one else, a regular who won a curt, delayed greeting as he was absorbed into the group around the bar.

With the exception of a woman in a dressing-gown who looked in from the back to complain, there were only men here. Yet it certainly didn't seem like a gay bar – unless it was some specialist working men's kind of ugly set. At last I nerved myself to gesture the barman down. Did he know someone called Cherif, French Moroccan, a docker . . .? At which he made a very clear announcement that what do you call him Cherif was not welcome there, or any of his type. I walked out at once and started back the way I had come, the same children turning and watching as I passed. The early evening was high and receptive and unsurprised.

The silence of neglect that enveloped the old church of St Nar-cissus was broken only by its hourly chime and – as I discovered that night – a six-hourly broken-toothed carillon, which donged its way heartlessly through a hymn that I hoped had ended each time it reached the irregular pauses of its missing notes. It had me awake at midnight and at six, with a stab of despair about last evening; I worked through wearying punitive fantasies about Cherif that fizzled out each time in shallow sleep.

At ten I went round, through a gleaming holiday haze, to the Altidores' house. They lived in Long Street, which ran out from the centre of town in an elegant, endless curve; I counted ahead of me and picked out No 39 before I got to it: tall and reserved, with a high basement and four or five steps climbing steeply to the black front door. I noticed I was repressing my curiosity about my future, coming to our first encounter with the empty mind and last-minute turn of speed that are a way of meeting a challenge; though all the time the boy's touchingly sullen image was in the air before me, flickered, like a subliminal projection, over spires and gables, while his surname exercised its glimmer-ing romance: Altidore, it was a gothic belfry in itself, or else a knight-errant out of *The Faerie Queene* . . .

Luc's mother answered my short but frantic-sounding ring; I stepped into an interior I had never guessed at, and which I saw at once was the shrine and workshop of an obsession. She must have been the most prolific needlewoman in Belgium. The hall, and then the sitting-room she pushed me into, were festooned with her work. Large-scale hangings, or saggings, depicting the sort of subjects – ships, timbered inns, corps de ballet – that are favoured in jigsaw puzzles for their monotonous difficulty rather than their beauty, were the mere backdrop for floral fire-screens, beaded and bobbled tablecloths and sofas so heaped with wildly coloured cushions as to leave only the tiniest area for the sitter's bottom. I ambled round amongst it all, giving speechless shrugs of appreciation, my gaze running for relief up to the high ceiling, though even there a woven affair, implying an almost Victorian suggestibility, extended like a growth down the chains of the chandelier. Following her politely through to the kitchen to get coffee I glimpsed the dyeing pantry, where hanks of red and orange wool hung dripping into buckets and giving off a raw smell.

Her manner was vague, disappointed and accidentally bitchy, so that I excused her rudeness or took it as a joke. Nearly six feet tall, in a mauve crocheted frock, with long lilac-stockinged legs and buckled witch's shoes, hair neat and lifeless round a small, pale-powdered face, brisk, apprehensive, humourless, painfully artistic: I saw the absurdity of her at once but thought I might grow to find her sadly sympathetic. When I declined a tiny sugared cake she said, 'Yes, you should lose weight, ten pounds at least, no cake for you', and put out just one for herself with the calm propriety of someone who would never be fat the way I was getting already. 'I am very busy,' she told me: 'I am working on a new altar-cloth for the Cathedral. You mustn't keep me for too long.'

I smiled and said, 'Of course not.' I began to wonder if Luc too might be very tall and skinny.

'I'm glad to see you alone though, while Luc is away,' she said, as if enlisting me in some operation that was peculiarly delicate and dreadful; though that 'away' was what echoed through my thoughts and resolutions. Away! So the pressure was off, the anxious gambits of the first conversation had been needlessly rehearsed. It seemed he had gone to stay with friends on the coast, no one could stop him, though Mrs Altidore had begged him to take some books, and held, frowningly, to the belief that he would be studying. She spoke about him in a tone of careless despair; but checked herself several times, to remind us both that he was clever, cleverer than almost anyone. He was wayward, troubled, unknowable; but then again he was gentle, introspective and beyond question a good boy. When she despaired I was full of conventional reassurance, modest confidence, I would see what I could do; when she withdrew into sudden solidarity with her son I found I was faintly jealous, and wondered how I could free him from her multi-coloured web.

She told me Luc had been a scholar at the college of St Narcissus, the province's oldest and most exclusive Jesuit school, where his friends were the children of various important lawyers and bankers whose names meant nothing to me. Last summer, however, following on an obscure incident, which it would be 'too great a waste of both our times' to go into, he had been required to leave. Now there was the worry of his finishing his education: Mrs Altidore thought she had persuaded him to try for university – perhaps in England: she had heard that Dorset had a European exchange scheme and a way with sensitive misfits. Luc himself was keen to go abroad. My task was to facilitate his escape – to polish his English conversation, already near-perfect, apparently, and to widen his knowledge of English literature: Milton, Wordsworth, Margaret Drabble and whatever further authors I considered significant.

Before I left she asked me what other pupils I had and seemed satisfied that as yet I had only one and so might really be able to devote myself to the cause of Luc. She wanted to know who the second one was; and raised her eyebrows and tilted her head when I said it was Marcel Echevin; she thought him a suitable stable-mate even if hopelessly dim. 'Don't try to cut corners by seeing Echevin at the same time as my son,' she advised. 'They are wholly incompatible. I hope I can trust you.'

*

18

The weather had turned breezy and hot, ideal September days, the pale-backed leaves quivering and glinting like spring, and I would have left town too, given the chance – joined my pupil at the beach in the flimsy pretence of studying a book. But I had the other one to see and my living to earn. It was hard to identify the impulse to work among the other sensations of merely being on holiday. I wrote a letter to my old friend Edie, telling her all about my rapid new start with Cherif but skirting round the blunt humiliation of the rendezvous at Wanne's bar. Also to my mother, but sticking more closely to matters of weather and diet. I felt them both in their different ways watching for me, half-hiding their concern at what I'd suddenly done. And once or twice I thought of them all, and the pub and the common and the whole suburban sprawl – half a map, half a picture, like the tourist hand-out here but infinitely draggled and banal – with a sudden heart's thump or two of longing.

Young Echevin came to see me after lunch: he was late, couldn't find the place, had disturbed the doctor's difficult old housekeeper (who asked rather pointedly that it shouldn't happen again), and sat pink and wheezing through the scheduled hour of our conversation. He was a severe asthmatic, as I knew from his father's letter, and had been absent from school for much of the previous year, gazing out from a dustless sanatorium near Brussels. I felt a twinge of pity for him, and remembered schoolfellows obscurely stigmatised by diabetes or inhibiting allergies. The same involuntary unlovely quality hung about Marcel; plus he was fat and anxious and maladroit. His asthma provided the main topic of discussion, and gave me glimpses of the boy's tame, glass-cabined world; it had limited his experience cruelly. Several staples of these lessons – sport, nature, what we had done in the pollinous summer holidays – were almost inaccessible to him; his own August had been spent playing video games (and for a minute his vocabulary took on an impenetrable self-confidence). A new drug had been his salvation – that and television, which had given him a certain scrambled knowledge of current affairs that he was too incurious and shortwinded to make sense of. Our primary rule – that we spoke only in English – was frequently broken; 'I do not know, I do not understand' was his timid refrain. And I was

19

recollecting my tutorial manner, out of the vacant social politeness that our chit-chat parodied, and a sudden pedantry or loss
of patience which alarmed him and brought him close to tears.
Of course his other tutors, for maths and history and so on, all
talked to him in friendly Flemish, they were local people who
shared his world of reference. It took me a moment to see how
alien I was – I felt myself being dreaded, in what I hoped was an
unusual way, and not being sure whether to live up to it or try
to soften it down.

Marcel wore bright-coloured kids' leisure-wear, as though he
was usually out on a bike or a skateboard, and had a huge
wristwatch with various rotating bezels and inset dials that
might have been of use to a sports coach, deep-sea diver or
trader on the international markets. He looked at it with dis-
arming frequency, so that I began to ask him each time how
long was left. I was as keen as he was for the hour to be up.

The shock came towards the end, when I asked him how long
he'd suffered from asthma, and if he knew why he had it, a two-
part question which I felt was unwise with a beginner, it might
fluster him and only one half would get answered. He looked
away and I saw a change in the colour of his unhappiness. 'Yes,
I can tell why,' he said. 'And when.'

I didn't quite make the story out at first, I was chivvying him
and making him repeat words without knowing I was taking
him back, like some kinder and wiser analyst, to the scene of a
childhood tragedy. It turned out he had been shopping in the
town with his mother: he was only six, it was ten years ago, in
the summer. They had gone into a florist's and were waiting to
be served, when he saw a bee hovering around his mother's
shopping-basket. He knew she mustn't be stung by a bee, but
she was talking to a friend and she told him not to interrupt. He
tried to flap it away, but only frightened it, and as his mother
turned to him it flew up and stung her in the face. She groped
for the antidote in her handbag, but she'd brought the wrong
bag. She fell to the floor in front of Marcel, and within a minute
she was dead.

His asthma had started a few months later, and was triggered
especially by flowers. There was a sort of pride in his possession
of these facts. He said that his father loved flowers, but had

never had them in the house since. I asked, with what was clearly a suspicious sweetness, what it was his father did; and learned that he was the keeper of the little museum of Orst's paintings, out on an edge of town I hadn't visited, but where five or six old windmills had been renovated on top of a high dike. Marcel said firmly that he did not like Orst's work.

I drank quite a bit in my room, tippling through my litre of duty-free Cap and Badge, and went out about eleven to the Bar Biff, a club in the basement of a house right next to the Cathedral. The unwary or short-sighted pilgrim might easily have mistaken it for the entrance to the Crypt (10th Century) and the shrine of St Ernest. The street outside was almost deserted, with an occasional late walker or pair of denim-jacketed boys pausing to peer through the locked grilles of electrical shops. Warm, too, with a scent from the trees that seemed to insist again on a last frail summery possibility. I felt quite good in my leather jacket, charcoal 501s and tipped, tight-laced black Oxfords; nervous, but adrift and irresponsible.

I'd seen the club extolled in a local listings magazine, and hovered with dismayed recognition over its central 'portfolio' of skinny lads in shorts and swimwear and reports on fabulous nights at discos: the flashlit shots of the two or three cutest boys there and the overweight barman with his arm round a peroxided stripling were indistinguishable from those in the British gay press recalling the great time had at Kid or Zoom! or Croydon's ritzy Blue Fedora a desolate few weeks ago. Once inside the heavy sound-proofed door with its little wired judas I was in a place so familiar that I would not have been surprised to see my old friends Danny and Simon reaching through to lift drinks over the shoulders of those obstinately seated at the bar, or stalking and jumping around the tiny dance-floor. There was the same mad delusion of glamour, the same overpriced tawdriness, the same ditsy parochialism and sullen lardy queenery, and underneath it all the same urgency and defiance. We none of us wanted a palace: we liked this humming little hell-hole with its atrophied rules and characters, its ogres and mascots.

21

Not that I could identify too completely. I was a newcomer, an unknown, a holidaymaker perhaps or shy débutant. A few heads turned, I thought, a few remarks were made. But as I got my bottle of expensively fashionable beer and wandered round I knew I hadn't gone down a bomb: something hard and proud in me wanted to shine, something homey and self-effacing was relieved I didn't. And of course your regulars don't all look for novelty: maybe they'd like to score with some strange angelic beauty but they know that heavy truck-driver with brown teeth and a famous dick will give them what they've been waiting for all week. The older men in the corner look with envy at the youngsters, but with a kind of disillusion too.

I leant against a mirrored pillar and kept my eye on a bunch of kids who hung around mocking and caressing each other, sipping quickly and shiftily at Cokes and beers and bopping about with a knowing coy beauty on the edge of the floor. They seemed more in their element than anyone in the dismal thin Euro-pop interspersed with tired, tired disco classics which to them perhaps still had point and exhilaration. Is it legal? I found myself wondering as I watched a muscly little lad in a string vest and baggy hitched-up jeans licking blond froth from the black down on his upper lip and holding forth hoarsely like a schoolyard gangster. He couldn't be more than sixteen, surely? But that was okay here, unlike at home; it was the classical, commonplace good sense of Europe. I thought I'd never wanted anyone so much. I upset myself by being obvious about him, so that his mates noticed me staring at him and he turned and made a gesture with his tongue behind his upper teeth. I couldn't quite tell if it was mocking or provocative, it might have been the sort of insult mentioned bafflingly in Shakespeare. I was absorbed in my own excitement and unaware of the routine spectacle it presented to others: I followed him when he went to the lavatory, but he peed in the lock-up stall and I heard him hawking expressively as he did so. I hung back and looked in the mirror at Edward Manners, the pudging, bespectacled English teacher twice his age.

Back in the bar and with another beer I had a man of flawless, dead good looks shift up to me and start talking with the banal sing-song that in the outside world would indicate a long

22

and comfortable acquaintance and here was used as a short cut to a short one. There was something fascinating about his blond blandness, skin stretched over wide high cheekbones, long hair starting forward and then swept back in a layered and possibly lacquered wave. It was hard to guess how old he was: his skin was perfect, but when he smiled it crinkled into a hundred lines around his grey eyes. Otherwise he was oddly classless and unmarked by normal wear and tear. His clothing was casual and yet dressy: over the V of a T-shirt a pink chemise with buttons, pockets and epaulettes, and pleated bum-hugging slacks that appeared to shelter, down front, something of remarkable, even tedious length. When he told me he was a model, it all made sense.

A man who is always smiling prompts a kind of mistrust. I wished Ty (as he absurdly claimed to be called) would allow himself more of the expressionlessness to which his features were suited, of which they were in fact the ideal expression. But he was orthodontically perfect as well, and perhaps he had calculated that that mattered more. Just how fastidious can you get? I asked myself and we danced together for a bit, though I broke off for a drink when a slow number was gloatingly announced by the DJ. I asked him what Ty was short for, and he looked at me as if I was being very silly, and said, 'Just Ty!'

We hung about together: though Ty was game for running through our earlier conversation a second time, and I pretended I couldn't hear him through the noise of the music. He was obsessed by his career and seemed to feel destined for success in London, and that I would somehow be able to bring this about. It was all arranged that I was going to look at his portfolio and let him know what I thought. We seemed to roam back and forth over a boundary between the functional nonsense of pick-up talk and some other elaborate fantasy of his own in which he was obliviously involved, and which turned around extended fashion shoots in tropical countries, rewarded by enormous fees. I took notice, though, when he started talking about the boys in the shadowy table-booth across the floor. I had deliberately kept my back to them but turned with false casualness, ashamed to feel ashamed: I knew it would be the kid I'd fallen for that Ty was pointing out. And there he was, curled up with a skinnier, long-haired friend and eating his face in the laborious public way that adolescents have ... leaving me eaten up too with envy and irritation. I swung back and muttered to Ty (I saw him uncertain if I was angry or joking); then kissed him, briefly, and got some consolation from that: he smiled, as if to say that his charm had now been acknowledged and succumbed to. We got another drink, and I was feeling quite drunk and had reached the stage of deciding to go with this guy, the all-too-common pragmatic decision. I was trying to see all that was best in him: the teeth, the skin, probably a good body worked on in gym and sunbed, which was more than I could offer, as was what he showed in his pants, and yet I felt entirely superior to him, with a kind of superiority I was too superior even to have given him a glimpse of. Then Cherif was standing in front of us grinning and leaned close to embrace us both at the same time. His breath smelt of dope.

I was cold to him and resisted his assumption that I would be pleased to see him. He ruffled my hair, and said with mock solemnity to Ty, 'Bonsoir, M'sieur Mouchoir,' and Ty laughingly but blushingly told him to piss off. 'So you've met up with my friend M'sieur Mouchoir,' he said to me; I supposed it was a tedious old joke to do with fashion and modelling – I merely shrugged. Cherif was nodding and chuckling and very slow. 'How are you, my friend Edward?' he asked.

I gave an unimpressed smile and said, 'I missed you the other night at Wanne's bar.'

'Oh, I can't go there,' he said, as if objecting to a suggestion I had made myself.

'It wasn't a very good idea to ask me to meet you there, then, was it?'

Cherif was absolutely opaque, and I wondered for a moment if he was struggling to repair some real lapse of memory; but his crude survivor's evasion proved he was not. 'Why are men with glasses so sexy?' he said. He looked to the handsome, I thought lens-wearing, Ty: 'What do you think, Mouchoir?' Ty merely shrugged in his turn.

'I don't like being made a fool of,' I said, but I was already warming to Cherif's hand moving gently on the small of my back and could see and feel the pleasure of going home with

24

him just as certainly as I could envisage the meaningless and un-arousing performance I might have gone through with Ty.

There was a period of semi-tactful adjustment, in which Ty's smile did overtime to mask the indignity of having me literally snatched from his arms by someone he knew already and who mocked him in such a childish way. But I wasn't at all sure why he had singled me out in the first place, or what feelings were hidden by his rather beautiful exterior. You'd think he would easily be able to score with some other person here – but it was true that none had approached him or greeted him in passing. He seemed to me suddenly isolated in his groomed preoccupa-tion and from the moment Cherif arrived I was aware of his seeking out another partner – his own reflection in the night-club's smoky mirrors. It was, I sensed, a relationship deeper than the one he might have with me or any other dancer in the Bar Biff.

2

Cherif thumped me awake next morning and excitedly told me to look out of the window. I was too slow, and missed the funny thing he wanted me to see. But a minute or two later as I was groping round and squirting a clown's beard of shaving-foam on to my jaw he called me back to where he was standing in just his vest at the half-open shutter. He had his friendly crooked hard-on.

Over to the right from one of the high barred windows of that institutional building which had so far remained silent and dark, three boys were peeing into the canal. They stood up on the windowsill, pressed against the bars, and directed their dying arcs up and out — presumably in a contest to see who could reach the furthest. I watched them finish and stand down whilst the shaving-foam thinned in an almost noiseless crepitation over my stubble. In a moment or two another trio took up their positions, we heard a command quite strictly barked inside, and the one on the left was away already. It must almost have been a false start. The other two followed a few seconds later, first in hesitant spurts and tinkles, but growing in confidence until for a while all three were at full cock, like a guard of honour. I don't think any of them reached our side of the canal, but number one made the finest impression and had the greatest capacity: he was still going strong as the other two's offerings dwindled and trailed home across the water and a breeze caught them and frayed their thinning plumes.

I understood for the first time that this patched-up brick barracks of a place was the school of St Narcissus itself and that today being the *rentrée* the young gentlemen were reasserting some immemorial right. Cherif and I watched a couple more rounds, until the novelty began to wear off and a hand-bell was

26

heard tolling. Then I realised that there would be this new element in my life, and that across the little lost garden below, where nothing but a blackbird ever stirred among the leaves, there would come week in week out the noises of a school: the bells, the blurred unison of lessons and chapel, the scraping back of a hundred chairs, the abrupt silences and eruptions of racket.

It was clear on the streets, too, as I walked over to the Altidores', that things had changed: a flat-footed straggler with his shirt-tails hanging out came panting past me and stopped, wincing with the stitch; two truants tugged off their ties before slipping into a video shop; in a sudden sally from a side-street a games-kitted crocodile lurched at a run into my path, headed by a manic bald master. It was the first day and there were the children caught up already in the severe rhythms of school, and looking back, like conscripts on a ship, to the lazy shore of home. For a moment I shared the truants' defiance and guilt and my heart raced with a long-forgotten panicky anticipation: I had to assert myself against the obscure medicinal hollowness of school. And of course my first assignation with Luc loomed and made me feel half master and half victim.

His mother got hold of me first, and took me into the dining-room. She hoped I didn't mind coming to the house, it seemed better discipline than sending Luc across town to me – and then she knew where he was. I was already imagining the squeaking board that gave away her presence at the door. She went on with a number of blunt and incoherent instructions, which I barely took in – I was pretending I hadn't seen him, just at the moment I entered the hall, behind his mother's back, skidding through to the kitchen, a towel round his neck, a glimpse of his bare heels, a vision of his undomestic size and energy.

She left me in the darkly panelled room, among the family portraits. I waited a minute under their humourless gaze, one above the other, prudent, black-bosomed, as if they had all been painted in widowhood. Feeling faintly culpable and unfit for responsibility, I went to the long window and looked out on the garden, a high-walled strip that ended in a canal with swans idling past and a little angular gazebo above the water, where I pictured Luc smoking or waiting for a tryst. Mrs Altidore's work was less evident in this room, just a kind of tasselled runner on the sideboard. Then I pulled out a chair and discovered the terrible industry of the seat.

There were footsteps, no voices, crossing the hall, and their brief hanging back to let the other enter first showed me they were both nervous too. Mother and son, side by side: I sensed the treaty between them and the unresolved cross-purposes.

'This is Luc,' she said. 'Mr Manners.'

He was pushing back his hair and his hand was damp when he shook mine.

'Hello.'

'Hello!' How old-fashionedly keen I was.

And he nodded, so that his hair fell forward again. Through the coming hour I would see that tumbling forelock dry from bronze to gold, and get to know the different ways he mastered it, the indolent sweep, the brainstorming grapple, the barely effectual toss, and how long the intervals were of forward slither and lustrous collapse. But for the moment, when we were left alone, I didn't altogether look at him; my eyes fixed uncomprehendingly on the sideboard, a hideous epergne, a sugar dredger, a tantalus of brandy.

He said, 'My mother's going to bring some coffee,' the voice light and mildly interrogative, the accent educated. Then I looked. He was lean and broad-shouldered in an old blue shirt; and I liked his big flattish backside as he walked past me, though his loose cotton trousers gave nothing else away. He was as tall as me (I could imagine him saying he was taller, and a laughing challenge, back to back). Did he understand that I was weighing and measuring him like this, or possibly envisage the tingle of desire that ran up my back when I saw his brown bare insteps between turn-up and low-cut moccasin? It was hard to know if something vain and mistrustful in his look was more than the ordinary wariness of a boy with his teacher, or of people starting cold at knowing each other.

To me of course he wasn't quite new, though when he took his place on the far side of the table and waited for me to begin I could hardly keep from telling him how different he was from his picture, how much odder and better. In his father's generation his features might have been thought ugly or exaggerated,

28

though now they had come into fashion and could be admitted as wonderful in their own way; he must have taken from his father the long nose and high cheekbones which gave him the air of a blond Aztec. His eyes were narrow and colourless – his mother's lost look given a new caution and sharpness; while his long mouth seemed burdened with involuntary expressiveness, the thick lips opening, when later I twisted a smile out of him, to show strong sexy canines and high gums. His upper lip was almost too heavy, a puckering outward curl, with no downward dimple in the fingermark beneath the nose, where it had a straight edge, as if finished off impatiently with a palette-knife. There was something engrossing, even slightly repellent, about the whole feature.

His mother knocked and brought two coffees in with a self-denying expression, as if to say that this would be her last intrusion on the serious work we had to do. Then the conversation made its faltering beginnings, and ran on for minute after minute, with topics artificially encouraged gaining a brief involuntary momentum before dying like an old engine in which too much confidence had been placed. We spoke about the geography of Belgium, the relative merits of the western plain and the south-easterly heights, and discussed the Flemish/Walloons question without reaching any very deep or new conclusions. It was a puzzling experience – I was fascinated by him, yet carrying on as though I'd been trapped with a bore at a cocktail party. Perhaps he really was a bore; there was no reason he shouldn't be, whatever his fretful mother had said. Or was I expecting too much too soon, and ignoring his steady merits, the schoolboy's vacant valuing of knowledge for its own sake? I felt I needed to find out about him, or like some subtle interrogator to beguile him into unnoticed indiscretions; I was slightly miffed when he started to give things away without much bother or self-importance.

He was looking sunned and well, so I asked him about his recent spell out at the seaside. He had been to the villa of a former schoolfriend, just over the French border, right on the beach at a village called St Ernest-aux-Sablonnières, to which, he told me confidently, the saint's body had been brought after his fatal crusade. Patrick something was his great friend there, another

29

rich kid I guessed, and they had often been together to this beach-house in the long holidays when the something family went out there. This time the fine weather on the very brink of the new term had tempted the boys to go there for a few days alone; or so I thought, and jealously hoped, until it emerged that there had also been a girl with them.

I fell into a rhythm of apparently pointless questions, so as to stretch his vocabulary; and under cover of these I went stalking through that seaside idyll that there had never been the remotest question of my sharing. First, how had they got there? In his friend Patrick's car. Ah, and what was that? A Mini! Oh; and what was the house like? It was white, it had only one floor, and its roof was flat. A verandah with white pillars ran all along the front. To my surprise he called it a stoa. Below the house there was a garden with trees that leant over and a gate with two or three steps going down on to the dunes. The nearest house was a hundred metres off. And what of the inside? There were at least four bedrooms (so perfect chastity could conceivably have been preserved). We itemised the linen, the duvet-covers in red and green, the sheets made from an uncertain fabric. The furniture there was built out of pine and oak; there were many books on wildlife and ornithology. The theme of birds was continued on the cups and plates, and on various other items in the kitchen, which he considered a delightful room. I wanted to get back to the night hours, and ask him what he dreamed about when the noise of the waves had lulled him to sleep; but something held me back. I felt I could pry no further just now, though he rose to all these challenges with only brief hesitations and a certain chilly pride. What had they done? They had walked, read, studied indeed, discussed various matters. Such as? Such as ... pollution, radio drama, the effect of wage agreements. They sounded like the dreariest people on earth. (They sounded like us.) Had they gone in the sea? Yes, although the water was quite cold. Then what had he worn to do so? A slip. Swimming-trunks, did he mean, or shorts? Trunks. And what colour were they? They were black. As it happened, he'd forgotten his own and had had to borrow Patrick's, and they were too large. So he couldn't keep them on? Oh he could, but it wasn't easy ... What, um, what had he read? He had read *Great Expectations* and something by Gramsci! (He seemed full of ideas on the latter but I kept bringing him back firmly to Pip, Magwitch and Herbert Pocket.)

When a little over an hour had elapsed there was another quick knock and Mrs Altidore stepped in and looked from one to the other of us, as if expecting a decision. There was a moment's silence. Then she asked Luc how it had gone, and he nodded and shrugged, accustomed to evading her fuss. I told her that he had very good English and she said, 'I know.' She then had Luc show me out, which he did with a telling mixture of reluctance and formality. I shook his big strong hand and he nodded his forelock forward and curtly said goodbye.

Out in the street I felt almost nothing. I didn't like to inspect my motives – I walked on quite briskly, looking about appreciatively, like someone at ease with himself and not denying a disappointment. Though the question insisted on forming, whether I had really come all this way for *that*.

I took a circuitous route home, past the Memling Cinema and down the street where the church of St Narcissus was. It had relatively up-to-date notices on the board at the front, though it was hard to decide whether an announcement of a pilgrimage (by bus) back in April was sufficient grounds to believe that the iron-spiked gate through which I was reading it would ever be opened again to the curious or devout. I noticed litter had gathered between the gate and the door.

Over the bridge, where my canal slid sullenly below, and there was the school. It was getting on for lunchtime. I heard a hand-bell ringing in an echoing inner courtyard, and as I crossed the road to look up at the tall, many-gabled building, its buckling purple brick braced all over with iron Es, Xs and Ss, I saw for the first time the historic uniform the boys wore: black breeches and stockings and black bum-freezers with wide collars and the yellow face of a narcissus flower picked out in braid on the pocket. Two of them who must have been quite senior were lounging in the gateway, like figures in an old print, and managed to look foppish and puritanical at the same time.

I wasn't quite sure I got this Narcissus business: Luc, in the hagiological phase of our chat, had said that the saint was an early bishop of Jerusalem, whose bones had been brought back by Godefroi de Bouillon from the crusade of 1099. But this plausible legend seemed to have been wilfully confounded with the pagan myth of the boy-flower. Not that I minded.

When Echevin came round in the morning he brought a verbal invitation from his father to dinner, if I was free, on that very day. As I was wearying of heating cans of this and that, and eking them out with milk and biscuits and the occasional burger from the McDonald's next to the Bishop's Palace, I accepted, and then found myself obliged to be very gentle and helpful with Marcel, whom I could hardly face over the dinner-table if I had been a bully to him during our lesson. I kept modifying my instinct that he needed to be pushed. He looked so miserable and apprehensive when he arrived – I was shocked to read on his big round face what a dragon I could be.

I was drinking with Cherif before I went – he was even at the bar before me with beers for both of us bought and waiting. I had the sense, both warming and disconcerting, of figuring in his plans, of a space being made for me; I thought, I mustn't let him fall in love, though I rode for a minute on the quiet high of his welcome, and half-relished the idea of a conquest; after the first excitement I knew that for me it wasn't falling in love, even if it had a nervous, mechanical similarity to that.

Then we sat and the talk didn't come very easily – we offered each other titbits of information and stared self-consciously around. It was almost a moment for a chat on Belgian geography. I remembered how I had planned to break free of the old routine of the pub each early evening, and here I was slipping already into the little comfortable hell of habit; the experiment seemed to be over. I set down my empty glass and gave Cherif a crumpled, sour smile, as if he was to blame for my weaknesses. I picked up a paper someone had left, and skimmed through one or two articles that vaguely interested me, explaining them to him in French – the British Conservatives were 'desperate for the return of Mrs Thatcher', the Flemish Minister of Culture looked for 'a new morality in the arts'. I wondered if it wouldn't have been better to have seen Cherif only once, and preserved the accidental sweetness of the first encounter, rather than pushing on into the stagnant shallows of the following days. But an hour later, when I had to go, would already be late, for the Echevins, we had rediscovered each other, his arm was round my shoulder, his dick was stirring comically in his jeans, and I would have given anything for another drink, or just to have taken him off with me to my room. I wanted to be fucking him and kissing the shiny brown backs of his ears.

Slightly pumped up with beer I had to go to the lavatory as soon as I arrived at the Echevins' and looked at myself in the mirror, pulling my face about into a respectable expression and tightening the knot of the blue silk tie which Edie had given me. I looked poor and improvised; the edges of my clothes were frayed and even my tie had a stain on it that I only now remembered, and which meant that I had no clean ties left. It may have been no bad thing to create a hard-up odds-and-ends impression on someone who was in a sense my employer, and I had always anyway loosely thought of myself as some kind of *artist*, who had a duty not to conform; but under my unhappy self-inspection I longed for a beautiful suit. Time was running faster than I realised. It was one of those lavatories with a flush which merely whirls the contents of the bowl around, removing selected items, and after a quick dry spasm regurgitates the rest to wallow reproachfully where it had been before. I stood cranking the not-yet-ready handle. The housekeeper had let me in and was still waiting for me when I emerged; she smiled sadly, but I felt from her too, as she led me up the narrow panelled staircase, a kind of disappointment. Or perhaps it was just my own sense of dislocation, out of breath after running between one world and another, a smoky bar with a juke-box and the silent elegance of an unknown house.

I had the sitting-room to myself, and wandered round it cautiously, as if I might damage something in the vague disequilibrium of drink. The panelling was painted white, as a backdrop to half a dozen Orst pastels, which glowed like oratory windows from frames three times their size: I frowned through the protecting glass at a prayerful face, the shot cerise of the afterglow. I was trying to remember the housekeeper's name, from what Marcel had told me that morning: she had been his nanny and as good as a mother to him since his real mother's bizarre death. Now I was in the house I thought of that bee-sting again, like the wicked intervention on which a fairy-tale turns, and of the survivors as existing under its long shadow.

Echevin was a late father, a handsome man in his sixties, pleasantly bald, and without the moustache I for some reason expected him to wear, so that his face had a sensitive, surprised look of some charm. His eyes were large, with oaky flecks in their pale blue pupils. He had on the grey suiting of a business man, but with unusual tucks and vents, which seemed to hint at his role in the arts. The housekeeper came back with a jug of punch (Mrs Vivier, Mrs Vivier) and he offered me a glass with a little murmur, as if he hadn't yet decided if we were going to be friends. I was hot and on edge and gabbled about Rubens and the charm of old brick in my most ingratiating manner, to which his answers, in rapid, unselfconscious English, were polite but brief. I told myself he didn't need to hear all this, but I was shy of bringing the interview round to the question of Marcel; in the end all he said was that the boy had never known the brief glad hours of childhood, or some such phrase, perhaps a quotation. Paternal love, watchful and removed, as I had known it and lost it myself, showed through for a moment. He saw he didn't need to tell me my behaviour had been ill judged and over-severe – I made an unsolicited promise to be kind to Marcel, and over supper beamed at him and joked in a way he seemed to find quite sinister after my earlier toughness. I didn't know if it was quite tactful to say to Echevin:

'Marcel tells me he's not an admirer of Orst's work.' It might have been a matter of contention between them.

'No,' he replied crisply. 'But there are other things in life than the works of Orst. And besides, they are not calculated to appeal to children. A taste for the *femme fatale* comes later; if at all.' Over the course of the meal a mild counter-argument to the effect that a boy of sixteen was no longer a child had been forming in my mind, and when I ran back to the romantic poseur I had been at the same age I thought I saw someone who would have revelled in Orst's private purgatory.

'I think they're really depressing,' said Marcel with a grin which showed this was a permitted house-heresy.

After supper, which left me feeling stuffed and clumsy, Echevin called me through to his workroom, while Marcel, to emphasise how they were keeping their side of the bargain, was sent to study his verbs. The poor kid came tolerantly in with Knowles's *English Grammar*, which he stuck under my nose and tapped before climbing on to the sofa and mouthing vacantly to himself, like a tiny child rehearsing imaginary friends. When we came back twenty minutes later he was leaning sideways and wheezily asleep.

I think his father's decision to show me what he was at work on was spontaneous, and so perhaps regretted: a moment of mid-evening confidence when a quiet chat, politely repeating itself and running down until it was time for me to go, would have been expected and even welcome. He had gone ahead, while I was saying to Marcel with a new fake-sternness, 'I should like, you would like', insisting on a pointless and unobserved distinction. I thought with surprising nostalgia of chasing velvety butterflies of vocab with Luc; and that in turn called up a summery haze of anxiety and desire.

Echevin's study surprised me by being where it was: he had entered what I thought could only be a cupboard in the thickness of the wall but when I followed I passed through a short brick tunnel and climbed two steps into a bright, crammed office on the first floor of the adjacent building: the director's office of the Orst Museum. I wondered if he regularly came back here after supper for silent work uninterrupted by the phone or the half-curious public chattering up the stairs that I saw through an open door beyond. A public brought in by the damp lowland weather, obedient to a notice in a hotel hallway or to a Michelin guide: what would they take away from these cryptic works of art? And what would their creator have cared for these chance visitors? Echevin gestured to a portrait photograph high on the wall: a lean-faced man of fifty, with a short, pointed silvery beard, sitting with cheek tilted towards the jewelled knob of a cane: the fastidious ironic look of the heterosexual bachelor, half dandy and half clergyman, and an air of steely enigma, almost as if he sought to outdo the starlit sphinx

35

he had painted, which now stood propped against the opposite wall with rubber corners shielding the coffee-coloured gilt of its frame. ('Just back from a Symbolist show in Munich,' my host explained, proudly, but as if it were a bore.)

And maybe it was a bore to work so long and closely with a man who looked so coldly down from above two thousand books and catalogues (in French and Flemish, German and English, Danish, was that?, Hungarian, and Japanese) that somehow, if only by a footnote, touched on him, or on his world and time. Echevin's note was less that of boredom than of a polite impatience, which I felt as I stumbled after him was directed equally at me and at Orst himself. Unsure quite what to do now we were there, standing side by side at the immense plain desk which took up half the room, he flicked open a folder and just like his son a minute or two before tapped the pile of photostats inside with a strong square finger. 'These should interest you,' he said, without complete conviction. He turned one or two of them over but didn't give me time to see them properly. 'His articles for the British press. There. "A Great Belgian Sculptor" – that was about Meunier – no, you may not know of him. That was in *The Studio* – and there, "Burne-Jones's Funeral", from *The Times*: did you know Burne-Jones was the first painter to be given a service at Westminster Abbey? A strange and admirable choice, don't you think?' He closed the folder again: 'Orst was once a famous figure in London, when England was open to the influence of Europe and when Belgium was the focus of the avant-garde. But that was a long time ago.'

'Yes, I'm afraid I'd never seen one of his pictures in the flesh until I arrived here.'

'That is perfectly possible. There are a dozen or more at the Tate, but they haven't been shown since before the war. There's an important one in Leeds, "Rêveries", some portraits in Glasgow, bought from the collection of Connal, one or two in Brighton' – *those*, I thought, I might have seen on some camp, windswept weekend, rising at lunchtime and wandering half-hysterically about with whomever I had in tow, full of wild plans for getting rid of him – 'and even a major drawing at your

36

mad little Corley-Cripps Museum in Eastbourne, which is always so conveniently closed.'

He looked at me unblinkingly and I said, 'Yes, I'm sorry about that' – then he gave an enchanting smile and a little giggle, at which I felt a sudden and unexpected intimacy had been reached. I had a warm glow, half a shiver, a tear in my eye-lashes, not enough to fall. I had seen the Corley-Cripps Museum years before with my gay uncle Wilfred, prospecting in the Newhaven area on some unexplained business of his own, and still vividly remembered the huge 1890s villa, with its green cupola and cars in a shed at the side that were almost as old as the house itself. We were admitted by a reluctant old woman in an overcoat, whom a pre-war photograph in one of the rooms enabled us to identify as Madeleine Corley-Cripps, daughter-in-law of the builder of the house. I might well have looked for a moment or two at a mystic panel by Orst, as I did certainly at the three Burne-Jones ladies and at blackened alle-gories by G. F. Watts. But their mysteries were dim beside the captivating dereliction of their surroundings – the click of loose tiles underfoot, the enormous moribund plants, the cases of damp-damaged memorabilia, the linings of the curtains tattered and brown and trailing on the floor, the view from the windows on to the garden, its statuary blistered and tarnished by the salt air.

He had only called it mad, but I hoped that my host, who must be a practised poker-around in odd and not always wel-coming places, shared my love for this one – and love, in the sudden flush of enthusiasm, is what it was revealed to be. I wasn't sure if the joke was already over. I wanted to say some-thing about the cars, and how my uncle and I, once Madeleine Corley-Cripps had closed the front door behind us, slackened our pace down the drive, halted, and without a word turned back and crossed to the garages, with hasty glances over our shoulders and at a disreputable near-run. All old Corley-Cripps's automobiles were there, three abreast and three deep: a sports Delage, an intensely rare Napier 90, a green Bentley, a long-nosed Isotta-Fraschini, a raffish little wasp-backed Bugatti – the other passion of that manufacturer of once world-famous pumps. And in what a dream light they lay, with the brambles straggling over the glass roof.

'The thing I recall even more than the Burne-Jones "Beatrice" there,' said Paul Echevin, 'was an eight-litre Bentley of 1931 (I think), the first saloon to exceed 100 miles per hour. It must have been untouched for a quarter of a century. One dared not lay a finger on it for fear that it might fall into a heap of dust.'

It was a night of stars and cloud, not late, the odd canalside bar still lit and, as I came by, the voices of the last regulars within, chatting and grumbling discontinuously, arguing out of habit. I was happy to be out in this beautiful little city, unaware if I was warm or cold after the last cognac – the one I had not been expected to accept. I felt full of energy, as I often did when it was really time to go to bed, the time when through my clubbing years we all of us used to come alive again and go purposefully on. I hung about in the Grote Markt and heard two quarters chime from the Belfry and smoked a cigarette between. The shutters came down on a restaurant as two of the waiters, with anoraks over their white shirts and black bow-ties, loped for the last bus, already impatiently champing on its air-brakes.

When later I crossed the road to the old doctor's house, I saw that the wicket at the side was open – I never left it like that at night, on firm instructions from the old doctor's housekeeper. And when I entered the yard I saw at once that the window of the top room on the other staircase was glaringly alight: my new neighbours had arrived. I climbed the stairs two at a time in a mood of affronted possessiveness. After I had closed my door I stood tensely in the near-darkness and heard, from that silent realm that lay beyond my wall of cupboards, the voices of the Spanish girls.

What could they be doing in there? At first I thought their unusually penetrating laughs and shouts must be the high-spirited noises associated with arrival and unpacking, questions volleyed from one room to another as to where such and such a thing, plucked incredulously from a suitcase, should go. But no other sounds were to be heard – no shuffling about or opening and shutting of doors. Perhaps they were just sitting there, reading their school-books or darning their stockings, looking up from time to time, unable to resist screeching some hilarious commonplace at each other. I wasn't sure of the layout of their quarters, and maybe they were quite unlike mine. I made a bit of noise myself, and in the middle of a long exchange which involved the singing of two or three verses of 'When I'm Sixty-four', marched along opening and slamming each of my cupboards in turn. Which made no difference whatsoever. In a moment of sudden despair I knew that they must have a guitar.

I got undressed and turned the light off and sat waiting for the next remark or the first explosive chord. Once or twice I thought I heard the first squeaking stoppings, the hunched rehearsal of the chord-changes before the right hand springs its hackneyed horrors from the box ... But perhaps it was just a distant creaking in the house or the bell of the night tram out by the station. After a while I could hear only my own indignant pulse and the hairs on my legs sliding together. Then the twelve o'clock carillon from St Narcissus, almost welcome, with its plonking hymn that had become a sort of malign lullaby. 'Yes, close your eyes up tight: You will not sleep tonight' – the dud note, the metrical space marked only by a rusty click, falling on the word 'eyes'.

3

Saturday, and a late start – waking in the usual cosy surge of memories and fantasies, the fantasies lacking in focus. It wouldn't quite work with Luc, I recalled a lad or two I'd seen about in the street, then hustled Cherif in quickly for the close.

I took a shower, maddened by the sudden shrinking of the supply, spinning the hot tap and getting nothing but a feeble rope of cold. I stood out on the floor, leaning in through the curtain to test it. Then there was a far-off whining and knocking from the cistern in the roof, and the hot came thrashing back in an instant devilry of steam. Of course! It was my new neighbours at work, their shower had some kind of priority over mine, they could draw my water off and leave me shivering with annoyance.

I mopped my little mirror clean and peered into it. It was absurdly small – it would almost have gone in a handbag; my face was cropped by its edges and looked rather good in it, I thought, like the features of any biker in the classic frame of his helmet. I swept my thick black hair around – my best feature, which people sometimes thought was dyed if they hadn't seen my forearms or bare legs. I imagined Luc might quite admire it, and see the claim it made for my being romantic and young. He ought to see it in this mirror, which left out all the rest of me. I thought of Cherif, with his comforting extra poundage, how he seemed to like all of me, and had no inkling of my steady disappointment at how I'd turned out and was likely to stay – never having looked fabulous in a swimsuit, caught in other people's photographs with a certain undeniable burliness. While my hair was still wet I combed it back, and it lay appealingly where I left it. It appealed to me, that is to say, though perhaps to other people it was the tell-tale feature of my self-delusion.

I went for a wander through the cluster of ancient buildings which formed the still religious heart of the old town – the Cathedral, the Bishop's Palace, the low dormered quadrangle of the Hospital – and out into the alleyways behind the Museum, to find that it was the day of the animal market. The vendors' pickups and trailers were drawn up tight against the wall, and in between, on low barrows or simply standing on the cobbles, were the rustling, rackety cages that contained their wares. There was a ripe, unhappy smell that I remembered from the circus that ran up one childhood summer outside our windows at Rough Common; and then, as I walked along through a light crowd that seemed oppressive in the narrowly overhung street, a smell of frying onions, sausages and chips from one van and of fresh whelks and shrimps from another.

I'd heard about this market from someone at the Cassette, and knew it was popular with the local children, who were here now, laughing at a marmoset sprinting in a wheel or trying to provoke some reaction from the comatose tree-snakes and elderly, moulting parakeets, who stood first on one leg, then on the other, looking cynically about. I saw lizards, kittens, carp, canaries; I saw a little ginger monkey rubbing its nose like a person who is embarrassed; I saw tiny fluffy dogs you might mistake for slippers and insects you might think were shrivelled fallen leaves. One old woman had a biscuit-tin of spiders, and a scientific-looking man stood behind a glass case half full of earth, challenging you to believe that it contained a pair of nocturnal burrowing voles. I hung about with the families, who were in a mood of subdued hilarity, and strolled among the boys who were standing with their bikes, their expressions mingling teen contempt with innocent absorption. Occasionally a few francs would exchange hands, and the purchaser of a rabbit or a piranha would walk off briskly, as from a shady deal; I was being very English, no doubt, but I wondered what heartless caprice could lead anyone to buy here. I avoided the sellers' eyes, and had the feeling that if I let them snare me with their sudden patter, or worse a huckster's wordless beckon and hand on the elbow, I would be shown some further unwelcome curiosity, something uniquely poisonous or malformed.

The animal-sellers were a collection as rickety as the animals.

Even the young ones had the weathered, impassive look of mar-
ket-people everywhere, silent for long periods as if without
expectation, then breaking into vaguely fraudulent animation.
From the signs on their vans and their registrations it was clear
that they came in from Holland, from the Ardennes, from
northern France, and for a moment I caught a glimpse of this
makeshift menagerie rattling from place to place across the
rainy roads of Flanders, a reluctant fraternity, showing up each
week or each month. There was shouting from further down
the street, the yap of a dog and one or two other voices indis-
tinctly raised. I couldn't see through the crowd what was going
on, but the way people turned and after a second or two resumed their conversation with a dismissive flap of the hand
made me suppose it was a well-known drunk or the flare-up of
some habitual old rivalry.

Then, shouting sporadic obscenities, a small bearded man in
torn and filthy tweeds came past, waving a stick and making
occasional growling sallies at parents and at their slightly
scared children, who I guessed were wondering if their mums
and dads also knew these wild words that were never heard at
home. In front of him hurried a black-and-white terrier, which
seemed partly to share in and partly to apologise for its master's
performance, and glanced at the animals that were for sale as if
to show a puzzled awareness of kinship. When the man wasn't
ranting the dog barked, so as to keep the noise more or less con-
tinuous. 'It's only old Gus,' said a man next to me; but his
bearing wasn't old – it had a certain mocking rectitude – and
when he glanced at me I flinched from a sharp-eyed hand-
someness lined and broken under matted hair and a week of
beard. He was old in the sense that a 'character' is old, and with
the premature old age of the destitute. Once he had gone past,
one or two of the boys had the courage to whoop a childish insult at him.

I had finished with the market but waited a moment until
Gus had gone before following him – wary of the man,
although when he did turn and brace his shoulders, or dart at
someone who embodied for a second whatever it was he hated
and raged against, the swipes of his stick fell short; and his
words could be laughed uneasily off. At the street's end light

struck in from the wider thoroughfare that crossed it and people stood talking in a weekend muddle of idleness and busyness. A nice-looking short dark boy, hands in the pockets of baggy blue corduroys, a guernsey round his shoulders, stepped backwards laughing just as Gus came up behind him. They both recoiled, the boy with momentarily delayed horror, Gus with the snarl of one who loathes above all to be touched; then silence and then a brown-toothed smile. He stepped forward, clutching with his left hand at the low, blackened crotch of his trousers. 'I know all about little boys,' he said, 'I know all about cocks and cunts' – so that the kid backed off and turned away fast, though with a mock-cheery shout to his companions. But Gus had already lost interest.

The indolent bunching of the shoppers, a parked van, the street corner with its hanging lamp and mutilated figure of St Anthony of Padua – all prevented me from seeing that broad-shouldered, strong-bottomed lad, and on impulse I followed him round the corner. He and his friends had cantered on for a bit, and it took me a moment to find them, stopped again under the iron and glass marquee of the theatre. There was my friend, and a taller fair boy beside him; beyond them, looking back at me, was a calm, wide-faced girl, hair cut in a shining bob. The shorter boy's hand rested above the small of the taller one's back, as if he had touched it lightly to reassure him or command his attention and then left it there in comfortable forgetfulness. It was a turning-point in my life, this second sighting of Luc. I knew at once how the shape of him lingered in me, like a bright image gleaming and floating on the sleepy retina: there was a kind of miserable excitement, a lurch of the heart. At the moment I recognised him and laid a hopeless claim to him, I knew I was observing him on the loose in a world that barely touched on mine: I had the clearest sense of his indifference, as he stood there with his back to me in a brown suede jerkin and white jeans, his back on which this appealing stranger was allowed to rest his hand, confident in some unguessed intimacy. Never love at first sight; but second sometimes – while I strode through the theatre colonnade, as if unaware of the three, and with a certain glamorous urgency bent on some objective beyond them, the singing echoes of my shoe-tips rang through a longer arched perspective, and seemed to summon up the skitterings of earlier loves setting out on their improbable journeys. The three had perhaps reached a natural pause in their conversation, though of course I thought their quite abrupt silence, when I was just by them but looking away at the long irrelevant announcements for *Henry VIII* and *La Siffleuse*, was virtually an act of aggression. I swept on stiffly to the Grote Markt, and crossed it as if they were still watching me, even following me. It was not till I got to the Tourist Office, went unhesitatingly inside and stood at a rack of cards, looking past it through the huge lettered window and found that they were nowhere to be seen, that I marvelled abjectly at how my sudden burst of feeling had wrongfooted me. I had lost the chance of an easy greeting, a display of the amiable equality of our dealings, a word or two with his beautiful friends. I could have put my arm around that broad suede back, just above the other one, and claimed the beginnings of a friendship just as intense. I plucked out postcards one after another and amassed them like a terrible hand at pontoon: the Belfry, the Belfry, a frozen canal, a mural from the Town Hall, painted by Edgard Orst.

I was in a dingy old bookshop, running my eye blindly over the stock, waiting for the storm in my head to pass: the place was a refuge, a bunker, insulated by its own dusty tedium and the bulkheads of paper and worn leather. I froze off the donnish assistant, who enquired as to my special interests and who may have thought I was a thief – I who had stolen nothing in my life. I worked my way into the remotest back-room, where there were three or four shelves of English books under the stairs, and crouched down in front of them with the feeling I was asking them for help.

H. E. Bates, *Hard Times*, Drabble, ancient abridged texts of *Gulliver* and *Crusoe* with the cancelled library stamp of St Narcissus, the ringed golden flower on the dull green boards ... The Poetry Section, Arkell, Armstrong, Arnold (Edwin and Matthew), it was like Digby's at home, where I'd had my first holiday job – a receiving area for dead and dying enthusiasms. Some local Anglophile of advanced years must have passed away. I saw my long-lost schoolfriend *Poets of Our Time*, and took it out and clutched it without opening it. I thought I would give it to Luc; we could study the Binyon and Bottomley and Masefield together, without his knowing how their phrases ran through my past, the melancholy secrecy of reading. It struck me I should buy him other books as well, they would be presents, too musty to be recognised as such, with invisible inscriptions. I took down an *Awkward Age*, a *Persuasion*, a *Love's Labour's Lost* with immediate firmness. And of course a tough enough reading-list would keep him busy, he'd have no spare time for his vacuous pawing friends, his day would be somehow mine; and the evenings – perhaps he would need to see me in the evenings to sort out his finer uncertainties, questions of motive and metaphor ... I ran along the shelf again and frowned to read the rubbed title of a novel; it took several seconds for me to be sure – it really was one of my Aunt Tina's, foxed and crumbly, on wartime paper, and priced as if the dealer knew the value it would have to one affectionate customer. There were family as well as friends here under the stairs.

When I didn't go to the Cassette I went to the Golden Calf, an old men's bar in the middle of town but so tucked away up an alley full of bicycles and beer crates that it could have been anywhere. The regulars either sat in unexpecting silence or spoke loudly and infrequently about what they'd seen on television. You could have been in a lounge bar in a market town in the west of England, or even in the George IV at home, except that here there was no music, which made it better for reading or writing letters. Today I sat with *Careful, Mary!* to distract me between the malty mouthfuls of a lunchtime 'Silence' – a flooring brew from Antwerp alleged to be made by Trappist monks. I felt obtusely proud of the filthy little book, and wanted to tell the old boy next to me how Christina McFie was my comical-tragical great-aunt.

Careful, Mary! was, or else wasn't, one of her best – it depended on whether you took her seriously or enjoyed her as a bizarre joke. Aunt Tina had spent a long childless adulthood in Africa, married to a Scottish coffee-planter, and her novels had come to her almost unbidden, like letters full of homesickness and childish make-believe. The more she wrote of England the more romantic her picture of it became — after three or four books it was barely recognisable; but her gaffes began to attract her a new audience, who loved the inadvertent comedy of her naively lofty style. For a while there had even been a Christina McFie fan-club, though it was never quite clear if she was fooled or if she took it in the camp spirit in which it was intended. I remembered the disappointment I'd felt as a child when she returned from Kenya and I discovered that she wasn't black, merely tanned and wizened; she had a sharp smell that struck a hugged six-year-old keenly, and wore trousers and smoked yellow cigarettes.

I had read *Careful, Mary!* when I was still too young to know what was wrong with it; it was the one in which she got muddled up and wrote about Bermondsey when she clearly meant Belgravia; the raffish 'Bermondsey set' were like figures from Thackeray oddly translated to the era of Victrolas and racing Bentleys. Still, why not? I thought. And then she had ended up in Chislehurst, in eccentric isolation amid some private fantasy of England.

I was quite taken by her portrait of the young Duke of Bermondsey and absorbed myself with deliberate enthusiasm in her topsy-turvy world. Then I finished my glass and the pleasure shrivelled. I closed the book and sat back with my head against the wall, drumming my fingers tentatively on the cover, half-smiling to myself with misery that this could have happened again. And with the excitement of a recognised necessity, too. Out in the streets I walked fast but aimlessly around, dry-mouthed and giddy with early-afternoon drunkenness under the glare of thin cloud. Soon I was in my street, I was in my room and closed the door. It felt warm and remote there, like a room left behind when everyone has gone to church: and there were the cold coffee-cups and old papers strewn about for a maid to clear in their absence.

Somewhere, now, Luc was . . . doing something. At home, perhaps, over lunch with his mother, eating well amid sparse conversation. She didn't understand how beautiful he was, she censured the sprawl of those long white-jeaned thighs under the table where he and I had sat for our hour. He was in the starry dream-orbit of his youth and she was trying to ground him with her worries and precautions. Or perhaps he had gone to a café with his two friends, they had got a bit drunk and excited on a bottle of red. The friends must love him and more or less openly desire him. I lay spreadeagled on the jangling bed to think, the back of a hand across my eyes. I heard St Narcissus strike three. When I woke the room was full of shadows and through the chambered thickness of the walls came the laughter of the Spanish girls.

It was not too early to go to the Cassette, and I had the makings of a bright, dry headache which could best be prevented by a flood of light Belgian beer. In the various streets and small squares around the Town Hall the markets were closing up now, the canvas was folded off the stalls, rails of clothes were trundled with flailing wheels over the cobbles towards waiting vans, a huge compressor lorry inched through the debris, fed at the back by teams of overalled oldsters ... The proper emptiness of the place was being re-admitted, surrendered to – and it filled me with gratitude and panic in rapid alternation. The annoying distractions were being removed, but the vacancy that followed left me impatient for company: company to hold and hint at my wild new secret amongst.

Cherif was already at the bar, apart at the far end, leaning on the counter, drunk and dejected after a couple of hours of TV football. On the screen above, pundits in white sweaters were analysing the game, and Cherif brought his fist down on the bar again at the slow-motion replay of an upsetting first-half goal. It took him a moment to refocus on me, and to accept the odd fervour of my kiss and embrace. I bought us beers and stood behind him as he watched the interview with the winning manager, and hugged him tight with my head on his shoulder. I sniffed up his smoky, beery slowness, and tucked my right hand in his waistband and felt for the clean beginning of the hair above his cock – what at ten or twelve, awed as children in a fairy-tale, we had called a 'forest'. How any groping, now, at

47

thirty-three, retained the freshness and the shock of those first twilight wanderings out of bounds, the first wonder of consent ... My left hand was in his left pocket, working on his dick through the rough lining, gently, so no one down the room would notice – until he twisted away and denied me with a little gasp.

Now that it came to it I didn't know how to make my confession. I took him off to a table in the corner, though I knew he was still looking from time to time at the TV screen perched beyond me and at an angle, so that he could only half make out the picture but couldn't stop trying to follow it. He couldn't see why we'd had to move, though I was so caught up in my secret and the acclaim that would greet it that I missed the note of bossiness in my own voice.

'Cherif, listen,' I said: 'I'm in love.'

He looked at me dully, then leant forward and kissed me on the lips. I felt quite pleased that I had his blessing. 'My friend,' he said.

'It's all a bit sudden, though I suppose I could see it coming.' He remained silent, incurious, then looked down as if feeling had for a moment made him shy; and reached in the pockets of his leather jacket for cigarettes and matches. 'I suppose you can guess who it is,' I said, with a little breathy giggle now I was so near to saying. He lit a fag and then offered me one, and though nerves tempted me and I was relishing already the shot of smoke and the gently crackling combustion, my hand was trembling too much to accept. He glanced up at the TV again and then back to me. I said, 'It's my pupil Luc', and he said flatly, 'I love you too', at exactly the same moment.

I had reached across the table to cover his fist for the announcement and in the silence that followed he looked down at this loose handclasp with a rather impressive contempt. He let me force my fingers into the curl of his, but I soon withdrew them. 'Of course I still want to be with you,' I said, like the clumsiest kind of adulterer – and for a second or two I hungered for Cherif and was mad with irritation at him and myself. After that he was in an angry sulk for the rest of the evening and was difficult company. I wandered and settled amongst the other people I was getting to know. Perhaps I forced myself on them – but I

48

presumed on a kind of queer camaraderie and drank so as not to notice.

For a while I chatted with Gerard, a young musician – very good company but somehow remote, the sort of person it is hopeless to fall for, as I quite did at first, with his hooting laugh and witty sentimental conversation. He told me he had been married at seventeen, but separated by the time he left university: she was a strong, demanding girl and had almost convinced him that he was straight. But after a year or so he found his thoughts were turning all the time to other men, as they had done before he met her. I could imagine the couple's self-absorption: he spoke of it as of some brief annoyance, like missing a train; but it was clear that it had troubled him more deeply. I put my hand on his shoulder and stroked his neck once or twice with my thumb, but we were no more intimate for that. He was still quite spotty, although probably about my age, and wore hopeless clothes – shapeless jeans, fluorescent trainers and complicated musician's knitwear; but he was beautiful, with his dirty blond hair and chestnut eyes. He gave off the sexy mood of youth going smoky and drinky: if too shrewd actually to be a drunk he was certainly a very drinky kind of person. He was girlish but unshaven; naked he would have been quite hairy, though I wondered if his body was slack or heavy and strong. He was relaxed and broad-bottomed but gave the impression he would be nasty in a fight.

Because I was in a state I knew I might give any contact a disconcerting charge of feeling and talked to him deliberately about his work. He played in a period-instrument band that met three or four times a week and gave regular concerts in the Cathedral and in other places across Flanders – I'd seen him come in a few nights before with the discreetly odd black case that housed his bombard, though it suggested a surgical device of the most specialized kind. They were called the Ghezellen van der Musycke – a name no more arthritic than most such consorts – and comprised singers as well as instrumentalists. Sometimes he brought one or two of them to the Cassette, but they sat apart, made childish jokes and left early. Gerard told me they had a record coming out soon and spoke about the ancient religious music of the town with such enthusiasm that I almost came to believe in his high estimate of the various masses and motets and other attainments of primitive polyphony that he was describing. A couple of drinks later he was still holding forth on late medieval life there, the unceasing round of ritual and worship, chants and processions, the festive days and offices. I drifted in and out of it; I felt he could be speaking to anyone. The image of Luc's back flared up again and again and made me gulp my beer down. Gerard spoke of the forever progressing Burgundian court. Sometimes brief highlights from Obrecht and Dufay were provided in the cracked croon that you hear on rehearsal records by elderly conductors. It seemed in May this year the Ghezellen had played their shawms and sackbuts in the procession of the Holy Cross and created some bad feeling among the conventional members of the town band. At Christmas they planned a re-creation of the festivities at the marriage of Charles the Bold and Margaret of York, in which the supper music was all performed by players disguised as animals: Gerard himself was to be a hare, and his colleagues would be lions, goats, bears and wolves. Seven monkeys would do a morris-dance. Apparently there had been a dromedary present at the original event, though it did not actually play. I looked over his shoulder to where the dusk was falling in the deserted street and in all the silent streets and courts beyond. I could picture my walk home, through the back lane called the Blind Fox and out into the floodlit square.

I started to tell Gerard about my father, and the records *he* had made, and about what it was like growing up in the house of a musician, the smell of starch, the hospital quiet, the cold suppers left under a cloth for his late return from a recital in Hove or an oratorio part in Guildford Cathedral. Gerard was torn between friendly enthusiasm and condescension towards this unheard-of tenor with a repertoire descending from Handel and Mendelssohn through Balfe and John Bacchus Dykes to *Oklahoma!* and the occasional medley from Lennon and McCartney. He shook his head and said, 'It's another world, isn't it?' – as if to marvel at my father's endurance and to re-move himself, as a musician, from any taint of association. I would have gone on to point out that Lewis Manners had brought far more happiness into the world than the Ghezellen van der Musycke were ever likely to do and that moreover he could sing, but I was distracted by Cherif climbing on to a stool further down the bar and twirling the remains of a drink with a look of moody disaffection.

Later I was talking to Matt. Matt was lean and pale, with slicked-back hair, and a cynical smile that never quite extended to the left side of his mouth. There was an affected calm to him; he looked at you with a glancing stare as if you had already come to an agreement. When I'd seen him here before he had been over-smart, and showed a spivvish self-consciousness about his cuffs and the creases in his flannels. I understood that he was something to do with computers, he was in the money, which explained his groomed composure among the transient youngsters of the bar and added to the static of sex and faith-lessness he knew he gave off. Tonight he was in clean new denim and a Tom of Finland T-shirt: a bulging biker arm-locked another across the shallow dip of his chest. He listened closely but impassively to my pained gauche hints about Luc and Cherif, then put a hand on my shoulder and talked to me quietly. His conversation was flat and narrow, and whatever he said took on the feel of a *double entendre*. He made my back prickle and my chest feel hollow. He talked about 'the best places to go': the best place was the Hermitage, some old gardens on the edge of town.

Matt and I walked up through the narrow stagy gloom of the Blind Fox and sat for ten minutes in a bus waiting for it to start. I looked around at the handful of other passengers, slack with tiredness or shaking newspapers inside out to find some last un-read announcement, and reflected on the ambiguous situation I was in. Matt was taking me to the Hermitage because of what I had told him of my troubles, of my day, and he thought it would take my mind off them; we were going there together – had left the Cassette glamorously together – but when we arrived we would have to look out for ourselves. I gathered Matt was pretty sure of meeting a builder from Leuven whom he'd had there the Saturday before; he wouldn't want me hang-ing around like a kid-sister, though I had a kind of comic dread that I would keep bumping into them as I prowled about. Actually I simply wanted Matt myself, but was powerless to tell him so as the seconds slipped away: we sat with our arms hooked over the seats in front and made sporadic remarks about things.

At the first stop I looked out and who should be waiting but Cherif. He clambered on and sat down at once at the front, next to a little old man: I didn't know if he had seen us or how conscious he was of being obliquely observed as he pulled off his awful tweed cap and sat with it rolled in his hands like a serviceman. I thought he was anxious as well as sulkily determined, independent but hopeful of mucking up our plans if he could. It was such a childish ruse that I knew for the first time in the whole fogged, giddy evening that he was truly hurt: I saw for a few minutes as we raced out on to the unpeopled glare of the ring-road that I was perhaps to blame, that I had stamped on some sentiment more delicate than he had been able to show, and that I was in fact the boor I had taken him to be.

Then Matt rang the bell and we sneezed to a halt at a shelter where tall and odorous limes towered over a high brick wall. A couple of boys, one stumblingly drunk, the other scratched and with thick sweat-soaked hair standing on end, waited in a loose embrace for us to step down into the road. It felt like arriving too late at a party, though it was only 10.30 or so. Matt, whose whole aim was sex, and who would not tolerate any lowering social embarrassments, muttered to me to let Cherif go ahead. Then we went on too, he suddenly shrewd, nervy, lighting a first cigarette, forgetting me or to offer me one. The walls swept inwards to big, curvy iron gates, which Matt immediately started to climb. I waited till he was clear and then was drunk enough to just do it, wedging my slippery-soled shoes into a haphazard ladder of bars and curlicues, and hoisting myself over the top whilst the gates rattled to their bolts. Another group of lads with bottles of beer gave almost whispered whoops as I swung down, and then said good evening with a kind of rowdy civility that cheered me up. I was in. I looked around for Matt, and smelt the iron on my hands; but he had gone.

I started down the avenue ahead. One of the boys called out

something, but I waved and went on, slowing as I lost the lights from the road and the mass of the trees closed out the sky above. There was a breeze from time to time and if I had been sober I might have found it chilly; the air was saturated with the woodland smell of leaves and earth and the rich shock of being in nature again after a week of brick and stone thrilled me. I stood still in the path for a while and listened as a cool gale passed through the wood from one end to the other. And my dear dead father singing 'Where'er you walk', with the words repeated a quite idiotic number of times, 'Where'er you walk, cool gales shall fan the glade, Trees, where you sit, shall crowd into a shade', and the expression of renewed wonder he managed at each repetition . . .

Beyond me the driveway framed a paler, slightly misty aperture, and as I emerged from the trees and peered about, convinced that the whole area was teeming with people, holding in their giggles like guests at a surprise-party, the immense three-quarter moon, close, just half a mile away, and yellow as brass, rose ahead.

In five minutes it had exposed the sorry remains of the Hermitage on my left and in front of it a wide field that narrowed in the distance to another avenue and a glimpse of water. There wasn't a sign of life and I thought for a moment that perhaps I *had* missed the party, or that if I had listened to the boys at the gate I would now be in the otherwise inaccessible place where the action was. All the same I felt self-conscious, and wandered along by the Hermitage as if I had come here out of purely architectural interest. There was a domed pavilion linked by a colonnade to a low, shuttered house. It was a fragment, crudely restored as a café and what might have been a park-keeper's store. Families came here all year round; beyond the buildings there was a sandy enclosure with swings and a climbing-frame. I walked back past them and looked in at a window of the pavilion, where the moon picked out the gigantic trophy of a tea-urn.

Away through the long grass, actions almost preceding the decision to take them, in the rampage of drink. Now I was in the mist that hung between giant beeches like dry ice in some romantic proscenium, tumbling slowly across the orchestra . . .

The two worn rococo lions could barely see each other, flanking the dark canal that lay ahead. I walked beside the water to the very end, learning to read my way in the obscured moonlight and the reflecting spread of the pond-mist, my heart catching sometimes at a waiting figure that was only a lichened Pomona or Apollo, its features obliterated – if not quite its promise. I couldn't know if I was nearing the place or trekking further and further away, to a region where all that stirred would be stoats and foxes and the odd rattled wood-pigeon. Matt had spoken of a kind of formal garden, almost a maze as I imagined it. I came back down the other side of the canal, beginning to think I would go home, longing for a drink.

I thought I heard music – a spacy androgyne popsong – but the breeze snatched it and dropped it like a waltz or shushed it under a long roar of leaves. I went towards it with clumsy determination, through the near-dark of the woodland, crackling over beech-mast and leaves, brushed by low undergrowth, lifting my feet up high but still tripping now and then on dead sticks. I must be making back towards the road. I ticked myself off in a muttering, good-humoured monologue for yet again taking so long, solitary and scenically roundabout a route to somewhere that was close by at the start: the luminous hands of my watch showed 11.20. I felt very far from home and stood still for a moment to test my sex-drive, like checking the oil in a car, decided there was enough for the time being and jogged on towards the music, and brief glares of light and boyish owl-calls on either side.

Someone had a torch and was roaming about, turning it on and off and provoking shouts and groans, and the occasional laugh. Or maybe the laughs came from the torch-carrier himself, drunk and tediously mischievous. For a moment I found myself at the fading limit of his beam, uncertain if I was visible, or if I wanted to be, if I was an intruder or a stumbling new arrival at the darkened pleasure-dome, grateful for the usher's glowing wand. Then the beam jerked to my left, and picked out two men against a tree, jeans round their knees, an arm round a neck, a hand roughly grasping at a white bottom – before they twisted back into the darkness, too far on to care much or protest. The torch went out and I stood still while the floating image, a glimmering ectoplasmic bottom, wandered and faded. In a minute the light struck out again and I saw the whole garden revealed for several seconds.

It was a wide circular clearing that would have been charming centuries ago, when the wood was no more than a nursery laid out in ranks and opening into tapering perspectives, but now was like something from a dream, with the huge impassive agitation of the trees above the circle of yew arbours, each with its gryphon-legged bench, and at the centre a brimming stone basin, mysteriously fed and clear.

One or two youngsters were squatting on the basin's damp surround: they had the ghetto-blaster, tuned in to some night-time station high on nostalgia – Herman's Hermits, then Village People, zapped from time to time by meteorite bleeps and whines and the continental jabber of adjacent wavelengths. I loafed out with all the smothered expectation of a teen date, hands in pockets. One of the boys called out 'Halloo, how *are* you!' and when I got to them we shook hands and inspected each other in the shadowed flame of a Bic lighter. Then darkness again. Someone said he'd seen me in the Cassette, someone else thought he had too. There was a mood of bland concurrence, as a large plastic bottle was nudged into my hand and Dusty Springfield mentioned smokily that she just didn't know what to do with herself. One of my companions sang along, anticipating the words and getting them wrong. Still, there was drink. I tilted the denting carboy to my lips and chewed incredulously on a mouthful of orange-juice.

Each yew-niche was a place of available secrecy, and I loitered round the circle, finding out what was going on. From some came steady little rhythms, or muttered encouragements, or deep, delayed intakes of breath, as pleasure turned serious. From some came girlish giggles and whispering. Some seemed empty and silent; or a solitary cigarette glowed and dimmed. I came round again, with slightly put-on carelessness, aware that I must be more visible to whoever was waiting there than they were to me. I got the impression from a smoker's ember-light of a fair-skinned mask, an upturned leather collar. I wished I had my leather jacket on, that I had planned all this. Was Matt still here? Had he met his builder? Was that beautiful man fucking a few feet away? Or was he off in the wood, beyond the torch-light, dead leaves in his hair and damp earth pressed into his back, mastered by his bricklaying colossus? I passed the alcove again, in a dither of lust and reluctance, and heard something murmured – just a throat-clearing perhaps, a manly Gitane-burble of readiness, of mere presence ... And where the hell was Cherif? A spasm of jealous annoyance carried me in.

You never knew what to expect. You never knew what they expected. You hadn't had the advantage of being at college to-gether, or persuading yourself you fancied him over drinks and supper, or knowing each other's name, or anything. The abso-lute black ignorance was the beauty of it, and the bore. Then afterwards perhaps there would be a match-flare of talk and in-formation, a number written down, too often only one ... It was simplest if they went straight down, or got you to: you were at it, you knew what you were doing, and it probably wouldn't last long. But then times had changed since the first anxious necessities back home on the common, at seventeen. There were new rules that didn't quite come naturally ... Sometimes these strangers got very lovy, tongue all over you, stubble-burn, sighs and moans. Sometimes they hardly wanted to touch, they'd hold you at a distance, like someone they were blokishly saying goodbye to; then a hand would descend and abstractly get about its business. Sometimes they liked to stand pressed up behind you, sometimes they wanted you to do that to them. Sometimes you wanted to, too. Often, of course, they were very drunk or stoned, and so were you, and it mattered less – anyway, you could hardly remember. Once in a while you had the best time you'd had in two or three years.

The cigarette was stamped out, though its smell lingered and grew stale around its smoker. I ran my hand quickly over a buckled leather jacket and down the stoutish legs as if I were frisking him at an airport. There was a lot of metal on him – the buckled jacket-sleeves, the thick chatelaine of keys at a belt-loop, the belt's own leaden buckle, rivets in the jeans. As I straightened up he ran his hand vaguely over my face, a nico-tined finger sour under my nose; then over my chest and stomach, soothing, noncommittal. I felt his head in turn, stroked behind an ear and pulled a lobe where three, four, rings clustered, and a further screwed stud. The hair was sleek and flat to the skull, and as he put his arms round me and hugged up close I traced it to a double rubber band and a silky foot of pony-tail. It was nice and warm being in there with him.

Even so I wasn't very keen on him; among my sighs and mutters I let out a great yawn over his shoulder, converting its final paroxysm into a shuddering, half-biting kiss of his manacled ear. I tried to imagine he was someone else, as he pulled out my dick – which was a bit sullen, a bit killjoy, wanted to be asleep – and as I duly prised out his own rather pushy, anonymous, straight-up little number. Suppose he was Matt, or even Gerard ... but I was growing used to the night, began to make out the dark oval of his face against the deeper darkness beyond, and when he rubbed against me, felt the chopped whiskers of a moustache. He knew I was holding back and out of friendliness or pure insensitivity he went at it the harder: there was a quick little ritual of groans, 'Oh yeah ... oh yeah ... oh yeah ...' and he shot off heavily up the front of my shirt. I closed my eyes. He hung on me for a while in hot-breathed recovery, and then returned to work on me. It was with a sense of conscious sacrilege that at last I admitted the idea of Luc. It was Luc standing behind me, his spent dick stiffening already between my legs, Luc's strong young hand firmly, almost over-fiercely, jerking me off, set on giving me pleasure, thrilled to do so: Luc who cupped his other hand to catch the warm splodge when it came.

I twisted slowly in his arms, the night wind carried a phrase or two of angelic tenorino Stevie Wonder on the crest of the forest's darker blind roar, the long grass ran and whispered, it was a rhythm of a runner's waterproofed legs whistling against each other, and the ambush of a flashlight a foot or two away. There we were – two men, drunk, ungainly, our spunk on each other's hands and clothes, and him looking at me with amusement while I winced and turned away.

4

'I saw you in the street.'

'When was that?'

'Saturday, at the market.' Luc's manner was warily reasonable and left him room to retreat if his first signal of friendship was rejected. I stared at the long, transparent miracle of his face, the slithering stack of hair, eyelashes still stuck with sleep, that brutally vulnerable lip. He was a slightly kitsch piece of work from an artist who carved in alabaster like flushed hard honey. The sleep-creases, a wisp of towel-fluff on a not yet daily razored jaw.

'I love you.'

He looked down at his exercise book and aligned his red, black and blue felt-tip pens with its upper edge. I pumped off a few more rounds of silent 'I love you's' – it took two or three seconds only. 'You should have said hello.'

'I'm afraid there was no time.' Had he sensed the clumsy semi-panic of my sudden stride across the square? 'I was with my friends.' Oh his friends . . . I thought of that well-favoured, self-admiring trio and of the trite intimacy of the shorter, darker boy and girl with my Luc, and was almost on the point of telling him about *my* friends. He mustn't see me as this lonesome crackpot. My heart was thudding, my own upper lip was dry, curled and stuck somehow to my teeth in a nervous rictus; I felt very warm.

We were in the dining-room again, not face to face as for the first interview, with its air of overdrafts, but cornerwise at the end of the table. I foresaw our legs touching, the pulse of a crossed leg gently knocking at the other's calf, if by the end of the hour we had pushed back chairs and talked. I had barely thought about it, but I had the light behind me, the rinsed light of the flatlands which illuminated Luc and made him frown

58

when once or twice the sun unveiled and struck across the sheen of walnut into those narrow, frankly unromantic eyes. I didn't see how he could be unaware of my feelings, which seemed to blunder and rebound around the room, hardly daring to fix upon their object. Surely I was behaving extraordinarily?

His mother came in with the two cups of coffee on their gilt papier-mâché tray, and they seemed a comforting little emblem of Luc's and my life together, tokens of its domestic normality that I saw repeated down the gallery of the coming months like the dwindling and vanishing servant on a bottle of Camp. She sampled our jerky conversation for a minute and retreated as if not quite happy with its colour and seasoning. When she'd gone I jumped up to get the sugar from the sideboard, alert now to her dogmatic little campaign that I should lose weight, and so made to seem defiantly flabby and rotten-toothed. But what the hell. I found myself reflected in the slanted glass of one of the blacker Altidore portraits, and I didn't look too bad: it was only in dreams sometimes that I turned out to be a true, short-winded fatso. I turned to offer sugar to Luc, who rejected it with a note of sleepy disdain; there was no spare flesh on him. I imagined him wanking in bed, perhaps half an hour ago, an intake of breath, the soft pearls tumbled at last in his pubic hair. I put the sugar-dredger carefully back beside the silver cruet, the grotesque epergne and the tantalus with its golden inch of cognac.

'So tell me about your friends.'

'Well, there is not too much to say.'

'I expect you have a large number of friends.'

'No, not so many.' He lowered his head to take a first slurp at his coffee. 'I have had some good friends at St Narcissus, but now I do not see them too much.' His voice, light, insistent, trustless, the heart-breaking Brutus of a school play; the occasional early-morning throatiness as if he were a smoker already.

'I can't believe they've all dropped you. Decided not to be your friends any more.'

'There are some, few, people who will always be your friends, even though you may not be with them often, and there are others who you see, whom you see, all the time who, sure,

59

they are your friends, but when life moves on you begin to forget them, and I find you do not have too much to say to each
other any more.'

'How very true.'

'For instance my friend Jeroen at St Narcissus, you know we
used to see each other every day, and so it was before then. His
father was at the very same school with my father, and I used to
play with Jeroen when we were just little kids. We both are,
well, quite good runners, but he became faster than me, and
perhaps I was unfriendly to him – not on the surface, you
know, but more on the bottom. Yes, underneath. But now,
when I see him in the town, like yesterday, I am actually quite
upset because we just say a few words and maybe I am embarrassed a little bit because I am not in the school any more, but
then I think he would like to be more grown-up and not to be in
the school too, even though he is now one of the top duxes – do
you say, the prefects, yes – and the captain of everything. So we
just laugh at each other for a minute and then we go away.'

My poor darling Luc! What hateful lessons you have to learn.
I grimaced avuncularly – not too avuncularly: the understanding smirk of a real friend. And it was cheering to think of his old
unappreciative friends dropping away, leaving only our little
corps of idolaters, unencumbered by other flatterers and time-
wasters (though schism and betrayal within so fanatical a clique
were a further danger not to be discounted). Even so there was
a certain grossness in my pushing the next question forward,
and I felt again for a second the interrogator's planned scorn for
etiquette, moved by the fiercer logic of his need to know.

'So who are your main friends, your best friends now?' And
my hand shuddered so that I had to return the cup to the saucer
untasted. A faint smile suggested surprise at a perhaps harmless
intrusion, registered the challenge of summing up so private a
matter and of setting about it in another language. But then, he
seemed to say, as he looked down and studied the dark swirls
and blooms of the walnut table-top, he wanted challenges, he
needed to excel, and I was right to test him so intimately within
the businesslike confines of our hour. I knew with a stab of certainty and regret that he would not have answered candidly if
he had thought of me as anything but a remote functionary,

60

whom he was well enough bred to treat as an equal. I had re-
ceded in a moment from Praetorian guard to the shabby
pedant-retainer of some remote and time-locked noble household.

The first person he described, Arnold, had been a frighteningly clever contemporary of his at St Narcissus, who had
passed his final exams a year early and was now at university in
Leuven, taking about ten different courses simultaneously and
aiming to graduate in half the usual time. He was unlikely to be
the handsome little chap of Saturday morning, with his rugger-
player's crop and bright but hardly intellectual air, and I interrupted after a minute or two's encomium of Arnold's
tremendous brain, his fluency in six or seven languages, his
almost negligent mastery of the organ and the cello, to insist on
the importance of a physical description. 'That's really what
you should have given me first, you know. Conjure up the outer
man, before getting into all this stuff about his *mind*.'

'Well, he is quite tall – '

'Ah.'

'Did I say something wrong?'

'No, no. Carry on. How tall is he? Your height?'

'He's a bit taller than me.' Luc paused, as if he might have
satisfied the requirements of the physical description clause, but
I pressed him a little further – kind of clothes, glasses, slight
speech impediment – to disguise my lack of interest.

'And Arnold's your best friend, is he? You must miss having
him around to tell you what's what.'

'What's what. Yes, that's correct. But we do write to each
other and he writes very long letters telling me about what he
has been reading and what music he is playing and so forth.'

'And what do you write about in your letters?'

'I tell him what I thought of the books he told me to read, of
course; and the music, but less, because he greatly loves organ
music, and I hate it very much.'

'Quite right.' Luc gave a grin, the first of our friendship, his
eyes almost closed, the long upper lip baring his gums, his moist
incisors. And then he seemed to notice how I stared at his
mouth, the grin went dead, he flushed and looked away deny-
ingly. Or was it mere self-consciousness at having acted for a

second or two so unselfconsciously? Without losing sight of the inquiry into his pals, I digressed briefly into music, and what he had been listening to. He said, depressingly enough, that he liked 'all kinds of music' – with the already admitted exception of the awful rumbling, blaring, warbling automation of the organ (he didn't put it quite like that) – and when pressed came out for Philip Glass (defiantly, as if he knew he wasn't any good) and for Schubert's piano trios (which Arnold was playing with a couple of university friends and insisted on Luc having in his head, in his system, as well). I thought back with a kind of despair to the days when I first got those trios into my head, and how I would never now hear them afresh. But that was half my life ago – when I was just at Luc's discovering age.

'And who are your best friends here in town?'

He took a moody couple of sips of coffee. 'Perhaps my best friend is called Sibylle.'

'That's a beautiful name,' I said airily, as if the ground had not shifted under my feet and there were not an ominous sifting of dust from the jagged crack in the ceiling. And like some creepy old hetero I went on, 'And is Sibylle as beautiful as her name?'

'Yes, I think I could say that she is very beautiful.'

'Fair-haired, I imagine?' I ponderously decoyed.

'Her hair is actually dark brown.'

'Tall and forbidding as a Sibyl of Michelangelo?'

Luc raised both eyebrows, stumped by that question, which I had indeed run out in a hammy double diapason, as if playing for the relish of some third, invisible, friend.

'She is not tall,' he said.

'The Sibyls were wise women, prophetesses. Michelangelo painted them in the spandrels of the Sistine Chapel, holding their prophetic books.'

'Yes, I know.' So you think you know what spandrels are, do you? But then, what are they *exactly* . . .? I hesitated and then pressed the door shut against the image of Luc with his latter-day Sibyl, meeting her in the empty afternoons, wandering the streets in a sentimental embrace, tea-time at a café, her on the pill, he priggish with first love. 'Is she still at school?'

'Yes, she is in her last year.'

'At St Narcissus?'

'There are no girls at St Narcissus. She is at St Opportune, near the Cathedral. It is an even older school, founded in fourteen – '

'Quite so. And – and do you know other girls there?'

'Yes, very many,' he said with a little defiant nod. And why shouldn't he know many, even very many, girls? I had known lots of them myself at his age, though fewer, somehow, now, away from the equal opportunities of school and university. And wasn't Edie in many respects my best friend? Hadn't we walked down Fore Street arm in arm and even loitered on occasion in Cricketfield Lane in a lovely sexless parody of boys with girls – daydreaming, nattering, full of camp confidences?

I wanted to know more, but dreaded hearing him say what I didn't want, above all, to hear said. 'Let's talk about food!' I suggested.

'Okay,' he said with a shrug, but then settled forward as if after all this might be quite fun. 'I will name fifteen kinds of fish.'

When the slightly fast clock in the adjacent sitting-room softly bonged twelve we had ransacked the slippery markets of St Andrew's Quay for a whole catalogue of eels, mussels, monkfish, dace and bream, and were growing almost hilarious as we hauled up odder and more doubtful species from neglected buckets and murky tanks. Luc's fish vocabulary was so comprehensive that I found myself learning from him; it was all good St Narcissus drill, of course, drummed in by some insanely thorough master, and I saw that though Luc notched up rarities like chad and wrasse to his credit he had no very clear idea what they looked or tasted like. Still, while the game lasted, we were suddenly closer, our awkwardnesses forgotten. The chase became a race. 'I'm surprised you should have overlooked grayling,' I said censoriously; and he slapped the table and said, 'Yes, and what about mullet, Edward, what about mullet!' so that I grinned and my heart sprinted at this first real naming, the first time I had become a person, my own name burning my face like some heartfelt endearment.

I expected his mother to come in and round things off, and got up and stretched and looked out of the window into the strip of garden with its tubbed shrubs and little pointed-roofed gazebo. Beyond was the canal, in whose sullen undredged depths fish undreamt of by Luc or me must live. I asked him if he knew my other pupil Marcel, and turned in one of the passing dazzles of sunshine to watch him answer, my shadow firm for a moment across the carpet towards him, its head in his lap.

'Only by sight,' he said, 'from school. I think he is a very kind young man and not a happy one. Sibylle . . .' I waited. 'Sibylle is a friend of his. I don't really know him.' He gathered up his notebook, in which he was yet to write a word, and clutched together the coloured pens. His mother came in. He rose and after a few exchanges did his duty of showing me to the door, but as if it were something he hoped he wouldn't always have to do.

5

I had arrived without knowing how on the street where the Orst Museum was, and sat down, suddenly exhausted, on a bench opposite. The quiet out here was subtly different from the quiet of the middle of town, the little brick squares where for a full quarter of an hour no car would pass and nothing alter beyond the pulling-to of a shutter, or a dog trotting along with an intermittent sense of purpose. Here the stillness was as deep, the grand brick houses equally steeped in silence and discretion, their windows silver-black above the stumpy limes. But you felt a freshness, the nearness of a larger sky, to which the line of windmills at the street's end blindly opened their arms. I watched a couple of tourists arrive at the Museum and recognised their mood of achievement, of having come out quite far, almost into the country.

In the Museum's dark, polish-scented hall I paid my admission fee, and bought a booklet, vainly feeling that the girl student at the desk should know that at other times I came here free, with the director, long after she had gone home. I laid a claim to it, somehow, because of the unexpected understanding I believed existed between Paul Echevin and me. It would have been pleasant if he had suddenly come down the stairs and spotted me; but I slightly dreaded it too, in case the greeting was cool and the girl student more in his confidence than I was. She sat behind the modest display of postcards with the defiant air of an intelligent person wasting time for a good cause. What hours, weeks, of nothing must happen in this hall, as the autumn came on. As I turned away she picked up a fat paperback and continued to read.

The first room was long and half-panelled, with the sparse furnishing of a house no longer a home — a pair of roped-off chairs, a writing-desk with a dozen dusty pigeon-holes, a tall

Dutch vase in the big black aperture of the fireplace. Cream cotton blinds were pulled half-down at the front, whilst at the far end the windows gave on to a sunless open porch and one of the city's high-walled secret gardens. A handful of paintings by Orst – each preciously isolated – hung in gentle diagonals of light against a background of worn heroic tapestry. I walked round the room three or four times wondering if it was all a mistake, if I should leave at once, but I clung to it in the end, almost fearing to be out on the streets again, the lulled, senescent streets, when I was so pierced with relief and exhilaration and lust and a sense of failure. I sat on an absent guard's folding stool as if stumbling to my corner, slugged by the boy's beauty and too stunned to see the beating still to come.

I made a forced decision to read the little history Paul Echevin had written. I knew I knew nothing about this painter beyond a few details on book-jackets, a decadent poster or two perhaps at university – his famous Sphinx that ramps and bridles and circles Oedipus' legs with its tawny tail; or the oddly appealing Purgatory where each gaunt figure stoops under the weight of its own Chimera, a domestic-looking hybrid like a mother's thick fur stole with feet and long-toothed head still on. The refined asymmetry and social elegance of the portraits in this room – all of members of his family, it turned out – came as something of a surprise.

I learned that Orst had been born in this house in 1865, the son of an eminent civil lawyer. His childhood had been secluded, the family pious and old-fashioned but not uncultured, the house cluttered and *démodé* in its furnishings and rich in the patterned and storied Flemish fabrics that were to appear so often in Edgard's pictures. We were to imagine him and his sister Delphine playing in the sequestered garden with its sixteenth-century mulberry trees, two introspective children lost in their own world of chivalry, playing sometimes quite apart, acting out their private legends. (At this point the various belfries of the town, slightly staggered and clangingly oblivious of each other, began to sound the hour.) In the far wall was the postern giving on to the outer defensive canal, a door always locked, but the source again, so Echevin proposed, for the repeated imagery of the doorway in Orst's work – a mystic threshold, apparently, on to who knew what, as in his master-piece 'La Porte Entr'ouverte'.

As a young man he went to Brussels to study law, but in a first surprising show of independence gave it up after a year and managed to enrol, on the strength of some romantic designs for *Hamlet*, at the Académie des Beaux-Arts. A marked strain of Anglophilia brought him to lodge in the quartier Léopold, with the British colony – and much of the success of his earlier years was due to galleries and collectors in London and Liverpool and Glasgow. Burne-Jones was an influence, an admirer and, in his last years, when Orst would spend the two or three months of the exhibition season in England, a friend. Orst joined, in its own final years, the group of Belgian Symbolists who called themselves, like the first squad for some irregular ball-game, 'Les XX'.

In 1898 he had made designs for *The Merchant of Venice* in Brussels and painted a life-size full-length of the Portia, Jane Byron, a Scottish actress with the abundant red hair and pale heavy-jawed beauty of the period. A scandalous love-affair fol-lowed (la Byron was suing for divorce in England, to the consternation of the Catholic Belgian press), and Orst produced a series of studies, portraits and outright fantasies over the heady six months before her death by drowning at Ostend in May 1899. The portraits and fantasies did not, it seems, finish with her death: furnished with passionate memories and several hundred photographs, Orst carried on painting her for another thirty or forty years – until he lost his sight in the mid-1930s.

In 1900 he left Brussels and returned to the abandoned city of his birth; his career as a portrait-painter was over (though he was persuaded to take the occasional commission, for instance to draw the King's children) and henceforth he devoted himself to his melancholy obsession. I imagined him spending his days in this childhood house, in this room perhaps; but apparently he had built a house of his own on the other side of town, a tall white *maison d'artiste* topped by a figure of Hermes who gazed out with a lofty challenge over the surrounding suburban gar-dens. (The house had been demolished after the war to make room for an important road.)

There were three pictures of Orst himself in the booklet. The first was by a fellow-student at the Academy, a hasty charcoal drawing that emphasised potential brilliance and potential tragedy. In the second, a photograph, he was seen in his studio against a background of tapestry and *objets de vertu*, already the cold-eyed dandy I knew from the picture in Echevin's study, half emerging, half held back by shadow. A pebbly pince-nez hung at his lapel. The third, taken in his last years, looked none the less like an experiment from the early days of photography, or like something indoors seen through a breath-clouded window, a wash of white light into which the blind old man, shawled in a wheelchair, seemed almost to dematerialise.

I was gripped by Orst's obsession with his actress. I loved the superior way he had renounced everything in its favour, and made such a show of retreating from view into the snows of a dream. Of course I was working it up rather from the few facts given in the pamphlet: my mind ran ahead and took possession of the idea. I imagined a life consecrated to the image of Luc, a shuttered house, the icon of his extraordinary face candlelit in each room – until I saw with a shiver that I had killed him off already, perhaps too high a price for either of us to pay. I went upstairs in search of Jane, standing aside at the first turning for the couple who had come in before me, and overhearing their firm Cheshire distaste for what they had walked all this way to see; I warmed to them and despaired of them at the same moment; then past the door of Paul Echevin's office, which was slightly open in approved Orstian style, his voice heard on the phone, trying to wind up a conversation.

And there Jane was. She wasn't entirely alone: other figures and various beasts paced and waited in the starry twilight, the jewelled Hades that she inhabited. But she was always the one on whom the drama turned or the mood centred. In a big triptych, hinged like an altarpiece, you saw only her ringed left hand scooping a train of crumpled satin, like a bride entering a carriage, but you knew it was her. In other pictures, cropped in similar startling ways, you were given only the firm-jawed lower half of her face and the hair spread out, or gathered round her like a shroud. A conversation-piece, where half a dozen women lazed on a terrace with tea and sewing and cigarettes while sunset waned through trees and spires beyond, turned out to be all Jane – full face, once smiling, once pensive, both profiles, a chicly bustled rear view, stretching, hands pressed to the small of the back, and a tender *profil perdu*, which spoke of intimacy and oblivion; in the mannered vastness of the flat gold frame, the words 'Léal Souvenir' were inscribed in red.

Just by repetition the face began to emanate a kind of power, though this was nothing to do with character or expression. Jane Byron might have been a versatile actress but all the roles Orst cast her in were enigmatic or monumental–the seer, the sufferer, the sphinx. Even the domestic scenes, depicted with photographic refinement, had an air of suspended animation, and seemed reports from a world of dreams. The face itself was a mask, heavy, almost matronly at times, and while I didn't warm to it in itself I was oddly excited by its pale proliferation. Though the pictures showed no concern at all with men (the occasional epicene boy was always in the end a Hebe or a bosomless girl-child) there was none the less something perverse about them which did almost as well. It was the sense of a passion that had taken the fateful turn into fixation, exploited by its own compelling mechanism long after its subject was gone.

It was quite a surprise after all this to find a group of pupils from St Narcissus on the upper floor, junior boys cross-legged in their capes and gaiters forming a semi-circle around the art master, a dynamic broad man built like a prop forward. I loitered on the further side of the room, looking with an adult eye at a row of tiny, almost invisible silverpoint drawings, but curious as a boy about the others and what they were being told. The master was explaining a set of landscapes: I heard how Orst had returned every year to the hamlet in the Ardennes where his childhood summers had been spent, and how he liked to escape from the studio and paint out in the forests and on the heathy uplands; how, in particular, he returned to a lonely woodland pond, which he had painted twenty or thirty times in different lights and at different seasons. I learned more about St Narcissus, too, than I had gleaned from the chants and odd emphatic phrases of lectures that crossed the back garden; I recognised the methodical presentation, the excessively clear

light thrown on obscure subjects, the mixture of free specu-
lation and arbitrary learning that make up a good
old-fashioned education; I saw the reasonable self-satisfaction
of the master and the concentration of the boys who were not
afraid to speak their minds when questioned, and not broken
by a reproof. And I thought of Luc out on this same lesson two
or three years back, attentive but independent, giving the best
answers, a big boy already in the dressy black uniform he had
worn until so lately, until whatever it was that happened happened . . . every teacher's darling, surely (though this one
looked a little fierce for darlings).

'What colour is this pond? Stevens?'

'Grey, sir.'

'No. Van Damme?'

'Lead-coloured, sir.'

'Correct. And what are these trees? Stevens?'

'Are they Douglas firs, sir?'

'Firs will do, thank you, Stevens.'

The faint terror of being back in school, but now as a forgetful grown-up among teenagers primed like guns, overcame me,
and I slipped back downstairs, leaving the ponds for another
day.

Paul Echevin was coming up, but something made me shrink
and look down as we passed, as though I might go unseen in the
oaky half-darkness; a second later I hated having flunked the
meeting I had already pictured to myself with pleasure, even excitement. 'Edward!' He had turned with a hand on the banister.

'Oh, hello . . .' I wasn't sure what to call him.

'You didn't tell me you were coming in.'

'I didn't know,' I said, with sudden force on the final word
which surprised both of us and made him pause a moment. 'I
didn't know,' I repeated more sensibly.

'Tell me if you're coming again – don't pay.'

'That's very kind of you.'

He started up the stairs again. 'Are you running off now?
Have you seen it all?'

'I have to. It's Marcel's lesson in half an hour.' I smiled and
shrugged to suggest that that was life, but that it wasn't a
burden.

'Ah yes. Well, come and see us again, won't you? Perhaps you'll join us for supper tomorrow. We'll have a couple of people in, but nothing formal. I'm a bit worried about you,' he said, nodding, whimsical but clairvoyant. 'I think we need to feed you up.'

I'd just turned into my street when there was an annoying pip-pip-pip on a horn, and a kind of jeep, metallic blue, with yards of chrome trim, triple exhausts and gigantic tyres, pulled up just past me. It reminded me of the uncomplaining toys which tumble over and right themselves all day long in trays outside Oxford Street gift shops. I looked in and Matt was leaning across, trying to open the passenger door. Our relations had been cool and abstracted on the night of the Hermitage, so I knew he must be stopping to show off his ridiculous vehicle.

'Hey, Ed!' he said. 'Jump in, let's go for a ride.'

'I can't,' I said, 'I've got a lesson.' The mistaken diminutive rattled me. My mother had insisted on the full Edward all my life, and so had I – though my uncle Wilfred was allowed the deviation of Ned. Yet there was a pleasure to be had from answering to it – a hasty, holiday intimacy. Ed was someone it might be a relief to be for a day, under a sunny sky. I felt a frisson of recall, just half a second of access to a keen, lost mood – a childhood summer at Kinchin Cove, my brother nagging me to put down my book and play rounders, a beach bully shouting, 'What's his name? All right, Ed, you're over there, Ed . . .'

'Is he the cute one? We could take him for a ride too.'

'He isn't, I'm afraid. Not this one. He's a fat little fellow with asthma.' I leaned in at the open door. Matt's right hand lay on the passenger seat still, its veins sexily fat and blue over the delicate bones, the nails shockingly bitten. I imagined it moving up my thigh as I sat beside him and we burned out of town.

'Where is it you live?'

'Just there. The white house on the corner.'

'It looks very grand.'

'Yes, doesn't it?' We gazed at it as if I was the lucky owner of the whole thing.

71

'And who's that?'

The wicket at the side had opened and an incredibly pretty boy with curly dark hair came out, checking his fly and looking pleased with himself.

'Oh, that,' I said wonderingly. Matt and I watched him go past on the other side of the street apparently quite unaware of our scorching attention.

'Another of your cast-offs, don't tell me.' He had turned and was craning through the polythene rear window of the hood to catch every last possible second of the sight of the young man. Then he swung back with a grin of lust.

'How did you get on the other night?'

'Okay, thanks.'

'You made out?'

'Yep. I got lost for a few hours, but I made out in the end.' He was nodding and staring: I was clearly meant to ask him the same question.

'How about you? Did you find your builder?'

'The fucker wasn't there. Or if he was he found someone else first. No, I ended up with your friend, the Frenchman, the Moroccan.' Matt looked at me narrowly, like a sadistic child, knowing his words would have some effect but unsure what. 'Ed, you ought to look after that man. He told me that he loves you, and he is *wild*. We fucked each other every which way.'

'Yes, Cherif's good,' I said, swallowing the passing heartburn of his remark. 'But he's not really in love with me. And you forget that I *am* in love with someone else.'

He looked at me sceptically, and revved the rough-throated engine a couple of times. 'What are you doing this evening?'

I thought of one or two lies (going to a dance in a barracks, supper with Luc at a country hotel). 'Oh, the usual,' I said. 'Chasing oblivion at the Cassette.'

'Have you been to the Town Baths yet?'

'Do you mean a swimming-pool or something else?'

'Yes, the swimming-baths. The Town Baths. Why don't you come with me for some hard exercise before your drinking begins?'

I didn't want to get more involved with Matt; I bridled, as I often did these days with beautiful men ('Don't bother about

72

me') – and I was a clumsy, nervous swimmer. But the thought of a distraction from Luc, an hour or two saved from a night that would otherwise be rushed and lost in drink, made a sudden appeal. And perhaps I did quite like the idea of being stripped out with Matt and the ten minutes afterwards in the showers, chatting like straight boys and sharing his shampoo. I said I'd come, and took directions to the place without being able to concentrate on what I was being told. Matt gave me a wink, I slammed his door; and it was only as I watched him fight his throttle and catapult through the empty street on some imaginary challenge that I doubted if I had any trunks with me. Then Marcel appeared, slightly anxious, but with a new comic silly-old-me look to him that was far from welcome.

I made every effort, through the hour that followed, to be helpful to the boy: I was becoming a friend of the family, which entailed certain obscure but real duties; and I had started to see how Marcel himself played a part in Luc's world and must be courted for access and information. I was quite alarmed at the thought of what he could tell me, the dreams he could unwittingly nurture or destroy. I'd lost the courage I had in questioning Luc, and paced the lesson carefully, making sure of each hesitant step, taking nothing for granted. The time was horribly elastic. While we toiled through basic irregular verbs, while I sat and waited for answers and gazed past him to the trees and church tower outside, the minutes and seconds seemed actually to slow. I had the sense that movement would be laborious or impossible, and that my voice would emerge in an ogreish growl, fractured into its separate vibrations. But when he lost me, when my mind ran over the whole story of Luc so far, when I thought jealously of Matt with Cherif, time looked dramatically condensed, it was all happening, fierce, bright and purposeful, like the top line in some great canon, whilst in the depths the basses pondered on the subject in inexorable slow-motion.

Suddenly, at last, St Narcissus was announcing the hour, its elderly clatter unleashing the rumpus at the school as lessons broke up and masters, half-relieved themselves, shouted their last instructions over the rising din. Marcel unthinkingly shut his notebook, in which he had been writing out the verb 'to forget', and beamed cheekily. He was still conditioned by the rules and stimuli of the school he had escaped; and seeing this I went to the window and questioned him amiably, as he packed up his satchel, about his time there and his friends.

'Do you still have some pals at school? You know, friends.'

'I have one or two.' And how unreal it must seem to be kept from them and their routines and gossip by this square of garden and this dull canal. It was as if one of the classrooms had floated off in a dream and perched nearby, filling its solitary pupil with a mood of privilege and anxiety.

'I should have asked you before if you knew my other boy, Luc Altidore?'

He mumbled, 'No, I don't really know him.'

'Of course, he would be older than you.' I turned and looked at him encouragingly. He was ready to go now and clearly waiting out of politeness, remembering perhaps that I was to come to dinner again, that he could never get away from me. 'You must miss it all, Marcel, don't you?' I urged. 'The companionship especially.'

'It is a very clever school, but I am not so very clever.' He shook his head, to say it was touch and go whether he was happier then or now; and I understood that he had not been happy either at school or out of it. I had known him from the first as a boy set apart by his illness, but I had at least imagined a hobby – in the simplest terms, stamps or model kits – and a friend or two he shared it with. But I could see that Luc himself would not be such a friend.

'And what do you know about Luc's girlfriend?' I boomed roguishly, appallingly, and blushed as I did so. Marcel shook his head and took on a dogged look, as if the lesson and its catechism were starting up all over again. 'What's she called?' I hammed on – 'Sibylle something?'

Marcel looked down and fiddled with his satchel-buckle. He was flushing more richly than I was. 'She is not his girlfriend,' he said. 'They are just friends.'

'Not his girlfriend,' I echoed quietly. 'No, I suppose he is a little young to have . . .' And what did Marcel know about girl-friends? 'Well, I'll see you on Wednesday. No, tomorrow night. That will be nice.'

'He was never interested in girls,' he said quickly in Flemish, as if the idea were too serious or shocking to manage in this difficult other language. I let the lapse pass, and hid away the longed-for but doubtful information to look at later.

A moment after the door had closed I felt quite humiliated to be acting the role of the buffoon, agonised into farce. I went to the front window and watched Marcel emerge into the yard below and break into a heavy run as if, sedentary and breathless though the boy was, he could hardly wait to reach the gate and be free of me. I knew instinctively the freedom that he wanted – not freedom to do some challenging thing, but to do almost nothing, to wander homewards through the mild afternoon . . . I stayed with my forehead to the windowpane and within ten seconds there was the slap of the wicket again, and back came the curly-haired boy Matt and I had seen earlier. He had been to the big supermarket and swung a carrier with a loaf and a bunch of flowers sticking out of it. He disappeared into the Spanish girls' staircase and something told me that in the bulky lower part of the bag were cheesy nibbles, Cokes and Sprites and a beer or two for the boys. The girls were out now, as far as I could tell, but when they got back they were going to have a party! For a moment my gloom swallowed up my envy.

I opened the hanging cupboard and got into it, tussling lightly with my raincoat and leather jacket and jangling the un-used hangers on the rail. I had a fatalistic need to know what I was in for, what crass intrusions of noise I was going to tolerate; as well as a complete curiosity about the boy, who seemed to me unswervingly beautiful and sexy just then in contrast to the shrouded and ambiguous merits of Luc, who was never interested in girls. But after ten minutes with my ear pressed receptively to the wooden partition, I had picked up nothing beyond the snap of a ring-top can, a few words, half-said, half-sung, and a smug reverberant burp. At last I thought I heard a gently rhythmic noise, and had him frowningly ex-ploring himself, until I realised it was the shushing of the pulse in my ear. I edged back into the room and shut the door.

*

My route to the Town Baths was vague enough in my mind to take in the street where Luc lived without forcing, but when I came past the house I looked down nervously, and only glanced for a second searchingly into the ground-floor windows. Evening was coming on, and I could see nothing in the front rooms beyond the heavy swags of Mrs Altidore's curtains. And on the first floor, something else, the gleam of a disc, like a lens, suspended just inside the glass and catching the light with a flash of animation. Better not to see him just now. The sudden ebbing of anxiety; and then the wallow as a questing wave of apprehension pushed into the inlet of my heart: perhaps that was what Wordsworth meant in a passage I would be teaching Luc much later on when he spoke of sensations felt *along* the heart – as if the heart were a sea-beach on which feeling rhythmically broke. I recognised a deep-suppressed cold fear of water and the schooltime echo of our high-raftered swimming-baths.

I would have missed the place if I hadn't seen a brisk little family with rolled towels under their arms turn off just ahead of me into a covered alleyway thronged with locked bikes. At the end a guichet and an inexorable turnstile gave admission to a further, darker passage, a region of brown paint and damp-eaten plaster.

I hadn't found any swimming-trunks, and so brought an old pair of army surplus shorts with button fly and turn-ups that some fantasy of summer had made me pack in England: they were my mowing the lawn shorts, my lying on the mown lawn with the Sunday papers shorts. They looked hopeless among the kids' darting Speedos and the trim corsetting of the dads. I stepped out gingerly through the lukewarm footbath on to the white noisy poolside.

Part of the misery of swimming was that you couldn't do it in glasses; the surrender to cold water followed immediately on the surrender to a world of vague distances and confused identities, and as I stood squinting down the lanes in the dim hope of picking out Matt's dark head I had a moment's foretaste of the fears of the old, as you see them smiling anxiously against imagined threats and half-heard ridicule. Then I jumped in like a child, straight off the side and holding my nose.

With my first kick from the edge the pockets of my shorts

filled heavily with water. After two or three more cautious strokes they were dragging at my hips and I had to dart a hand down to tug them back ... I felt with my feet and could just stand tiptoe. Not daring to haul myself out in a rash denuding surge at the side, I hopped and then toilingly strolled towards the shallow end, startled by the shout of a strong swimmer swimming laps, a wordless bark was all he had time for as his head plunged in again and I sprawled backwards to get out of his way, knocking into a stout woman with a stately, slow-moving head held high and a kick under-water like a mule.

I stayed crouching and randomly splashing in the shallows, exaggerating the bruise the woman's kick had inflicted, and whining inwardly like a child who wants an excuse to go home. I moved around enough to bring any of the other men who were waiting or resting between laps into the welcoming circle of my close vision, but there was no one I knew, there was no one special, until at last I saw Matt and waved and gave a derisive, laddish shout. He stared for a moment, then turned his back on me as I roamed towards him and I had almost put my hand on his shoulder before I realised it wasn't him. Then some kids came threshing past in the fury of a race and a fight mixed up together, and mixed up in their wake a further shout and rush, an arm from behind throttling me, thighs locked piggy-back round my hips as I stumbled forward and under in a horri-fied welter.

When I struggled up, gasping and mad, the grip relaxed, he slipped off my back and turned me in his arms quite lover-like. 'Matt, you stupid fucking cunt!' He was dazzling with his hair flattened, the cheap flash of a sapphire ear-stud and his un-apologetic sideways grin. I wanted to slap his face, but just held back as he said, 'Did I frighten you?' and splashed some snot off my upper lip. We were standing a few feet in from the end almost in an embrace; the pool was navel-high.

'I've got to get out,' I said. 'My trunks keep coming down. Well, they're not trunks, really – that's the point ... ' Matt was running a finger inside the sagging waistband, rubbing the back of his fist against the water-logged crotch. 'For god's sake, man. We're not in the Bar Biff now.' I made off towards the little lad-der the timid and the oldsters used. But Matt was with me, creamily kicking across on his back, lean and effortless. When I got out and the water streamed from my pockets and turn-ups on to the poolside he didn't laugh; he even hopped out too and walked with me to the exit: he had on weightless, silkily synthetic black shorts.

'I'll buy you a drink later,' he said. 'I've *got* to do my 2,000 metres.'

'That sounds like quite a lot later. Okay, you know where I'll be.' He squeezed my upper arm before he turned, jogged back and up-ended without a splash into the rippling blue. He was interestingly white, as if he couldn't be bothered with the vanity of tanning or had spent the hot late summer in some more worthwhile way than most of us. I was sorry to have passed up the chance of soaping his back.

The showers were functional and fierce, a yellow-tiled room with six fixed nozzles and high up in one wall a narrow strip of meshed window that could be tugged open at the top by a chain. I was amazed to pick up, through the crash of the water and the suck and wheeze of the drain, the putter of a boat's engine and a brief reek of burnt fuel. A canal must lie just outside, perhaps lapping against the very walls of the bath.

'Have a good swim?' said a shampooing dad opposite, with the nice unintrusive openness of the people here.

'I haven't got the right clothes,' I said and hurried to get out of my shorts.

'You want some proper swimming-trunks,' he said. The conversation was unlikely to soar, but we chattered on for a minute or two while I washed, about indoor as against sea bathing and about the Belgian beaches. He was very enthusiastic about Blankenberge, though what he praised in it, the crowds, the cheap food, set me against it. I stayed on for a while when he'd left, the hot water thrumming on my shoulders, then went to the doorway and screwed up my eyes to read the changing-room's electric classroom clock. It was already ten past eight: seriously time for a drink.

I towelled myself down at the rubber-matted threshold of the showers, and I was largely dry when I heard a whoop and a couple of lads came splashing in through the footbath, a nicely curvy dark one and a skinny one with long fair hair twisted up in a knot like a girl. They ran straight into the showers and fell against opposite walls, panting and laughing at each other. Without hesitation I flung my towel aside and went back in, unstoppering my conditioner bottle and preparing to wash my hair all over again.

I hadn't seen them since that first evening at the Bar Biff, the hot little loudmouth and his friend, his lover, who now unknotted his hair and shook it over his shoulders as if he were Jane Byron herself; and it did give a scatter of glamour to his hollow-eyed face, still blurred by spots around the forehead and jaw. The dark boy, who wasn't plump but would never perhaps be thin, was as hoarsely sexy as possible: I flickered a look from moment to moment over his square full-mouthed head, like a Roman street-boy's, the soft black hairs on his upper lip – and one or two already on his broad-nippled chest – and down to the bow in the draw-string of his trunks, the string hanging and diverted across the neat sideways jut of his cock within the tight red fabric. Yet it was his scrawny friend, just beside me, who gave me again the feel of those lost months of self-discovery, the first possession of the rights of sex. The dark boy would always be sexy, even when he ate himself into middle age, and, who knew, into marriage and its infidelities; but the blond one – not blond even, but a sort of no-colour that took body in the wet – I saw as a common scrap irradiated by love and confidence. I remembered how the whole world changed, how you were suddenly inside the great luminous concourse of human happiness, and how you thought you would be there always – though now, fifteen years later, I found myself glancing myopically in from the limbo of baffled hopes and bad habits that was always ready and waiting just beyond.

My boys didn't actually wash or strip, just lounged around and laughed. After ten minutes or so their unembarrassed possession of the place was tiring me and I had washed so frequently and industriously that I began to feel like the victim of some traumatic guilt, who must wash and wash till his skin is chafed away . . . Then at last the fair one had finished, and hurried off into the changing-room – I couldn't quite catch his remark. He had on knee-length trunks in phosphorescent orange, lime and mauve, nightmare colours from my own child-hood that seemed to be fashionable all over again. His friend grinned in appreciation, in anticipation, but stayed behind. My heart stepped on the gas.

By now I was simply lolling under my jet, as if to get the maximum benefit after several unusually demanding hours of exercise. When I looked up, the boy smiled at me.

'Excuse me, sir,' he said in English. And then, stumped as to how to continue, went on in Flemish, 'Could I borrow some of your shampoo, please sir?' Seeing that I understood and held out the rather precious phial of Coward & Rattigan's herbal haircare, he smiled broadly and came forward to receive it. If he had been one of my pupils I would have pointed out that what he borrowed he must expect in due course to repay.

He tilted out a greedy palmful and stood in the middle of the room, rubbing it into his shortish hair; then handed the bottle back and came in under the jet next to mine. Long drools of suds flooded down his easily muscled back.

'Did you have a good swim, sir?' he asked.

'Yes, great, thanks. I feel quite tired after it.'

'That's when it does you most good. What did you do? Hundred lengths, sir?'

I could have done without all this 'sir' business; it made me feel like an old gent in the hands of a keen young hotel porter with his eye on a tip. I only wanted to appear his equal, almost his coeval, and he was calling me 'sir' every third word. I wondered for a moment if he had mistaken me for a master at his school. 'Not quite that much,' I said, 'though I'd have liked to have done. My name's Ed – Edward, by the way.' He nodded, and jutted his face into the column of falling water. Then he stepped back, breathing in sharply two or three times and at long last toyed with his draw-string and tugged off his little red slip.

An odd thirty or forty seconds followed – me with a helpless and untouched hard-on, the boy quite clumsily doing some sort of improvised act, turning and bending under the shower, join-ing his hands behind his head to show off quick young biceps, sighing like someone simulating pleasure in a film. Thirty or so seconds before I understood. I was out of the shower in a moment, snatching up my towel and going at an angry stride through the changing-room, suddenly alert to my own naked-ness, and abruptly shrunken by my sense of stupidity and loss.

I had picked a locker in an odd corner, an alcove almost. The fair boy, the skinny lover, was in there now, back turned, a towel over his shoulders. I must have said something – just a swimmer's bark perhaps – and he twisted round with my wallet in his hands. Beside him the locker-door was open, my wet shorts still hanging from the pin of the key, revolving slowly and dripping on to the concrete floor.

He threw the wallet on to the bench as if it were distasteful to him, as if he had been tricked into picking it up in the street; and came round me quite fast, tossing his damp hair back off his face. He couldn't have run far in the state he was in, but he might have headed back to the pool, where it would have been harder for a diffident foreigner to make a fuss. I'm sure he would have dodged me in some way, if his friend hadn't come pounding along the alleyway of lockers and hanging coats, grim-faced but with a trace of chancy humour still in the eye-brows, ready in case the situation could be saved with a joke. I imagined a good deal of crap was about to be talked, and a lot of conning extenuation produced to block my path to a proper complaint or report. But my dark young decoy didn't have to claim a part in this, he could have played ignorant, and when he came marching to his friend's aid, his strong little cock bob-bing, I was obscurely touched and confused in the midst of my anger.

'Has he taken anything, sir?' he asked, a hand on my shoulder, looking at the rifled locker. The 'sir' had a different sarcasm now, like a policeman's. I stepped forward and snatched up the unbuttoned bill-fold. There had been little enough in it, anyway. 'I haven't got any money, you stupid bas-tard,' I blurted out. 'You've really picked the wrong person.' I knew I'd come out with a few hundred francs for drinks and perhaps a sandwich or a pickled egg. There was nothing there now.

'I didn't take anything,' said the thief, with a brief insulted smile. I stared in silence, my hand stuck out. 'It was like that when I came along.' His friend moved close to him as if to

81

whisper something through his hair, slid two fingers into his waistband and tweaked out the money, the two shiny leaves with their High Renaissance portrait, my survival-kit. 'What the fuck are you doing?' the boy said, bewildered, thinking himself betrayed. But I had a hunch that the other was a better criminal than his accomplice, who had taken so long and been so miserably caught. 'Here's the money, Edward,' he said. 'Listen, I'm really sorry about this.' I fumbled with my towel and fixed it round me like a skirt. I was more wounded by my own idiocy than by the tawdry little crime, and raised my voice to cover my shame.

'That's all very well,' I said. 'I'm afraid I shall have to report this. You just *can't* . . .'

'Hold on, Edward,' said the boy, looking around him to assess the damage my outburst might be doing and perhaps to make sure that he had no audience for the rest of his act. Again the hand on the shoulder, and this time the side of his body pressed lightly against mine. 'Sit down a minute, you know . . .'

'There's no point in sitting down,' I snapped. And then, 'Oh shit, where's my watch?' – my dear father's gold watch with the stop-hand that had slyly timed many a *Messiah* and *Gerontius* . . . I rummaged in the locker, grateful at least that I had caught the offender and that that above all could be saved. But it was still there, rolled in my sock in the toe of a shoe. I turned round almost panting at the waves of pain and apprehension these kids were so wantonly inflicting on me. At the same time I was aware of not speaking in my own voice, of being betrayed by anger into routine threats and dead formulae. The skinny boy muttered 'Mark', but Mark stared at him and then slowly sat down; and there was something about that slowed pressing together of the slatted pine bench and the boy's naked bottom, maybe something calculated, maybe not, the momentary heightening of his nakedness by contact with the inanimate, hard world, the fore-image too of the faintly flushed stripes the slats would leave when he stood, as if after some delicate accurate thrashing, that tilted the balance for him. I sat down in turn and so after a moment did the other boy, opposite us and wary. He shivered slightly and hunched the towel around him.

82

Mark looked me straight in the eyes and reddened as he said, 'I'll do anything you like, Edward.'

Telling Matt the story as we hurried in the early hours from the bar towards his flat, I had trouble conveying the keenness of the dilemma, this particular boy sitting naked beside me, breathing through his mouth into my face, his wet hair releasing sudden trickles down his neck, and making fabulous proposals that I had grumpily to reject. 'You should have brought him back here,' said Matt. 'We could have taken turns with him.' He gave his short nagging laugh, that always sounded bitter or unmeant. 'Yeah, we could have fucked him at the same time. You ever do that?'

'Oh yes,' I said, 'but not since I was a kid myself . . . ' He looked at me admiringly in the street-lamp's masking glow.

'You're really wild,' he said.

'Everybody's wild if they're given the chance,' I announced, too pissed to care if I was right. 'There's this place I used to go to when I was about, well, twenty or so, it was like a sauna, but just in someone's house – you'd never have known it was there, it didn't have a name or anything: people who went there called it Mr Croy's. Though I must say there was never any sign of Mr Croy himself.' The thought of those wild afternoons had me catching my breath to find I already had such epochs in me, and that I could look back through the drizzle of wasted time to arcadian clearings, remote and full of light and life.

I stopped and called Matt back. 'Just come down here a moment with me. I want to look at something.'

'Come on, man, it's fucking half past one.'

I took no notice, and doubled down the side lane that led into Long Street. It was only a quick couple of minutes and I was standing across the way from the tall house, gazing up reverently, like a young man in a Schubert song, at the sleeping beloved's window. Not that I knew which window was his. Curtains were closed at every one, and the discreet illumination of an old-fashioned lamp, highlighting the black shine of the front door, lost the upper floors to the night. Where I had been shy before, I gazed hungrily now, with anxious exhilaration, at each shadowed opening, up to the dim roofline and the stars that stood beyond.

'What's this?' said Matt, coming up beside me.

'In there, a beautiful seventeen-year-old boy is asleep.'

Matt shook his head. 'Is that all we've come to see? Or do we get the seventeen-year-old boy as well?'

'*Please!*' I grinned at the Altidore residence and somehow brought Luc to light in my mind, dreaming, lips parted, in near-darkness – pyjamas, for some reason, but the jacket unbuttoned and twisted under him, an arm across his stomach unconsciously repulsing the possessive duvet.

I spoke to Matt for a while, incoherently, trying to bring him into my mood, but glad in the end that he wasn't drunk or romantic enough to get there, and that I possessed it unviolated. He had a hand round my waist, under my jacket where I was a bit fat above the belt; when a taxi came by the driver commented on us to his fare – and when they had gone the silence left me awkwardly alert to the noise we must have been making. I remembered nights at home woken by drunks, passing or stopping for half an hour outside our gate, loud and heedless with drink, sometimes women's wild recriminations . . . I pictured Luc stumbling, half-cross, half-curious, to tweak back the curtain, seeing us propped up and talking rubbish in the doorway opposite. Then Matt started undoing my fly.

6

'You're wearing a truly astonishing tie.'

I beamed. 'Yes, what do you think?' There's no denying one's tie, no standing back from it. Mrs Vivier nodded at me to show she had taken in the phenomenon but was too polite, too little *au courant* with the whole tie scene, perhaps, to venture an opinion. I went towards the over-mantel mirror with the backward-leaning prance of an actor made up fat, and was more startled than I had expected by the gaudy flash of the main motif.

'I'm not sure I'd want one myself,' said Paul Echevin, considering it too in the mirror's safe distance. 'Isn't it the wrong way round? I mean it's right in the mirror.'

'Oh.' I squinted down at it uncertainly.

'But do tell me where you got it.'

'A most extraordinary clothes shop in I think it's Tanners Street, aptly enough. Masses of leather, and jewellery made out of knives and forks.' It was the campest thing I'd said to Echevin, but he laughed intelligently. 'There's someone there who paints these art-ties.'

The dry buzz of the doorbell was heard – Mrs Vivier called out from the kitchen, and Echevin went down to let in the other guests. I was alone with my tie for a few moments, and with the puma-pounce of love that made me gasp and go white and then go red. I felt so raw and mad that afternoon that I had bought absurdly in the little shop, spent to soothe myself, a kind of proxy giving to Luc. And I had considered getting him just something, a neckerchief, a death's-head ring, a silver lurex *cache-sexe* . . . When the doe-eyed assistant in jodhpurs and smoking-cap had peeked through the curtains to ask if I needed a hand getting into some oddly unelasticated swimming-trunks that he had recommended, I thought perhaps I should bring the boy along for a fitting – remembering how he had told me, the first day we met, of borrowing from his friend Patrick a costume that was too large, that, like my shorts, had promised to peel off. In the end I took the trunks, and a shirt so lobelia-blue you could scarcely look at it, and the notorious tie. I imagined wearing it to Paul Echevin's house as a badge of my inner turmoil as well as a distraction from it.

My fellow guests were a man called Maurice, his coolly humorous wife Inge and their daughter Helene, a serious young woman I took a moment to recognise – the one who sold the tickets at the Museum next door. Maurice was a firm dogged little man, quite good-looking, who flung himself into a chair with a sigh as if he lived there: he was a schoolmaster, it turned out, and he had certain schoolmaster's character-istics: in some subtle way dislocated from ordinary adult society, squeezed between vocation and routine, dull yet with a habit of enthusiasm. I remembered the mystery of masters' marriages, the way the poor wives had been figures of lust or ridicule to the filthy-minded boys. I wasn't sure which the plump, unageing Inge would be. She was half-German, half-Swedish, she lived in Flemish-speaking Belgium and had been for years an interpreter in Brussels, at home in the lexicon-limbo of Community administration. She told me her story at dinner, without much sense that I would be interested in it, and the drunken excitement I showed as each turn of her career unfolded may well have sounded forced or even mock-ing. But by then I had discovered that Maurice was no ordinary teacher, he was the head of English at St Narcissus, and so the source, if I handled him right, of exquisitely pre-cious information. He and his wife were to be courted and heeded as they had never been before.

The start was a bit rough. Maurice made himself so com-pletely at home that I was left out while he gossiped with Echevin. Inge was busying into the kitchen to swap notes with Mrs Vivier, and Helene and I found ourselves back in the role of children, who, if discreetly ignored, might well get on to-gether. We were still dry, to my dismay, and I stood with my hands in my pockets while Helene fiddled with a ring on her left hand.

'You're engaged!' I said; and she blushed when she said yes. That happy confusion, coupled with some remote tribal relief that in that case I wouldn't have to marry her myself, and indeed was honour-bound not to flirt with her, made me suddenly warm to her. 'Are you an art historian, I suppose?'

Again the solemn discomposure. 'No, no. Oh, you mean the Museum. No, I just help out there from time to time when Paul asks me to.' How often I misread a face, an attitude, and credited strangers with intimidating powers they didn't have or want. 'I do bits and pieces. Baby-sitting I don't mind at all, and helping with censuses. I've done secretarial work for my father, and even invigilated exams. But no, I'm nothing really.'

'You like jobs where you can read a book.'

'They are the best,' she said, with a shy chuckle. There was something so sensible and tender about her that I began to feel quite jealous of her husband after all, her husband to be. I thought of asking her about him, although I tended to mistrust the accounts young women gave of their intendeds, their wonderful jobs and looks. But in rushed Mrs Vivier with the claret-cup and glasses on a tray. At which Maurice looked up and said, 'I've just noticed your Orst tie.'

'Oh yes,' I said, smoothing it over the largely imaginary stomach that it caparisoned.

'So Paul's selling these now, is he?' – at which Echevin merely hummed. 'It's the Athena, isn't it? Not here, though, not next door. It's in the Town Museum, surely?' He stood up and peered at the tie – on which Orst's Athena was indeed reproduced with a certain additional gold and glitter and with the illusory depth of a hologram. 'What is it William Butler Yeats says? "Maud Gonne at Howth station waiting for a train, Pallas Athene in that straight back and arrogant head" . . .' He looked up, stirred by his own brief delivery.

'Waiting a train,' I said.

'Maud Gonne at Howth station waiting for a train.'

'Yes, it's waiting a train – no for.' He looked uncertain, not altogether pleased. 'It's an aphetic form of *awaiting*; or perhaps more strictly an aphaeretic one,' I went on like a complete arsehole. 'You know, deliberate docking of the first syllable.'

'I can see you're going to have to watch yourself with your quotations, dear,' said Inge, with a mild air of vindication.

I glanced self-deprecatingly around the room, actually quite shocked myself to have brought this blare of kitsch into a place where real Orsts, of incomparable delicacy, were hung.

We sat down to dinner without Marcel. 'Gone to the pictures with a friend,' Echevin said. '*Bloodbath 4*, I think it's called. Will it be all right? It's so many years since I saw a film ... I have an idea perhaps I should be protecting him from something.'

'I'm sure it will be fine,' I said. It wasn't my kind of thing, but I had a proper reverence for the ripped pecs of Kurt Burns, the subhuman star of the whole successful series, who had reared up all over town in the past few days with oiled bust and machine-gun aflame.

'How's the little fellow getting on?' Maurice asked robustly, across the table.

'He's fine. He's a lot happier,' his father said, which gave me a keener sense of just how unhappy he must have been before. 'He's still a bit wheezy. But if you think what he was like a year ago ...'

'Is he showing any inclination to read books?' said Maurice, not quite gently enough.

'The poor child has been so slowed down with drugs, Maurice,' said Mrs Vivier, 'it is hardly surprising if his work has suffered.' It was an unexpected flash, which Echevin appreciated even as he smothered it.

'You'd have to ask our friend Edward about that,' he said.

Maurice turned to me after a second's bafflement, and I hastily confessed that I was indeed Marcel's English tutor, and was doing what I could to ... 'He's getting on fine,' I said loyally. 'What he needs most is confidence.' (And there was the simple substance of a million end-of-term reports.)

Maurice ducked to his soup, and took several spoonfuls rapidly and without appreciation, as if it were the school food he must be used to. 'So when are you going to let us have him back?' That was when the coin dropped for me; within a few moments the two of us had been revealed to each other as colleagues of a kind, though he stood at the centre of the great self-exalting machine, whilst I was picking up the damaged and difficult fragments that its noisy shuttling shook loose. Perhaps at dusk, with closer attention, I would be able to see him from my window, pacing the illuminated classroom and holding forth on Yeats.

'I'm so sorry,' I said. 'I hadn't realised that you were at St Narcissus.' I hadn't realised, in fact, that the staff of a Jesuit school need not all be cold-eyed clergymen.

'We'll see how he's doing at the end of the spring,' said Echevin.

I was so keen to ask about Luc that I fell completely silent. I felt that if I even mentioned his name I would turn crimson, or my fly would burst open, ricocheting buttons off the wine-glasses, or the Athena on my tie would turn and give a wink. I wouldn't use that lolling monosyllable itself, of course; it would be 'the Altidore boy' or some such crisply pastoral phrase. I drank with a need, and was touched to find that Echevin, who was a cautious drinker himself, remembered my habit and reached out to me frequently with the sharp, appley wine I had guzzled and praised on my first visit.

'Helene tells me you've had some great excitement at the Museum, Paul,' said Inge. 'I didn't *quite* follow it . . .' His expression lightened beautifully: here was a man familiar to the point of weariness with his own job, his own rather airless and enervating cabin, suddenly wresting open the corroded porthole and taking deep breaths of his forgotten purpose.

'I've been on the phone for days, trying to bring it off, and it *looks* as if – as if I've been successful.' I nodded at him approvingly. 'I'm reassembling a triptych that was broken up before the war. We've had one wing of it for years, the woman looking into the mirror. You remember you only see the woman's face in the reflection, cut in half by the edge of the mirror.'

'That must be the most popular postcard we sell,' said Helene.

Her mother said, 'It's the very dark one; isn't it almost all in the dark?'

'It's very *ténébreux*,' Echevin agreed; 'there are extraordinary effects of candle-light on the woman's robe – well,

89

it's like a sort of cope – and the hair, of course, is given a lavish treatment.'

'It's a Jane, I imagine,' said Inge, with a tolerant chuckle like her daughter's.

'It's a Jane,' said Echevin. 'The whole thing is called "Autrefois", which in itself has been a problem, since Orst produced about thirty pictures with that title. Fortunately, however, I had a photograph of it, when it was still in his studio at the Villa Hermès. Not a very clear photograph: it's at the back among various other works, but it gives enough to go on. I could be pretty sure when I saw something whether or not it was it.'

'Why would anyone break it up in the first place?' I asked.

'It was sold quite late on; the old man was rather pressed for cash in the thirties – he was out of fashion, of course, and going blind and not producing any more. One or two collectors rather preyed on him, I think; his whole inclination was to hoard things but he did let quite a lot go. This particular work was bought by a Bavarian-Jewish manufacturer who hung on as long as possible before fleeing into Switzerland with almost nothing, *except* a wing of the triptych – the other one, which is completely different and I believe a lot later. I've known about it for two or three years now: it's an astonishingly beautiful seascape, nearly abstract, just three zones, sea, sky and shore, very brooding and intense.' We hummed appreciatively.

'I wonder what the connection is between that and the woman at the mirror,' I said.

'Ah well . . .' rumbled Maurice.

'It is rather one of his things,' said Echevin, smiling to cover the implication that I might have been expected to know. 'You probably noticed several pieces next door where he frames apparently unconnected subjects together. Sometimes there is a clear symbolic relation between them, sometimes the poetry I suppose lies in their mysterious difference, like images in a dream. He speaks of them as being shrines of a mood or a memory – he hoped for an attitude of mystic contemplation in the viewer.'

I nodded. I sort of did know that; and was sorry to have

90

forced the recital of the point. 'I want to hear about the middle bit, then,' I said.

'Now, the middle bit,' said Echevin again with the sweet glow of discovery, a warm crinkling about his large pale eyes, 'is what I found almost by accident when I went to Munich in the summer for the big Symbolist show. I met a man at a party one night and when he heard of my Orst connections he said would I go to his flat and look at a painting he had bought in a sale in Czechoslovakia which had the EO monogram on it. I must admit I hesitated. The owner himself clearly wasn't an expert, he was a perfectly nice dentist, but the odd provenance made me wonder, and the idea of treasures in Eastern Europe suddenly rising to the surface and becoming available was attractive too.'

It was clear how the story was going to end and we sat with expressions of placid encouragement and poked politely at the thick, off-white fish on our plates, a fish that must figure somewhere in Luc's catalogue, though I couldn't put a name to it myself. And that had me sunk for a heart-gripping ten seconds in the sensation of Luc: abruptly in his presence, I was starting to unbutton his shirt . . . 'It wasn't quite so easy,' our host was saying. 'He took me off from the party in a taxi, he wanted to know straight away, it seemed. We drove and drove, and then we were on a sort of motorway and it turned out he lived in what was virtually another town; I was getting a bit restive, and I could see how anxious he was that I shouldn't get anxious, so there was a rather difficult kind of constraint. Eventually we reached a magnificent apartment block – absolutely brand new, he was evidently a very rich dentist – and went up about ten floors. He lived there with his fierce old mother; she emerged in her dressing-gown and shawl, looking very disorientated and very possessive.

'The apartment was stuffed with art, most of it rubbish but with occasional little things which it might have been worth getting down and looking at carefully. There were some Puvis drawings for instance. But the picture he wanted me to see was very much in the rubbish category, a crude portrait by someone who couldn't paint, which Orst, whatever his faults, decidedly could. I looked at it and pronounced upon it perhaps a little . . . firmly. It didn't even have the promised monogram. The mother stood around suspiciously, despite the son's urgings that she should go back to bed; it was only when I said I must return to my hotel that she shuffled off.' Echevin's eyes rested on me for a moment. 'I'm so slow to understand,' he went on. 'I popped into the bathroom before I left, and when I came out, wondering if I had enough money for the taxi back and imagining an embarrassing moment as I asked the dentist to help me out, there the dentist was, but now *sans* jacket and tie, waiting in the doorway of a dimly lit bedroom. I suppose I must have given some signal earlier on, or misunderstood something when we were talking at the party: my German's by no means perfect.'

'Oh, my god,' said Maurice; and Helene and I laughed appreciatively. I could imagine how Echevin's nice looks and his neat, shy, independent manner might encourage this kind of confusion.

'The awful thing was,' he said, 'that over his shoulder, and indeed over the bed, I could see a painting that made my pulse quicken just the way the poor dentist must have hoped it would when I saw him. It was of course the Orst he wanted me to see, it had all been a front with that other awful daub; and despite the shadow, I could see that it was very like the middle panel in the old photograph – one of his deserted gothic townscapes: actually the dimness made it very like the photograph. And I had to get into that bedroom! That was a testing ten minutes . . .' Echevin noticed his food, and set to catching up.

'He must have been pleased to find he owned a valuable picture, though,' said Inge.

'Oh yes, he was – in the end. One could see the tussle of greed and hurt feelings. It was unsigned – had belonged to an uncle – our Bavarian industrialist, of course. The man *liked* it very much, which was why he had it in his bedroom. And why it has not been at all easy to get him to part with it. I've had to be quite flirtatious on the phone. However, I believe he will now lend it to us, and as the wing from Switzerland will arrive on permanent loan next month, we might well be able to re-assemble a major lost work by the end of the year.'

'What a ghastly experience,' said Maurice.

'He was quite a handsome dentist,' said Echevin with a teasing shake of the head. There was a moment of mutual adjustment, of taking the ethical temperature. I was feeling terrifically queer tonight, but none the less anxious not to alienate the strait-laced Maurice or lead him to suspect that under the benign curiosity I would show about Luc I was aching for the boy's arse and touch and lips and tongue and tits and legs and salty toes and involuntarily spurting cock. The talk ambled and clumped through dessert, prompted and set askew by drink. There was that common dinner-party sense that no one truly knew what they were talking about, Helene, who played the piano, keen but clueless about music, Maurice with his fudged quotations and half-forgotten stories from the evening news, and me pretending to have half-forgotten books I had never read. Echevin, of course, truly knew about Edgard Orst, but when the talk turned to football and boxing, on which Inge had vigorous views, he was soon feinting and conceding.

For a minute or two I played a game of introducing the name covertly into the chatter, as I remembered doing with long-ago infatuations, asking or rather telling Helene about Gluck, or swapping Cavalier quotes with Maurice, jealously watching him shape and just exactly mispronounce the word Lucasta, the darting buss with which it began, the upward and downward flicker of the tongue against the teeth. Then he said, firmly and uncorrectably, 'If I have freedom in my love And in my soul am free, Angels alone, that soar above, Enjoy such liberty.'

It was only when we returned to the other room and stood around with our coffee-cups, filling the contented pauses with long looks at the paintings, that I at last brought out my question: 'I wonder if you taught my other pupil, the Altidore lad.' Even to my ears it sounded deranged, bumblingly casual for the first few words and then, as the sacred name approached, slipping the gears with a reckless snarl. I tried to pass it off as a smothered belch, cough and sneeze.

'What's that? Um ... No.' He took a sip of coffee, and looked around.

'Don't be ridiculous,' I felt like saying; but waited and then prompted: 'He seems a very clever fellow.'

'Yes, I believe he always did pretty well. I only take them for the last year, as a rule.' What a miracle, I thought, that Luc was not even now writing an essay on Lovelace or Suckling for this busy, musty-smelling man, who was turning and raising a hand to signal to his wife and so perhaps about to leave.

'It must have thrown him a good deal to be chucked out,' I hazarded.

'I'm sure you'll keep him up to the mark,' he said, with the sudden warmth of someone who is going and wishes to leave a friendly impression on a person whose company he has not enjoyed.

Blessedly, Inge had heard. 'Who's he going to keep up?' she asked.

'Oh, it's just another boy I'm teaching, Luc Altidore, and I wondered if Maurice remembered him from St Narcissus.'

'Well, *there's* a story,' she said, plus chuckle.

'You mean his being expelled?' I said rapturously.

'Quite so.' Again there was a scary pause, in which I foresaw the conversation being hijacked by some intolerable boring other thing.

'I wasn't quite sure,' I said dawdlingly, 'from what his mother told me, what actually happened.'

'Well, I don't suppose anyone knows exactly what happened, do you,' she said with a jolly-stern tucking in of the chin ' – except the boy and the sailors themselves.'

I don't have a clue how I took this. I think I smiled, smirked probably, under the creasing pressure of horrified excitement. 'The sailors,' I said at last, rather crossly, and as if I'd always expected the worst from them.

'I mean, that's all I know, maybe Maurice knows more' – but Maurice had already turned away and was calling something to his host – 'the boy, what's he called?'

'Luc,' I said weakly.

'Young Luc was found on a ship out at the port, playing cards or whatever with a bunch of Norwegian sailors, at, like, 3 a.m. . . .' She shrugged. 'Isn't that it?'

'Mm, that's all I know,' I agreed.

'And it's *probably* enough.' Now there I couldn't agree. And happily she said, 'But if you should find out more, it might be rather fascinating to know.'

'I don't think I could very well ask him,' I said, already wondering how it could be done.

'When you're better friends,' she said, so that I thought she had seen right through me. 'I rather love these dentist-sailor stories.'

7

Matt lived in a servant's flat draughtily tacked on to a large shabby house on the western side of the town. If you got to bed late there you only slept for an hour or two before container lorries bound for the port rumbled past the end of the street, making the windows rattle and the bed-springs distantly vibrate. You woke and found you needed a pee, and groped in the half-light from outside into the small cold bathroom, the floor a tangle of dirty underwear, the glass shelf cluttered with Matt's creams and conditioners, pep-pills and prophylactics. You stumbled on something as you made your way back and for a second or two Matt's snoring stopped; then you slid apologetically under the bedclothes and the snoring started again, and you lay there with just a shiver of longing to be back home. Then the alarm-clock started beeping, it was seven already, and Matt rolled over behind you and pushed his hard cock between your legs.

I had been amazed on my first visit at the chaos in which he lived, the chairloads of clothes, the tumbled boots and kicked-off loafers, the old socks and pulp novels mixed up in the bedding. Dirty plates and glasses were rigorously taken to the grim little kitchen but, once there, amassed in the sink until a particular item was needed, when it would be gingerly extracted and run for a moment under the flaring and popping hot-water geyser. Much of remaining space between, under and on top of bed, wardrobe, chairs, table and TV was taken up with Matt's computer stuff: the stacked boxes of components, disks, spare keyboards – as well as other electrical goods, video games and hundreds of blank tapes. Yet out of this unconscious shambles he emerged each day, each night, clean, beautiful, sweet-smelling, and giving off an air of masculine order.

The house he was at the back of belonged to an elderly and

96

reclusive woman, deaf and cat-loving. Matt, it appeared, was not allowed to use her front door or to go into her part of the building at all; so access to his rooms was through the back yard and a glassed-in porch full of half-dead plants. It was odd that we both lived hidden away behind old people whom we never saw; comforting too, as if it allowed us to be children again, free and disadvantaged. Matt in fact had no respect for the rules, and my first time at his place he worried me by swaggering down the hall and into his landlady's kitchen to find some brandy I had said I felt like at two or three in the morning. The cats gathered round him discriminatingly, as if they knew him well or expected him to feed them.

I was astonished, once I had sobered up, to find that I was Matt's lover: I thought it might have come about through something Cherif had said to him, an inadvertent testimonial. When I looked at myself in Matt's bathroom mirror I seemed to be greeting with new respect an acquaintance I had long thought unlikely to succeed. But then it was an odd sort of success: lover, perhaps, was hardly the word for my role. Matt was like someone beautiful I might have met on the common and counted myself lucky to have ten minutes with under the trees. There was no sentiment to it, beyond the minimal trust of two people pleasuring themselves together; when my instincts homed sleepily towards love I felt him hold me off, cold-eyed, as if my sheltering embrace had been a threat or lapse of form. For all his trickiness, there was no romantic con. I wasn't even sure he had much grasp of friendship. He seemed able to sustain that pure detachment of sex from feeling that normally crumbles with the loss of anonymity or the chance of a second meeting. It threw me back to my great sex-period, the days of saving up for Croy's. And half the time I saw it suited me; with Matt I did the dozen things I couldn't do with Luc.

I stayed at Matt's for most of that week, partly because of the Spanish girls – not so much their noise as my fear that they might make a noise, intrude some unwanted disturbance on the nervy, luxurious disquiet which was mine already and which kept me pacing about, drinking and after a while smoking, reading a paragraph a dozen absent times, gazing from the window when the day waned as if trying to decipher some truth, or rather some hope, from the trees and clouds and time-blackened brick. In the little lost garden below the first leaves were turning. At Matt's there were no such distractions. I would be there as a rule only after the Cassette had shut, drunk and demanding, and each visit described a slowing arc from fucky oblivion to parched and anxious waking, stumbling, dressing and going home. It was the hours of half-sleep that were the longest, and through which the green figures of the alarm-clock, between tiny spasms of dreaming, kept their steadiest vigil. Time was tearing along, but it would never be morning.

Cherif had gone off somewhere – to Rotterdam so Ivo, the camp and caring barman, said, though Cherif in his blunt, hurt way had said nothing to Matt or me. I should perhaps have been worried, but his absence seemed to offer one of those undeserved respites from guilt and obligation. Then I noticed that it left me feeling lonely; Matt was lean and fit and fierce, I liked the gymnastic sex that had me sweat-soaked and out of breath; but when I woke to his rattling snores I began to think back tenderly to Cherif's comfortable hug. I was writing a long and often interrupted letter to Edie, saying how Cherif had said he loved me and how I missed his dusty clothes and serious kissing.

I was too self-absorbed to realise at first just how criminal Matt was. The little raid on the pantry should perhaps have alerted me; and later in the week, when he went in to find an electric fire to allay the new coolness of the nights, his landlady's back could be seen through the kitchen door as she washed up and dotingly harangued her cats. He was in love with his own boldness; when he came back with the fire I could see his cock was half-hard in his jeans – and in his face I saw bravado suppressed by the con-artist's cynical and touchy blankness. Then one evening when I came round I found him folding dirty underpants in tissue-paper and putting them in a batch of Jiffy bags with address-labels printed in capital letters. I made no comment on this and played up my latest Luc news in a show of blind infatuation which easily screened the fact that I had noticed. Not that Matt hid what he was doing: he was a competent operator. The whole thing stirred long-forgotten anxieties, uptight disapproval fighting with randy, craven admiration.

My news was fairly momentous too. By now I always took in Luc's street in my walks across town and went past the house fast but brazenly, with a look of friendly expectancy that would have appeared slightly potty to another passer-by. I saw how my routes for simple errands were tugged into wide and tiring loops by the pull of that street and that house. The cheery tourist map was traversed by new trails, and a new and unsuspected shrine had been drawn in. A general restlessness kept me on the streets a lot by day, and I began to recognise stallholders and groups of kids and certain afternoon walkers who kept regular hours. I aimed always to go past the Altidores' in the early evening, when the lights might first come on in the house and Luc be seen at an upstairs window towelling his hair. But so far it had never happened, and I would go on with slackening pulse, through further streets already impregnated with a mood of bafflement and anti-climax.

That Thursday, after my lesson with Marcel, who was making progress and described the plot of *Bloodbath 4* with a new determination, I went out, drifted round the shopping-streets, spent a while in the photography section of a bookshop browsing the fashionably retro albums of athletes and swimmers, and then guiltily slipped into the Golden Calf for a bottle of Silence. I felt fizzy and reckless when later on I turned into Long Street just as the lamps twinked on above, pink and mauve and flickering like a favourite vice.

I was still some way from the house, but I had it casually in my sights and knew just how it fitted in the rhythm of frontages opposite, glassier and posher than its immediate neighbours, the house before it having an illuminated cross in an upper window. Luc's front door opened and two figures came out sideways on to the top of the steps and then Luc himself, taller and protective, emerged between them: the Three! I knew Sibylle's smart look at once, and the boy too, of course, snug and strong. She reached up and kissed Luc on the cheek. I saw as if an inch away his flared lips kiss the air beside her as she did so, and he and the boy slid an arm round each other and left them burningly there through a last brief reprise of their talk.

99

I faltered. Could I be seen in the uncertain light? I should go on with a quick wave and greeting, even, ideally, stop and be drawn into a loose embrace of conversation – introductions could be made, fast friendships charmingly inaugurated. But I stopped where I was, twenty yards off, pressed against the wall, watching their joking and agreements in the doorway with the hunger of a ghost: I felt like a nothing, a mere emanation of weathered bricks and mortar. Fatuously, I crouched to re-tie a lace, but looked up helplessly in the youngsters' direction, and saw the guests disengage themselves, come down the steps and turn away with a further sung-out goodbye. They strolled off for a few seconds and Luc called, 'Hey, Patrick', and when the boy looked round made a nodding jump, like heading a ball, and they both grinned. Then the boy, Patrick, went out into the road and bent to unlock a car: the Mini, the mauve Mini. I wandered dimly after them as the car pulled out; the engine wasn't firing properly. I tried to remember the number plate: KYF, KYF ... a Cherif-like syllable. The door had closed behind Luc by the time I came by, and I didn't even glance in at the window, swamped in my renewed sense of failure and imbecility.

There were running footsteps behind me and Luc touched me on the shoulder. He was ravishingly flushed and pushed his hair back and for a moment I thought he was going to hit me.

'Hello, Luc! I was just . . .'

'Edward, what really good luck! I wanted to ask you something and I didn't know how to get into contact with you.'

'Oh.'

'Then I saw you actually walking past the window at the very moment I was thinking about you!' He was agitated enough not to notice perhaps how oddly I responded. 'Don't you think that must be a good sign?'

'I certainly hope so.' I wondered if he was going to ask me in, and I glimpsed an evening utterly changed, even if just a drink with him and his mother and high baroque trumpet-blasts of power and lust breaking out soundlessly above us.

'Well, I hope very much you will let me change my lesson tomorrow, because I want to go away out of the town.'

'Oh, of course, well, where are you going?'

'I am going to the seaside, I think I have told you about it before, to where my friends have a house.'

So that was what the three had been planning ... And already the old city began to feel irksome and desolate without them, without him, as it might have done centuries before when the court that Gerard had described to me moved on and took its revels with it. 'How long will you be gone?'

'Only till Sunday night or Monday. I can see you on Monday, perhaps in the afternoon to be quite definite.'

'Yes, okay. As long as you make sure you take some books with you. We've got a lot of books to look at, you know; you can't get too casual about this.' I had the astonishing image of him in my mind frowning through smoke and drinking vodka in a cabin on some rusty old tanker, dealing cards to a ring of blond sailors in singlets, who exchanged glances and chatted about him in a language he couldn't understand.

'You bet, Edward. I will be reading *The Poets of Our Time* in each free moment.'

'Good.'

There was a pause in which we simply looked in each other's eyes and his grin of self-congratulation seeped away and he was shifting and waiting to be dismissed. I had never seen him so childish – it was a sign of trust, maybe, that he wasn't bothering with his usual indifference, though he must have known too that keenness and high spirits won adults' hearts and persuaded them that there was goodness left in the world. Then when he turned and jogged back to the house I thought I had never seen him so manly – so broad and so slimly heavy and incontrovertibly grown. I went on towards Matt's, the street-lights warming and yellowing as the twilight fell.

8

I panicked again under the huge sweep of sky that opened up. The city was suddenly behind us; I looked back, and above the warehouses and estates the cluster of extravagant towers rose into view again; they became the city; then they dwindled and were blurred in haze. We were leaving fast, the engine was shouting, the wind tore over the windshield and whipped the hair about on top of my head. I wanted to be back where we'd come from, late in bed or strolling out for a pre-pre-lunch beer. We overtook lorries and family cars with luggage on the roof, new from the ferry. Here was all the rest of the world, and my old world too, the Brits still cautious on the blind side of the road, looming ahead and then for a few seconds alongside, the roped tarpaulins jabbering loose, the drivers anxiously alert to the flashy blast of the jeep. But I was a Continental by now, and looked on them with pity and dismay as they fell behind.

There was a certain brown obscurity in the sky ahead, like rain falling out to sea. Matt was wearing bottle-green dark glasses and frowned as he drove. A few miles later it lifted and dissolved; and the further we went the more radiant and old-masterly the air became, so that the whole mad, worrying escapade began already to feel out of time, steeped in a dream-ether of its own. When we crossed into France, and Matt turned off and pulled over in a country road to check the map, my gooseflesh smoothed and the October sun was almost hot on my forearms. We went on the last four miles more stealthily, my left hand tucked for childish comfort under Matt's thigh. Then we dropped to a wide view of current-silvered sea, with several big ships standing off; and a sharp turn of the road presented us all at once with a straggle of houses, a massive, squat church with a spire, and the sign – St Ernest-aux-Sablonnières.

We dawdled along the street, me slunk down in my seat with

one of Matt's baseball caps not disguising me much, dreading to be seen or for us even to be noticed, and the jeep farting uproariously at each touch on the accelerator. There was a grocer's, a bar, a novelty shop, a few old stone houses and at either end new brick ones with steel security blinds and unmade gardens just as the builders might have left them. Between them you saw the sea, and other houses lower down, and when we turned and came back we took a narrow lane to the left and emerged on a sand-blown track that I knew was where we had to be.

A string of modest villas, bungalows with lawns running down to the dunes. An air of mild neglect – scabbing stucco, rusted house names, woody buddleia breaking through the garden fences. An air of between-the-wars, of chic whiteness and empty space and cocktails on the glass-screened terraces with sunset views across the Channel. And of being in a place now forlornly unchic, a little colony half-abandoned to encroachments of sand and wiry grass.

We pottered along past the ten or twelve houses to the end of the road, where there was a small concrete car-park looking out over the sands like a gun-emplacement. A few new vehicles were waiting there beside a derelict and plundered Ami, and down the beach a few figures could be seen. Were the Three amongst them, intimately corralled in one of those striped wind-breaks, or careering down to the shock of the sea? We turned again, and drove back, and it was only going this way that I caught sight of KYF, tucked in a rose-tangled carport, the carport of . . . Les Goélands. I was now virtually on the floor of Matt's jeep and urged him to go on. He pulled up in the next entrance-way and asked me just what it was I wanted to do and why we were here. He wasn't angry but he was used to getting results; he wasn't imaginative; he wasn't shocked by the whims and oddities of others – the odder the better, as I was coming to realise – but he needed an objective. It was hard to explain that I just wanted to *be* here, just wanted to see the house.

'So we're going to spy on them.'

'Well, how can we? If I go on the beach I'll be recognised.'

Matt disregarded this. 'But you want to see him stripped out. You want to know what's going on with Les Trois' – he took on my term without a flutter – 'and whether your kid's fucking with the girl or the boy. Or both.'

'Or neither.' It was not unhumbling to have it so spelt out.

'You must remember I've never seen any of these guys. They'd better be good.'

I sat feeling wretched for a while, bruised by my alliance with someone so alien and unsuitable as Matt. Then he turned off the engine and jumped out.

The entrance-way we were in was overhung with sprawling trees; the gate, meshed against dogs, sagged under a heavy chain. Inside, clumps of cupressus had been allowed to grow and grow, and obscured the house; their young tops swayed in the breeze. I watched Matt leaning at the gate, his polo-shirt hanging out. Then he scrambled over smartly, showing a white quarter of naked back, and disappeared down the driveway. I stayed where I was, at last confident of disaster.

This was an older house than the others, maybe the first that had been built out on the dunes below the village. It was shuttered and weatherboarded, and at the bottom of the neglected garden another gate under a rustic arch gave on to the beach. Matt had moved the car to the park, where it looked fractionally less conspicuous and almost sensible – a fun-truck, a beach-buggy high on testosterone. Anyone who saw it there would know at once that it belonged to some sporty young fools miles down the beach with a ghetto-blaster and a badminton set. And here we were, stalking through the prickly shrubbery, peering into the back garden of Les Goélands. There seemed to be a whitewashed wall in the way, and nearer the house a dark shed with a tarred roof. You just couldn't see in, and you couldn't hear anything, either.

I gave Matt as accurate a description as I could of the little group. 'They're all beautiful,' I said. 'Sibylle is small and self-contained, with glossy reddish-brown hair, and Patrick is stocky and square-faced and unhurried, with short dark hair that sprouts out at different angles; and Luc . . . well, I've told you all about Luc.'

'You certainly have,' said Matt, with a stylish little sarcasm he didn't normally rise to.

I sat at the end of the garden whilst he cruised off down the beach in his black swimming-shorts and a singlet. It was like teaching, in a way, knowing how to catch his imagination, to set him tasks he might take to for the pleasure of them. Now he was my eyes, he had to find and recount for me, and my mind's eye followed him over the loose horizon of the sandhills and into the field of play I absurdly couldn't enter. I kicked around in a low-walled patio overgrown with grass and bindweed, with built-in benches warped by sun, and the black griddle of a barbecue that might have been used quite recently: maybe parties stole in from the beach — there were beer-bottles tumbled in a corner and holding their scant few inches of rain. I smoked a cigarette and fizzed the stub into one of them. It was very still, with the lull and whisper of the sea nearby but out of view, and hot sunshine that was a miracle in which the Three uncannily took part: they had known of it in advance, and known, almost without thinking, what to do. I unbuttoned my shirt and lay on one of the benches, breathing the seedy vanilla smell of a bush on which half a dozen late bees still dropped and toppled.

Later I walked round the house, and peered in at a couple of places where the shutters were broken, but my own head cut out the light I needed to see by. Upstairs at the back was an old-fashioned sunroom, with a view that must clear the dunes through wide salt-bleared windows, at each of which a pale venetian blind was lowered and closed. On the hard standing below a small sailing-boat lay upside-down on bricks; I twisted my head to read the blistered freehand lettering: *L'Allegro*, and wondered idly if its sister-vessel was laid up next door. Perhaps Luc was half-heartedly caulking it right now.

My heart raced when I heard footsteps coming up behind: it was Matt, hair still wet from swimming (though quilled and looped a bit by the breeze), and sand drying in the dark hairs on his calves.

'You've been ages,' I said. 'Couldn't you find them? Perhaps they're all in the house.'

'No, I found them.' He half-turned from me, pushed down his waistband and pissed fiercely into the bushes; then stood for a while slapping his dick in his palm as a doctor smacks a vein he wants to rise; then with a snarl of regret stuffed the stiff thing back so that it jutted awkwardly and then slowly slumped.

I was hungry to know what had happened, and also just plain hungry. It was high lunchtime. 'Shall we go up to that bar and get something to eat?'

'Yeah, you go,' he said. 'I had a beer and a sandwich on the beach.'

'Oh. Well, thanks for bringing me some.'

He strolled off a pace or two and stood with hands on hips looking up at the house. 'I'll tell you something,' he said. 'That boy is wild.'

A shot of pain and acclamation went through me. 'Well, I told *you*,' I pointed out. 'I told you he was a golden dream made solid flesh.'

'No, not the golden dream one,' he said. 'Well, he's okay, he's a bit skinny, a bit weird . . . those lips? No, the other kid, Patrick.' Matt looked at me and shook his head. 'I'll tell you something, that boy has got a *whopper*. A total fucking monster between his legs.'

'How do you know?'

'Man, you only have to be a hundred yards away to see that. He's running round in these little swimming-things, he's got this big fat strong arse sticking out the back and this unbelievable package out front. The whole beach was just, like, fixated on it.' Matt gripped himself between the legs and shivered.

'I'm glad you've enjoyed yourself,' I said tartly but truthfully too. The lesson was working. 'I'd like to see him myself. What was Luc wearing?'

'What? Oh, sort of trousers, like sailing trousers, long trousers but short.'

'He wasn't swimming in long trousers?'

'He was reading a book.'

Oh, my obedient Luc, taking my instructions so simply to heart.

'Are they still out there?'

'Yes, they'll be there for a bit. Then they're probably going to take a boat out this afternoon. They've got this nice little dinghy.'

'Mm. I shouldn't let your imagination run away with you.'

106

Matt came back to me, put his arms round my shoulders and kissed me on the nose. 'That's what they said they were going to do, anyway.'

'You mean you actually overheard them talking.'

'Ed!' He shook me. 'I've just spent the last half hour with them. We've been playing frisbee together – well, the girl and Big Boy and me. The professor was studying . . . And then they very nicely shared their light lunch with me.'

I backed away. 'How can you do this?' I said, amazed and angry and eaten out with jealousy.

He sauntered along the side of the house, and I watched him stoop at the back door and rattle the handle. He walked haltingly round, bare feet on pine-needled gravel. When he'd done his circuit, he said softly, 'We'd better stay here tonight', and sent me away down the garden again, so that I shouldn't see what he was going to do. I began to feel that he could do anything he wanted, just by not caring about it.

When I stepped into that house and the back door scraped shut and a family of mice whizzed and froze over the kitchen floor, it was with a whisper of reluctance that could hardly be heard. Matt beckoned me through a shadowy doorway and we were in limbo; the quick adrenalin of the crime was calmed by the still, stale air; the twirling shafts of light from the cracked shutters only stroked our legs as we passed and left me with a feeling of mysterious safety, hushed and remote as the sound of the sea.

In the entrance hall the two oars and paddles of *L'Allegro* were propped in a corner and a 1987 calendar with an image of the Virgin and the compliments of a Citroën garage in Dunkerque was pinned up above a telephone – which Matt lifted, listened to and laid on the table-top, as if we had no wish to be disturbed.

The owners were called Rostand, rather impressively, but the cold, intrusive shock of seeing their name on a spew of dead mail, a gardening catalogue for each year, seasonal circulars from St Ernest, was allayed by the long passage of time, almost as if they had given up any rights in the property by leaving it alone so long. I envied them their holiday home and remembered how possessive I had felt of the bungalow we took each year at Kinchin Cove; how I liked the second-best, third-best furniture, the formica-topped table, the patched armchairs, the shell-covered lamp just like the Rostands had, and how I hated the last day, the bed-stripping, the tidying-away, the final retreat to the back door, wiping the floor as we went and effacing the last footprint of our presence.

Matt had gone on upstairs and I followed in a dream; though most of the house was in a twilight murk there was a brightness at the end of the landing, where a door was open on to the sun-room, and Matt called softly, 'Ed!' The closed blinds were luminous with the sun outside and the air held a dry old smell of warmed woodstain, like the inside of a cigar-box. Matt was kneeling on the low windowsill and as I came up beside him he tweaked down a slat of the blind and I glanced through with the sudden vertigo of a crane-shot in a film, clear over the tangle of the shrubbery to the long white stoa of Les Goélands and the white steps and the rectangle of sloping lawn. He took his finger away as if to say, it's there but you can't have it yet. 'So what's my reward?' he said, standing up.

I went down and nosed and kissed his balls through the sleek black nothing of his swimming-shorts, and lifted them on my tongue and let them drop. I glanced up and he was sighing into the distance as if he could still see Patrick – I knew it was hardly me he wanted. He pushed the shorts down to the top of his thighs and waited with hands clasped on top of his head whilst I tugged his balls free with my lips and tongue and little careful cat-nips of the teeth. The gauzy inner slip of the trunks was damp and still held grains of sand; he tasted salty between the legs.

He shuffled backwards as I helped him from the fleeting encumbrance of the shorts, and spread himself on the mouse-pillaged cushions of a wicker sun-bed. I came after on my knees and licked and pulled and sucked on his balls whilst he stroked himself off and ploughed my hair back over and over with his other hand. Sometimes, my hair tumbled forward and was trapped and yanked in the steady piston of his fist. 'That hurt!' I felt like saying, but he was choking both balls into my mouth to swallow on as he came, and I only produced an ill-mannered grunt.

108

While he was out at the shop, I drifted through the house, only half-curious about the Rostands and barely conscious that I was doing wrong. At the other end of the landing was a door with a boyish notice, 'Julien, Privé, Danger de Mort', and as I opened it I saw for a fraction of a second a fat little boy with glasses earnestly coming to terms with The Police or Duran Duran. But as my eyes adjusted to the gloom there was nothing but a bare mattress, and a child's deal desk on which lay some Astérix books and a die-cast Ferrari Testa Rossa and a long-since shrivelled inflatable globe. I felt Julien must be a bit younger than Patrick. Had they known each other, played with the boat each long summer, been transformed one after the other by puberty, Julien anxious and awestruck by his Belgian friend? Maybe Luc had known him too, and maybe that earlier, simpler threesome had come up to his room to fight and boast and hold the stilted talk of adolescence.

We camped out at the house, eating floury apples and pâté and olives from a jar. Matt escaped a couple more times and swam again in the late afternoon when even he admitted that the sea was hurtingly cold. I liked having the house to myself and lay about in the diffused light of the sunroom, blindfolded with daydreams and drifting into sleep. I made a slight adjust-ment to the angle of the slats and from time to time looked through. Once the long windows on to the porch were open, and towels and trunks had appeared on the line: I had missed their return. Later the doors were closed and lights reached out across the lawn; but we were at too obtuse an angle to be able to see in. Later still, at one or two, I went out along the beach myself and loitered by the white palings of their fence. There were no lights now, but a hazy three-quarter moon picked up the glimmer of the dunes, the small vanishing lines of the wave-crests, and, when I turned, the white villa itself and the hanging towels and the dim, sea-bleached hydrangeas. Here was the gate, jammed open in the sand, and then the stunted thorns, clipped by the wind into arrows pointing at the darkened win-dows. Why not step in? Suddenly I knew the house would not be locked, and that I could ghost through it and hover over each sleeping face, him with her or him. But I didn't, I wouldn't. I kicked and stumbled back through the dunes, my heart spurting with longing. I had left a candle burning in the kitchen and shielded it upstairs with its dumbshow of shadows and startlements to where Matt was already snoring and striking a sympathetic echo from the old cupboards and bare floors. I hovered over him for a minute, his arms pinned in a camphory cocoon of blankets, his beautiful, cynical face agape and faintly senile. Then I stole across the landing and lay down fully clothed in Julien's room. For a long time I watched the candle burning, the flame tugged away by a harmless draught. When I blew it out and saw the thin-walled cup of wax at the tip cool into darkness I thought how for centuries the world had fallen asleep with that sweet singed smell in its nostrils.

I woke in horror and disbelief at having overslept and missed the beginning of an important exam. Half an hour late already, and none of my clothes ironed, nothing remembered, all movement slowed and spasmodic ... Then I woke again and groaned at the vestigial gleam of my father's watch-dial – 'illuminous' I had called it as a child, taking it from his wrist and hanging it on a lamp to recharge its brilliance. Five and twenty (as he always quaintly turned it and as I sometimes affected to do), five and twenty past four: the worst wastes of the night at last admitting the possibility of dawn. There was some noise in the room, intermittent rustles and distant scratches, the same as always, or perhaps with a squeak of caution at the slumbering Gulliver in their midst. I decided I didn't mind, worried briefly and blankly about my life and everything I was doing, and then I found it was quarter to eight and the window-square was illuminous with excluded sunshine.

Businesslike Matt was already up and out and I had the holiday impulse to catch the best of the day as well. Then I ran the scene of a chance meeting through my mind and paled with sickly embarrassment. I kept a regular check from the sunroom, but the tenants of Les Goélands were clearly making the most of their unhindered, unsuspecting Sunday morning. A bell from St Ernest rang demandingly and then stopped and still they slept on, or woke perhaps with drowsy smiles and gummy kisses and hotly did again what they had done before they slept. It wasn't till after ten that a window opened, and Patrick came on to the porch with a mug of coffee and stood scratching the back of his head and looking unexpectantly at the sea.

I tried to make out this famous dick, but he was wearing baggy old cords as he had been the first time I saw him, and a sweat-shirt with writing on, not tucked in. I didn't really care; it was Luc's cock I cared about and endlessly imagined. In my fantasies it changed, sometimes modest and strong, sometimes lolloping and heavy-headed, its only constants an easy foreskin, a certain presence, and a heather-honey beauty to it. He stepped out from the house behind Patrick and stood for a moment with an arm round his shoulder.

I recoiled from the window as if from the flash of an explosion, and then came timidly back. Surely I couldn't be seen, they would never notice the adjustment of the blind, it was the last thing on earth they would expect. I felt the need and the humiliation at once, and it took a while to learn the voyeur's confidence of being unseen. A hundred metres apart, Luc had told me the houses were, which only went to show how little he cared for accuracy, or how little he had ever noticed, or imagined that his pointless answer to a pointless question would ever be checked and charged as it was now, that it would be the distance between him and me. He was twenty, thirty yards away. He had vanished. When he came back it was with Sibylle, and a plate of white bread rolls and a pot of jam. The three sat barefoot side by side on the steps and I could hear their voices, though not what they said. Sibylle competently sliced the rolls in half, daubed them with jam, and passed them along to the boys, who hunkered forward to avoid the crumbs. I hadn't seen Luc eating before. When he had finished, Patrick looked him in the face and said something and Luc's tongue came out and licked up an apricot stain.

Then there was a little spat, Luc nudged Patrick like a naughty child at table, and almost pushed him off the edge of the step into a japonica bush. Both boys stood up grinning and shielding their faces with their hands and Luc capered backwards down the lawn. I had the strongest sense of his just having got out of bed and pulled on that thin blue jersey with perhaps nothing beneath, and those old red calf-length ducks. I watched him ankle-rocking until he saw that the game was over and dawdled back to the house. They all went inside, leaving the plate and a coffee-mug on the steps. Oh, they were only kids, they were only camping out: if Patrick's parents had been there, they would have had a table, a tray, napkins, a cafetière. It touched me terribly the way they just roosted in the place and did without the adult protocols.

Time passed. The sun climbed and cleared. Flies buzzed between the blinds and the glass. And still the window on our neighbours' porch stood open, the cup and plate sat on the steps, yesterday's towels swung slightly on the line. It was like a memory game. I felt challenged to find something that had changed. I thought Patrick's black trunks perhaps had been taken in. When Matt came back I snogged with him fretfully for a minute downstairs. Where were they, he wanted to know; what was going on? He'd been for a long run down the shore, families were out, there was a small crowd round a van selling frankfurters and frites, beach-balls were a-bounce, and still their little fucking snot-nosed lords and ladyships declined to come out and play. He was cheerily angry, like someone covering up a mischief of his own. I picked up a wodge of *Paris Matche*s and took them upstairs to thumb through, nervously waiting for a possible appointment. We played a desultory game of following the fortunes of actors and models, seen together in a night-club in my copy, married in the later issue Matt was already throwing aside, agreeing a separation in a special exclusive two or three months after that. And who were they with now? Matt lost interest quite quickly and went prowling around.

It was voices that alerted me, and I sidled back to the window with abrupt and gloomy excitement. Another fight was going on, with Patrick asking Luc a question, accusing him of something but embarrassed already by possibly being wrong; Luc shook his head in a mime of disbelief and backed away – then turned, slung out a hip and pushed his trousers down to show a strip of blue undershorts. Such a saucy, commonplace little mime it was: I didn't like it. Patrick went back into the house, and Luc hung about for a couple of minutes by himself. I felt he was self-conscious, as if distantly aware of being looked at. I

112

began to pick up on the odd tempo of the voyeur's day, the scattered sightings, the extended lulls, the great patient investment of time, the eerie, more than social intimacy with figures utterly detached and unconscious of you; they were the twitching puppets of their own routines and whims, immune to your muttered urgings, your baffled telepathy, your shielded stare. I'd known it before, once or twice – and half-ashamed – watching a boy next door waste a day, his expanses of day-dreaming, his occasional inscrutable actions. I remembered the texture of the thinnish, slow time in which he existed, the one-sock-on, one-sock-off doldrums of a morning alone. I hated the Donningtons – not for any particular reason, just in that keen, general way one hates one's neighbours, with their boat and their extension – and as I trained the binocs on young Gerry, whose round face was being brusquely thumbed, pinched and generally rethought by the gods of puberty, I felt I was taking a secret revenge. I shut myself in the bathroom and watched and watched. It was like a corrupt privilege granted in a dream or in an ancient public school.

'Let's have a look.' Matt came up beside me, bored, rather brutal. I was still peering at the empty lawn.

'There's nothing to see at the moment.'

A flesh-mantled finger with a tiny oblong of lost nail pushed down the blind-slat, and the leathered cylinders of a massive pair of field-glasses slid into position.

'Man, you can see everything with these.' How did he do it? I was ineffectual again, a mere blundering inner man, protected and outwitted by my cold-hearted friend. Another blunt finger rocked the milled focus-wheel. 'Incredible. You can count the blades of grass,' he said. 'If you want to.'

'Let's have a look.'

His whole identity was obscured by the glasses, and his grin might only have been the sneer of a face screwed up against the sun. 'You could count the pubes on his balls.'

'He doesn't have pubes on his balls. Now can I have a look, please?'

'Yeah ... yeah ...' – a concentrating tongue peeped and havered. 'Oh boy. Here comes Big Boy. Just look at that ... Looks like they're going boating again.' I squinted through, somehow convinced that without the binoculars I wouldn't be able to see a thing, though there of course Sibylle and Patrick were, encumbered with paddles and a bailer and boxy pink life-jackets.

'Now where's your little friend, I wonder? He'll probably stay indoors to do his reading, and you won't see him at all, which will be your fault.' I gave Matt a blow in the ribs – just like the boys fighting, I saw – and he cackled and said, 'No, hold on, who do we have here?' And Luc was back again, awkward on the steps, as if unable to give help when it was expected of him. 'If I was young . . . Luc,' said Matt, 'I'd be getting a bit jealous of Big Boy and the girl.' When I got the glasses at last though, and caught the pair as they scuffed out on to the beach, there was an angry firmness about them. They looked unlikely to enjoy themselves. I took off my specs and twiddled the focus to my shorter sight. The lenses were powerful, ocean-sweepers proved perhaps in some war-time conning-tower, treasured later for their ability to capture shore-birds' markings and charming movements. The heavy casing was chipped, the leather was frayed and in the paint the name DHONDT was roughly scratched.

Half an hour raced and drifted by before Luc appeared again. Then things began to unfold with a canny momentum of their own. He came on to the porch and I had the field-glasses on him: he was startlingly clean and close, palpable but also stylised in the flowing depthless picture-plane. When I shifted my position the picture twitched uncaringly to various greenery, a nodding sapling's top, and I had to run the glasses down and across in a worried blur to find him strolling over the lawn, just beneath me it seemed, like a figure in the flattened foreground of a Japanese print. I didn't dare open the blinds further, and the picture was hazily occluded above and below by the unfocused slats. They gave an edge of mystery to the brilliant image they framed.

He spread out a pale blue towel with tattered edges, an old towel kept for the beach, for tar and sun-oil. Then he paced around it in a territorial sort of way, and looked out towards the dunes. I thought for a while he might be going on to the beach instead and that I would lose my almost supernatural vantage-point. But he resolved on privacy and I saw at once his shy, clever dignity – it made me love him even more. He tugged off his jersey and lay down, reaching out for a cloth bag: I watched him take out some lotion and read the bottle before deciding he wasn't likely to get burnt; the sun was bright, though, and he put on visor sunglasses, their arms linked behind by a short embroidered band. Then he rolled on to his front and opened a book, he was looking away from me and I refined the focus over his shoulder and made out a typical page of *Poets of Our Time*: he must have folded a pencil in as a marker, and he was soon underlining words and scoring the margin and then for about five minutes he worked on a dense, formal doodle – I think it was on a Roy Campbell page. The thing about Our Time was that it was really Our Fathers' Time. I wondered at my own impulse to keep him back with me in a shared childhood of unfashionable lyrics and discredited rhetoric. I studied his naked brown back more closely than I had ever studied anything – the wide plates of his shoulderblades, the slight boyish dip between as he leant on his elbows, traces of pink scratches on the shoulders, the shaped, back-swept golden hair stacked in the embroidered sling of the shades-band.

When I put down the binoculars to take off my trousers I was confused to find myself indoors, in another house, and not kneeling just behind his open legs ready to fuck him or tickle his feet. I came back to my vigil to find him standing up and looking around, and I thought perhaps he was giving up already. Matt was quite wrong to say he was skinny; he was lean but no more skinny than Matt was, and his chest was surprisingly big, with wide milky nipples. I knelt there teasing the air with my tongue and teeth, and working my jaw in imaginary kisses.

He was taking his trousers off.

I can't go on about the next hour. Luc on the grass in his shallow blue shorts, rather discreet; the tan-lines of the summer, of his red ducks and of longer shorts than these, marking comical sexy stages up his long legs to the whiteness I just glimpsed where the hem rode high by a finger's breadth on the rise of his buttocks. Already the little creases and blue nodes of veins on his inner thighs. Nothing about his cock, but a couple of seconds' vision of crinkled scrotum (I may have imagined that).

The discarding of *Poets of Our Time* and the getting on of a yellow Walkman. Its not being Schubert. The scary challenge of a look my way, half-sitting up as if alerted by a noise or the glint of the lens, then lying back again, fingers in his waistband. My envy of his hands as they cupped his head, or flicked at an insect or a tickling grass, the light scratches with the back of a thumbnail. My envy of a long-toed, dirty-soled foot rubbed against the opposite calf, then sliding slowly down till it lay by the other and tick-tocked to the beat of the music.

He had to move as the sun swung round and the shadow of our house advanced across the lawn; the steep roof and the lower sunroom took an ominous form, like the blind head and paws of the Sphinx, I thought. Twice he picked up the towel and resettled himself further away, frowning, the subject of an experiment in light he seemed not to have grasped. Twice Matt brought me off. I needed both hands to hold the heavy glasses without shaking. I was rather tied up, head and hands in one place, heart and mind out there where my pupil lay and day-dreamed and shifted from the advance of the cool tide of shadow.

9

I must have been early for the lesson. I was approaching from
the other side, on the streets I associated with disappointment,
the pilgrim's reluctant departure from the shrine, sores and
deformities still unhealed, though this way round the sombre
landmarks took on a new aura of hope and apprehension. I was
calming my nerves with tricks against stage-fright that my
father had taught me. And there was Luc, walking ahead of me,
not running but clearly anxious not to be late. I was bucked up
when I saw him look at his watch; my authority was manifested
in that quick gesture – undiminished, maybe even heightened,
by my tolerance in rearranging the lesson. Then wasn't I pained
too to know what a distant figure I was to him still, the martinet
of dead poetry and strict time?

He had turned a corner and when I came round it twenty
seconds later I saw him talking to a man who must have
stopped him. They were holding on to either side of the unfolded tourist map and Luc, taller by a head, was stooping
across it in the search for a street, I assumed, that the man had
asked for. I heard him groan with annoyance and giggle with
shame at not finding it; while the visitor wore a calm, almost
gratified expression, finding himself not so stupid after all. To
ask the hard question is simple, I thought.

I didn't like the look of this man – fortyish, fit, with curly fair
hair receding above a long boring face. I could imagine people
saying he was good-looking and he gave the impression of
believing this himself. He had a neat little knapsack with a cape
packed across the top.

I stopped before I got to them, determined to reach the house
after Luc, and staggered too, seeing him only feet away, to
think where I had been, in mind and body, since we had last
met. Only yesterday I'd come twice across his naked legs – or

117

rather, on to a cushioned window-seat and a sprawl of time-crinkled TV magazines in a derelict house — but still it had seemed to me as if we had made love, the intimacy was so prolonged and detailed; I knew his body better than he did himself. I saw now that it wasn't quite fair, incredibly he didn't know, he'd been reading and listening to music at the time. The man was excusing Luc for his failure, his free hand grasped his upper arm consolingly. 'Don't worry, it's a very special, odd interest of mine,' he was saying in English as I stepped forward and gripped Luc's other elbow in an involuntary challenge to the stranger's claim. How dare he foist his special odd interests on the boy?

'He wanted to know where the Fratry of St Caspianus is,' Luc said as we walked on the last hundred yards to the house. 'I know I ought to know that, I have learnt it once.'

I could have told him, god knows. It was a dingy, patched-up little place on the edge of town, close to where Matt lived; I passed it every day and never saw a sign of life. Only the most insatiable antiquary could ever have dreamt of going there by choice. I could have impressed him, even gently squashed him with my knowledge, which wasn't even monk-knowledge, just a part of the accusing streetscape of the morning after. But my mouth was as dry as cloth and my features had a rubbery stiffness, as if I had been terribly wounded by an old friend and didn't know what to say. Luc glanced sideways at me, but thought perhaps I was merely angry, and that he was in for a difficult hour. I was on the brink of tears just to be walking beside him in the real world, the two of us in our black jeans and smart today with light sports-jackets, though his was costly and Scottish whilst mine was American and second-hand.

'So whatever did happen to your glasses?' Luc asked with new informality as we sat down in our regular places at the dining-room table.

I fingered the cracked bridge and the side-hinges stiffly fixed with tape. I wanted to tell him how when he had finally gone into the house and left nothing but the silvered oblong on the grass where his towel had been spread I had stood up and wandered desolately over the half-seen floor, treading on the spectacles that I had discarded to make love to him and inflicting the damage he could now see. 'I fell off my bicycle,' I said absurdly: 'or more accurately I was knocked off.'

'I hope you weren't hurt, Edward,' he said with eager sympathy, almost more eager than sympathetic, but he was only seventeen and what did he know? 'Everybody rides bicycles and I think they can be very dangerous.' I shrugged to show that I was fine. 'I didn't know you had a bicycle,' he said.

'It wasn't actually *my* bicycle,' I admitted. 'It was a friend's.' I could see myself being pressed further and further into deceit rather as a lying quick answer to a barber's question, incuriously followed by a further question, can lead in minutes to a crazy-house of invention and non-sequitur. 'I won't be riding it again,' I emphasised. 'It was a complete write-off.'

'A write-off. Yes. Anyway, I think of you as a walker,' he said. (So he *thought* of me.) 'I have often seen you walking along this street, when I am working in the evening, and it reminds me to work even harder.'

He had seen me ... And was there controlled anger in his cool delivery, a new tone in our affairs? I lobbed the blame clumsily back – 'You can't have been working very hard if you were looking out of the window' – and heard what a leaden censorious jerk I sounded, and grinned to deflect his hatred.

'Perhaps you don't know all about our little mirrors in the window, which are present in most of the old houses. We can sit and do what we want to do and then we just look up quickly and we can see all along the street.'

I blushed and nodded with genuine enlightenment. Of course I had seen these spying-glasses; but I hadn't realised just how routinely nosy these people were. I began to feel that everything I did might be observed and censured from within the dark old windows of the town. 'How was your weekend?' I said.

'Oh, it was very good, thank you.'

'You'll have to remind me where it was you went. I know you said it's where a friend of yours has a house?'

'Yes. It's in a small village that is actually in France, called St Ernest-aux-Sablonnières ...'

'Of course, I remember now, where St Ernest etc ...' He nodded, and looked at me with slight concern, as if I might really have forgotten the whole rigmarole of our first lesson. 'You must have had good weather – you even look a bit browner; if it was anything like it was here, you could almost have done some sunbathing.'

'I find it is too boring, sunbathing. But yes, the sun was shining and all was right with the world.'

'So.' I pondered this vain concealment. 'Tell me what you did. Who was there?'

'Oh, it was just me and my friend Patrick. I think I told you before it is his parents' house.'

'Just the two of you, then?'

'Yes, it was very quiet, we could just relax and well, do our work.'

'How cosy.' And he looked away as if I were insinuating something, though in fact I was baffled by this lie and hurt to be lied to and had a will to chase and expose him. His mother was out today at the Cathedral, and we had no coffee to fill the pauses and neutralise our embarrassments. We were alone in the house . . . I stood up and walked to the window and made a frowning survey of the garden, two Japanese maples with twisted limbs in a combustion of bronze and crimson. My long, disappointed silence bothered him.

'I have done the reading you told me to do.'

'Good . . . good . . .' I came back and sat down. I needed to re-establish the reality of the weekend. 'We might as well be very British,' I said gravely, and watched his forced smile fade into unease. 'Tell me again what the weather was like.'

Relief and boredom. 'The jolly old weather again! In the morning there was some . . . fog; then it went off and there was only small cirro-cumulus formations.'

'Aren't your friend Patrick's parents worried about leaving their house unattended?' I was brooding on the dream-mirage of yesterday's sunshine on white stucco, a door left open, and he was adding and taking away, smuggling Sibylle out of the picture, touching in the stratospheric clouds that I had never looked up to see.

'They aren't worried. My friend's father, Mr Roger Dhondt, goes there quite often. He is a writer and, well, he does his writing there.'

'So your friend Patrick's surname is Dhondt?'

'Yes, have you heard of him? Roger Dhondt has had published books about nature and – *ecologie* . . .'

'Ecology. No, I've never heard of him.'

'You know he used to be at Het Zwin, with the wild fowl. He is *very* interested in birds.' I glanced at Luc, and saw he was troubled by my frown. 'In fact,' he said encouragingly, 'their house is *called* Sea-Gulls.'

'I know, I know,' I felt like mumbling, as even the vacant charm of that boarding-house, blue-skied name tarnished.

'Sometimes in the summer there are people living on the sand. But they are bums and we are not worried about them.' He grinned like a child who has no access to his parents' puzzling sadness and tries to entertain them, while they exchange a stony intimate look. 'Sometimes they go into another house there, which has been empty for many years. We know they sometimes go into the garden, which is fine, okay, and make a fire and have a party. Now, my friend Patrick thinks there are people living in the house, but I don't know.'

'And why would he think that?' I said vaguely. 'I mean, has he seen people there?'

Luc was vaguer still. 'He said he heard noises in the house, which is next to ours, to his. There was, you know, a *guy* around, that we kept seeing; he was a stranger, but I think he was a nice good-looking guy, quite rich, and not a bum who would break open the house.' I stared at him, and saw him stir himself again – but as though not certain it was worth the effort – to a further pleasantry. 'My friend Patrick says he could hear the sound of someone snoring, in fact, coming out of the house. But I think it was only the sound of the sea.'

It was on the journey back from St Ernest that Matt told me he would be going out of town for a week or two. He said it in so casual a way that I knew it must be something important, into which I shouldn't enquire.

'I'll miss you,' I said, and was surprised by the truth of my words.

121

He said, 'Yeah', in an ambiguous murmur; and after a moment mentioned some business things he hoped I'd look after for him. He fiddled in his breast pocket for a fat roll of notes and tossed it into my lap. I didn't like to count them while I was with him, but I felt a surge of undeserved good luck, whatever was involved. I'd been ignoring the money problem, burning up my good but sparse teaching-fees in drink and wasting my small reserves on romantic unnecessaries like my lobelia shirt – I had sort of decided that after the weekend I would make a decision to decide what to do. Then it turned out we weren't even to spend tonight together; and as he was leaving the next morning I was unexpectedly bereft. I wandered back to my room feeling wild and lonely.

An envelope with beautiful, imaginative writing on had been slipped under my door, and lay on the threadbare rug. I tidied away an ashtray, a crusted coffee-mug, a bottle of milk precipitated into caramel grounds beneath faintly blue water – all out of respect to my letter and the capricious hint it gave of a finer life I could be living. I had no real idea who had sent it; I hoped it might be an invitation – someone's offer to look after me for an hour or two. But hardly anyone knew where I lived. I was dying to see Cherif again, but doubted if his writing, which I had never seen, could possibly be so rococo. Marcel's, I knew, was loopy and backward-leaning. And then my first idea came back, against my better judgement: that it was from Luc. Something he was too scared to say to me face to face – a kind of Valentine in a fancy script, or its opposite, the astounding note that said everything must end.

It was from Paul Echevin, and I adjusted after a moment to the pleasure of that. Did I want to earn a bit of money by helping him out at the Museum? Sometimes it would be Helene's job of reading a novel in the hall and occasionally selling a ticket or a postcard; mainly it would be paperwork, checking references, proof-reading the English text of the Orst catalogue that he really must get finished before the coming summer, that was so many years overdue.

I felt charmed, and a little intimidated – even though he laid the letter out as an inventive uncle might for a bright child, with a sketch at the bottom of himself disappearing under stacks of paper, and his name written with streaming tendrils for serifs, like the visiting-card of the South-West Wind in a children's book I'd had. I felt the ghostly oppression of work, the wrong way you had to do for money what you wouldn't do otherwise; I was thinking like a child who can't see the point of things, but whose questions to a jovial grown-up touch even so on some uncomfortable flaw. Then I saw myself, still about nine years old, sitting at Paul Echevin's immense desk, chin on forearm, in the first week of wintertime, in the teatime lamplight and gloom and the busy adult silence, lost in a world of words and pictures.

It was dark on the stairs, dark in the room at the top, but the darkness there was like the darkness in films, where sleepers lie in blue shadow; or there was a phosphorescence in the air, the curtains, the sheets and pillowcase were mildly luminous. I stepped cautiously over dropped clothes, a screwed-up dress shirt, upsettingly jokey boxer-shorts, anxious above all not to tread on a pair of glasses. Luc was asleep, on his back, his pyjama-jacket open, his nipples wide, brown and rough, he held back the greedy duvet with a leather-gloved hand. I thought if I could unbutton that glove at the wrist and coax it off those long, nervous fingers it would be a very beautiful achievement. I perched on the edge of the bed and looked minutely at his stomach as it dropped with the long-delayed breaths of deep sleep, the tongue-tempting crevice of his navel. His anatomy was grand and somehow luminous itself, and where the blue veins thickened in his neck they seemed transparent, as in a model or a chart. The model of a man . . . I pressed back the bedclothes devoutly and saw his cock asleep in the heedless gape of his pyjamas. It was heavy and warm in my hand, silky, the skin slid back with an intimate moist whisper. When he opened his eyes I was the first thing he saw. He was too moved to smile, it was love like a tranced levitation, cosy and radiant like divisi strings, a saint's vision perhaps of the timeless in the humdrum. It was ours. His arms circled my head and brought me down to him.

123

When I opened my eyes the first thing I saw was a pair of shoes, made of webbed orange-coloured leather, shucked at forty-five degrees, the heel of one on top of the other, like a first position in ballet. They were intensely horrible, alien in design, scuffed and lopsided from wear. I was lying on my side at the mattress's edge, the bedding just reaching to the line of my shoulders and hips. I was afraid the weight of my stomach would topple me over on to the floor. The shoes were the focus of my dry misery, and I closed my eyes again and ran yearningly back through the dream-fade to catch and remember everything I could. How he had loved me. How he had clung to me.

I was fixed in my position by the rough heel of a foot pushed against my calf and the lightly adhesive pressure of a biggish bottom pressed against my own. I tried shoving slowly but firmly backwards, but met with unconscious, heavy resistance. Squinting at my watch on the floor I saw it was only 6.15; day-light was hardening on the wall and all I longed for was warmth and oblivion. I slipped out of bed, walked round and climbed into the cold welcome of the other side. The pillow there had the yeasty smell of dried semen – fresh and stale at once.

I looked at the big stubbly face of – who was it? Frits. From Holland. A keen uncritical lover of English literature. Perhaps the coppery lighting of the Cassette and the benign warp of drink had lent him a glow as he stood against the wall reading *Of Human Bondage* – misled himself, I suspected, by that potent noun, but still stubbornly hoping after two hundred pages. He'd looked shelteringly big and artisanal, with a touch-ing mixture of clumsiness and adroitness about him; I imagined him doing something expertly with wood.

He seemed pleasantly surprised when I asked him back to my place, as if our talk about Maugham might have been an end in itself; as if I were offering him a lift that took me somewhat out of my way. 'Thanks very much,' he said. It was clear to me as we walked across the empty town that I had picked up a pretty heavy bore; every time I pushed the conversation gratingly towards men and sex he said 'Yes, yes' as though he didn't quite understand, and then went on in his dogged English about Richard Adams. I began to wonder if he knew the Cassette was a gay bar.

124

And then the Spanish girls, the voices in the woodwork, mur-
muring and shrieking in what felt like derision as I sat in Frits's
lap in the armchair and slipped my hand inside his denim shirt
and jiggled backwards and forwards on him until he had a big
fat hard-on. 'Yes,' he said, 'I began to know that the life of
being in an office all day, every day, was not for me. I then
needed to take time to find out what it was that I really wanted
to do. I wanted to read good literature, and travel around the
place. I had to get out of the mouse-market, Edward.'

I lifted the bedclothes a little and looked at his sleeping body
in the greyish light, slumped, hairy, held in, it almost seemed,
by a long brown hairless scar, the plump bud of his cock shifting and stiffening as he rose himself into the light of early
dreams.

10

'Hello.'

'Hello? Matt?'

'Matt's not here, I'm afraid.' A thoughtful pause.

'Oh yes.' The line went dead.

I carried on sorting out the orders, clipped pink slips on which products were tactfully referred to by number. A good sprawl of post awaited me each afternoon on the floor of the porch – the business letters addressed to Matt, and occasional envelopes for a certain Wim Vermeulen, which I set aside and which aroused my curiosity more. I supposed he must be one of his old lovers or partners, or perhaps the previous occupant. Something kept me from opening them – I wondered raffishly if it might be thieves' honour.

The letters from Matt's subscribers were often several sheets long, full of secret enthusiasm and not easy to read. 'I can't thank you enough for introducing me to young Casey Hopper,' one of them began. 'What a "doll"! I've quite fallen for him. It's such a pleasure to find a lad of that age who really likes to take it from an older – and bigger – man. And Casey, I am pleased to say, is certainly well set-up himself. He has such a pleading look as he lies there spread out, when his arms and legs are tied to the bedposts and I can gaze at his secret treasure. Sometimes it is "all over" then, before anything else has happened.

'Perhaps I should tell you a bit about myself. I used to be in the agri-business in Ghent, where I have lived all my life. I am sixty-seven by the way, and have retired now, so I have plenty of time on my hands, and will certainly be getting in touch with you again. I like young men, eighteen to twenty-five or so, well-built, with *short* hair. I do *not* like boys with obviously dyed hair or who are effeminate in any way and wear ear-rings or jewellery. As you can imagine Casey Hopper tops my bill!

'You may think it strange, but I have never much cared for sex, despite what I have been saying; nor would it have been easy for me. I live with my mother, who is now ninety-four but has only recently become fully blind. I have always relied on the clean and easy practice of what used to be called self-abuse. I'm proud to say that I have climaxed at least once every day since 1937.

'*Hot Hunks 12* certainly lived up to its name! Please let me know if you have any further films with the admirable young Casey in . . .' The writing was clear, slanting, impatient. His was in every sense a busy professional hand.

I could hardly think of a less appropriate person than Matt to confide in, though I understood the scientific attitude with which he would read a letter like this. His was a service industry, which entailed a certain respect for the fantasies it serviced. I had seen him at his silver-screened lap-top intently answering such queries; and listened to the muted rattling runs that followed the pause as he thought through some cruder provocation and gave a little cackle or a throaty 'Oh yeah . . .' The trick, it seemed, was to be both direct and archly metaphorical, the result having an enthusiastic, illiterate tone, in its obscene way not unlike the work of my Aunt Tina. Love was blindly introduced and as a prefix was fully interchangeable with fuck: love-poles were destined as a rule for love-holes, and at the end it was geysers of white-hot love-juice that (paradoxically) cooled the lovers down. I answered one or two of these enquiries myself and discovered a natural aptitude for it: 'Pretty-faced Lance soon gags on Chad's massive love-meat, and Chad turns all his attentions to the youngster's pleading love-hole.' Later on I tried variations drawn from Gerard Manley Hopkins: 'Rick worships Cody's massive mansex . . . Doug and Darren dauntlessly double-fuck the freshman's dewy down-side . . .'

I felt a little uneasy, though, in the half-world of Matt's room, treading on so many things. The long knots of the bedding looked a bit too squalid without him, lean and white, sprawled amongst them. I noticed more than before the musty smell of the bathroom where the soiled underwear that he stole

and sold collected behind the door and stopped it from opening. There was something eerie, as the deaf woman banged and
sang through the wall, about finding the right fuck-film and
copying it on to a new tape on two parallel VCRs. I perched
among the junk, wrapping stained jockey-shorts in tissue paper
and adding an authenticating ticket whilst the machines
worked almost silently, with steady red lights, and the ritual
imagery of love-meat passed along the cables.

The phone rang again.

'Hello.'

'Hello! Matt's not there, right?'

'Did you ring before? Is that Dirk?'

'Oh yes it is.'

'You probably want to know if he's got anything for you,
don't you? Well, he has.'

'Who is this, please?'

'My name's er – Casey; Matt's left me in charge of his
things.'

'What, like Casey Hopper. That's really great.'

'Like . . . I don't think I know him.'

'Oh, you'd like him. Actually he's very popular.'

'I've got something very special for you. I think you know
what it is, don't you?'

'If it's what I hope . . . Is it from a certain young man?'

I consulted a clipboard Matt had left. 'It is. To be precise, it is
from – Master David K – '

'Shush, Casey, don't say it.' I felt I'd entered a secret place. I
wondered if my interlocutor, my customer, was naked. 'Please
be so kind as to describe it for me.'

I reached down at random for one of the items. 'I hope you
will want this, Dirk. Matt has gone to great trouble to get it.'

'Of course. Anything of . . . David's . . .'

'Well, it's a white pair of briefs. Calvin Klein.'

'Such vanity,' Dirk whispered.

'Medium.'

'Mm, mm,' Dirk affirmed. 'Is it, is it enriched, autographed?'

I twisted it round rather gingerly, and noticed the red name-
tape of one P. R. Maris. 'It has a firm primrose signature in the
front panel. It seems he dresses left, by the way.'

128

'I *knew* it.'

'It will be quite expensive, though,' I said, looking at the price Matt had underlined on the list. 'It has the front marking, about the size of a franc, very rich, but also a clear . . . rearward indication.'

'Oh the wicked boy!'

'Yes, a proud stripe.'

I could feel a flush coming down the line. 'Such youthful haste and high spirits.' I let the sagged item, with its legend of juvenile incontinence, drop to the floor. 'Do you know, I saw him, the other day, coming out of the school gates as pretty as you please in his breeches and I thought, little do you know, my angel, that I'm wearing your shameful little soccer-shorts at this moment – so tight and small they were.'

'Quite so. Well, wait till you see these. Which you can do when you send six thousand-franc notes to the usual address.'

I heard him absorb the insult of the price, just for a moment humiliated by the extravagance of his need, then considering that only he and I need know of it. 'I may have to ask you for other things, too,' he said.

'By all means; but I'm afraid I can't come down on this price.' I swivelled round to where Patrick Dhondt's black swimming-trunks were spread, sleazily lustrous, on a plinth of empty boxes. 'Many people are prepared to pay far more than that for the top items. For god's sake, Dirk, it's a hazardous business.'

'You look rather tired.'

'I haven't worked so hard in years.'

'Are you not enjoying it?'

'I can't quite decide. The first day's bound to be a little anxious, perhaps.' I grinned at Helene, who smiled capably back, and then looked down. 'Do you want to go out for a drink?'

It was the sort of offer she didn't regularly get, and she showed a shy person's brave readiness to take it up. She was holding a bag that contained the day's slim takings and I waited while she ran upstairs to the safe with it. In the corners of the hall, and in the shuttered room of family portraits beyond, the red spots of the alarm-beams blinked on and off with vigilant intermittence. When Helene came down she activated them from a panel in a cupboard, and we had thirty seconds to get out, which gave us a suspiciously hasty look.

'Do you know somewhere round here?' I said, not keen on a long walk before my drink.

She frowned at me humorously. 'There's nowhere here,' she said. 'But if it's urgent, I've got a car.'

I weighed it up quickly and chose the Golden Calf. She drove us there in a yawing 2CV which had various things wrong with it. I chatted in the forced informal way of a passenger in a virtual stranger's car, whilst she frowned through the windscreen and stamped on the pedals alternately.

She seemed disconcerted by the bar, by its high brown gloom and inartistic décor, which were wonderful to me and a relief from everything else. We sat down beside a pair of arthritic domino-players, and when the old waiter came I ordered a large beer and she asked – with a certain polite democratic negligence – for a coffee and a glass of sparkling water. I watched her watch the waiter's retreat, the impatient haste with which he denied or overrode some deformity of his foot.

'Is this where you normally come?'

'I come here from time to time, as a change from the other bar I go to, where I know a lot of people, who would be a distraction from talking to you, which is what I wanted to do. At the Cassette there's a juke-box, and great scrums of young people shouting their heads off. Here there's no music and everyone's over ninety and they don't talk to you or even quite approve of you and it's all rather restful.'

'Yes, I've been to the Cassette,' she said. 'Jan, my fiancé, has got several gay friends, who used to go there all the time.'

'I see.'

'It's quite good fun, isn't it, but there are so many handsome young men and I know the last thing they are interested in is me! But perhaps, as you say, that is rather restful.' And she blushed at the sudden shift of level and the mimicking airiness with which she brought out the last words.

'Did you know I was gay the first time we met?' I asked.

130

She was blank-faced. 'Oh, I thought you were wearing a great big badge saying I AM GAY in enormous letters.'

'I . . .' I stumbled, laughed and blushed for some reason in my turn. 'I wasn't absolutely sure if Paul knew – I assumed . . .'

'You don't want to worry about that,' she said, as the drinks were brought and the waiter stooped into our conversation. 'Paul loves you anyway.'

I was terribly pleased to know this. 'Well, I like him very much,' I said, raising and holding my glass as if drinking to him. 'It's very flattering, because when we first met he made me feel rather a fool.'

'You perhaps had too much to drink,' she said, dipping to the mocha-freckled froth of her coffee with the same fastidious air that she had turned on the bar as a whole. And of course, as to the drink, she was probably right.

'He was quite stern again today. I suppose he wanted me to start off on a proper work-footing.'

She smiled. 'At least you had work to do. Down in the hall I was dropping asleep over my George Meredith.'

'He is a rather yawny author.'

'Oh, I'm glad I'm not wrong.'

'Well, if you are we're both wrong. Which is *very* unlikely.'

She glanced around the room, photographs of a fifties football team (whose right half was now the morose, memorialising landlord), one of those fake paintings of settecento cardinals enjoying a joke. 'What work was he getting you to do?'

'Well, stuff on this grand catalogue of his. It has to be finished by next spring, apparently, in the English version first. Orst produced such quantities of work, and the provenances are a nightmare. I'm speaking as if I knew what I was talking about, but of course I don't, which makes it more interesting in a way, even though I'm not doing research myself, I'm just checking the English text.'

'It sounds as if that might be a little bit yawny too.'

'Fortunately I'm a terrific pedant, a fallible pedant, I'm sure, but I know how to spell words like daguerreotype and de Nuncques, and I love noticing when 1869 has come out as 1896 or even 1968.'

'You speak Flemish very well indeed, for an Englishman.'

131

'Thank you. My mother's mother was Dutch, and we had a certain amount of it at home when I was little.'

'Yes, that's right – you speak Flemish with an English Dutch accent!'

'Aha,' I said, slightly rattled. 'I didn't realise your middle name was Professor Higgins.'

She leant forward with a serious look. 'No one really expects Paul's catalogue to be finished by the spring,' she said, almost embarrassed by him, or perhaps on his behalf. 'It's actually a bit of a famous joke. It was supposed to be published at least five years ago; but for some reason he can't bring himself to finish it.'

I felt inclined to disregard this, or to think that she couldn't really know. I wanted to see it through to the end before I left town, before next year's unimaginable summer. I sensed for a moment the awful opacity of the intervening time, the winter we all had to go through, when things would develop and decay and become my past and Luc's – and Jan and Helene's too. They would be married in St John's in November, beneath its great brick scary tower. Perhaps she would invite me and I would come out dressed as smartly as I could with the bells booming and see with a pang the boys with their push-bikes who had stopped to watch the crowd and the bride and were laughing distantly at her. And Luc . . . we were good friends by then; I had failed to win his passion, it was a rather earnest friendship, full of my morbid suppressions and his apologetic compensations and constructive ideas.

'I wonder how long you've known him for,' I said.

Helene's answer was quietly conclusive. 'Oh always. Didn't I tell you that he's my godfather? Well, he is. He and my father grew up together, during the war – they used to be sort of best friends, though I think they stopped being *them* a long time ago. Paul's still very sweet to Maurice, but Maurice seems to have dried up somehow in recent years and isn't very sweet to anybody. Of course he does speak almost entirely in quotations, which is exhausting and drives poor Mummy mad.'

'I'm a bit of a quoter myself. I don't suppose he'll forgive me for correcting his Yeats,' I said.

'No, he probably won't.'

132

I seemed to have finished my beer and wondered if I could actually have been given a full glass. Helene knocked back the rest of her mineral water, but when I offered her something else she said, 'Why don't we get out of . . . here, and perhaps have a walk by the canals.' I looked at her aghast. 'Then I will go home, and you can get back to some serious drinking.'

The evening was cool and grey and I let Helene steer our course, across the deserted arena of the Grote Markt and into what I had seen described as the *ville sainte*, the city hidden within the city, the narrow courts and alleys and cloisters around the Cathedral and the Bishop's Palace. I had walked there before and perched on the steep brick bridge that linked two covered walkways across a canal, and felt almost out of breath with sighing; so it had its mood for me, a black undertow.

'No, it will be interesting to see what happens about the catalogue,' Helene resumed. 'I'm sure there's still a lot to do. Has Paul shown you any of the very late pictures, painted when Orst was going blind?'

'No, but I haven't really even looked at all the pictures in the Museum.'

'There are hundreds more up in the old storage attic. Sometimes you see a very big one that's going to an exhibition being winched down outside on the hoist, in a great big box, of course.'

'What's special about the late ones?'

'Paul doesn't like to show them. They're not really finished, at least not like the earlier ones which are so brilliantly painted, they're almost like photographs – well, of course, he based most of them on photographs as you know. Then at the end he tried to paint what things actually looked like as he was losing his sight. The landscapes became blurred and clouded over, and you have the sense he couldn't really see the canvas, either. I think they're very moving – in a way I like them more than the other ones, which slightly bore me after a while' (this said with a pretend-guilty wince). 'But Paul for some reason can't decide about them.'

'So are they going in the catalogue?'

She gave her touching, oddly sexy little chuckle. 'I wonder.'

'Well, I must find out,' I said stiffly.

'Mm, do.'

We emerged through a gateway at the edge of a wide canal-basin, where half a dozen glass-roofed tourist-boats were tethered one beyond the other. There was a delicious sense of being left behind, the season over. We leant on a railing and looked down through dropped brown chestnut-fans into a shadowy saloon.

'I think Orst's death must have left . . . a mark on Paul's mind. I think that may be something to do with it.'

I shook my head, aggrieved at my own ignorance. 'I've no idea what happened.'

'I'm sorry, I don't know what you know. Yes, Paul, as he's probably told you, used to know Orst, he used to go and look after him when he was a boy, and read to him, I think. Orst apparently never saw Paul, or said he thought he could see him sometimes through a mist. He used to get him to describe things to him at great length, including his own pictures, which must have been like doing the catalogue already, and Orst could remember them all . . . Then he was murdered by the Germans, and it must have been a bit like losing a father, or an uncle perhaps, for Paul.'

'He was murdered by the Germans. It doesn't say anything about that in the booklet at the Museum.'

'I know.'

'But it does sound a quite major point of interest in the painter's story . . .' Helene raised her shoulders for a few moments. 'Was he Jewish, I suppose?'

'I'm sure he was partly. You'll have to ask Paul about it.'

'It doesn't sound as if he's very likely to tell me.'

We swung round and looked back over low roofs to the rival towers of St John's and the Cathedral, already silvery and shadowless in flood-lights against the dimming sky.

'Actually I think it may have been a mistake – or he was arrested and died anyway. He was old and I think extremely ill. It was just before we were liberated,' she said with a somehow comically offhand identification with that earlier generation and that deep event: 'Paul would have been about eighteen.' I thought, if this was the Second World War, what would Luc be doing? I didn't know yet if he was merely a follower, subtly in-stitutionalised by his St Narcissus training, or if his breaking away showed some more decisive and unstable quality, the in-explicable gift of shaping his own life, as he was shaping mine. When Paul took up with the blind old painter, he was a boy, he might have been someone that someone like me might have taught; and he was making a life-decision – no one knew at the time, perhaps it was mildly worrying to his parents who con-doned the charitable impulse but regarded the artist in his eccentric villa with superstitious unease. Who could say? But if he hadn't recognised that necessity, well, I wouldn't have been perched on this canal-side railing now. It was an oddly satis-fying few minutes, under the great wrecked chestnuts, looking back at the gables and towers and the evening lamps, and seeing how Paul's altruism and Luc's wild truancy fed into the empty vortex of my own life.

'I'm quite envious of you working *upstairs*,' Helene said, with a little gasped laugh at her own candour.

'I won't always, you know. When you're not there I'm going to be on the front desk, with the Meredith.'

'Well, we'll see.'

'It would be nice if we could both be upstairs,' I said cour-teously, masking my new sense of disquiet that I might have taken a job from her and that this little stroll was being used by her to let me know. 'You know so much more about it all than me.'

'Well, I wouldn't be useless. It's not that I really warm to the paintings themselves, just that I seem to have known them all my life. It's Paul's direct connection with them – it makes me a little proprietorial about them in my turn.' She stood off a pace or two and we went on, through an archway under a lamp that gave it the look of a convent or a hospital and through a chain of silent courtyards so obliquely linked with dog-leg alleys that in each one it seemed we had gone wrong and had come to the end.

'What did you think of Orst's pictures when you were a girl?' I said, quick-marching for a moment to keep up.

'I found them quite frightening, but also very fascinating. You know how you *make* yourself look at horrid things to burn

135

out the horridness – some of them were all right of course, the wonderful portraits; but the Medusa with all the snakes in her collar made it hard for me to enter that room really until quite recently. Some of the others were less sensational, but I thought they were even more disturbing by being vague about what was going on.'

'It did seem quite odd to me when I saw a whole party from St Narcissus in the Museum.'

'Oh, we were always coming in from St Opportune, as well, with Miss Van der Menge, our mad art mistress. We had to choose something in a picture and copy it and write about it. I remember I was very keen to get my own Chimera. Then you had to do some research: what is a Chimera, what does the artist mean by it etc, what does it eat?'

'You really are much better qualified.'

'I always had an advantage, because I was shown round with my parents sometimes after hours, and Paul would get out beautiful drawings and prints the other girls had certainly never seen. He even showed us some of the white paintings then.'

'The *white*?'

'It's what I call these very late pictures I was telling you about, which are in different shades of white, just verging into yellow or pale blue. Don't you think it's a good expression?'

'I can see that it *could* be offputting . . .'

We had come out into Trumpet Street, to my surprise, a few yards away from Helene's parked car. Away to the right the carillon of the great belfry began the maundering Catholic hymn with which it made its devotions before striking the important hour of six.

'I'll see you next week.'

'All right,' I said. 'I'll look forward to that.'

'I've got to go home and work on my dress.'

'Oh . . .'

'Mummy and I are making a fantastic wedding-dress. You can hardly see us when we're doing it, with all the yards of stuff. It's like being in a cloud.'

'A cloud with pins in, I should imagine.'

She gave her funny laugh, shuffled forward and let me kiss her on both cheeks. Wedding-dresses, white ones, made me think in old-fashioned terms: had she kept herself for Jan? Had she kept herself from him? How unimaginable to walk in trembling purity through the tearful, admiring crowd.

11

The next time I went to Luc's house, the door was opened by an anxious girl like a cockney parlour-maid, who eyed me up and down before standing aside: I stepped in over various boxes and the flex of a floor-polisher. Luc was trotting down the stairs.

'Frightful bore,' he said, in his most startling Englishism so far. 'My father's coming to visit us, and all is on its ears.'

Mrs Altidore came out of the dining-room. 'I can't have you in here,' she said, frowning at us in turn and giving me at least a feeling of being linked with Luc in some wonderful delinquency. Luc himself was gaping and shrugging exaggeratedly, gently taking a rise out of her panic and its thin veil of disdain. If I hadn't been there she might have raised her voice or given him a harmless hit on the upper arm. She stooped and snatched up a small rug and shooed us towards the stairs with it. 'Take Edward Manners up to your room, darling, and let Rosa and me get on.'

'But . . .' – Luc was beginning some further broad objections, just coloured, I thought, with a real unwillingness to have me up there. I thought for a flash of Julien Rostand's room, out at the coast, the protocols of an adult-free zone – 'Privé, Danger de Mort'. I looked down, pained by the situation, a hot sick stripe of excitement in my chest. We were both perhaps fixing on the same embarrassments – the unmade bed, and where I would sit, the helpless revelations of childhood that a young man's bedroom always makes, his sudden consciousness of them. When he saw that it was inevitable he loped up the stairs, two, sometimes three, at a time, leaving me gesturing to his mother and then turning to follow. There was a hint of spurning and unmarrying in the way he sprang on ahead, it was no companionable face-to-bum ascent. We had never walked up a flight of stairs together before.

On the first-floor landing I hesitated, and walked on into a room – twin beds, dried flowers, pale sunlight scalloped through lacy curtains over silver counterpanes, the guest-room mausoleum. Time was muted there, the empty months extended, and close by Luc was growing, bounding up and down the stairs all day past this half-open door. He was calling out, hesitating on the turn of the banister above. As I came up he gave me a tense smirk of reluctant welcome.

Luc's room . . . I walked through it with an open-minded air, as if I were being shown it by a house-agent, and looked down into the street from the window, noticing the smaller globed reflection of the view in the mirror that hung beside it. Luc's room didn't have that much character: a battered old desk with a secretarial kind of swivel chair, bookshelves above with school-books, English, French and Flemish novels, several volumes of a cheerful and unlovely children's encyclopaedia; a mini sound system with headphones plugged in and a stack of tapes, the yellow Walkman too; fawn carpet, magnolia walls with a framed school photograph and a poster from the Town Museum (some chaste Memling); a single bed hastily covered with one of his mother's gaudy bedspreads, kicked-off moccasins seen beneath its fringe . . . If only it could happen now, my hand in his hair, the whole length of him pressed against me, our tongues rolling over each other. He was wearing very baggy desert-coloured trousers, pinched in at his slim waist with a useful-looking belt; his shirt was almost a jersey, with three buttons at the neck – the effect was quite feminine, and had me imagining his cock with more than usual hunger and wonder.

We danced a clumsy excuse-me in the middle of the room, and I fetched up in the chair whilst he retired to the bed, and sat nervously at its edge; I glanced across the litter on the desk beside me, and read the beginning of a letter, 'Dear Arnold' in big disconnected writing, 'How are you getting on?' – at which point inspiration seemed to have dried up.

'So your father's coming?' I opened with.

'Yes, that's right, my father. We don't see him for ages, and then, bouf!, he just goes and turns up.' He blew out a puff of air

139

and nodded illusionlessly. 'Then my mother gets very worried and we have to clean up the house.'

'I'd have thought it was immaculate already.'

'Yes, of course. But I would not suggest that you tell her that. She is not listening to things too much today.' I couldn't tell if he was really got down by all this.

'I can't remember how long you said they'd been . . . apart.'

He almost jeered the answer: 'Four years,' and stood up. 'I don't see any reason why we can't have our coffee,' he said. 'Do you want some?'

'Um . . . thank you. But . . . Shall I come down?'

'All right,' he said, but then turned back and looked at me as if I might be a liability, or as if he wanted to save me from the ludicrous trouble he was about to stir up. 'Perhaps it will be better if you don't come' – and he was out of the door, leaving me, already, alone.

For a moment, to my surprise, I was frozen with sympathy for his poor mother, provoked by her son when he ought to have been at school and she was at her most vulnerable. Then I thawed under the hot blast of illicit opportunity: perhaps Luc didn't mistrust me after all, it was only a guilty projection of the love he had never even suspected. He was so unknown, he was still all possibility, unopened cupboards and drawers and hastily straightened single bed . . . I took a step or two and the boards cracked loud enough to be heard in the street.

I looked down on the bed I had dreamt about. The crimson bedspread was worked elaborately in twining gold thread, long art-nouveau filaments that blossomed at the head into crumpled white lilies; I thought it might have been a dry-run for one of his mother's altar-cloths. I pulled it back and stared at the bolster in its loose sleeve, pummelled and askew, shoved round, perhaps, in a spasm of dreaming or in the clumsy fight of waking up; and the white duvet with blue piping, rucked and bunched and bursting at its buttons. I stooped to breathe it in, laundry and cotton and the merest hint of manscent, a lost trace of sleep and dull boy's breath. I pulled the cover back to where it had been, and sat on it for a moment to re-create the hollow he had made.

In the top drawer of the desk the last thing dropped in was a bright paper wallet, showing angled family snaps on the out-side, and letting slip from within a glossy stack of lightly curved colour prints. The nervousness of sixty or seventy seconds earlier had left me, and I shuffled through the photographs with a burglar's certain hand. And up they bobbed, one behind the other like bathers rising and dropping on the incoming waves – Luc, Patrick, Sibylle, Patrick, Patrick, Luc, Sibylle, Sibylle, Sibylle. The boys in singlets, or bare-chested, mock-heroic, she very composed, self-aware, conscious of her beauty; the boys were conscious of their own, as well, it showed in every caper-ing gesture, even when one was pointing at the other, who stood cross-eyed, with his tongue sticking out. Then there was a picture of Luc so mythically beautiful that my mouth went dry and then I found I was flooded with a little sob. He was looking through me, eyes narrowed but translucent in sunshine, sea-wet hair pushed oddly, darkly back, lips apart but firm, as if trying out his own name, naked to the bottom edge of the photograph, just below his navel, and his long hands stretched wide, some ordinary gesture caught half-way through so that he looked like Nijinsky resting in the air. I heard the quick stride of his ascent on the flight below and as I thumbed and squared the photos back I slipped out the strands of negative in their crinkled wrap-per and tucked them deep into my inner breast pocket. When he came in I was sprawled in the chair with one of his story-books and sucking the ear-piece of my twiddled spectacles. I did detect a certain anxiety as to what it was I was looking at.

'There will definitely not be coffee,' he said. He looked quite pleased and amused to have made the effort and carried out his plan with such provoking reasonableness. He sat on the bed again, and rubbed his hands together. I wasn't sure if we were allies in this tiny episode, or if it was all his own. 'What are you reading?' he asked.

I didn't have the wildest idea, a glance at the page gave nothing significant away, I proffered the book with a bored smile. It wasn't a very attractive book – it turned out to be a history of the Crusades, in a fortified school binding.

'I never could sort out one crusade from another,' I said.

Luc grunted. 'That's one of my father's books,' he said.

141

I took it back with kindly dim interest, not sure what I was looking for. 'It doesn't seem very . . .'

'All those ones are published by him,' he said. 'Of course I never read them, but he sends them all, and I think it makes him feel better.'

Then Luc told me about his father's business. A meticulous account, something he had worked out for himself rather than something half-forgotten he had been told. He said, 'I call it The Fall of the House of Altidore.' I was so flattered and sympathetic that I found it quite hard to concentrate. His great-grandfather Guillaume, apparently, had created a little publishing firm in the 1890s, and produced small and luxurious printings of belles-lettres and poetry — part of Maeterlinck's work on bees, collections of verse and essays on Flemish art by Verhaeren with beautiful brown plates. I hadn't realised how wealthy and grand the Altidores had been: the publishing was just a *jeu d'esprit* of Guillaume, who presided at the family's modern apogee, and was a great collector too. Now the original Editions Altidore were worth thousands of pounds, but the mercantile empire that had financed them had dwindled away. Luc's grandfather had been a gambler, with little interest in shipping and copper. He liked to travel and have house-parties, and had built himself a house to have them in, a little frescoed château in woodland near the coast and the casinos. He lost a fortune in the Congo; and a good deal more in the Depression. The only thing he made money on was publishing, and he broadened the list to include many of the more popular writers of the day. Ten years ago Luc's father had inherited a moribund business but one with a long backlist, dull in the main but studded with steady sellers. He had poured in a lot of his rich older wife's money and in the boom of the early eighties things picked up. He had visions, said Luc, of their regaining something of their turn-of-the-century grandeur. Workmen had been sent to repair the roof of the little château. Then things turned down again, and Editions Altidore, like so many others, was bought up by a huge conglomerate. Luc's father kept some decorative, pretend position there, was enormously rich again from the buy-out, and over the course of a year or so of irregular commuting removed himself from his home and his family and lived a fashionable life in Brussels instead. He had never sought a divorce, in the four years since he went, though Luc knew that he lived with an actress – virtually a teenager, he said with disgust – and his mother had been difficult ever since.

I was struck by his unfriendly strength of feeling as he told me all this, and dismayed by the high-principled severity of the young, that was a focusing perhaps of other fears and doubts. I felt quite abashed, sitting there holding his father's book, as if I were somehow involved or to blame; like when a friend recounts to you an argument he had and enters into it again with such vehemence that you start to feel you are yourself the butt of his remembered anger. I smiled.

'I am very well disposed towards my mother,' Luc said solemnly. 'I don't want you to think I am not. I get annoyed when she is making so much fuss about him and imagines he will come back, when it is obvious that he won't. Most of the time I can look after her, but when my father is coming there is not too much I can do.' How poignant and humbling suddenly to see Luc as the watchful support of this woman I had always thought of as absurd, and now began to picture as the heartbroken dupe of a husband far younger than herself. 'Already', he said, 'I know enough about love to understand why she does it. But still . . .'

I stared at him for an agonised few seconds, then blurted out optimistically, 'So you do get on with your father?'

'I do, of course. And you see, he is very amusing and full of life and so forth.' He looked down at his two squared fists, which he was knocking nervily together. 'I used to think it was possible he did not want to have a child. Now I am not sure – I think we are better friends now that we never see each other.'

I didn't know how to follow so muted and painful a statement. I think he was as surprised as I was at everything that had come out. I leant forward, I might easily have stroked his hand and coaxed the fist into a grateful clasp.

'Have you met the . . . actress?'

'Yes, once at a party with both my parents. It was a long time ago, I think before this love affair began.' He looked round, as if he might stretch out on the bed, but then thought better of it. 'But how can we tell?'

143

I don't think he expected an answer. 'Oh, we can't tell.'

'She was in a film on the television which was in two or three parts, which I could watch if my mother was not in the house.' Again the thoughtfulness mixed with mischief. 'I must say that she is very beautiful, even if she is a very bad actress. You might fall in love with her yourself if you saw her, Edward.'

'I wonder.'

'I think I am right that she was only seventeen when he met her.' I couldn't tell if he was looking at me pensively, abstracted by his picturing of the girl, or if he was speaking with deadpan cheek. 'Anyway, he told me once that it was love like a blow of lightning for him, though not for her, which took much more time.'

All this talk of love from him suddenly, it was as if he had just learnt the word: he used it lightly and consciously like a new swearword packed with untried power and provocation.

'And what about your grandfather's château? Have you ever seen it?'

'We all went when I was small, perhaps when I was . . . eight. No one had been there for a long time, and it wasn't all that safe. I think it wasn't built correctly.'

'Oh.'

'All I can remember well is a round room, do you say a rotunda, with paintings on the ceiling of my grandfather and all his rich friends, who were idlers in fact, dressed up for a fantasy. My grandfather Theo was dressed up like an Indian prince with a long sword.' Luc looked at me openly. 'I also remember I was very frightened of his picture.'

'And what's happened to it now?'

He shrugged, denying his disappointment. 'It's still there, with the windows all blocked up, and there is a metal roof over the top, because of the rain.'

I wanted to go there with him and help him get it back. It was just another strand of longing to know about the dereliction of what should one day be Luc's Little Trianon, and about a certain baffling shittiness in the last downward flight of the Altidore family history. At the same time I had the image of my own history like a locked and rotting pavilion too far off and too unsafe perhaps for Luc to want to visit it. These lessons

144

were simulacra of conversations, my part pained and inquis-
itive, his merely reactive and polite. Once or twice I had
mentioned my father's singing or my great-aunt's novels, both
equally forgotten, or spoken reassuringly of my own school-
days and their various failures. His reaction was a tolerant
blankness, a pause.

Sometimes the pressure was almost too great, having him
there in my sight, looking at me, moistening that fat lip with a
hesitant tongue, pushing back his hair with the hand that later
would undress him and make free with him. I got up abruptly
and asked to be directed to the bathroom.

It was on the floor below, next to the marmoreal spare bedroom. Luc showed me in and gestured at the various opulent
appointments. After I locked the door I thought he might wait
outside, as Mrs Vivier so patiently had at Paul's house once,
and I listened until I heard the creak of the stairs as he went
back up. I leant against the door and looked at myself pityingly
in the wall of mirror opposite, thinking I must say something to
Luc, I couldn't just let this go on. I felt I might as well have a
pee, since I was there, and did so, able to watch myself, as you
sometimes can in trains, with a certain admiration. I washed my
hands, and noted the mingled bottles on the basin's mosaic surround – the mother's lilac talc and cleansing lotion, the son's
canister of shaving foam and Donald Duck toothbrush, caked
with pink paste; I remembered it so well, your things took the
place of your father's, you became a kind of couple in your
turn. The dry toothbrush tasted of nylon and dead mint.

At the end of the long white bath with its tall, perched and
somehow vigilant brass taps was a gingham-lined clothes-
basket with a lid. I rootled lightly among its contents – again
the mixture of silvery slips and bras and sweatier boy's things,
grimy-necked shirts, inside-out socks and underwear. There
were some white Hom briefs, tiny, damp from a towel they
were bundled in with. I picked them out and covered my face
with them. They seemed spotless, hardly worth changing for
new ones, with only a ghost of a smell. When I rolled them up
they were almost hidden in my fist. I buried them at the bottom
of the basket, but then some awful compulsion made me plunge
my arm in for them again.

145

Before the end of the hour we heard the pneumatic scrunching and electronic whine of a big car being parked in a small space. I saw Luc studying the window spy-glass, and saw the nose of a grey-blue Mercedes swelling towards the front door in the mirror's convex surface. As it happened I was making another attempt to tell him something about myself, but I watched his attention waver and go.

'Yeah, my father's here,' he said. 'I think I'd better . . .'

'Let's call it a day,' I said, and we both sprang up. He had a look of anxious excitement that made me feel both protective and *de trop*. I thought in a way I *should* meet his father; there should be some mutual recognition and professional understanding, as it were, over Luc's head. Then as we got half-way down the stairs I was simply embarrassed to be a stranger towards whom distracting courtesy would need to be shown at a moment of family greeting and tension. But Luc, though he was ahead of me and so precious to me as I let him go, didn't forget me. He leapt down the last four steps and, as his father looked up from a muttered exchange with his mother just inside the open front door, wrapped an arm round his neck and kissed him on the lips. Then he half-turned and extended his other arm towards me. 'This is Edward,' he said; I came forward with a silly expression of shyness and pride, as if I were someone he wanted to marry.

His father and I exchanged only a few sentences, bantering around his absence and uncertain responsibilities, reassuring ourselves with the facts of Luc's excellence at English and the inevitability of his good results. I was startled by Martin Altidore's appearance. He was so young. Though I knew he was younger than his wife I had still somehow expected a burgherly figure out of one of the family portraits; but there was nothing of their prudence or their warning glint of power. He was darker than Luc, more animal and compact (Luc's legginess came from his mother), but with the same long nose and almost the same big lips. And he was in the same stretch of life as me — well, a little further on, but surely only forty. His dark suit was beautifully cut, his off-white shirt and blood-coloured tie were silk. You knew at once he was a fucker. If I'd met him in a bar

I'd have wanted him. I was trying to please him, playing to some cockteasy quality he had – charm I suppose, a kind of shallow intimacy; something Luc incuriously lacked – and at the same time to stay in with Luc; and then to be good to his mother, half-forgotten just outside our little male ring.

12

I went out to the station to greet Edie and had to wait half an hour, pacing the platform systematically and then sitting with a coffee and a cigarette in the nearly empty refreshment hall. It was one of those vacant interludes, when pleasant boredom mixes with anticipation, and six or seven minutes of anonymous sex in the mopped and deserted Gents is what you would like best – you come just as the tannoy chimes and the fast train is competently announced. But there was nothing doing this morning: a few stout minor businessmen in belted macs, an elderly lady with a cart of luggage and a look of foreboding. I was tense but weightless, oddly comforted by the unknown plans and problems of the others. The long hand on a digitless clock-face clunked from minute to minute as the trim red second hand busied round. I gazed through the enormous windows, back towards the city – nearby a little guard-tower with a pointed roof and drooping chequered flag, and beyond it an impression of walls and spires like a city in a book of hours, only blurred and brightened by the gold of horse-chestnuts turning and the paling yellow of limes. It was a good moment for my old friend to see the place.

In fact when she arrived she found everything wonderful: the clean, late train, the absence of people, the sleek inter-war grandeur of the station with its fawn marble and redundant spaciousness, all seemed hilarious and entrancing to her. We had a fierce hug and I was carried along for a while on the surge of confidence that came from being with a real old friend, whose friendship outlasted and diminished my other frets and misguided wanderings. I balanced up her several bags like an experienced bellhop, and we set off into town on foot. She was travelling with a hat-box.

'I want you to see it this way, as if you were an old pilgrim, or you couldn't afford the tram.'

'Heavenly.'

I led her over a bridge, through an escutcheoned gateway and into the first little square; silent houses and a statue of a nineteenth-century man with swooping moustaches – she ran forward to read his name.

'I've no idea,' I said.

'But darling, I thought you'd know everything by now.'

'Sorry. I do know one or two things, but . . . not that.'

'I see.' She walked round the statue on its high plinth as if my ignorance made it more interesting or problematic. The nice thing about the man was his thoughtful, almost unhappy expression, as if he felt himself unsuited to the eminent perpetuity of statuedom. He might have been a good doctor or a minor devotional poet. Edie imitated his posture, mocking it gently, and caught the eye of a young boy who came trotting past and stopped in surprise to see a man with a hat-box and a striking dark girl in black tights and tunic and slouch-cap, like a Stuart page-boy in mourning, standing stock-still; while to me it had an older resonance, the busy longueurs of photo-sessions when Edie was still at fashion-school, when we would go on to the common with a suitcase and umbrellas and sheets of tinfoil and one or two of her inventive friends and create our gleaming static happenings, which patient passers-by would stop and puzzle over.

I was bursting with things to say to her; she was an indulgent listener, not like rivalrous old men friends who fought you for the conversational advantage. But I wanted to let the city enfold her first. As we walked on I would point out a church or house or a glimpse into a courtyard, but we hardly spoke. I felt the place was mine, I was proud of it, and of more or less knowing my way through it; and I knew the quality of Edie's different silences, from the violent to the serene, and that we were together in this one – as I hadn't been together with anyone since I came here.

We were at a famously pretty point, with a view of the Belfry beyond a canal, leaves fluttering on to the water, a long quay to the left with three receding bridges stepping from the empty sunshine into the narrow lanes of the middle of town.

'It is absolute bliss,' Edie said. 'You're so lucky, and so right to have come. I couldn't see why before, to be honest I thought it was quite potty, but you're absolutely right.'

I swallowed the blunt admission. 'Voilà.'

'I must say it is rather peculiarly *quiet*.' She looked at her watch. 'I mean we've seen three people in the past twenty minutes, and now there's nobody in sight at all. That sort of *might* get to one.'

'Yes, things have been a fraction on the dull side since about 1510. But we do what we can to make our own entertainment.'

'So one rather gathered from your letter.'

She was not ungrand, Edie. My mother often said she came from 'a very good family', which was her way of glossing over Edie's more gavroche and boozy qualities and suggesting I was lucky to be friends with a de Souzay at all. The de Souzays were great liberal philanthropists, though not, by and large, as keen as this one was to get in a pub and talk, at some length, about men and what they liked to do. She had an emphatic contralto speaking-voice, and a certain *hauteur* – undercut by a vulgar laugh that could set other people going in a cinema or café.

She always used the same scent, a beautiful fragrance that was abbeys, aunts, tapestried country houses, dulled petals in china bowls before it was . . . whatever it was, the discreet phial put up by some Mayfair herbalist for powdered dowagers in black court shoes. It didn't go particularly with what she tended to wear – often made by herself and usually sexy, theatrical and vaguely disconcerting: she was my earliest experience of glamour, of bold exposure matched with dazzling concealment. Fifteen years ago I had seen her squeeze up her bust like a sou-brette in a Restoration comedy, and watched with awe as her face, with its long nose and downed upper lip, was painted and dusted into a challenging and ironic mask. Even then she wore her mysterious perfume, so that to breathe it again now in my rooms was to go back through half a lifetime passed alongside her. It overwhelmed the yellow roses I had bought and stuck in a jug in the middle of the table.

'I love it, dear,' said Edie, opening the cupboards into which

I'd tidied things away. 'You could have a great romance in here.' She went to the long back window and gazed down into the secret garden.

I felt buoyantly rich with the money I'd been given by Matt, and loved being able to make Edie completely my guest. She kept offering to pay for things, as she had often had to in the past, and I would sternly but suavely refuse her. I took her out straight away for lunch at a gloomy and highly praised restaurant in the main square, where we drank three bottles of Chablis and ate mussels and turbot and apple pancakes. The subject of Luc was palpable just beyond us. I felt more reckless and confessional as I drank, but I kept clear of it till coffee: I thought it would take my appetite away and then the meal would be a waste of money. I asked her about things back home with the feeling I'd been away for five months, not five weeks.

'Everything's *pretty* much as you left it,' she said. 'I was at the Common last weekend – just seeing Ma and Pa, but I popped into the George for a glass of Guinness and to pick up the gossip. One hears your old friend Willie Turlough has had yet another baby.'

'To think I could have been his baby,' I said, as though envisaging some wild new form of surrogacy. 'Still, he's bald now, isn't he?'

'It's a glorious great pate, by all accounts. Not that he could ever be less than humblingly handsome . . .' She leant forward and pushed a hand through my thick mop.

'Anything else?'

'I went into Dawn's shop, it's all outrageously expensive. He said no one had even rung the bell – you know they've got a buzzer now for security – for *two days*. I bought a pair of old china candlesticks for about the price of a world cruise, it was sort of a mixture of charity and madness, like so much of one's existence.'

'Are you pleased with them?'

'Not at all. I'm just longing for someone to get married so that I can pass them on.'

I twiddled the stem of my wine-glass. 'I never long for that,' I said. 'And what of Dawn himself?'

'Well, I was amazed to see him looking so fit. Colin took him to Algeria, which was apparently somewhat hairy with the riots, but did mean he got nice and brown; and he's put on a bit of weight. The AZT seems to have made him rather hilarious.'

'I so want him to be all right,' I said — it seemed still worth saying.

'I'm afraid I didn't see your ma,' said Edie after a pause. 'I don't suppose she'd expect me to call if you weren't there.'

'I had a ten-page letter yesterday. She's fine. At least if there isn't an upset in the later pages. I've never quite finished reading one of her letters before the next one arrives.'

We were late, perhaps loud with drink (one never knew), and the sole survivors of lunchtime. The waiter who was left to us gave only a curt nod when we asked for a second pot of coffee. 'So what about this breaking heart of yours?' said Edie. 'Or am I exaggerating?'

'God, I wish you were,' I gasped, tears suddenly in my eyes.

'Darling. Perhaps it will be all right.'

'Of course it may be all right . . .' I lit a cigarette, it was from a packet left behind in the bar, an American brand, thin and sweet — the shock of finding what other people buy and like.

'Have you actually . . . made a move?'

I shook my head. 'There are the most tremendous bars and forces in the air. Sometimes I'm only eighteen inches away from him, our feet are virtually touching as we sit at the table for the lessons, I can smell the milky coffee on his breath. And yet I'm completely immobilised.'

'Well, you could hardly start groping him in a lesson.' Then, 'How's it going to end?'

'That — that's too logical and impossible a question. How it is is all that counts.' Edie said nothing. 'I'm so empty and aching for him, he affects everything I do and think, and it's very hard to believe that maybe he doesn't even know. It really makes me feel quite mad at times. When I go round for the lessons, you know how it is, at first I feel absolutely mad simply being with him, then after a few minutes I kind of subdue my passion with words, things get normalised, their banality somehow shows through for a while – of course there are spurts of hot heart-burn – and then as the end approaches it becomes unbearable again. I feel my face is stiff with all the pain he doesn't even know he's inflicted: it's just that basic biological thing, you can't stand being separated, and for minutes after he's said goodbye your heart is thumping and thumping and you feel full of despair and shock as if you'd just witnessed some great accident. And you *have* to have a drink.' I took a deep pull on the cigarette and stubbed the whole thing out. 'Ah, coffee.'

The waiter set down the copper pot, and busied and obstructed us removing the ashtray and at last empty glasses. 'Which way do you think his thoughts turn?' Edie asked.

'Anights? Well, it's hard . . . Did I mention the Three? They enhance each other's mystique no end. They're all beautiful and well off and give the impression of being crazy about each other.'

'You know what they say . . . "Un trio n'excite pas de soupçons".'

'Well, my soupçons have never been more excités in their lives.' I hesitated, and then drew out the wallet of pictures from my inside pocket. 'I can show you.'

'Oh.'

I shuffled through the prints and laid out half a dozen in front of her. She seemed deliberately to take a detached line. 'So this dark one is Patrick? He looks a real little thug, I must say. Quite nice though.'

'He *doesn't* look a thug. He's got a gigantic cock.'

'Sibylle is lovely, I agree. Beautiful eyes, and mouth; and colouring.'

'Yes.'

'She looks very sophisticated and irresistible.'

'Quite. Thank you.'

'And this must be him.' I looked away and then back to the upside-down image and waited for her reaction. It was the faun-like picture of Luc on the beach.

'Don't you think it's very ancient Greece that one?'

'Mm. Where was it taken?'

'It's at a place just over the French border where the Three

153

are always going. I followed them down there with my friend Matt and we kind of spied on them.'

'I see, you took this.'

'No, no – no. I stole the negatives and had them printed.'

Edie raised an eyebrow and I wondered again, as I had in dense hours of meditating on that picture, just who *had* taken it and at which of his friends that complex gaze of Luc's had been directed.

'That must have been rather difficult.'

'Terribly easy. I've stolen lots of things. I'm wearing a pair of his pants at the moment, and one of his vests and one of his socks.' I stuck out my feet beyond the tablecloth and she looked with concern at my one blue and one green ankle. 'The blue one's Luc's.'

'Darling – I mean . . . you do seem to have gone *complète-ment* bonkers.'

I tolerated this remark, I wasn't sure if it contained a hint of congratulation. I drank a cup of coffee in quick insistent sips, and Edie kept looking at the photos. 'Are the others any good?' she said.

'There are some others I wasn't going to bore you with.'

'*Bore*? I love other people's photographs. They're the only ones that aren't disappointing.'

I gave her the packet. 'There are those rather odd ones, where they're acting or something. That one where Patrick has a sheet over his head, and Luc's waving a poker round like a sword. Most peculiar,' I said, drily and enviously.

Edie frowned over the print. 'It isn't *that* peculiar. They're only larking about. Just because you can only imagine them gazing into each other's eyes and having sex all day long, you seem to have forgotten that they're only kids, who still do childish, rather kooky kind of things, and like dressing up and being silly. You may not have heard about it, it's called fantasy.'

'You haven't even met them.' She held my hand across the table. 'You haven't said what you think of Luc.'

'Well, he's lovely, darling . . . odd-lovely, wouldn't you say? His upper lip is very large and over-luscious.'

'When you see the point of him it's the upper lip you love

154

most of all. You go from disliking it to accepting it to . . . adoring it.'

'The other thing I think', said Edie, 'is that he's too young for you.'

'Well, of *course* he's too young for me,' I said in sudden miserable annoyance. 'Still, it happens, it happens.'

Edie was a hit in the Cassette and shook hands with people and made funny conversation, much of which was over their heads. She wore black shoes and tights, a thick short bunched red skirt that stuck out, a black leather jacket and her hair pulled up inside her black cap: she looked like an interesting young man during that brief phase when skirts for men were considered a possibility. She wasn't a fag-hag (if anything, she claimed, it was I who was a hag-fag), but an emotional aloofness, the afterspace of several short, obscurely unhappy affairs, made her at home among gay men; they were abruptly intimate yet made no deep demands on her, and she followed their doings with close attention and a kind of caustic merriment, as at some gratifying old melodrama. She would go into the George IV at lunchtime, but never at night, when she thought the boys should be left to make their own mischief, which she could hear about next day. She was kind, too, when she needed to be: she had looked after friends of ours who were dying. Dawn was one of them.

She and Gerard took to each other and had a long lively talk, while I sat it out on a bar-stool and made occasional interjections implying a closer relationship with Gerard than was really the case. I suppose their witty chat, with Edie like a louche minor royal showing a radiant fullness of interest in her interlocutor's stories, stirred some clumsy jealousy – and I remembered Gerard's old ambiguity, the early marriage, and didn't quite trust him. I bought us all another drink and he dropped the subject of Burgundian court music like a flash and said, 'How's it going with Matt, then?'

'Fine!' I said.

Gerard looked around the room and said, 'Yes, a lot of people were quite surprised when you went off with him.'

'Too hot for me, you mean?'

'Well . . . And then he's not very interested in the things you like.'

'I'm sorry', I said, 'but we seem to have quite enough in common to be getting on with. Perhaps you believe in the narcissist theory of gay attraction; I've always loved it with people who are different from me.' I was sounding cross and turned cosy for a moment. 'He's been away for a couple of weeks, should be back tomorrow.' I looked down. 'I've missed him a lot actually.'

'I hear he likes pretty kinky sex.'

I said, 'Yup', and Edie said,

'Is this the person you've been working for?'

'No, no,' I said, with the warm mendacity of tone I knew she would understand – in fact she had named it the Manners Disclaimer years before.

'You wouldn't want to work for Matt,' Gerard explained to Edie: 'he does very shady dealing, and is often in the jug.' We laughed, and he added, with a spoiler's relish, 'As Edward will tell you, Matt isn't even his real name. He's really called Wim Vermeulen.' After a moment of narrow-eyed scepticism, I nodded and sighed in confirmation. 'He changed it recently when he came out of prison. Apparently he thought he looked like Matt Dillon.'

'I think he looks just like him,' I said.

Later on Edie and I slumped together on the banquette in the corner and half-watched some stubbly frenching going on across the room. 'Is this Matt really a crook, as your musical friend says? It does seem rather odd if he's changed his name.'

'Gerard's just madly jealous of us,' I said as I realised the symmetry of the thing. 'Actually he is a crook, yes. And I'd more or less come to the conclusion that he'd been inside. Though I confess the Vermeulen thing is a surprise. I thought he was someone else he knew; letters come for him. I'd even started getting a wee bit jealous.'

'Do be careful.'

'It's nothing serious, what I do isn't. He has a lot of business with computers which as you can imagine I have nothing to do with. And then this other stuff . . . it's rather shaming really.

He's a sort of fetish merchant. Well, he sells porn videos, very cheaply, by mail – he buys them and copies them, which I suppose is illegal. And he also sells people's clothes, which must be illegal too, and is much more profitable.'

'Why's that illegal?'

'He steals them first. There are guys out there – in here, for all I know – who are prepared to spend a fortune on, say, a sixth-former's Y-fronts or a really sweaty kind of yucky jock-strap.'

'I hope you didn't spend a fortune on your one blue sock.'

'No, no, I helped myself to that. The thing about Matt's items is that they're a con. Actually he does sometimes genuinely work to a commission; but as a rule he just passes things off as, say, the young postman's rather heavily soiled smalls, or the lycra shorts of the national schools squash champion, who just happens to come from our very own St Narcissus. He goes to the Town Baths when they are in for their swimming-lessons and helps himself to a handful of the dirtier pieces.'

Edie had the open-minded expression of someone on holiday good-naturedly learning the rules of a foreign national game.

'So the soiling is the important part really?'

'Oh, absolutely. And pubes. They up the price phenomenally. And there you do have to be a bit careful.'

'It seems to be very school-oriented.'

'Yes, it does at the moment – it may just be the rush of the *rentrée* that's got so many of the perves on edge. There are older people too who have their following – some of them soil professionally; the cynical foul, I suppose you might call it.'

'It's all a revelation to me.'

'Isn't it? It's a kind of alchemy really. You take something of only slight practical value, but give it a magically arousing association, even if of a kind most people would consider revolting, and you're minting gold.' And I had a hard-on myself at the grip of Luc's tight little knickers and feeling the hard-ons he must have had pushing against the very cotton that now constrained mine and his balls thoughtlessly snuggled there all day long.

'I suppose you haven't met any of your customers.'

'It's all done by registered mail. They write of course, these great fantasies about porn-stars – some are illiterate, some are obviously the work of leading academics, they're rather like Henry James, they put all the rude words in inverted commas; some are always bragging about the size of their own equipment, which I don't believe. And then there's the phone. It's all new to me but I find I make quite a good phone-fraud: I work them up in a slightly grudging way, as though I might not let them have what they want so badly. As an opportunity for speaking stilted English to foreigners it beats conversation-classes any day, and the pay is far better.' I glanced to my left and saw Frits, heavily alone with his book. 'Don't look now,' I said, 'but I'm quite keen to avoid that person standing reading.'

Edie looked at once, and just happened to catch his eye as he was turning the page.

'Well, I hope you're a Somerset Maugham fan,' I said, as he came gratefully over and offered us another drink.

Much later, in bed, an almost pre-adolescent clean cosiness except we must still have smelt of beer and smoke, Edie like one of the von Trapp children in pyjamas that looked to have been made out of old curtains, and me in brand new boxer-shorts, still with a lot of dress in them.

The lamp was out and only a ghost of light showed her form between me and the window. The Spanish girls were at rest, only sometimes the loose purr of a car over the cobbles rose across the intervening houses; and at one o'clock Edie said she would be disturbed by the hours sounding from St Narcissus, which I no longer noticed.

'I rather like Frits,' she said drowsily. 'It ought to be the Flemish for chips.'

'I rather like him, too. I like the way he's genuinely surprised if you find him attractive. You have to egg him on a bit. And of course he is an absolutely stupefying bore. You have to keep reminding him that what you want's his dick and not his view of Hugh Walpole's Rogue Herries novels.'

'Well, I don't want his dick. I thought he was sweet and rather thoughtful, unlike some of the others you introduced me to.'

I sighed. 'You'll probably hate Matt, if you meet him. He isn't sweet at all. He's a great connoisseur of other people's foibles.'

'Thank heavens I don't have any,' said Edie, snuffling and shouldering into her pillow.

There had only once been trouble between us. I had been silly about a blond with very good manners called Robin Stannard, who was perfectly friendly and pretended not to be aware of the mawkish strength of my feelings about him. Edie had been my confidante in the whole non-affair, and strengthened me in my fantasy until I found out that she had suddenly got off with him herself: I greeted him with yearning bonhomie and smelt her perfume on him. It was a betrayal so stunning that by the time I had adjusted to it their little fling was already over; and after a few days Edie was coming round, too shamed to be able quite to apologise. It was ten years ago, but it pressed round me tonight with something of its original force, and kept me awake long after she was unmistakably asleep.

Next day was Saturday, autumnal and clear. I had offered Edie a round of essential sightseeing, the Memlings, St John's, maybe even the Orst Museum if we had the stamina. She got up early and did some alarming exercises, but I had woken resistant already to the plans I'd made, the shine had gone off them, I almost let it be seen that I was longing to spend the day, waste the day, in some other fashion. 'I don't know,' I said, 'what would you like to do?' I was on the edge of that bad territory of scuffed-over promises.

Edie loved climbing things – castles, cathedrals, follies with a view of five counties, the wind-shaken iron lookout towers left in public parks from forgotten expositions. It was partly the fact that I didn't, that after counting fifty steps in a dark spiral staircase I began to feel more than merely breathless, felt threatened and starved, that had kept me from paying my few francs to climb the Belfry. I'd even felt a mild panic yesterday when I'd seen Edie set eyes on it, and inwardly mumbled some childish magic to prevent her from asking me to go up. But there was no avoiding it. This morning in the square she craned up at its pinnacled top until she almost fell over backwards. The sky was azure and endless, it was an obvious day for the ascent.

'We must do it,' she said, and didn't see at first my misery at hearing what I most dreaded proposed by a friend with brutal high spirits. Then she was telling me not to come, she'd wave from the top, I could wait 'like a grown-up' at the café across the square. I stood back and wincingly scanned the exterior. I admired it of course in a picturesque way, but to the prospective climber its odd construction, like three tall church towers stacked in narrowing sequence, heightened the sense of the ordeal by dividing it into three phases. In each the stairs would doubtless be narrower, the sense of entrapment tighter, the occasional glimpses from tiny windows the more terrifyingly remote from earth. The topmost part was an airy octagon in which the bells could be seen hanging over nothing.

The first phase wasn't actually too bad. The stairs were broad and well lit. It took a while for the tower to disengage itself from the great squat gothic hall which it surmounted. At the top we stepped into a gloomy chamber that housed a museum of local history, and out of sheer relief I looked minutely at the decrepit noseless or fingerless manikins in historic costume and the scale-model of the town at the time of Charles the Bold, with its fallen-over toy soldiers and web of canals covered in dust.

The second section was more testing. Edie kept saying how incredibly brave she thought I was being and why didn't I go down; and I don't know what perverse machismo pushed me on, like someone just behind me with their fist pressed into the small of my back. 'I wouldn't tell anybody back home,' she said.

'I want you to tell everyone back home that I did it,' I panted, recoiling from an arrow-slit image of old roofs far below and a horizon of ploughed land.

In the bottom of the third part was the carilloniste's office, deserted at the moment: we looked in through the roped-off doorway at the keyboard and the framed photographs of various celebrities who, amazingly in some cases, had climbed this far and shaken the carilloniste's hand: King Leopold II,

Montserrat Caballé, a man in furs and regalia who looked like Eric Sykes. It was cosily appointed – one half-expected to see a gas-ring and kettle. Then the real horror began.

The stair was not much wider than a person, and very steep and dark. I became hilarious, shouting snatches of poetry, which Edie took as a good sign until I was groping and gripping at her heels, the calves of her trousers. I longed to turn back, but wouldn't have dared go down by myself. Then voices were heard ahead of us, whirling footsteps, numbers shouted out, eighty-three, eighty-four, high-pitched taunts and boasts. What sounded like thirty, forty children were going to come past us. Before I saw them I pictured them as red and black apprentice devils, capering gleefully with their forks over rooftops, clouds. When they came there was just squeezing darkness, airless bombardment. I lost my grip on Edie, my outstretched hand grasped at cold black stone, children's knees, knapsacks; someone trod on my fingers; I clung to the notional central pillar, the inner tapering edge of the steps wasn't wide enough, I saw myself being dislodged by the heedless barging onrush of youngsters and dropping into a black funnel.

'There, that wasn't too bad, was it?' said Edie as she hurried up the last few stairs into the sunlight.

'Edie . . . Edie . . .'

She turned and ducked my head like a baptism under the low lintel. A doorway for dwarfs, for god's sake . . .

In front of me lay the rinsed expanse of the leads. I was unhappily aware of Edie springing across it and snorting in one view after another through the generous loopholes in the parapet. 'It's glorious!' she shouted, jamming down her hat against a surprisingly tough little wind, undiscernible at ground level, sent to bother those who dared the heights. I thought if I could gain the central flagpole and hang on to it, I might be able to cope. I ran to it as if expecting sniper fire, my legs like rope. Clasping it behind me in both hands I stood and considered my position. It was hard to believe I wasn't play-acting, no one could be so silly about heights; yet my knees were fidgeting with fear and I couldn't breathe deeply for the black knot in my chest.

'You must tell me what everything is,' called Edie.

Slowly, holding me like a difficult drunk, she brought me towards the parapet. I wanted to do it, but had already the sense of scrabbling for existence on the edge of a cliff. I couldn't have done it with anyone but her. Well, Luc, perhaps could have beckoned me on. The long hexagonal apertures opened at diaphragm height and one could grip the stone on either side. I did give her a perfunctory pointer to the Cathedral and St John's; and there was the lantern of St Narcissus, of course, the school with its two hidden courtyards beyond, and that must be the steep old roof of my own room, with the front dormer just visible: Edie looked along my trembling finger to find it. If I tilted my view too steeply down I panicked and drew back. 'Gosh, look at the docks,' I said. The sea-canal was bright and empty, and in the distance were raised cranes and beyond them the glimmering line of the coast. I saw the derelict industrial suburbs, roads swinging out across the flat farmlands, and far-off masses of poplar and beech.

On the other side there were the shadows of cities towards the horizon, there was the station, and the modest outskirts of the town, and then a beautiful golden wood. It took me a moment to recognise it as the Hermitage. Seeing it all at a glance inside its high wall I could hardly believe how I had wandered in it that night for so long. There was the tea-house; and that long break in the trees must hide the endless, misty pond. And where was the clearing with the yew-niches? Some-where there, among the autumn magnificence.

I wanted to look for Luc's house, but it was too close: I felt faint as I traced the far end of Long Street and had to step back and sit down. I lay out flat for a while and closed my eyes while Edie bounded about. As well as the animal fear I felt a kind of humiliation at seeing the quaint labyrinth of the city contracted below me, and my futile little circuits laid bare. When I opened my eyes it was worse – swinging blue vacancy, the tip of the flagpole with its oxidised lightning-spike. It was like being on top of a mast. Then, with annihilating loudness, eleven o'clock began to strike.

*

162

'Now you must do something for me,' I said. I was stamping and lurching about on the lovely flat ground, giddy like someone who has just been robbed of his autonomy on a scary ride at a fair. Surely passers-by could tell that I had left their dimension for a while and had come back to it with a vow never to leave it again. The warmth! The sensible calm! We went into the Golden Calf and had a settling gin.

We didn't get to Orst that day, but we did a very quick tour of the Town Museum: Edie had an intense, photographic way of looking at pictures, unlike my lazy day-dreaming habit. I showed her the spot in front of the Bosch where I had met Cherif, and I was lyrical about him: so sexy, so ready . . . And where was he now? Rotterdam, was it still? 'He's probably being ready and sexy down there too,' said Edie, sceptically but not unkindly.

We drifted out and round the corner, among a thin crowd, and there in the narrow back lane was the animal market again. I told Edie she must see it, perhaps in turn not noticing her reluctance, but after a few yards of terrified mice in wheels and tethered hawks hopping and snapping at their leg-chains she turned away tense with anger and distress. 'I'm sorry, darling, I can't . . . I don't know how you can.'

'No, let's go somewhere else.'

I took her arm and we went to the lane's end, and left into the square by the theatre. 'This is where I fell in love with Luc,' I said, doggily marking each place with an amorous association.

'It's like a bloody Jubilee Walkway,' said Edie. 'Except you've only been here five minutes.'

'Sorry to be a love-bore. You just happen to have caught me on my last mad fling before old age sets in.'

'Hmm.' She swung away to take in the buildings. 'Are you treating me to the theatre tonight?'

'Well, we could. It does take up a lot of valuable drinking-time.'

'I have a hip-flask.'

'And I don't know if you'll like it. There's an opera season – Saint-Saëns's *Henry VIII* and Grétry's *La Siffleuse*.'

'The second one would be lovely. It sounds like something for Sir Perry.' This was a reference to our local old man of letters back home, Sir Perry Dawlish, known, up to a point, for a monograph on 'Whistling in Literature'.

We ambled past the side of the theatre, drawn by the noise of a piano and a woman's voice. From an open rehearsal-room window a melancholy soprano came floating down: 'Dans cette brumeuse Angleterre je meurs sous un pâle soleil . . .' We listened until a stamp and a cry of 'Shit!' precipitated a bad-tempered reprise.

'It must be poor dear Catherine of Aragon,' said Edie solicitously. 'One knows how she feels.'

'Have you been writing anything?' she asked, much later on, in the Cassette. This was a reference to our local young man of letters, Edward Manners, groomed early for a career in print, and already considered by most to be a lost cause.

'What a very insensitive question.'

'Sorry, darling. Do you want another beer?'

'After that I certainly do.' And it had caused me a genuine twinge of bleak unease.

Left alone, I gazed down the busy bar and thought how attractive and interesting everyone looked: it was the onset of anything-will-do time – often of course (one tended to forget) a mutual compromise. There was a parting of the crowd and a couple shunted through: I dwelt on them for a second or two before I placed them. In front was the shatteringly pretty lad I suspected of servicing the Spanish girls, and propelling him with a hand on his neck was the assistant from the camp clothes-shop – I'd seen him there before – the one who had sold me my bad-taste Orst tie. 'He's not queer, he's not queer,' he kept saying excitedly.

They shouldered into the bar just by where Edie was standing, so I slouched over. Shop was still sheltering Shattering with an arm round his back as if otherwise he might panic and run off, or else be pinched and spoiled by the inflamed clientele. I said to Edie, 'This boy works in a fashion shop in town, you ought to meet him', and then told the boy how he had once fooled me into buying some deviant swimwear. Never having

164

worked in a clothes shop, I imagined the staff must fondly remember everyone who went in. 'You were wearing jodhpurs,' I said, to seal it in his mind. He stuck a hand in his fine dark hair, widened his large dark eyes and then dubiously exclaimed, 'Of course!' He was slight, mobile, playing on looking so young, unfairly eclipsed by the beauty of his friend.

Edie passed me my glass and stood looking politely at the boys, who had half-turned away to catch the barman's eye and obviously thought our conversation was over. 'I'm Edward, by the way,' I said. The shop-boy looked back uncertainly. 'Edward. Me Edward.' I stuck out a hand.

'Alejo,' he said; and then compelled by Spanish courtesy: 'This is my cousin Agustino, from Bilbao. He's not queer.'

'And this is my friend Edie from England. She's not queer either.'

Agustino looked terrifically cheered at this, and shook hands fervently with both of us. I held his gaze until his grin faded, he looked down and I let go of the fingers I was still absent-mindedly clutching. I felt almost sorry for him having to carry the responsibility for such deranging beauty through life. His short dark curly hair, his quick dark eyes, the slightly everted lips and the little lines made by his smiles, the small ears, the unblemished fineness of his skin set off at the neck by the upturned collar of pale old denim, all made one long to kiss him and fuck him. I was hollowed out with envy of the Spanish girls having him on the other side of my wall.

I got Alejo talking with Edie. She said something about an embroidered black waistcoat he was wearing, and I saw her finger the work on it. He brought to mind her camp young friends of 1980 or so, her fellow-students at the Central School of Fashion, when she was my entrée to London, to the West End, and we would all go drinking together in Soho, which waited on the other side of Oxford Street like a barrio of risky enticements. It was dear old New Romanticism then, the boys were growing pony-tails, dressing in braid and buckles, voluminous pants and sleeves; they were crazy about girls, they thought it was fabulous what you could do with them and a few yards of taffeta and ribbon.

I was making reassuring conversation with Agustino. So,

how long had he been over here? Nearly a month. And what was he doing? He was employed by a Spanish wine-warehouse ... they had an outlet in Obrecht Street ... I should come to a tasting. I'd absolutely love that, I said. I noticed a certain self-consciousness in his answers, caused by our physical closeness in the crush of the bar, and by a drunken extravagance of my own that I was barely aware of, and by the way he found me watching his face and the beautiful opening of his mouth. What a piece of luck that his cousin should also be living in the city! Yes it was. Were they close? Well, Alejo's branch of the family still lived in Trujillo, which was very remote (a sweet misunderstanding of the question, this, that had me puzzled how Alejo had made the journey from remote Trujillo to a postmodern northern boutique). I said, 'I wonder if you know some other Spanish people in the town, who live on St Alban Street?'

He seemed startled by this, as though I were in possession of classified information. 'That's remarkable indeed,' he said. 'At present my sisters are living in that very street. I have been staying there sometimes; it is better when my cousin has his boyfriends and lovers in his room: he doesn't want me to be there.' (Now that was hard to believe.) 'So I go to my sisters and sleep on the floor, oh dear' – and he made a mime of rubbing his shoulder and stretching his back. His sisters ... the floor ...

'I wonder in my turn', he said, 'if you know an Englishman who lives on that street, who is my sisters' next neighbour ...'

'Oh,' I said.

'A very mysterious man. They say they have never seen him but they hear him late in the night, swearing and singing and banging the doors or something. He is always very drunk and though it is disturbing for them they are frightened to speak to him.'

'Have you heard him yourself?' I asked, hoping I could discount this as scandalous hearsay.

'Oh yes, I have ...' and then I watched it dawn on him with a lovely blush and a kind of setting of the face against his mistake. He took a long draught of beer, and with the oddly magnified attention I was paying him I saw his open lips very clearly through the glass and his teeth refracted through the pale beer, which slid into his mouth in three deep swallows.

'I often am very drunk,' I admitted, placing a heavy hand on his shoulder and shaking him matily. I glanced aside to Edie, who was sculpting around herself for Alejo's benefit some imaginary bustier, and who topped it off with a sceptical *coup d'œil* in my direction. 'And to be absolutely honest, your sisters *can* make quite a lot of noise themselves.' Oh, the ghastly give-and-take of life.

One or two others were hovering, as if hopeful of an introduction to Agustino, whom Alejo had never before been able to persuade to come to this place: they were raising their eyebrows at him over Alejo's head while I clumsily tried to keep him with me. But I had had my turn. Alejo was kissing one of the newcomers and tugging his cousin away to meet him.

After a blurred further hour of drinking and more than my ration of cigarettes, Edie and I found ourselves outside again with the two Spaniards. It was refreshingly cool, though they were wearing less and were less numbed by drink and paced about as we said goodbye. Alejo was going on to the Bar Biff with five or six others. He kissed Agustino with sensible fervour on both cheeks, which seemed to give his friends a licence to do the same; the boy stood there like a reluctant bride as his new acquaintance filed towards him. Then we three were alone – of course it was a night for him to be away from Alejo's. I was their escort . . . We rambled home under brilliant stars. I dimly recall one or two diversions to show them historic things, my voice echoing off the darkened houses, Agustino standing in a street-lamp's soft gleam, shivering and expressionless.

Much later in my room, sitting with Agustino, Edie already in bed, flat out with drink and fatigue. The boy must think we're a couple, or he wouldn't have come up to see, and accepted a cup of whisky. My Uncle Wilfred's motto going through my mind: 'You don't want girls around, spoiling everything' – not always true, that. Whole quarter-hours passing in two or three minutes. Agustino is worried about his cousin and the life he is leading – he doesn't disapprove, it's not like that, though if his aunt and uncle in Trujillo knew . . . I tell him it is all fine, I am talking up the overall excellence of Alejo's lifestyle and the things he likes to do, as if I had known the boy and taken an interest in his welfare for years: it seems to make me more trustworthy . . . Agustino is scared by stories he has heard – he speaks superstitiously of drugs, pornographic films, disappearances. Perhaps a friend of Alejo's has been kidnapped. For a while I concentrate on him so hard that I can't take in what he's saying. It's like sometimes you can't understand, when people speak too clearly. I am devastated by his beauty, which seems to me on another plane from when I first saw him.

He tells me 2.30 has just sounded from the church. We are standing at the top of the stairs and I ask him with laborious irony if it is all right to go disturbing his sisters at this hour: it has been very quiet there. He says it is fine, they are both away for the night in Antwerp. 'Oh,' I say, with a muggy sense of opportunity. I take his left hand between both of mine and stroke the back of it for a moment. I lean into his anxious breath and trace with my fingertips the quick-pulsing blue vein in the miracle of his neck. He pushes me to arm's length, frowns a disappointment that cuts to the heart, and holds out a hand. We shake once, twice, and he springs down the shadowy stairs without a word.

A Sunday morning swim was what Edie always had. She rose from the bed like a zombie at 8.30 and I heard the flush of the loo and the humourless rhythmic grunts that accompanied her exercises. Incredible how she did it. I pulled the duvet over my head, thinking with satisfaction that I was too lazy to become a creature of habit. I didn't seem to have a hangover yet. I wanted to go back into the shallow dreams of old friends, brought to mind by all the nostalgic talk we had been having . . .

She was standing at the bedside with a mug of tea. What a brick. 'Time to get out your deviant swimwear,' she said. What a fiend. I writhed and kicked and bawled but it was no good. 'And shall I give Agustino a knock?'

Agustino!

I lurched into the other room and got into the cupboard. There was the faint sound of a radio-voice, something beginning – oh, I knew it, K361. Had I done anything truly terrible? Surely not, though there was a lingering sense of pain. He'd have to be a bit of a prig to hold it against me. Had I tried to kiss him? Awful guilt-circuit of years ago. The music snapped off and then a door slammed. I went to the front window and looked down into the yard, and saw him go busily out. It was only for a moment of course, but he seemed to have displaced Luc at the summit of my mania.

Edie said, 'I thought we'd agreed long ago that you didn't get involved with straight boys and I didn't get involved with queer ones, since it was in either case a recipe for heartbreak?'

'You are right,' I said, standing unguarded, paunchy in my boxer-shorts. In a spirit of mortification I went to look for my swimming things.

I did feel a little queasy by the time we reached the Baths, what with the rash drinking and the anticipated misery of swimming, memories of last time, and the sense of hearty purpose in the echoing din after the quiet streets outside. The air in there had the morning-after chlorine smell of nail-varnish remover and stale cigarette-smoke.

The changing-room was busy and there were a lot of dads with their sons and friends' sons, kids screeching about, running into me as I winced and wove through the room. I found a locker and started to undress. I got my new trunks on and they seemed okay, just not very supporting: they had a good sleek feel. They were perhaps rather conspicuous. I was pulling my shirt over my head when I heard a voice I knew and then another. My heart leapt, I had no time to plan an escape: for a second or two I thought I might keep my head hidden in my shirt, and move off somewhere else like a defendant leaving court under a blanket. But I nerved myself, tugged my arms free, and looked. Luc and Patrick were sauntering towards me, and just behind them, smiling to himself, was Matt.

I was so appalled by this grouping, and what it implied, that I simply sat back with a sigh and a smile. The group themselves showed no concern, however: they were relaxed and cheerful. They didn't see themselves as a tribunal for my complex, shaming crime. They had come from the shower – the teenagers in long towels tucked round their waists, Matt naked, but holding his towel and wrung-out shorts in front of him. Luc was the first to notice me, and stepped forward with a big grin and shook my hand as if he was really fond of me, or as if this bleak male place demanded classic camaraderie.

'What extremely good luck, Edward!' he said.

'Yes, amazing.' He was a hundred times more wonderful than Agustino. The pictures of him were rubbish. Despite my looming humiliation I was thinking that he wasn't wearing any clothes, only that towel, and that he was about to take it off. I stood up and felt the warmth coming off his chest and face, and saw that his arms, even so, had gooseflesh.

'This is my friend Patrick, by the way, who, whom I have told you about.'

Meeting them both was like meeting filmstars, their aura and beauty put weights on your tongue. Patrick shook my hand too and nodded and said he was pleased to meet me; he spoke English easily, though without Luc's tendency to parody an English accent.

Matt had been observing this and I shot him a warning glance over Patrick's shoulder. Perhaps if he didn't acknowledge me the day could be saved; each of them was busy at his locker. I wanted to be out of there and hidden in the water: at the same time I longed to dawdle and see Luc naked – I had to see that. Matt came across and said, 'Hello, my friend', and swiped a hand across my shoulder and down my upper arm in a laid-back greeting.

'Hi,' I said huskily.

'Crazy swimming-trunks,' he said, and then under his breath, 'Your own?' – and winked as he turned away.

Luc noticed and said, 'Does Edward know Matt?' in a tone of surely affected bemusement.

'Yeah, these are the guys I was telling you about,' said Matt. 'The ones I met down on the beach that weekend.'

'Oh ... I ...'

'Yeah, *he's* the guy *I* was telling *you* about,' said Luc tediously. 'I said there was this young man on the beach at my friend Patrick's house and ... you know, the house next door?'

'How extraordinary,' I said. 'Do you mean you were both at this tiny place no one's ever heard of at the same time? You see I've forgotten the name again.'

It all depended on Matt's next sentence; I don't know why I

thought I would be let down except for my jealousy of his friendship with the lads and my hang-over paranoia and the heresy of last night. I was holding on to a look of distracted marvelment. 'Yeah, that time we broke into the old house.'

Patrick looked up with triumph, even admiration: 'So you did break into the house?' and Luc frowned at me.

'You mean you both?'

I would have blustered and given myself away if Matt hadn't ended his game and said, 'Not him, no – I was with an old friend of mine.'

'We never saw *him*,' said Luc coolly. 'Or her.'

'Perhaps you snore a lot?' suggested Patrick. I thought hollowly of the other losses, and how stupid Matt was to rely this much on his glamour and his lies. The boys seemed so innocent in his company, unsuspecting, flattered by the attention of this lean swimmer ten years older than them with his casual sharp knowledge of what was what. That was how con-men worked. The boys didn't see the stiff-up hard-on he flashed at me as he turned and pulled his jeans over his naked arse – how he was turned on by danger and deceit. I watched Luc absorbing the fact that a man might not wear underpants, and thought aloofly of the things I'd eased up that same backside.

Patrick pursued Matt with a few more questions, slipping out of his towel and drying his arse so that his cock swung back and forth. It was a sumptuous monster, with a lazy confidence of mastery about it, a veined softness and sheeny bloom that suggested astounding powers of extension and engorgement: in fact the whole genital ensemble was just about the most breathtaking I had ever seen. But it wasn't the right moment for me. I was utterly on edge for Luc (I spotted his smiling glance at it). He was taking an age piling his folded clothes on the bench in front of his locker, which was just too far off for me to keep up easy chat from in front of mine. I was spinning the thing out in the most dreamy way, whilst vainly trying to hold my stomach in – I only had my glasses, watch and socks left to take off. I affected a concern with the state of my toes, and peered between them as though for signs of athlete's foot. I made a clumsily cheery interruption to what seemed to have become an

absorbing conversation between Matt and Patrick about football, I hadn't been able to pay attention. I remembered Edie,
several determined laps into her routine. And would Luc never
drop his towel? What was he so shy of? I thought of perhaps
setting fire to it, or asking to borrow it.

The moment came when I had to take off my glasses, the last
thing I put into my locker. Now I would need to get really close
to him if the vision when it came was not to be a mere blur of
pink and gold. Then:

'Hi!'

It was a voice I knew, and I prickled with displeasure even
before I figured who it was: the pushy little Englishman who
had detained Luc in the street on the very morning after the St
Ernest escapade. I reached for my glasses again. Yes, it was him,
fit and compact, dripping from the pool.

'Oh, hi!' – Luc's indiscriminate pleasantness, like a dog; it
seemed to rob our lovely earlier greeting of half its value.

'I saw you in there,' said the man, nodding and making little
muscle-shifting hunches. 'You're pretty good.' Luc smiled and
vaguely shook his head. 'But you're not getting those turns
quite sharp enough.' He put a hand on the boy's shoulder as if
to say that it was only a small thing, he'd help him get it right if
he liked; then glanced down at me, taking in the fact that I was
here, on the scene, again; and dropped his arm in a gesture of
temporary concession. 'Well, better take a shower!' What a
world of exclamations he lived in. I looked at him coldly as he
retreated.

'I think you've got an admirer there,' I said, shamed and
somehow treacherous. At which Luc frowned. And then the
bastard was back:

'Oh, I found the Fratry, by the way.' He smiled as if this
really was their own private success. 'Absolutely fascinating!'
And Luc now not knowing how to react, whilst his admirer, my
hateful and forward rival, gave a little wave and darted off.

'When is it we meet again?' I boomed out wretchedly. But
somehow Luc failed to hear. He strode away from his empty
locker with all his clothes in his arms, entered one of the four
changing-cubicles preserved, I had imagined, for the clinically

insecure or for those who perhaps for some religious reason . . . and bolted the half-door. Ten seconds later, like the rape of Danaë, there was a scattering of coins from an upturned pocket and a smothered 'Fuck'. A few centimes came spinning towards me across the damp tiled floor.

13

A day of steady rain, a constant whisper in the street, rising in a hiss and then fading when a rare car came past. Sitting under a lamp at Paul Echevin's desk I imagined the indolent persistence of the rain out along the roads of Flanders and at the coast, on hotel porches and empty esplanades. Paul saw me daydreaming – I think, hard worker though he was, he had caught the mood of it too: we exchanged a wistful smile above the stacks of cardboard folders.

I turned the pages of an album of Orst's prints, looking for a reference but lulled and taken care of like a child with a picture-book. It was a subtly different world from that of the paintings: a haunted domain of gleams and shadows and briar-tangled paths. In some of the little etchings people were hinted at in the dark hatching but not quite defined, like figures seen tilted against the rain in the blur from a moving car. There was 'Le Carrosse de l'Archevêque', where the spidery last light came in at the coach's window, but it was hard to know if the dark bulks on either side were benighted travellers, cloaked and veiled, or merely spectral presences against the dim upholstery. There were glimpses of legends that I didn't know, or maybe no one knew: I had to take them on trust like manifestations from the beyond, to be scried and construed according to my needs. Often the titles were mere phrases, taken perhaps from a tale or poem, 'Il resta debout devant la troisième porte', 'Encore dans la chambre de ma vieille parente'; a scene in which a man stumbled down a spiral ramp into deepening darkness bore the frightening inscription, 'Que fera-t-il là, l'insatiable?' I had a sense of mysteries without solutions, or sometimes of ecstatic solutions to problems that had never been formulated. There was a series on 'The Kingdom by the Sea: d'après Edgar Poë', that had no bearing on my memory of the poem, and another on 'The Kingdom of Allemonde': the instinct for lost realms and haunted, ailing royalty was deep. Allemonde was a dream-terrain of sunless forests and ruined towers, steeped in a mood of fate, though somehow without causality; the groping figures on cliff-tops and stairways seemed too passive to be tragic – at times a flare lit them against the dusk and lent them a certain pathos, like marionettes.

I had pages of the catalogue beside me in typescript, with their scrupulous details of date and measurement, and provenances that often trailed into appropriate vagueness, present whereabouts unknown. I had to confirm some quotations from a volume of *Légendes flamandes* that Orst had illustrated. It had just enough purpose to it to keep up my self-esteem: that is to say now and then Paul had made a mistake, an extract was not from the page his note claimed it was, or a name was mis-spelt – little lapses in scholarship that made me useful and were changing my understanding of him. We both seemed to know that this dusty, fiddly checking was in a way intimate work, it steadied some private tremor: just the years going by, perhaps.

I was reading the story of the False Chaplain. A great Knight was married to a beautiful Lady, and they lived in a castle by the sea. The Knight went out hunting and generally doing good, and the Lady walked in her garden or sat with her women and made lovely tapestries. All seemed well, but as the years went by they were troubled by one thing: they had no children. And however hard they prayed, nothing could alter that fact. The Lady was sorrowful and spent long days in supplication to God, asking her Chaplain how she could atone for the great sin in her heart which God was punishing her for in this way. And the Knight was angry; and then he too would ask the Chaplain for absolution.

At length the Chaplain, who was a fair and soft-spoken young man, said to the Knight that he must go away on the Crusade that was about to set forth and seek forgiveness from God within the walls of Jerusalem itself. Only then, he said, could the Knight and the Lady hope to be blessed with off-spring. So the Knight armed himself and rode off and left the Lady in the care of the Chaplain to wait and pray.

Now praying was not really what filled the Chaplain's

thoughts, for he had conceived on the first day he saw her a great passion for the Lady, the more terrible for being damned by the highest precepts of his order and his honour. And as the weeks went by he worked upon the Lady, and slyly disclosed his love to her, as if he were speaking only of God's love. And she, who liked and trusted the Chaplain, found her feelings soured and disturbed by the young man's passion. Then one day, when they were sitting in the garden bower that over-looked the sea, the Chaplain said that if he himself were to lie with her, then God's will might surely be done, and her womb would flower.

When she saw the true nature of his love she shrank from him, and kept apart, and met with him only at the hours of their daily devotions. But the Chaplain's fever burned all the more fiercely for her spurning. And as the weeks turned into months, he found ways of being with her, banishing her women with terrible threats of God's vengeance, and ordering the Castle as if it were his own. He visited great humiliations on her, but always she prayed, for her husband, for herself, and for the Chaplain too, that he might repent; and always she turned him away. Then for days he would deny her food, or keep her in a guard-room without light, saying it was God's will that she should mortify herself. And he would put wild animals with her at night, snakes and toads that the local children trapped in the woods. And still she said no. And still she prayed. And at the day's end he would make her come to him to confess her sins.

Then, when a year had passed and another spring had come, word reached the Castle of the Knight's return. He had ridden to Jerusalem and prayed for God's forgiveness at the Holy Sepulchre itself. Within the day he would greet his Lady, and their union would be blessed with children.

When he heard this the Chaplain was filled with fear: his heart was so eaten up with his love for the Lady, however wicked it might be, that he had never given thought to the day when the Knight should come back. But the Lady was joyful and filled with God's blessing, and rose up proudly, for she knew that when her husband returned not only would her womb flower but her heart too be lightened of all her sufferings at the hands of the false Chaplain, and the Chaplain would be banished for ever.

Now the Chaplain came to her humbly and begged her for God's love to say nothing of the treatment she had had of him. But she said that in God's eyes no sin was hidden, and that all should be known. He fell upon his knees as though he were praying to the Mother of Christ Herself and implored her with tears in his eyes to keep tight the secret of his great love. But all she said, as she had said to him a thousand times, was 'No', and 'I cannot'.

Seeing this, he withdrew silently, and came to her again meekly at the day's end, at supper-time, and offered her a beaker of good Burgundy wine to drink. And she drank it joyfully, as a health to her husband, and to the child that should be hers. And not a moment had passed before she fell to the floor, crying out with her hand upon her heart; for the false Chaplain had poisoned the wine with an ichor drawn from a toad's brain, that she might not tell the Knight of his wickedness, and never more be her husband's if she might never be his. And as she lay there a footstep was heard on the stair, and the Knight entered laughing and calling out for his wife; and when he saw her there he took her in his arms and she looked on him and then she died. And the false Chaplain said a blessing over her and prayed for her soul.

I looked out of the window at the drifting gleam of the rain against the purple brick of the gables opposite. The limes had lost their leaves now. My thoughts about the ragged injustice of the story dissolved into the inhospitable weather, with its calm and comforting insistence we should stay inside – a frisson of childish safety. I turned back to the crackling quarto with its precious powder-blue wrappers and enormous margins, and then read Paul's comments on the three illustrations to the False Chaplain. He pointed out how the theme of constancy was one which recurred in Orst's work, and the disturbing way in which the artist seemed to admire the constancy of the Chaplain's obsession with the Lady, more than that of the Lady's love for her husband. She was the focus of all the engravings, white-faced, pale-eyed, swirled in her own hair – a premonition of the Jane Byron figure. The first picture was simply an icon of her, though formally displaced, her head at the top left-hand corner, the rest filled with the oscillations of her hair and the vertical plunge of her gown. In the second she was sewing with her (oddly similar) women and the dark folds of the tapestry lifted in their hands set off the mystic pallor of her face as she paused and stared. In the third she lay on the brink of death in a kind of skewed pietà, the wings of the Knight's cloak sheltering her; his face, though, was out of the picture and the black figure of the Chaplain rose exaltedly behind, with upraised hands and eyes. It was a very *fin-de-siècle* subversion of an old tale going back to the thirteenth century, and found beyond Flanders in French *fabliaux* and Italian collections. Its unusual ending attracted Orst, and he had simply had his way with it, giving a hint of perverse sexual triumph to the shaven phallic upright of the priest, and the supine surrender of the female, lips parted, eyelids lowering over eyes that still cast an ecstatic light.

Note too the use of the fortified tower of St Vaast as a basis for the sketch of a castle which forms the *cul-de-lampe*: a word that disturbed me for a moment, Luc being a backward offering of cul, Luc's cul a dream palindrome – the two round cheeks of it and the lick of the s between: I was nonsensing and spoonerising it in my mouth all day long. I paused to note the publisher's colophon, *achevé* March 13, 1897: Editions Guillaume Altidore, and the monogram, a Secessionist GA conjured into a hoop, that I had passed by unsuspectingly amid the exquisite discretion of the cover. 'So,' I thought, closing the book and laying my hand on it. It felt very remote from Luc, but at the same time gave me the illusion of closeness to him, a share in the glamour of the family history he felt so surprisingly proud and bitter about. My love-struck need for shapes and portents was eased by the curving together of two stories.

'Have some lunch here,' suggested Paul a bit later. 'Lilli's away, we'll have to throw ourselves on the mercy of the fridge.' We went through the door between the houses and into their austere little drawing-room, still coloured for me by an obscure sense of social discomforts, of embarrassments probably only I remembered. 'As you must have realised, she's very much a country person. She goes off once a week to her sister-in-law's farm and stays the night. Even when she goes for a walk it's along the edge of the town, so that she can smell the fields.'

'Having grown up on the edge of a common I know what she means. I smell the meadow in the street, as Tennyson says.' I picked up the *Flemish Post* from the kitchen table, and while Paul looked worriedly at various dishes in the fridge, read about the kidnap of an industrialist's son: there was a sullen photo-booth snap you knew you could never recognise him by.

'It's a wintry day, isn't it, let's have some wine.'

'Yes please.' This was almost slatternly by Paul's standards. 'I see the *Légendes flamandes* were published by Guillaume Altidore, who I now know was the great-grandfather of my other pupil.'

'Of course, I'd forgotten that.'

'He was telling me all about the family's decline.' And my hand shook as I lifted the glass from the table.

'I suppose they have rather declined. I expect you've seen their old house, just near here? It's offices now, no one could live in a house that big.' He stuck a finger in something and licked it. 'I'm afraid Martin Altidore's no good – the boy's father. And the mother's rather pathetic, isn't she? I had a difficult time over one of her altar-cloths. As secretary of the Antiquarian Society I had to write and say we *didn't* think it appropriate.'

'Poor woman. I'm not surprised though.' I recalled her ironic first reactions to the name of Echevin.

'The Altidores were always marked by eccentricity, or whimsicality. And I dare say the combination of that with immense wealth was not a very sound ... recipe. Unlike this curried chicken salad, I suppose it is. Let's eat.' He went out into the hall and warbled 'Marcel!' up the stairs in a sweetly silly way. There was a distant impression of dropped objects and going to the lavatory.

'I gather your last lesson went well?' he said.

I was still thinking of the Altidores, and my last lesson with Luc came back to me with a twinge. Then 'Oh, yes, fine. Yes, he's getting much more confident.' (Was he? Really he seemed much the same to me, but relations between the three of us depended on this pleasing fiction.)

179

'What *is* the Altidore boy's name?' asked Paul when we had all sat down. As always I found it difficult just to bring it out – it was heralded by such inner flutterings and gongings.

'He's called Luc,' said Marcel.

'Now did Luc tell you about his much older forebears, in the sixteenth century, for instance? They were more interesting in a way. One sees how the family fortunes have gone up and down, very wealthy in the fifteenth century, then, as you know, the old sea-canal silted up and most of the money-makers moved out. They stayed on, living on the past, as their prosperity slowly declined. It was only with the Congo business that they suddenly shot up again, I believe, and that wasn't for long.'

'Luc's father seems fairly well-heeled.'

'Luc's father sold a Memling. To Japan.'

'Ah.'

'A Nativity specially painted for his ancestor, for the altar of the private chapel of a guild, a kind of noble confraternity of which he was a member. There was an outcry – a private sale, no one knows how many millions. I'm sorry, my dear Edward, but the man is a barbarian.'

What an impressive and senior gust of anger. I tended to forget that Paul was twice as old as me, he had a lifetime's lead on me. Still, I did rather lust for Martin, both in himself and in the reflected glow of my longing for his son.

'She's got lots of money,' said Marcel, with his mouth full.

'I'm wandering,' said Paul. 'Anthonis Altidore was the very odd one. He had the fantastic idea that he was a direct descendant of St James the Less, Our Lord's brother – or, as I've always thought it should be, half-brother. Still, he went to great lengths to establish the thing historically, he was obsessed with genealogy and employed teams of antiquaries to draw up bogus family trees – at least I assume they were bogus, one imagines some pretty murky areas around, say, the third century. And he collected innumerable relics – the usual bones of course, you know, could be a bit of old dog, and I believe a tongue, and various memorabilia, part of his cloak and a wooden staff that is still in the Cathedral, if you know where to look.'

'How very funny.' I knocked back my wine, getting out of

control on all this Altidore adrenalin. The thought that Luc might actually be related to Jesus Christ was slightly unnerving.

'The obsession seems to have stuck too. When you go to Brussels you can see an early Van Dyck painted for it must be Anthonis's grandson. Actually it's a Holy Family, bringing in St James the Less, a little unconventionally – you can tell him by his very splendid moustaches, the head is apparently a portrait of Altidore, who was very proud of his bristly ... excrescences.'

'They're all incredibly vain,' I said, with a treacherous thrill.

'The boy used to be very good-looking, I met him once,' said Paul. I had to put down my knife and fork.

'I suppose he is in a way,' I conceded.

'I felt so sorry for his poor mother, who was having to cope by herself, when that business blew up on the ship. I think that's what may have turned her colour sense.'

'*Arctic Prince*,' said Marcel.

'I beg your pardon?'

'*Arctic Prince* was the ship. Orgy on *Arctic Prince*.'

'Darling, it didn't say that. Actually Altidore managed to keep it out of the papers almost entirely.' Paul looked with amused reproval at his son. 'Marcel knows all about it from his, I'm not allowed to say girlfriend, *friend*, Sibylle de Taeye, the daughter of the Minister of Culture, who is something of an Egeria to young Luc, I gather.' And Marcel blushed as he had weeks before when I'd blundered into this patch. Of course she wasn't his girlfriend – he was up against some pretty stiff competition if that was his idea; he was blushing to have his fantasy disclosed.

'She's *not* my girlfriend,' he said.

'She is very sweet to you though, isn't she?' said Paul optimistically.

'No she's not!' said Marcel, and a big tear gathered in his eye. I thought, just you wait till your next lesson. The vocabulary of the orgy. You're going to tell me everything just as you had it from Sibylle.

Later I was reading about Edgard Orst's now demolished villa, which had stood so conspicuous and so secretive on the edge of a suburban housing park. Paul had given me an English journalist's account of a visit to it in 1904:

We were privileged last month to be received by M. Edgard Orst at the Villa Hermès, his splendid new residence-*cum*-atelier, whose designs our readers will no doubt recall from their publication in these pages some little while since. Indeed, the house has been three years in the building, and though M. Orst has regretted the delay, it cannot be denied that every detail of the structure and its appointments speaks of the most especial care in both design and execution; the artistic visitor will be bound to exclaim with us, 'How should it have been done sooner?'

In external appearance the Villa is tall and somewhat forbidding, its severity of openings and the plainness of the elevations, however, being mitigated by the fine patterns that are scored into the stucco along the coigns and lintels, the whole being given the most delightful brightness by virtue of being painted a dazzling white. Atop the foremost gable, of course, stands the figure of the alert young deity whom M. Orst has invoked as the guardian of his house – an admirable piece in bronze gilt from his own studio.

Arriving a little before the appointed time, and having dwelt on the exterior, we rang the bell and were obliged to wait for some minutes before the opening of the door. This door itself, let it be said, is a thoroughly imposing one, massively enriched with nails and fine furniture; and it gave rise to not a few reflections on the solitude into which M. Orst has chosen to retire, and on the strength, so to speak, of the fortifications which he has thought necessary to protect that solitude from an undeniably curious world. For in M. Orst, unlike other artists of the 'Symbolist' school – we think of that exquisite dramatist of the impalpable, M. Maurice Maeterlinck, with his avowed enthusiasms for the beer-hall, the velodrome, and the ring – in M. Orst, we say, we find the aesthete *par excellence*. As we stood at his door on that April morning (and in a light rain that had just begun to fall) we were at once in possession of the gauge of his claim to be considered the *doyen* of all the artistic recluses of our time. It was for us to ponder at what cost to his seclusion, and so to his art, an invitation like our own might have been made.

Our readers will know something of the unhappy circumstances that have befallen this remarkable painter in the years since his last exhibitions in London, and will be in a position to understand the dictates, in his life as in his art, of a heart, and an eye, subjected to so violent a shock: his has been, in the words of one of his contemporaries, 'un veuvage précoce' – a premature widowhood, indeed; and one that has imposed upon him its own high and unwavering demands. There are those (a few in Belgium herself, though more, we admit, on our own neighbouring shores) who continue to question M. Orst's standing in the first rank of modern artists; and some who are all too ready to consign his productions to the midden of depravity, along with those of M. Félicien Rops and one or two others, to be spoken of only as one speaks of the art of the criminal or the madman. To be sure, that M. Orst's paintings – and his admirable sculpture in plaster and gesso, not to mention his abundant work on the stone – have value as testimony to a fertile mind subjected to pressures of exceptional severity, cannot be denied; what we do deny, absolutely, is the inherent unworthiness of his subjects or of the dark sensibility which all his work reveals.

Some thoughts such as these, as we say, passed through our mind as we waited at the doorway of the Villa Hermès; which, in due course, was opened by a young woman in a pale costume (reminiscent of the hygienic dress of Ancient Greek maidens, and styled according to M. Orst's own design), who indicated to us to enter. We gave our name, and she withdrew soundlessly – we had already been apprised that all the servants of the house are encouraged not to speak, and to make themselves understood, as far as is possible, by gesture.

We found ourselves detained in the long and somewhat sepulchral vestibule, which runs to the full depth of the house, and off which open various small rooms. At a number of these a curtain was drawn back to reveal a fragment of an Attic frieze, displayed on a high plinth, or a drawing from the hand of Giovanni Bellini or Sir Edward Burne-Jones. In all the rooms of this ground floor, it should be said, the windows are either placed too high to permit one to see out or else are filled with coloured glass, which serves to create a magical play of symbolic light.

The young housemaid returning and beckoning to us, we left the hall and climbed an imposing flight of shallow stairs which brought us at once to a domed ante-chamber, in which a most beautiful bronze figure of Andromeda, chained to her rock, is reflected in a marble pool. Through an archway beyond we were able to glimpse, between curtains of fine old brocade, the lofty space of M. Orst's studio. In front of these curtains runs a curious brass rail, somewhat like that in the sanctuary of a church, which ensures that no one enters unless at M. Orst's express wish; in which case a mechanism causes the barrier to retract into the wall.

Being so favoured, we pressed forward into this principal room, which indeed occupies the full height of the back of the house, with the exception of the basement, which on that side is reserved for household offices. We can say at once that the impression of the studio, with its great north window and the accumulation of magnificent and exceptional works displayed on its walls against the sympathetic background of antique tapestry, was superlative. But our closer and more prolonged inspection of the pictures was deferred by the arrival of the painter himself, who stepped forward and greeted us most cordially, as a friend, he was pleased to say, from a country he had long held in especial regard. It was a sign of that regard that he wanted at once to have news of acquaintance of ours in England, and that he seemed content to talk of those bygone days quite as if we had no other purpose in being there. Our fear of disturbing him at his work proved groundless; he was finely dressed and did not, as so many artists do, advertise the nature of his craft by appearing in a pigment-daubed smock and with his palette on his thumb. Indeed, it is said that M. Orst has never been observed at the easel by any stranger.

He led us into the dining-room, whose white walls formed a fitting background to a cycle of his paintings on the theme of the Seasons of Life; it was here, over a generous collation, that he spoke to us of his feelings about the Villa he has built as a shrine to his own calling. It was only in the course of designing it, he said, in the incessant small changes to his plans, in the conjuring of the perfect solitude from light and space and the exact positioning of *objets d'art*, that he had worked out to his own satisfaction what it meant to him to be an artist, and what the life of an artist, once so impetuously embarked upon, might in the end demand of him. It was not hard, under the spell of his gently modulated delivery and pierced by the momentary glint of his sharp eye through a heavy pince-nez, surrounded, what is more, by some of the most striking products of his genius, to feel the incontrovertible hand of his particular destiny.

When we left the dining-room, in order to be shown M. Orst's library, we were witness to a most surprising ritual, in which after every meal not only the various dishes and plates but also the table and chairs, and in fact the whole furniture of the room, were removed from it by the servants, leaving it as an unsullied temple of his vision.

The study of the Villa Hermès is a charming room, in which M. Orst conducts his business with those connoisseurs who follow and collect his work, and which contains the large cabinet in which he keeps his prints. We remarked that the drawers of this cabinet were somewhat cryptically labelled with Hebrew hieroglyphs; and it was with some humour that M. Orst, noticing our eyes upon it, declared 'that no one would ever know what lay in there', and that many a rich collector had offered him a fortune for a chance to choose some item from among its contents. He did, however, throw open a further door into his 'dark room', most magnificently equipped for the treatment of photographic plates, and which seemed to us indeed to be the dark crucible of his art.

I turned to the photograph at the head of the article: it was grey on grey, the windows pewtery and opaque, the dead light of certain spring days. The young trees in the garden in front were orderly, suburban. 'Une petite forteresse de rêve', one old acquaintance had called it; another saw it as a crystallisation of Orst's cold, loyal nature, his 'British' reserve and desire not to be too intimately known. For some reason I found myself thinking of it on the morning of his death: I imagined Paul running, cycling, to the house and hearing the news, a doctor making a brief last visit; and then the servants who communicated by gesture, stunned into natural silence, closing curtains and shutters, while the telephone rang, and the tables and chairs were left in the dining-room all day.

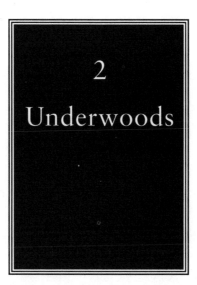

2

Underwoods

14

Rough Common is a common and also a small town, south of London. The town was nothing much until the 1790s, when its principal inn gained importance as a posthouse on the way to fashionable south-coast resorts. A watercolour by David Cox, done in 1812, shows the white weatherboarded cottages with spindly verandahs that run along the common's edge; and in the brief broad progress of Fore Street, with its pollarded limes and Wednesday market, there is still a hint of the Regency sense that a good time might be had there.

The post-road itself is now swept off into a chasmal by-pass, crossed by high footbridges that lead to new, remote parts of the town. I'd been there at night sometimes with people I'd picked up. The cars thrumming past below added a certain desolate glamour to my vertigo. The old part of town is all the quieter, as if its hubbub were subsiding to the wind-gusted calm of the common itself.

The common has always been there, in its modest, unstinting way, rising beyond low railings at the end of Fore Street to rabbit-pitted sandy heights and thicketed folds. At the top it is suddenly steep – a scribble of path, a concrete bench and the blunt monument of a trig-point against the sky. From here, you look over a large pond, sandy-edged but black-hearted, and the beginnings of a wood that runs in a long dense belt to the common's further end. On a clear winter's evening the view from the trig-point takes in surprising distances of sombre downland and the skyward glare of the Kent and Surrey suburbs.

The town stretches out along two sides of the common, westward past the Regency cottages on a socially aspiring curve that takes in the de Souzays' small mansion and other large houses before reaching the leafy dead end of Blewits, home of Sir Perry Dawlish; and eastward, descending past the row of mock-

189

timbered villas where we lived to the crumbling thirties hous-ing-estate, the Flats, with its useful late shop.

I let myself in and shrugged my bag to the floor. In a few minutes I would lose the surprise, the disconcerting and exact sameness of everything in the house I had lived in all my life. My mother was out, it was dusk, and this was the silence that had been around us all the time, and that I had left her to. The rattle of the loose parquet, the jiggle of the door-catches and hesitant tick of the clock were sounds I had always known, echoing from surfaces my father had kept bare and polished for acoustic reasons. My mother had changed almost nothing in seventeen years – a new telly, a new Daihatsu Charade: and there were different library books on the hall table awaiting re-turn, the latest issue of *Common Knowledge*, the local advertiser, caught in the letter-cage of the front door. I looked into the sitting-room, a smell of polish and lavender, the black mass of the piano, shadows thrown across the wall by the street-lamps and the tall unhusbanded privet hedge rocking in the wind.

I hadn't meant to be back so soon in my room, with its wall of second-hand books, its air of determined privacy and make-believe. I glanced at the squeaky single bed; and there were the forlorn fauna of childhood, the one-eared rabbit and the drop-sical trousered bear, passed by but still pathetically alert. I stood by my desk, where I had written a thousand adequate essays, and not a few sonnets, and looked down into the Don-ningtons' garden. Gerry had a rowing-machine now; the white buttock-scoops of the seat held pools of rain which gleamed in the unshielded light from their kitchen. As always, I opened the window before I lit a cigarette.

It seemed Colin's car had gone out of control on the Brighton road: it was the 6-litre Craxton he'd had done up, he should have known the problem with it in the wet, with just a bit too much speed the tail swings round on a bend, then you're spin-ning across the lanes; you might be lucky and cartwheel down a high bank and thwack to a halt in earth and grass; or you might catch five or six other cars light ruinous blows and come out shuddering and vomiting with terror but okay; or you might shimmer sideways, seem to hover for half a second alongside

190

the blurred rain-sluicing roof-high tyres of a twelve-wheeled juggernaut, then crumple under and be sliced to death.

Edie had seen it happen, the whole thing in the time it takes to turn up the radio or glance aside at your companion. She was a bit behind Colin and Dawn in her Peugeot; she braked and zipped through on the hard shoulder to avoid the bucking and careering of the lorry, and then ploughed into the bank to dodge the front of the Craxton, with Colin in it, as it shot out from beneath. She sat quivering and weeping, gripping the wheel, and felt the thump in her back as the severed rear end of Colin's car exploded, fifty yards behind.

It was a couple of hours later that she got me on the phone, at the Orst Museum. She described running along to the wreckage, ready to plunge in for Dawn, but the flames took her breath; she ran back for Colin and he was all over the crushed cabin as if he had been detonated; something in the engine was still churning and banging, the radio still going, 'The Pavane of the Sons of the Morning from *Job*': she coughed up the words as if horrified to have known what it was, and having to tell me, and dropped the phone, but I could hear her wailing and gasping.

They had been to Hove to look at a long-case clock that a friend of Edie's father wanted to sell. Edie, as the intermediary, had led them down, Dawn accompanying Colin for the run and a change of scene from the eventless shop. The clock was a good one, and Colin brought it back in the car – you just could with the passenger seat folded forward and the whole thing wrapped in blankets. Dawn had had to sit in the back. Colin knew the way home, and when they hit the motorway he overtook and powered ahead. Edie, slightly oppressed by this male challenge, had done her best to keep up. She thought they were doing about 85 when the spin happened.

Dawn's real name – unreal, it seemed to me, when I read the newspaper report – was Ralph, which was romantic and adventurous and didn't suit him, but which he managed to accommodate by the age of fifteen to his strain of boisterous schoolboy shyness. Then he took part in the school reading competition, judged as a rule by a stone-deaf old actor, a pupil of the school during the Great War, well-known for his portrayals of clergymen. Each aspirant would take the rostrum, like a witness, announce his name and his selected extract, and then deliver it in a sufficiently loud and commanding manner to get through to the judge. Ralph, flushed and nervous, appeared at the lectern and immediately began a rather sensitive account of the Gordon Bottomley passage he had chosen from *Poets of Our Time*; it was not until he had confided three or four lines of it that the old actor cheerily called out 'Name?' and Ralph, humiliated, bellowed 'Dawn . . .' adding a 'by Bottomley' that was lost under a roar of laughter.

The first day people tried out Bottomley, which seemed apt, as Ralph was a sturdily bottomly boy; but it was Dawn that stuck. After initial petulance he let it happen and blossomed into it, like a drag-name, much as he came to understand that his bottom wasn't a laughable encumbrance but a majestic asset. He never used the name himself, and up to the end would say on the phone 'Oh, it's . . . er . . . Ralph here', with a hesitation like someone you might not remember, someone you had swopped numbers with in a club. And his dim manly father, though he accepted its currency, only ever said it by accident, choosing generally to speak of Ralph-ie, as a kind of token cissification. But his mother, a cheery, cynical woman who had worked at the BBC, took to it straight away, as if it explained things.

I went up over the common with my mother next morning. It was grey and blowy and our macs were stippled once or twice with flung raindrops, threats of a storm we saw stagger aside and discharge in a slanting fume a mile away. She had the disconcerting habit of talking indignantly about something other than the obvious subject of concern: in this case my elder brother and whether she could afford to visit him in Melbourne. She felt very keenly that Charlie's wife had stolen him away from her, that she had set out deliberately to break the mother's bond with her son ... They were married within a year of my father's death, so grief and joy were followed again by grief when Lisanne ('Always a calculating cow,' said Edie) abruptly cancelled visits, in due course kept the children from their grandma and finally persuaded Charlie (who was an electronics boffin) to go for a job almost as far away as it was possible to go. My mother pined for him and the two little girls terribly; they were twelve and fourteen now, they wouldn't recognise her, she said. Charlie promised they would fly her out for a lovely long visit. Then Lisanne had written to say they couldn't afford it this year, Charlie wasn't doing so well ... 'Charlie's so weak,' my mother said, and gripped my forearm as we started on the steep top path to the trig-point. She seemed somehow grateful that I at least would not get married, and so would spare her this particular pain. I remembered how at five or six I had said that I only wanted to marry her.

We reached the top and turned briskly to look in each direction, as was the habit, saying 'Yes ... yes ... yes' as we checked off the different views. The church-tower was clad in grey polythene. The nearby belt of trees, referred to as Condom Copse in a recent letter to the *Knowledge*, was almost leafless, its secret underwoods laid bare. 'Fall, Winter, fall,' I said flatly, not really wanting my mother to hear.

'You won't have any hills like this where you are,' she said.

'No,' I said, and breathed in heartily.

'You've made some friends, though?' – as if the two might be obscurely related.

'Masses!' The thought of them was too agitating, a flare that made me clench my face for a second. 'Paul Echevin, who I work for at the Museum some days, is frightfully nice, he's rather taken care of me and had me round for meals.' For a moment I just wanted to tell her I was in love with Luc, give her the whole stupid thing and watch her grasp it. There had been spells of candour before, and she rose to them pluckily; but I knew she would rather not know.

'The loop?' I nodded. This was the basic family walk, followed times out of number, that avoided the far end of the common, and brought one gently down through patches of alder and thorn towards Blewits, before turning back sharply and running home parallel with the road.

I said, 'I rang Dawn's parents this morning.'

'I ought to. I don't really know them.'

'She seemed quite calm.' She had spoken in a slow, drugged, but practical way. They thought he died instantly, but then with the fire . . . well, what was left of him? 'She didn't say so, but I got the feeling she wasn't sorry he'd gone like this, rather than . . . in a few months' time perhaps. And then *he* came on, I've never known how to cope with him at the best of times, he actually said, "Well, no one can say he died of AIDS, Edward." I suppose it will strike them in a day or two, some griefs are too big to take in all at once.'

'Poor things.' I knew my mother had a sick worry about me not being careful – not having been careful. One of my candid moments had been when I told her my negative test-result.

'She asked me to choose something to read at the funeral. It's rather difficult . . . not "Dawn" by Gordon Bottomley, anyway, I think.'

After a pause, she said, 'I love the end of Gray's "Elegy", I remember I read that a lot after your father died. It reminds me of all our walks. Or you could do a bit out of *Lycidas*.'

'That might be too moving. I've got to get through it.'

'And what's happening about his friend from the antique shop?'

'She didn't say. She may not know. People are often rather miffed if there's another death at the same time – it's as though it's been done deliberately, to steal their thunder.'

'Who wants thunder?' my mother said.

I wasn't in the same house as Dawn; I was in Raleigh, which had a strong tradition of smokers, beauties and abstract expressionists, while he was hidden away in Drake, a dour, disciplined house that smashed everyone at rowing and rugby sevens. The school wasn't old or great, which perhaps explained why it had chosen such creakily historic house-names – Sidney, Frobisher: portraits of these ruff-necked adventurers hung in the stale air of the dining-hall. There was something touchingly childish about it.

He had arrived a year before me, but I was streamed straight into 4A, whilst he, who had spent a year in the Remove, trundled up into 4B or C: so we didn't meet. I knew his parents lived near the school then and he cycled in on his sports-bike each day. I was a weekly boarder: every Monday morning and Friday evening I made the twenty-minute stopping-train journey out and back to Rough Common's tiny rustic station, a kind of *cottage orné* with an acre of commuter car-park. I can't remember much about him then. The only image is the end of a Colts match against Lancing, dutifully clapping the teams in, an air of madness and gloom, the clatter of boot-studs on the path, and Dawn in the midst of them, socks down, heavy thighs slashed with mud, sweat in his black hair and blue eyes, the nice heft of him – we crowded them consolingly and for some reason I patted his hot damp back as he passed.

My great friend was Lawrence Graves. We went through school in tandem and both wrote a lot, though he always assumed, with his combination of names, that it was he who was destined to be a major literary figure whilst I would fill some ancillary role: in one of his fantasies I edited his poetical remains after his mysterious early death. He had the *Lawrence–Graves Letters* out of the school library on permanent loan. (There wasn't much demand for it.)

Graves pleased me at the start, and even slightly unnerved me, by knowing about my father. He had heard him give a re-cital of popular Schubert songs in St Leonards and let it be known that though he had certain reservations it hadn't by any means been a washout. He already had autographs of Ronald Dowd and Elly Ameling, so one knew that his standards were high. Later my father sang the Evangelist when the school Choral Society put on a *St Matthew Passion*: he was in beauti-ful voice then, and sounded like a great singer against the scrawny background of child violinists and choristers uneasy in dynamics below mezzo-forte. I sat at the side of the hall in my own vortex of anxiety and pride, sometimes mouthing the words as if he might forget them. Occasionally, when he rose for his next oration and stood waiting, his eyes would sweep over me without apparent recognition: I told myself that he saw me all right, that he was bound by the exalted protocols of art, which dictated the ritual stance and the glazed formality of tails, black cummerbund and patent-leather shoes – the extinct indoors garb I would sometimes pick up for him from the cleaners or menders. The concert lights glowed on his oiled black hair and black-framed spectacles.

I felt this event should make me too a figure of some consequence, and Graves hung back afterwards to get an autograph; but even so there was something risible about my father's fame. He had appeared on one or two uncool telly programmes, supporting a talentless 'star' through various sickly ballads; and his record of seasonal music reached No 3 in the album charts in the lead-up to Christmas '71. For a moment there was talk of his having his own show, and our house was in the grip of misery for a fortnight. But the screen-tests didn't go well, he was too shy and serious; he came home hopping with shame and relief. I fantasised about his having a success that transformed our rather careful lives, but I loved him best for what he loved best, the patience-shredding hours by the piano, my mother stoutly accompanying, as he worked and worked on a song or a recitative. None of this meant much to my schoolfriends stuck in Mudd and Slade. After the *Matthew Passion* one of them gave a strangulated parody of my father's performance, not from malice but it brought tears to my eyes. A doubt had been entered, that could never wholly be expelled, that he was a figure of fun.

Of course he didn't always have the alien rectitude of the concert platform. He loved getting out of his frac. At home he was a quiet ironist, closer with my brother Charlie than with me, though I was the one who inherited his habit of sitting and gazing into the middle distance. A tiny bedroom had become his office and often you would pass the door and see him leaning at the window, watching the wind over the common. Hundreds of hours I sat pretending to read, but sharing music with him, anything recorded by Beecham, whilst he read the score or peered into infinity through the blank above the picture-rail. When I first brought Graves home he won my father's heart by his morbidly detailed knowledge of Delius, but then

196

risked losing it by conducting when a record was on. I had to take him for a walk to the trig-point to explain my father's conviction that if Sir Thomas had already conducted it there was no need for anyone else to.

In our second year at school Graves and I shared a study-bedroom. He was too camp and snobbish to be popular, but I had fallen swiftly under his influence and he had correspondingly formed a keen dependence on me. No one else made any claim on us, and though part of me longed to be billeted with one of the fabulous Raleigh rebels, I consigned that plan to my thriving fantasy folder, and settled in with Graves and his record collection instead. He was tall and heavy-boned, with wavy brown hair and a long intelligent face made thuggish by adolescence. He loathed what he called the 'plebeian' use of Christian names, and we addressed each other as Graves and Manners from the start, and till the end.

Graves was going to be a great conductor as well as a great writer, and the double demands of his destiny were enacted daily in the narrow space of our study, when he would leap from his desk, pen in hand, to 'bring them through' an especially devilish test of ensemble or stab out the climactic chords of whatever record was on. The walls were soon spattered with ink. He was working on a play, *Noble to Myself*, in which all the characters had titles, and I would be required to take three or four parts in read-throughs, improvising ever more clipped and drawling accents.

His parents lived in Somerset, and seemed for all practical purposes to be a good deal more remote than that. Often he came home with me for weekends, though my mother didn't warm to him or his nocturnal habits, and my brother mocked him behind his back; my father, who found the thought of his visits oppressive, was irresistibly caught up in talk about music and would sit up with him after the rest of us had gone to bed, listening to Bax or Busoni 'quietly'. My father's memorabilia included an inscribed photograph of Beecham, and one of his batons, which Graves used to eye yearningly as he sat on his hands on the sofa. Sometimes, in conversation, my father would illustrate a point or remind us of a song by singing a few bars; it was lovely, but we all found it embarrassing.

197

He'd been dead so long now that he moved in my mind like a figure from another age, a life in evening dress. Even at the time, when we heard him on the wireless, singing in the Daily Service or in a request for Three-Way Family Favourites, I remember the feeling that his voice was being brought to us from the beyond, from a cavernous other world screened by the tarred muslin of the speakers. We had been early possessors of a stereogram, a monstrous and luxurious teak coffer with discreet lights and grilles and a lid it was impossible to drop: some cushioning mechanism arrested its fall and brought it noiselessly to rest. It had good bass sound, which my father used to turn up to cover the hiss and crackle the machine exposed on his treasured old records. There it still silently stood, at the beginning of November 1991. And there was Beecham's baton on a stand like a pen-rest; and the ugly canterbury stuffed with music, Bach cantatas, Victorian parlour-songs that were enjoying a kitsch revival when he died; and the shine of the parquet around the subfusc bulk of the sofa and chairs and under the black promontory of the piano. Nothing had been altered, nothing renewed. I felt the sense of return oddly exaggerated, as if my childhood went back further than it did.

I sat about my room in my vest and pants, smoked a last cigarette and flicked the stub into the Donningtons' bushes – lilacs that would crowd over the fence in early summer and waft up to my window. Something awful had happened last week: I'd left the dining-room in the middle of Luc's lesson and gone upstairs for a pee, as I always did now, I'd become a reckless addict of the laundry-basket. I had the negatives on me and planned to run on up the further flight to Luc's bedroom, return them to the wallet in the desk and be back at the bathroom again in fifteen or twenty seconds. It was a simple but bold idea, and as the time came on to put it into practice I was less and less able to concentrate on the passage from Milton we were talking about. 'A herd of *Beeves*,' said Luc. 'I'm not so sure what is a herd of *Beeves*.'

'I'll explain it in a minute,' I said, springing up with the look

198

of comic distraction that signified 'Need to go', and slipping out of the room. I had a feeling there must be a downstairs loo, and I didn't want to give anyone time enough to tell me about it. Up I went, in swift strides, past the bathroom and then on to the further flight, keeping to the inner edges of the talky old treads. The door of Luc's room was ajar, I slid round it and was half-way to the desk before I fully understood that I wasn't alone, that Patrick Dhondt was sprawled on the bed in his black school breeches, reading a book.

'How ridiculous!' I said. 'I was looking for the bathroom.' I felt myself going as red as I have ever been, disastrously compromised. He looked at me with faint surprise. 'Hel-lo!' I exclaimed. 'How are you?'

'Very good,' he said, and then smiled. He was unquestionably in possession of the room, of the bed. I backed towards the door, and he looked down to his book, in part to hide a flush and grin of his own. 'It's downstairs,' he said.

I got hot thinking about it now – one of those torturing moments you masochistically recall from time to time for the rest of your life. I unzipped the side-pocket of my bag, took the photographs out and climbed into bed. Why hadn't he been in school? Why did I have to be the bore who took Luc from him for an hour? What had they said to each other afterwards, when Luc jogged back upstairs and ragged on the bed with him? Or had they just dismissed me from their minds, leant close together and solemnly begun to kiss? Luc's hand ... I choked the vision off, and sorted out all the pictures that had Patrick in: I didn't want to see him, or the girl. Two snaps of Mrs Altidore at work on a tapestry and smiling dimly had struck me none the less as having some subtly accusing quality, and had already been eliminated. I tightened a magic circle round the young man.

The picture in which he appeared like a faun of the dunes disappointed me now. I looked at the others that I'd tended to neglect, even the silly shots with the soles of two feet gigantic in the foreground and the supine body unfocused beyond had some information value. Could one read the soles of the feet as one could a palm? Was that dirt-filled crack the line of destiny, that callused declivity the line of love? He had long prehensile

199

toes, I remembered from the Baths – and he had told me he ran very fast over short distances. I couldn't quite imagine it; whenever I saw him he was moving with the confident slowness of the beautiful. Even his jogging was somehow in slow motion.

Here was a glancing shot under his chin, with the tiny nicks of inexpert shaving; an armpit, with sandy sun-bleached hairs; the broad nipples needing to be twisted and hurt. Here was the white watch-stripe on the tanned arm, the circle of the absent dial off-centre, sloped to the wrist-bone: time was away and somewhere else ... Here he loomed in a kisser's blurred close-up, his molten trumpeter's lip. Behind him, in the clear irrelevance of a background, was the house next door, a slat of a sun-blind kinked down for a hidden eye.

I lay in the dark and jerked off glumly. I thought, here is the room I left Dawn to come back to on all those nights, hot-mouthed, clumsy with disguised fatigue but high and alight with love. I could melt still at the memory of his back, when I pulled his shirt over his head, and pressed kisses on his shoulderblades and neck. No one ever looked nicer from behind. His back was the tapered shield, the figure of my love for him, too simple, too confounding to be put into words. I knew there had been a good deal of boredom and pretence, he hadn't perhaps been interesting to me in himself, and yet I also knew he was the motor of my grandest feelings and most darting thoughts, the ground bass to those first intense improvisations. At moments I felt lonely with him; at others, never so excitedly at peace. And what had there been since then? Nothing quite the same. Everything in some way melancholy, frantic or foredoomed.

The first person I was in love with was called Mark Lyle. I was ten, and a day-boy at a pious little prep-school I could walk to on the edge of town. Mark Lyle was perhaps three years older – too old to be a friend to kids like me but equally too young to be acknowledged by my sixteen-year-old brother and his set. He occupied a fascinating limbo, his voice had broken, in my eyes he was a man already, but clearly not a man in the full, self-important way that Charlie was. When he left my school, his parents couldn't afford to send him on to Stonewell, and in my imagination he became a kind of outlaw figure, whom one might expect to find living under canvas in a dell of the common. In fact his father was an epileptic who had lost his job, but to me it seemed that some dark, perhaps ancestral secret had exerted its pull. Ancestry was much in my mind at the time; I was at work on my first book, 'The Manners Family of Kent', fed with boastful anecdotes by my great-aunt Tina and rather more disillusioned sidelights from my Uncle Wilfred, sometimes quite hard to understand; I described how the glory of a family grew, until it was crowned with genius like my father's, who sang on the wireless and was certain of a knighthood. Seen in this perspective Mark Lyle's family clearly suffered from some critical defect. It even seemed possible that Mark Lyle was a drop-out, something of which there was a lot of talk at the time.

One or two of the older boys heard from him after he'd moved to the comprehensive, and bragged discreetly about the contact. Occasionally I would see him myself in the town and watch him with the considerate pretence of indifference that one accords to the truly famous. I was anxious about his new friends, giants of fourteen or fifteen with fluffy upper lips, waiting at the bus-stop with ties undone and shirts bagging out and a No 6 on the go; like them Mark Lyle was growing his hair in thick dirty bunches swept behind the ears, and this seemed to me both wrong and beautiful.

Late one afternoon I saw him walking past our house, and ran out and followed him. I had shorts and sandals on – one didn't go into long trousers till the Sixth Form – and he had his black blazer hooked on a finger over his shoulder. I wasn't close to him, but still as I walked along I found myself in a heady slipstream of Old Spice. He must have been drenched in it, perhaps he was addicted to it in some way: I knew one of the prefects at school was a keen user, too, and had heard him drop thought-provoking hints about its potency.

I trailed Mark Lyle down the hill, having to stop and dawdle from time to time to prevent myself from excitedly catching up with him. He was clearly in no hurry to get home, wherever that might be. I wanted him to do something definite – meet a friend, enter a shop or a house – so that I would have something on him, and could go back home and ponder it in the context of my other, patchy, research.

I'd imagined he would turn left into one of the residential roads lined with flowering cherries where some of my schoolfriends lived, but he ambled odorously on until we had come in view of the Flats and I began to get worried. The front range of the Flats was built above a row of shops – a ladies' hairdressers, a newsagent, the dry-cleaners where I took my father's tails, the Indian grocers that stayed open till 8 o'clock – and overlooked a broad oily forecourt, where residents worked sporadically on cars with long-expired tax-discs. But beyond that, it was unknown territory to me. The Sharps and Flats my father called the place, as if we lived in the cloudless Naturals of Life. I don't think I was actually forbidden to pass through into the grassy courtyard or even to enter its long white buildings with corroding metal windows. It must have been a self-imposed prohibition, a social fear that was activated again when I understood that Mark Lyle's parents had now been reduced to a council flat.

That summer holidays I got serious about Mark Lyle. In my fantasy he became my protector, and introduced me into the thieves' kitchen of the Flats as someone to be respected or they'd have to answer to him. At the same time I was to have a redemptive effect on him, leading him back to the life from which fate had deflected him. I would often ask insouciant questions about him, and my brother would say, 'What are you always going on about Mark Lyle for, stupid?' and my mother would say, 'That poor family, I don't know...' She was inclined to charity work, but they seemed not quite to qualify. I imagined going down there with her, taking blankets, and meals under tinfoil.

A lot of the day I was out on the common. It was harmless and healthy, and though I'd overheard remarks about leathery old Colonel Palgrave who sunbathed in the long grass by the woods with nothing on, I never had a sense of danger. Sometimes I tagged along unwelcomely with Charlie and his friends as they stumbled round complaining and calling things bummers; often I played out complex romantic games on my own,

202

or dared myself to clamber up trees, giving instructions to an imaginary person following me. Once or twice I stumped around on the edge of a group that included Mark Lyle, ready to drift off if they got threatening. We had a huge, friendly dog at that time, who ran away if I didn't keep him on a lead, but who was a good way of meeting people. I was embarrassed to tell boys from the Flats he was called Sibelius, and pretended his name was Bach, which led to one or two jokes but by no means eased the problems of discipline. I became increasingly excited when I saw Mark Lyle, and my early troubles of manhood about that time took him as their object and even as their cause.

One day he was up by the pond with some other boys and a couple of girls. They were trying to fly a kite in the intermittent breeze, but after a few dips and a few spoolings-out of the thread it would smack to earth. Then the thread got snagged in a sapling pine, and the others suddenly lost interest in the whole idea of kite-flying and sloped off. With heart thumping, and not knowing what to say, I came forward and started to disentangle the cotton line from the little tree. Mark Lyle looked at me and didn't say anything either. We worked it clumsily free, managing to ravel up the rest of it in a series of loops that tugged into knots as we tried to pull them straight. Still not speaking except in grunts of concentration and annoyance we bundled the whole lot up and went off to the bench to work on it.

'This is a fucking game,' said Mark Lyle after a bit. It was fantastic to be spoken to like that. I perched there in the swirl of his swearword and his Old Spice, looking into a new life of almost frightening pleasure. I glanced at him shyly; his shirt was half-unbuttoned and I could see a brown nipple as he leant forward. Sometimes our hands touched as we rolled the cleared thread on to the plastic reel.

'That Dave Dobbs is a fucking cunt,' he said.

'He *is* a fucking cunt,' I agreed, and Mark Lyle gave a big bright laugh. He had a wide sun-tanned face and a large mouth with one or two spots by it that he should have left alone. When we'd more or less finished, he patted his thigh and asked me if I wanted a cigarette. I blushed and said no.

'Mind if I do?' he said, with surely unnecessary courtesy. Actually I was terribly worried about him meeting an early death from lung-cancer; but I was overcome by the glamour and intimacy of the occasion. I watched him raptly as he smoked an Embassy to the filter. Each frown, each wincing inhalation, the way he balanced the smoke between his open lips and then as it escaped drew it back up his nose, the two or three different fingerings he essayed, all were written on my mind like a first exercise in sexual attraction. I thought Mark Lyle was the most handsome man I'd ever seen.

Later that summer I saw him again. The friendship I had envisaged had not blossomed. Indeed he'd vanished altogether for about three weeks, leaving me full of forlorn agitation. Then one evening I was rambling homewards from the Blewits side of the common through the long dry grass when I saw his unmistakable mane of fair hair. He was sitting on a bench with his back to me, and I dithered for several minutes just a few yards behind him. He wasn't aware there was anyone there. Occasionally he lifted what looked like a beer-can to his lips. I looped round and came back in front, pretending to notice him at the last moment. Following our convention I said nothing, but sat down beside him and waited.

He can only have been fourteen, but he was managing to grow real sideburns, a more gingery colour than the rest of his hair. He was wearing a Cream on Tour T-shirt, and tight high-waisted shiny brown trousers with generous flares. You could see the stub of his cock very clearly.

'I wondered if you'd been flying that kite again?' I said at length. 'I should think it's a jolly good one.'

Mark Lyle tilted the last of the beer into his mouth, swirled it round and swallowed it, then belched so that I could smell it. He seemed to have forgotten about the Old Spice. 'I'm fucking pissed, man,' he said, and dropping the can on the ground stamped on it violently two or three times. Again the conflict of excitement and distress. In a way this was the opportunity I needed to put my redemptive impulse into operation, but when it came to it I wasn't at all sure of myself.

It was one of my mother's phrases I used: 'There can't be any need for that.'

He looked ahead and laughed mirthlessly. 'Yeah, fuck off now, there's a good little fucker.'

Tears came to my eyes; I wanted to blurt out, 'No, no, I love you, I love you, I didn't mean that, don't say that.' But he got up and stumbled away. I couldn't watch him. I sat picking at the edge of the bench with a thumbnail. I let ten minutes go past, calming myself only to be shot through again with the awful words of rejection. I tried to sound out the note of merely friendly exasperation in them, but it was soured every time by the fierceness of the rest. No one should be spoken to like that, I thought. Then I leapt up and ran the last few hundred yards to home.

Edie had gone to stay at her parents' flat in London: she needed to be looked after. I spoke to her father on the phone and he said she was sleeping, she'd been given some mild sedative. They would all come back to Rough Common for the funeral. It wasn't every day you saw two of your friends killed. 'No, indeed,' I said.

I drifted through town. There weren't many people about, and the side-streets had the watchful echo I'd grown used to in a bigger, older city. But in Fore Street the market stalls were up, fruit and veg, cheap skirts and blouses, huge slabs of chocolate under plastic sheets. I looked at a rampart of fraudulently flawless produce (they always served you the sad stuff from behind): red peppers, red apples, pouchy tangerines with dark green leaves, dense purple globes of cabbage, a pyre of parsnips, trimmed, stowed end to end – I thought, Dawn will never see anything like that again. 'Yes, sir,' the stallholder called confidently, but I found I was crying and turned away with a half-spoken rebuke to myself.

I walked on, past the George IV: I didn't want to meet people there. Past Levertons the jewellers, with their arcane boast 'Belcher and Curb Chains "Our Forte"'; past the rain-warped barrowloads of books outside Digby's Second-hand and Antiquarian: the stock looked unchanged since my school holidays, just more spotted and bleached. On the corner was 'Colin Maylord – Antiques' – an original shop-front, the door set back in a welcoming embrasure. The sign said 'Open', but it was wrong. I peered in, shading my eyes against the reflections in the glass. Normally spotlights drew richer gleams from the mahogany and old oak and heightened the sense of historic abundance receding unaffordably into the tapestried depths of the shop. But today the tallboys and chairs, the card-tables and clocks and dressers laden with Coalport huddled in the natural gloom, too much furniture, cluttered together as if somebody were moving house. I looked abstractedly at the figurines of musicians in the window, their price-tags demurely averted.

I didn't know Colin well, hadn't much liked him, couldn't see why Dawn should have liked him – loved him – either. He popped into the back bar of the George sometimes, forty-fiveish, lean, straight-looking, in honey-coloured cords with turn-ups, suede brogues, striped shirts. He was plausible, unamusing, a genuine connoisseur of English furniture. Dawn more than hinted that he was no thrill in bed, but had the sweetest nature; he was certainly an angel to him in his first big scare, when he thought he was going to die. But he was not a terminus I could ever have predicted to the line of lovers in which I was the first and over which I kept a futile, regretful watch.

Dawn was at ease in the shop. The last time I talked to him he was pottering around there, and we sat among the merchandise, me in a snug little Windsor chair with a £700 price-tag, him in the carver of an eight-piece Regency dining suite which crowded vacantly behind him and was marked at six thousand. At one point I watched him nearly persuade an American couple to buy a commode, and smiled at the dumb camp with which he pulled out the drawer with the china po still *in situ*. Later we stood in front of a time-foxed mirror, and I hugged him loosely, beefily, from behind. He was thin, seemed breakable, like something priceless he was selling. The mirror was meant for a mantelpiece, we should have been toasting ourselves at a big log fire. Our talk had been blandly constructive, but it faltered rather as we held each other's gaze in the spotted depths where everything was reversed. I thought, he is looking at his death. He slipped free and started talking antiques.

He knew a lot by now; and if the journey of his heart was inscrutable to me I could follow the steps of his career more

206

confidently. Perhaps it had all been a slow winding down towards this precious shop, its still, polish-scented air, caught in the tradeless doldrums of a deep recession. But for a long time it had seemed a different progress.

He didn't work hard enough for his degree at Dorset; he got muddled up doing French and Film Theory and Vernacular Handcrafts and came out with a Third that caused considerable tension at home. His father was a workaholic insurance-broker who stubbornly thought Dawn should be the same. Instead he took a menial job with the Acomat Carpet-Cleaning Co. For a year or more that great rear presented in bedrooms and sitting-rooms in the Croydon area as Dawn moved around on hands and knees, applying his Deep Foam Cleanser to the wine and cigarette damage of innumerable teenagers' parties. Once or twice he found himself removing stains of which he was himself the author. In time a friend of Edie's gave him a call and he was magicked up to London to be a picture-researcher on *The World of Chandeliers*. I didn't see much of him then, though I knew from Edie about the editor of the magazine, and the affair he had had with him.

When the affair was over, so was the job. Dawn was on the loose then for about a year. I had a sense of his giddy footing and fucking around, of the various older, richer men who needed to look after him. It was 1983. When we met again he was different, flamboyant, high on sexual deceit. Then it started to go adrift – a lover of his died with incomprehensible swiftness. Suddenly he didn't have any money.

For a while he was the young man who holds up the clocks and vases on the plinth at Christie's as the lot-numbers are announced. He wore the porters' maroon apron with a certain flair, as if it might catch on; but would blush terrifically with a hundred or more covetous pairs of eyes on him or at least on what he held in his hands. One such pair of eyes belonged to a sexy Italian dealer with shops in Bath and Tunbridge Wells who picked him up at a sale of antique chronometers and fucked him within five minutes in the customers' loo. That relationship lasted for five years, with Dawn in the end running the Tunbridge Wells establishment. To me he was still a boy, but he must have had a business nous I didn't quite like to think of his

207

acquiring. Then very quietly he made the transition to Colin. It almost looked as if he had been passed over, in exchange perhaps for a lovely bureau that hadn't been tampered with. But Colin knew he was ill. He fell in love with him and he had the kind of love Dawn needed just then. You wouldn't have known it as you sat bored rigid by him in the pub and smiling wanly at his pleasantries, but Colin found himself in giving and sheltering and taking care.

In my third year at Stonewell Dawn started to appear on the little train. His family had moved to a village a couple of stops further down the line from Rough Common. He would put his bike in the guard's van, or sometimes just stand with it across the end of the carriage; he was fiercely attached to it. When we arrived at the school he would slip past the straggle of boys on foot with a quick ratcheting of the gears, head lowered, buttocks hoisted on the narrow perch of the seat. One Friday evening he took an empty place by me as we clattered through the leafy sprawl of suburbs homewards and we talked briefly of the merits of the different French masters. He was rather put out to learn that I and Van Oss, a tall pretty boy in the Lower Sixth, also had Dutch lessons from one of the French masters' wives. He couldn't see the point of that. Squashed up by him on the dusty moquette I got a bone-hard erection, though I'm not sure I put it down specifically to him. Any physical contact at that time was arousing, there was nothing you could do about it. But that may have been the moment when it began.

Graves and I had stuck together; indeed, Graves and Manners had become an established schooltime partnership, like a famous textbook or a make of biscuits. Being nicer, weaker and more sociable than Graves, I was aware of an occasional disadvantage in the coupling. I'd have to disown him sometimes for the sake of the late-night hash and rock parties in one of the Raleigh rebels' studies; and the return engagements tended to be flops, with Graves coming back unexpectedly, full of sarcasm and envy, and making us listen to Vaughan Williams. Even so, he was my habit, and he couldn't be broken.

We egged each other on into a language world of our own. It was Graves who located and nourished my vein of pedantry, and together, like mad academicians, we established a complex of unwritten rules and forfeits, making even our Latinist house-master uneasy about entering our study. The discovery of French Classical drama was a major step: after a term with our A-level texts we were recycling alexandrines and spoke with a marked sense of the caesura. Graves was very taken with the *précieux*, plonkingly translated into English: anyone who offended him was said to have 'soiled his glory', and it was rare for him to refer to his feet as anything but his 'poor sufferers'. This fitted well with our pained avoidance of monosyllables and abhorrence of abbreviations. In a school where a typical notice might read 'All RHJ report to BOC at 3 for TP' we held out for old-fashioned queenery and unnecessary effort. One year for the whole of Lent there were fines for using the first person singular: at weekends I would run up on to the common shouting 'I, I, I, I, I' like a madman with a terrible stammer.

And we wrote. Graves had abandoned his plans for the stage and was at work on an experimental novel, a completely new tack, the characters not only having no titles, but also no names: the men were identified by numbers, and the women by the various voiceless additional characters on the typewriter, such as # and [. He typed it at immense speed, with music on in the background, the carriage-return bell sometimes fitting in felicitously. I remained loyal to poetry, and alternated masked *vers libre* fantasies about the prefects with Wordsworthian son-net-sequences on the seasons, the months, the weeks . . . I even started a sequence on the days of the year, each poem to be written on the day in question, but had dried up by early February. 'The Months' was printed in the school magazine, and received Graves's most particular criticism. Aunt Tina read it there and worked up a mood of acclamation at home, sug-gesting, for some reason that seemed cogent at the time, that I should go and see Perry Dawlish, who was a friend of hers, and find out what he had to say.

Dawlish would have been about seventy then, and was con-sidered locally to be a famous author. If ever he showed up at a fête or sale of work he would be photographed for the *Know-ledge*; and his rare appearances on TV programmes about writers of the twenties and thirties were also flagged in the local press: '"I knew Merrifield well", Sir Perry says, and goes on to recall his three marriages and his lively sense of humour, which he claims some people could find disconcerting!' Dawlish was a baronet, but this didn't discourage a general supposition that he had been knighted for his services to literature.

He had had poems published in the *London Mercury* when he was only fifteen (my own age at this first meeting) and Squire had included his work as a brilliant new star in his *Selections from Modern Poets* a few years later. He had written novels, too, which had a reputation for candour; and slender apprecia-tions of Tennyson and Patmore. All that local people would have seen of his work was the *Memoirs*, remaindered inex-haustibly in Digby's window, and the thin bookmaking ideas he had taken up more recently – the text to some pictures of Royal London, an anthology of 'The Kentish Muse'. I knew little of this at the time, of course: to me he was the spruce aquiline old gent I saw hurrying through the town, looking up with embar-rassed good humour through bushy eyebrows and smiling at strangers as if they had recognised him. Once or twice he had come into a shop at the same time as me, and I was aware of an unconscious heightening of tone, a kind of feudal relish on the part of the traders that I found silly but moving. Sometimes I passed him on the common. He had a neurotic papillon spaniel that aroused Sibelius's interest and would hurtle down the leaf-strewn slopes so that it and the whirled-up leaves seemed one. He would say 'Good Morning' or 'Good Afternoon', but I never for a moment thought he knew who I was.

Much of his mystique for me came from his house. Blewits was named from the lilac-gilled mushrooms that grew in profu-sion in its dank spinney, and which he gave almost at random to people from the town. When I was a little boy my mother re-ceived a basket of them, and I remembered her anxiously pondering if they were edible, the gift of a good or bad spirit, and then hastily putting them in the bin. Gigantic beech-trees whelmed above the house on the common side and roared thrillingly on windy nights. In winter you could look down through them at the steep red roofs and shingled gables, the air full of rooks and bonfire smoke. In summer everything was hidden; the drive twisted through laurels and rhododendrons, the light was speckled and private. To visit the house was to have the magic access of a dream fused with the proud ordeal of winning a prize.

It was late May and the mossy outbuildings were roofed with fallen horse-chestnut flowers. I thought they would be fun to explore, those sheds with small cobwebbed windows and sometimes a chimney: more fun than talking to Sir Perry Dawlish. 'Good afternoon, Sir Perry,' I kept rehearsing, on my aunt's anxious prompting. 'No more cake, thank you, Sir Perry.' I had a high regard for 'The Months' but even so was not fully convinced that this famous old writer, who had actually known Gordon Bottomley, would want to spend much time on them.

The house was very gloomy inside. I was aware that it was a romantic kind of Victorian house, which accounted for the dark oak and stained glass of the hall. At first I could hardly see and was impressed by the confidence with which Dawlish moved around. He had the busy air of someone unused to dealing with children but determined to make a go of it. His voice was high and enthusiastic, with the lost vowel-sounds of an earlier age.

We sat in a big muddly room at the back, a sitting-room-cum-library that merged into a conservatory with doors open on to a derelict-looking garden. Again I had the sense of his being utterly, blindly at home here, whilst I was stepping cautiously between stacks of books, parchment-shaded standard lamps, little cluttered desks with only an inch or two left to write on. He sank on to the end of a sofa that was slumped and shaped to his person, and gestured me to a hard button-backed chair that resembled a corseted lady.

'It's very kind of you to ask to see me, Sir Perry,' I said. 'My Auntie Tina sends you her . . . best regards' (I couldn't quite come out with 'love').

'How is the dear woman?' he said, with a shrewd, humorous look that suggested we both thought she was a bit of a fool.

'Very well, thank you.' (This was far from being the case, I recalled at once: in fact she'd just had a cancer of the throat diagnosed.)

'What a gifted family you are. Novels and belles-lettres: that's your aunt. Lovely singing: that's your father. And now poetry too. You must feel you live on Mount Parnassus.' I looked away, abashed by the tribute, and running my eye along the bookshelf beside me: George Merrifield's *Love and Earth*, *Ochre* by Violet Rivière, Robert Nichols's *Aurelia*, *More Verses* by Wayland Strong. The dust lay thick along their tops, like blue-grey felt, but still ... real books, by real poets. I knew Merrifield's sonnet on 'Cider' from *Poets of Our Time*; indeed Graves claimed I had cribbed from it in my own 'Autumn'; but to see the full majestic volume of the man's work was to come a step nearer to the fountainhead. I noticed a thin book of V. L. Edminson's and thought perhaps Sir Perry could clear up a bitter dispute between Graves and me as to V. L. Edminson's sex ... 'Do you walk on the common?' he asked.

'Oh yes, sir, we're always going up there. I particularly like it at sunset. It can be quite glorious then.'

'*Glorious* – can't it. I don't know what I'd do without the old common. Paulette loves a run-around on the tops. My dear little dog,' he explained. I decided against owning up to the bullying Sibelius. 'So many different aspects to it, don't you find, the steep bits, the flat bits, the woody bits, the open bits ... There's a bit for every mood out there! At this time of year the hazelwood is too lovely.'

'*Lovely*,' I agreed, not actually sure which the hazelwood was, but caught up in the nervous enthusiasm.

'Don't you think? I wander up there and sort out my ideas, as I call them. I dare say you do the same. Work out a poem in your head, then scamper back and write it down?'

This was exactly what I did, and I felt privileged to know that Dawlish did too. At the same time I was fractionally put out to think that the nature-mysticism I had evolved around the common's numinous gullies and heights was not my private cult, and had other, older adepts. 'I feel as if I'm in direct contact with the Muse up there,' I said. And when I sat in my special tree and waited for the folding star I did, I did ...

'*Direct* contact, absolute "hot-line", I quite agree.'

I didn't think I could better that. 'Have you been writing a great deal, Sir Perry?' I was making it sound as if a new book from him was what I wanted most – we all did.

'Well, d'you know, I have? I've got a new selection out next week; and I have enough poems already for two more books after that.'

'That's wonderful,' I said, imagining retailing these potent, probably confidential, pieces of knowledge to Graves and one or two others.

'Well'; he shrugged and burbled something about *tempus* something, which I took with a sympathetic smile. 'Things start coming back to you at my age. I've been writing a lot about dead friends – and about my brother Tristram, he would have been a *great* poet, of course.' He gazed at the floor. Should I ask about Tristram? 'We all jolly well had to be writers, and thank the Lord we all started young. I don't know if you know, but well, *Tennyson* . . .' And off he went into an account of the Dawlishes, the bishops, the generals, the poets, Swinburne, Henry James, Robert Bridges (his godfather), young T. S. Eliot, that certainly put the Manners Family of Kent in its place, and held me enthralled in the musty gloom. Even so, after twenty minutes, I felt my concentration ebbing, my features locked in a kind of sneer of astonishment, my poems in their plastic folder still clutched in my lap, like the programme to a different concert. I felt painfully ignorant of Swinburne and Henry James; we didn't do T. S. Eliot till next year. I was flattered but also somehow hurt that he had misjudged me and poured this well-rehearsed torrent of stuff over me.

Later we went into the kitchen together, as if not quite sure what we'd find there, and managed to make a pot of tea. Again it seemed an honour to be doing these homely things with a great man, and so soon after meeting him: it would have been less impressive if he had had the servants I'd expected. There was no suggestion of cake.

At last he made me hand over 'The Months' and leaving me to browse went off to a chair at the brighter end of the room. I got out the Merrifield volume, which bore the inscription 'To Perry Dawlish from "the Old Rogue" – George Merrifield, May Day 1928: knowing that he will go far . . .' I turned to the list of contents, hoping to find 'Cider', which I knew by heart anyway (it was the unobvious rhyme of *oozing* with *refusing* in the sestet that I had stolen); but it wasn't in *Love and Earth*, which was perhaps an earlier collection. I realised for the first time just how large Merrifield's output was.

I was awed by the book and its associations, and wondered why its author was known as the Old Rogue. I imagined him like Toad of Toad Hall, with goggles and a cigar, motoring recklessly from one Sussex alehouse to another. I kept peeping towards the window, trying to read Dawlish's reactions. He was in profile, and partly canopied by a broad-leaved plant that sprawled across the glass above him. He seemed to be paying each sonnet the very closest attention. Or had he perhaps fallen into a quiet doze? It occurred to me that he might have died. No – another page was shuffled under. I wondered which month he'd reached. I was aware that some months were stronger than others, which was why the sequence began with September, like a school year. I thought it unlikely that he would be very critical of them, but I would have to be sensible and take his criticism with eagerness and resolution when it came.

One time I glanced up and found he was looking at me and slowly nodding, pausing to find the most tactful opening. 'Marvellous,' he said. 'Simply marvellous, you've really got it. Really. I do congratulate you. You *understand* the sonnet, as few nowadays do. And every one of them has some memorable effect. "When all is frozen to the rover's call" is a splendid line.' And he said it again, to bring out what he heard as the 'wintry echo' of *all* and *call*. I thought it was the best line of the lot myself, and saw it gaining something like proverbial status with Dawlish's endorsement. 'There's absolutely no doubt about it, Edward,' he said, with those gestures of regret that sometimes heighten the effect of praise, 'you are a writer. A born writer, I would say. I see a very bright future for you indeed.'

Hunting moodily through my books for something to read at Dawn's funeral I came across *Poems Old and New* by Peregrine Dawlish, with an inscription to me, and beside it the copy of Merrifield's *Love and Earth* that I had felt bold enough to ask to borrow that day eighteen years ago, and had never returned. I felt dully guilty about it, but it was too late now. Flicking through the Dawlish I remembered that he had been a good Georgian poet with a tight lyric grace; it was later that he mistook his gifts, made painful attempts to get modern, shrilly took on free verse and low-life subjects and made a fool of himself. You could see why Squire might have praised him at fifteen: I suppose he used the same words as Dawlish had solemnly addressed to me. Looking back, I thought I could make out the suspect emotion of that afternoon, the old man's vicarious excitement in acclaiming talent he had only imagined, the tone of foolish self-congratulation. But at the time, it was so much what I wanted to hear that I took a nearly erotic pleasure in it. When, after a moment's hesitation, he lent me the Merrifield, and capped it with *Poems Old and New*, with the further wingbeat of wonder at finding what Perry was short for, I felt as if I'd been received into a succession. There was something about the light that day, the penumbra beyond which he sat in the leafy window, that fixed what he said in amber. I could still hear his hollow augury now; like the words of a fairground palmist, hard entirely to discount.

Early that summer holidays I wandered up on to the common after supper. Charlie was just home from Cambridge with a Third that no one quite knew what to say about. His line was that he was a maverick genius, that exams weren't where he shone. There was a sort of smothered row (we never had any other kind) about his waist-length hair and its probable impact on anyone who might interview him for a job. He had a girl-friend at last, whom he deferred to on everything: 'Lisanne says you shouldn't boil vegetables', 'Lisanne thinks Schubert's really boring'. After a couple of days Lisanne had become an invisible antagonist in our house, the subject of Charlie's veneration and everyone else's keenest loathing. We almost longed for her to come and stay, so that we could answer her back in person.

Charlie let me know that it was what he called 'the full scene', and came into my room unnecessarily to extol the virtues of Lisanne's breasts and the miracle of the pill. I didn't care about them, but being made to think of them only worsened my holiday blues, the sense of being sundered from the boys I felt and thought so much about. It was hot and tedious at home; my father was out of sorts and depressed and seemed withdrawn from us in a new and unaccountable way; the few friends who lived in the town had been whizzed off to Skye or Montpellier or Corfu with their families. I went up the hill a lot, semi-spying on sunbathers semi-hidden in the long grass, and thinking of Mawson and Turlough and El-Barrawi transforming whatever holiday thing they were doing just by being their enviable selves.

My favourite time was soon after sunset, when I liked to catch the first sight of the evening star, suddenly bright, high in the west above the darkening outlines of the copses. It was a solitary ritual, wound up incoherently with bits of poetry said over and over like spells: sunset and evening star, the star that bids the shepherd fold, her fond yellow hornlight wound to the west ... It intensified and calmed my yearnings at the same time, like a song. In one poem I'd seen that first star referred to as the folding star, and the words haunted me with their suggestion of an embrace and at the same time a soundless implosion, of something ancient but evanescent; I looked up to it in a mood of desolate solitude burning into cold calm. I lingered, testing out the ache of it: I had to be back before it was truly dark, but in high summer that could be very late. I became a connoisseur of the last lonely gradings of blue into black.

This evening was windless, with high grand cloud that the afterglow made into dream-towers of pink. A hawk went over in the dusk as I climbed to the top, then there was a nagging squeak – I thought of a small night animal, but it was only a boy on a bike, braking and juddering around the steep rutted paths. Well, others could share the twilight too. There would sometimes be a couple with a dog, relishing the cool, or kids from the Flats, not quite ready to go in. Charlie said the queers went up by the wood at night, and I imagined them with a mixture of distrust and fascination. I leant on the trig-point, and saw the bike approaching again. What an effort to have walked it all the way up here, even if he came by the gentler climb from the other side. I was aware of the wheels wobbling by me, the squeak of the brake again, a plimsolled foot scraping for balance. It was Dawn. He fell against me, hand round my throat to keep him steady, so that I choked for a second, like in a fight. He let the bike slither under him across the path and hopped free of it while a wheel still lazily spun. Then there was a second embrace, an arm round my shoulder in apology and surprise.

It seemed we were being matey: Dawn's arm stayed heavily where it was, his fingers absent-mindedly doodling on my collar-bone. We gazed out at the glimmering pinky-mauve crag of cloud that stood motionless to the west. He was very warm from exercise, and lightly sweaty in a tracksuit – not the sleazy multi-coloured modern kind but the soft old navy-blue kind that was like a rugged form of undress, like slumberwear worn out of doors. I always felt disadvantaged in sports gear, and envied boys like Dawn who came to life in it. I was analysing the slight discomfort in our stance, a hollowness in my stomach, an ache down my thighs like I got on a high building. I raised my arm and rested it on his back.

'I should have known I'd meet you up here,' he said, with a hint of routine school jeering, and a hint of flattery too, as if I figured in his thoughts, a poetic type from the Lower Sixth who might be worth wary emulation.

'I'm always up here,' I said, to counter any suggestion it was his place, not mine.

'Yeah, I come over on my bike sometimes, since we moved. We should arrange to meet up.'

I loved the idea of that, perhaps we both had these great vacancies – these *grandes vacances* – to fill. On the other hand what would we talk about . . . We hardly knew each other; he was already coloured in my mind by being in Drake, with their drab plum strip. He was handsome, he'd been a rather hopeless Orsino last term, but his strong physique and violet tights had given the role another kind of interest. He turned towards me and jutted his chest out, with a body-builder's deep breath, and hooked up his other arm. 'Feel that,' he said, nodding at it. The light was failing, there was a moment's uncertainty. 'Go on.'

I ran my hand over the gathered biceps, then played down my approval – actually, I wasn't interested in muscles, except as part of the knot of manhood and the tightening hold it had on

217

me. He rocked his bosom against mine, as if he had a girl's big tits. I could feel his hard nipples through our two layers of cotton. It was the sort of dumb sport you imagined them passing the time with in Drake. I was dying for him.

He reached down quickly and grabbed at my stiff cock. 'What do we have here?' he asked facetiously as I ducked backwards with a giggled gasp of protest. But his hand was still on my shoulder. 'Oh, come on,' he said in American, and pulled me slowly back towards him. 'I saw you getting a root that time on the train.'

'When?' I said.

'I had one, too.' This was too much what I wanted. I thought, I am in a higher form than this person, I'm writing a lot of sonnets, I can speak Dutch, in fact I'm going to write a sonnet-sequence *in Dutch*. He took my hand gently and rubbed it against his tracksuit, where his cock was a hard ridge held sideways in tight underwear. Why was I ashamed to be seduced by him? 'Let's do this,' he whispered, right up against me, the first time I'd ever heard anyone breathe my own thoughts like that. There were voices close by, and I broke away.

An oldish couple who might have been standing in the gloom for ages. I sort of recognised them. They admired the sublimity of the sky, some stratospheric wind just teasing the top of the cloud over into an anvil point, the lower parts darkening through lilac to powerless storm-grey. Oh, *why* didn't they just fuck off? The man, in a cap, half-stumbled on Dawn's prostrate bike. 'That must be the Ashringford road,' the wife said, gesturing at distant lights. I looked at Dawn, and found he was looking steadily at me. This was the real thing, we were going to do it. Our expectant silence must have been palpable to the others; as they disappeared down the steep path I heard the wife's crisp 'I don't know', and wondered what the murmured question had been.

We stepped back together and he kissed me with closed lips, as if shyly soliciting an answer in his turn. It was the gentlest thing I'd ever known from another boy, blasphemous and unhidden. I reached down again and rubbed him through his pants and he just let me. 'We'd better go under the trees,' he said, and went to pick up his bike. 'Don't want to lose that.' I thought to myself, 'But that's where the queers go', imagining some nice distinction between what they did there and whatever we were going to do.

I felt the minute of physical separation keenly, skirting the pond, Dawn walking the bike between us, the proficient idling of its wheels; I wanted things to start again, and then, as we stepped under the nighttime of the wood's edge, was quite afraid, too. This was the 'dim woods' of poetry for real. I cannot see what flowers are at my feet. The forest's ferny floor. I'd threaded the paths there often by day, but now it was mazily different, the underbrush of August was thick and tangled across.

Dawn had stopped to lodge his bike against a tree, and whispered loudly, 'Hey, Manners ... don't go too far.' Perhaps I was trying to lead the way, as if I often did this. I came back towards him and we bumped into each other. I just couldn't see at first, and then began to make out tree-trunks and bushes against the relative brightness of the open common beyond. We hugged for a kind of confirmation, and I passed my hand shyly over his face (he kissed it!) and through his short curls. My mouth was open and sour with need when his lips nudged over it and his fat shocking tongue pressed in.

When we came out of the wood I knew I was late, and must hurry down. The towering anvil of cloud had become a ruffled palm-tree of darkness against the other darkness of the sky. I longed to be alone, longed for it to happen again. Dawn sat astride his bike and leant on my shoulder to steady himself. It was a firm, slightly painful grip, through which all his weight and balance seemed to communicate themselves, as if we were an acrobatic act. Then he circled swiftly across the turf. I ran up to the trig-point and watched the rushing field of his front light and the red glow of his back light as he jolted and swung down the hillside and was suddenly out of view.

Geoffrey and Mirabelle Turlough were great friends of my parents, though I was never quite sure why. Geoffrey was a wiry man with a depressing grey beard and no sense of fun, whilst Mirabelle could have represented fun in a pageant and was huge and outgoing, with short dark hair and glasses on a chain. He was in charge of the local planning office, but had been a fine amateur tennis-player just after the war: one could picture him doing months of practice serves. They had met at the Tennis Club where Mirabelle often umpired the ladies' matches. Later a shoulder injury had forced him to give up, but Mirabelle, who was no player, retained a passionate interest in the game, one that he seemed rather to resent. In my teens he was always in grey flannels, jacket and tie, when she would be wearing white daps and sports shirts with pockets right out on the end of her breasts; she would often be tugging the shirt down over her hips in a jolly, let's-give-it-a-go sort of way. Each year at the end of June she would appear on the television in uniform, glaring down the tramlines and howling 'Fault' whenever possible. 'She shouts so loud', my father once said, 'you hardly need a telly to pick it up.' Even so, those two weekends late in the summer term were always spent with the curtains drawn and the tennis on, not from any particular interest of ours in the sport, but rather from the hope of seeing our friend crouched behind the muscled legs of the receiver. The next week the Turloughs would come to supper, and Mirabelle would reveal the best of the scandals she had picked up about the players – particularly sexual ones of a kind that were never talked of at home, and which all of us, including Geoffrey, took rather stiffly.

I knew from early on that Mirabelle was somehow in tune with sex in a way that I couldn't believe my parents were. On the other hand she seemed to have no real rapport with her husband, whereas my mother and father were clearly linked by some deep if reticent bond. Geoffrey was a decent, disappointed man, who would ask you about your O levels, whilst Mirabelle called you darling and winkingly cross-questioned you on your non-existent girlfriends. They seemed to embody some mysterious thing – perhaps a flaw, perhaps a principle – about matrimony and the unimagined later centuries of adult lives. She was always pumping me for information on their heavenly son Willie, who was in the year above me at Stonewell and fancied by absolutely everybody; and it was a disturbing moment when I overheard her saying to my mother how easily she could fall in love with the boy, and my mother replying, 'He's too young for you, dear!' Alas, Willie took after his father in conscientious dullness, and was aloof to all pashes and advances. Later, when it became clear to my mother that I was gay, it was Mirabelle who helped her come to grips with it, and spoke of it as an enviable state of being, the opportunities . . . She brought it up all the time, with slightly wearying good-heartedness.

After my father died, she kept close to my mother, and developed the habit of dropping round for coffee three or four mornings a week. For years she was associated in my mind with our neighbourly sitcom doorchime, which didn't so much ring as brightly announce impending good-fellowship with its halting ditone. Once it had been an incongruous interruption of my father's practising. But later, when nobody else much came, the words Mirabelle and doorbell became almost synonymous with each other.

I was sitting at the kitchen table with my mother, looking at Gray's 'Elegy' in *The Golden Treasury*: I was amazed to find how little of it I remembered. I didn't see it as especially appropriate for my dead friend, who blushed, but not unseen, and wasted none of his sweetness. I thought she must just like its tone of maxim-studded consolation. 'It's the end,' she said, and pointed to the verse beginning 'One morn I miss'd him on the custom'd hill'. Then the bell ding-donged. 'Ten fifty-five,' she said, with irony but no resentment.

Mirabelle was sixty-four now, a year older than my mother; but whereas my mother never aged in my eyes, and remained at an ideal forty of competence and prettiness, her friend struck me, after a couple of months' absence, as abruptly an old woman. The hugeness had become wheeziness and powdered underchins, and the odd compromise of her marriage, it turned out, was under unexpected strain.

At first she was all cheer, subsiding on to a startled kitchen chair, and examining me closely. 'It's lovely to see you, darling, but he's looking a bit pale, a bit black under the eyes, isn't he, Peg? I expect it's the late nights out there.'

'I think he *has* lost weight,' my mother answered obliquely.

'I expect you've got one of those lovely Dutch boys, haven't you, with blond hair, *grey* eyes – very *friendly*.'

'I'm not actually in Holland,' I said, shying away from the complicated truth.

'He's here for the funeral – you know . . .' said my mother.

'Darling, it's too unbearable. Poor you, poor them, oh dear . . . You know Willie's had a third, a little boy: they *couldn't* decide what to call the little chap, they've just called him Number Three or something silly like Marmaduke, which I thought was in danger of sticking. Anyway, now they're going to name him in memory of your friend.'

'What, Dawn . . .? I'm not sure that's . . .'

'No, Ralph, silly.'

'I think Ralph Turlough would be a very good name,' I said, though feeling that Willie had somehow managed to miss the point.

'I'm sure they'd love to see you.' She hesitated, and took the coffee my mother was passing her. 'I've been taking refuge there myself, of late. Well, I can help with the baby.' And then the story came out – how Geoffrey, within weeks of his recent retirement, had gone into a resolute depression, had claimed that their life together was pointless, that he had never loved her, never even liked her much, and that he knew all about her affairs with numerous other men, including, one rather gathered, my own father. 'And I never!' she said, in Dandy Nichols cockney. 'I never!' My mother smiled confidently. 'Do you know what he said to me today?' she went on. 'He came into the kitchen and said, "Good morning, evening and night, and now I don't think I need speak to you for the rest of the day." And he just *sits* there, you know, with his fingers in his beard.'

'Don't you think he ought to get help?' I suggested.

'I'm the one who needs help, ducky. The fact is, if I may digress, that when he grew his beard I thought "Oh, no", but then he couldn't play tennis any more, which was very hard for him, he had to have something to do. And after a while I got used to it, it even came to represent, ghastly though it was *in itself*, a kind of scratchy comfort and security. But now . . . I keep wanting to run up behind him and just chop it off! Never grow a beard, darling. There's a lot more to a beard than meets the eye.'

As she talked I was increasingly drawn under by a current of recollection that her presence, and the lines from Gray, had obscurely triggered – the desert air of that summer of 1976, in which she and Geoffrey had somehow played a part, a memory of sexual loneliness, which would later pull so much I did into its own fierce patterns.

I remembered the day after that first time with Dawn, coming downstairs with a kind of wary astonishment, feeling I'd been given access to a world that lay just on the other side of the parquet, the fridge, the radio, the piano declaiming in the sitting-room. I looked covertly at my family, wondering if they too were inhabitants of this thrilling dimension. Perhaps Charlie was; but his accounts of life with Lisanne seemed oddly to leave out any mention of it. I felt both irritable and supremely tolerant at the same time, sulkily looking over my mother's shopping-list, but then when I got outside, dancing to the baker's like a character in a musical comedy.

It wouldn't have been an early start. Throughout my adolescent holidays I got up wastefully late, as though to make up for the austerity of school mornings, the wintry dressing in the dark. Sometimes it would be 11.30 or 12 before I came down for a cup of coffee and was warned off spoiling my lunch. They were hours of luxurious tedium in the half-light of the bedroom, reading for a bit, dozing in and out of songs coming from downstairs, *Schöne Müllerin* all that summer, my father flagging and dissatisfied. I evolved fantastic sexual situations around boys at school, dropping off in the middle of them, then waking and putting them through some further fabulous depravity. My mother's weary, unwitting half-joke, 'Are you getting up?', would be shouted from the hall, and I would reply with my comprehensive euphemism, 'I'm just having a think.'

Now that I had actually made love, more astonishingly now that I had been made love to, the fantasies were subtly undermined. It had been awkward, a bit scary, my legs were stung by nettles, we'd only kissed a lot, really, then quickly stroked each

223

other off, but it was wholly different from the heartless occasional jerk-offs at school with someone who called you a queer
afterwards. Next day my head was full of the heat of it, the
lovely certainty we did it for each other. When we met tonight,
it would be a step further into the dreamy underwoods of love.
By the time I went out for my walk after supper I was prospecting far into the future. I had coached Dawn to some surprising
exam results, he had moulded me into a runner and swimmer
who commanded respect. I wrote long letters to an imaginary
friend abroad, dotingly detailing Dawn's sweetness and beauty.
For all our open-air beginnings I had him closeted with me in
des Esseintes-like privacy, in a sealed world of silk and fur and
absolute indulgence.

But Dawn didn't come. I sat on the bench reading Tennyson,
but not taking it in, looking up every few seconds for a bike or
just for him in dark running gear. It was breezier than last
night, the wood was stirring in tumultuous slow-motion, the
pond broken and bickering. I waited through a muffled sunset
till the wind had blown off the cannon-smoke of low cloud and
opened up a sky of densening stars. Of course we hadn't said
we'd meet. I walked nervously under the wood's edge for a
minute, and looked out the way I thought he would come, for a
light swivelling over grass and bushes. But there were only the
lights of planes, high up, climbing out of Gatwick, the intermittent yawn of their engines, and when they'd gone just the
gusting of the trees. I was shivery in a T-shirt, and jogged home
for warmth, working out a story about how I'd come back
safely along the road.

Next day I was desolate, and even coaxed out a few tears in
my room, which I found impressive and almost cheering. I
knew I had to ring Dawn, and got up suspiciously early to do
so, hanging about in the hall with a book, until I thought the
coast was clear, and then swiftly dissimulating my intention
when my mother or Charlie came heedlessly through. I was
more and more nervous the more I deferred. I didn't know their
routines or anything about them; the phonebook gave me their
address and I worked up an image of 12 Sands Road – by the
sound of it pleasant enough – as a household severely unwel-
coming to phone-calls of any kind, much less those from boys

who wanted to fuck their son. I imagined Dawn denying all knowledge of me, hanging up on me, or just giving me some casual putdown. I had actually started dialling when my mother looked out from the kitchen and said, 'Can't it keep till cheap time, love?' And I accepted her objection with only a show of reluctance.

From 5 o'clock on I was locked in a parched rehearsal of my opening remarks, which involved an optional parent-charming paragraph (always say who you are and apologise for troubling them) that snagged on the question of how I should refer to him. Then I had to say 'Hi! Dawn? It's Edward ... yeah, great . . .' and hope to catch the warmth in his reply and if at all possible lead him on to propose a meeting himself. By six these simple phrases had become a kind of hysterical gibberish in my mind, as though they'd been passed round the room in a game of Chinese whispers. I went to the phone, but thank god someone rang up for my father just at that moment, and I put it off till 6.30.

After supper I said, 'I'll just make that call now, Mum', and went and did it so quickly that the adrenalin only caught up with me at the moment someone answered: a girl, rather sultry and bored. He must have sisters. They were all out, she said. Or put it another way, she was there all by herself. She almost sounded as if she'd like me to come round and fuck her instead. She said she'd tell Ralphie that I'd rung, and repeated my number sluttishly wrongly before she got it right.

Then I set out into the high-summer wastes of longing. Dawn never rang back. I missed him on the customed hill, all right. I missed him everywhere. Some days it was as if nothing had ever happened; on others I felt ruined, I'd been given a sip of some marvellous elixir and then had it snatched away. I knew it was absurd to fall in love after ten minutes' breathless smooching, but that only added an element of hysterical determination to my passion. Everyone noticed I was moping, but there were larger glooms about the house that rendered mine unimportant. My great-aunt Tina was very ill; Charlie kept deferring his visit to Lisanne's parents (who weren't at all sure it was a good idea) and tinkered pointlessly with circuitry in his room; and though nothing was said to me, it was obvious my father was doing less work and that there was a new caution about money. He had begun to cancel engagements. He was pale and withdrawn. I would ask him if he was okay, and he would push out his chest as if about to sing and say, 'I'll be all right – a bit out of sorts.' But our fortnight at Kinchin Cove was off that year; and the trading-in of our rusting Humber Snipe, a suffocating monster which, if never entirely new in our experience, had been a sign of prosperity six years before, was again deferred: it began to resemble one of the broken-voiced old hulks on the forecourt at the Flats. I had always been thrilled by cars and was deflated and embarrassed. I was told that my school-fees cost more than a car, and knew that I wasn't allowed to complain.

After the first week, I took to ringing Dawn's number two or three times a day from a phone-box in town, though there was never any reply. They must have gone on holiday: he was somewhere different entirely, showing off on a beach, chasing his sisters, picking them up and spanking them, being clumsily macho for their protesting fun.

I felt trapped in the house, but didn't want to miss a phone-call if it came. We had a smart, trilling phone but it was on a party-line, and I imagined Dawn baffled and kept at bay by the engaged tone as our talkative neighbours (whom we knew only from the inane fragments of chat that obstructed us when we tried to ring out) were maundering on. I began to hallucinate the cheep of the phone in the routine undertones and overtones of the house – in the burble and chink of the fridge, inside the dreary howl of the hoover, in the tinkling drops of a filling cistern. Perhaps I was going mad with desolation. I lay on the floor a lot, gazing across the landing to where the sunlight slanted along the carpet of the front bedroom, showing up various boxes that had been stowed away beneath the bed. Once when everyone was out, I went into the sitting-room and stormed up and down on the piano, which I had refused to learn, with clumsy ferocity – Sibelius standing thoughtfully beside me, as if ready to turn the page. Those were rare moments of *faute de mieux* togetherness with the dog, which otherwise owed all its loyalty to my parents, and still if I took him for a walk would run away.

Sometimes a postcard came from holidaying friends and I

examined the grim communality of the beaches with burning interest. That lad in black trunks, half a centimetre high in the middle distance at Rapallo or Cagnes-sur-Mer, looked pretty hot. It was so sexy there. Here there were only some beery lads on the grass, or old gents with their shirts off sitting on benches, listening to the cricket on tiny trannies. In town I found things taking on an absurd sexual significance: I tramped round and round on imaginary errands so as to see a butcher's boy with a spot-crossed full-mouthed face joking in the doorway with his workless mates. I knew where in Digby's the second-hand manuals of photography and volumes of obsolete sexology were shelved. Even the square-jawed beige mannequins in an outfitters' window, with a generalised mound between the legs, possessed a certain power of suggestion, as did the surreal cross-sections used to display underwear, as if the erogenous zones had been cast life-size in milk chocolate. Being in love seemed to license and heighten random desire all around; I felt guiltily untouched by the conventional wisdom of never looking at another man.

It was into this dispirited household that I remember Geoffrey and Mirabelle coming, quite often, as if determined to brighten us up. There was a sense of an impromptu party being stirred into reluctant life; they would arrive with a half-bottle of Beefeater or a batch of meringues in a tin. The idea of Geoffrey brightening anyone up had something incongruous about it that added to the forced sense of fun. He made a genuine effort, he smiled a lot in a rather loopy way, he even once told a long humorous anecdote, followed by an expectant silence in which Mirabelle quietly provided the proper punch-line and pointed out an error earlier in the story which altered the meaning of the whole thing. It was Mirabelle really who made the going.

As well as her line-judge's shout, she had a lovely liquid singing voice, which I imagined being refined to its bright clarity in the great stills of her bosom. She was always rather shy of using it in my father's presence, and made pointless remarks about how she couldn't sing at all, but then would break into a phrase or two from Cole Porter inadvertently, out of pure tunefulness, when carrying out the plates or pouring a drink. What sometimes happened was a duet with my father, which seemed less

227

presumptuous on her part, though he would much rather have just listened to her or better still had no singing: 'I will if Lewis will too,' she would say, which may have been the basis for Geoffrey's festering jealousy all these years later.

My father had a great aversion to character-acting in songs, any rolling of the eyes, putting hands on hips or wringing out of humour. He tended to sing like a sentinel, sworn to some higher purpose. Mirabelle, however, was much given to caperings and routines which spoke of a thwarted desire for the stage and could be rather overwhelming in the confines of the sitting-room. She knew several of the drunk songs from operettas and *fin de siècle* musicals and sometimes did 'Ah, quel dîner', from *La Périchole*, in a recklessly 'French' manner. But her party piece was a song 'I'm just a wee bit boozy', from a forgotten show called *Her Cousin from Kansas*, in which each verse was slightly more slurred than the one before; at the end she would pretend to stumble against the piano or even fall to the floor. My mother, who accompanied, always had a look of forlorn sobriety after this number.

On one of these sad restless evenings that they came ding-donging into with such puzzling gaiety my mother muttered to me not to go out after supper. I was immediately certain that this was the night when Dawn would come back. I saw him, bronzed, heavy with sperm, roaming the common into the small hours, maybe meeting someone else . . . But Charlie had boorishly slipped the net and gone down to the pub, and I was being relied on to keep up some sense of occasion. The Turloughs had brought a bottle of cherry brandy and I drank several little glasses of it and felt annoyingly careless and witty.

We went into the sitting-room, and I sat by the door, so as to get to the phone first when it rang. It was extraordinary the certainty I felt, one of those baseless whims, a slight chemical thing perhaps, that changes your whole attitude. Geoffrey, as a rule needlessly discreet, gave a detailed account of the machinations behind the current bypass proposals. Then my father went to put a record on the stereogram. I knew that he hated background music, and that this was a ploy to prevent anyone from singing. But the moment he lifted the magic lid Mirabelle exclaimed, 'Oh Lewis, my love, why don't you sing to us? I can't bear a record on, when you don't know whether to talk or listen to it.'

'I really won't tonight,' he said firmly but with a smile. And then what could he do but add, 'But if *you'd* like to . . .' I think she agreed less out of high spirits than from a sense of duty.

'I shan't sing "I'm just a wee bit boozy"', she said, 'because actually I am, and I'll probably get muddled up with the words.'

'Ah well,' said my father.

'But can you play . . .?' She had a whisper with my mother and after five seconds' modest thought broke out in a deeper, sexier voice than usual, 'A home is not a home without a man – He's the necessary evil in the plan . . .', at which Geoffrey looked quite uncomfortable. My mother accompanied anxiously, making it sound like a metrical psalm. When it was finished I clapped for too long.

'Thank you, darling,' said Mirabelle with a bow. She had on black linen bell-bottoms that added a further curve to her outline and low-cut slippers which showed the little pinched cleavages of her toes. 'What would you like me to do next?'

There were no immediate requests, and the general answer might well have been 'Sit down and shut up'. 'Beggars in Spats,' I called out mischievously. This was a comic number from the Broadway of thirty or forty years ago, a genre utterly antique to me but treasured by all these adults as the glamour music of their youth, and so absorbed by osmosis into my own. It was another of those things that gave me the ghostly sense of having grown up in an earlier age.

She did sing 'Beggars in Spats', which was about a couple getting married with only a nickel between them but somehow managing very well; it was a long song, in which everything happened several times over. 'And now I've done enough,' she said, turning her eyes on my father. 'If I really can't persuade Lewis to join me?' He shook his head. 'There seems to be a bit of a matrimonial theme. We *could* round it off with "There's Nothing Like Marriage for People" . . .'

'I'm just not up to it tonight.'

'Oh, go on, Dad!' I said, bounding across to his chair and tugging at his hand. 'It's always so funny when you do it in your American accent.' And Sibelius, noticing the activity, lurched to

229

his feet and clittered round the parquet giving short affirmative barks. I appealed to my mother, who looked mournfully at my father, not knowing what to hope. Mirabelle doodled the first two lines sweetly, *sotto voce*, 'Imagine living with someone Who's longing to live with you', and winked at me as he got up, with an alarming look of stifled wretchedness, and took his place by the piano. Mirabelle slipped her arm through his and sang the lines again, still very sweetly. ('Oh god, I imagine that every minute of the day,' I thought.) 'Imagine signing a lease together; And hanging a Matisse together,' my father replied, but in stiff English. She took it up, in English too, 'Oh what felicity In domesticity!' and he capped it, with a sternness that was comic in itself, 'Let no one disparage Marriage!'

It was all very strange. Geoffrey stared at his wife expressionlessly. Was he angry with her for pretending to be getting married to my father? Or was he merely stuffily hiding his admiration and assessing the song as though he had never heard it before? I wondered if I was so self-absorbed that I'd missed out on something important that had been said. The accompaniment was oddly inadvertent. Mirabelle was nursing the thing along by sheer, even exaggerated, force of personality: 'Hurry, let's call up the minister!' – head thrown back. A second's delay, 'Why be a sinister Old bachelor or spinister . . .' My mother had stopped and I turned to her irritably. Her cheeks were wet with tears, and she was fumbling at her cuff for a handkerchief. Then she jumped up and ran out of the room.

My father called 'Peg' and went after her, half-tangled up with the doleful but excited dog. Mirabelle looked horrified at what she had brought about. Geoffrey nodded towards the door, and she drifted into the hall, biting her lower lip. The two of us were left alone. The shock of the first moments was yielding to a childish urge to cry too, the contagion of misery, however little understood. Geoffrey got up, walked to the window, and stood glaring into the dusk and the privet hedge.

'I'm very sorry about your father's bad news,' he said, raking and smoothing his beard. 'I suppose it's as well to be prepared for the worst. Let's hope they can hold it off for a few more months, eh?'

*

I did ring Willie Turlough, god knows why – perhaps out of that same sense of desolation that had welled up from the past and seemed to me, as it can in certain lights, to be our real environment. We talked against a background of white noise, he was impossibly distracted; I pictured him holding a wriggling bundle like the baby that turns into a piglet in *Alice*. What people put themselves through . . . I shouted that I would come round after supper, and had the impression that he agreed.

I was in the pub first. It didn't seem to them to be all that long since I had left. To me it did, so that I was reluctant to go in, and then hurt at how little fuss was made of me. The deaths of our friends were in the smoke-soured air, of course; they were still being talked about with original shock, and with the occasional hilarity that came with shock and brought a tear to the eye that the indulgent reminiscences failed to raise. From time to time someone would have the muffled excitement of breaking the news to a new arrival who hadn't heard. I noticed how the story was changing as each teller patched it together.

I bought lagers for my old chums Danny and Simon, who must have known me well, we had drunk so much together and talked so much, up and down the scale between murky confession and the permitted embellishments of tales of conquest, the two of them drily puncturing my more preposterous flights; but I had an eerie sense of having broken with them, of looking in with envy on their steady and self-sufficient affair. The utterly unchanged bar, some of the men I had slept with at one time or another, even Dawn himself, existed in earlier, closed-down precincts of my life. When Simon asked me some perfectly straightforward question, I felt it had been run through a scrambler. What was the scene like in Belgium? You mean the scene . . . in Belgium . . .? I couldn't think of anything to say.

Willie and Alison had given up expecting me by the time I made it out to their house. She appeared in her dressing-gown, holding the baby, little Ralphie, whom she had just fed into fat-faced sleep. Willie was hurrying about in his socks, holding chewed toys, a stained cot-blanket. I felt I was interrupting something arduous and intimate.

'What sort of time do you call this?' he demanded cheerfully, and gave me a sympathetic kiss on the cheek. Actually it was

231

only half past nine, a time at which I normally comforted myself with the certainty of hours of drink to come; but when you entered the lives of young parents you were in another time-zone, pale faces came to meet you in the half-light, abstracted with fatigue. 'It's like some awful kind of training,' Willie said, 'where they wake you up at odd hours of the night, and you have to put an engine together, or defuse a bomb.'

'I didn't know they did that.'

'Don't they? I *thought* they did . . .' He yawned like a dog, with a whine too.

Alison had gone upstairs and didn't re-emerge. I imagined she'd just fallen asleep where she was. Willie looked mildly bemused by the silence, the social call from the outside world. He was piecing together what it was one did. I said, 'Would you rather I went?'

He was dismayed. 'My dear Edward!' Slightly ponderous now. He frowned and smiled, and I realised he looked so much balder because he'd done the sensible thing and cut it all off short. Last time I'd seen him there had been fatally middle-aged wisps. His features were so good that he looked even more handsome without hair than with it. As he wandered round through the debris of plastic bricks and scribbled scrap-paper I couldn't help thinking back through his shapeless casual clothes to the naked prefect he had been, his magically unblemished skin, the blue veins that ran over his upper arms, the idle beauty of his big cock and balls. Not for the first time I thought what an excellent homosexual he would have made. 'Would you like a drink?'

'Mmm. Perhaps the merest rumour of Scotch. The merest *hearsay* . . .'

'I'll bring the bottle.'

I swept the rubbish from an armchair and sat down and still got a piece of Lego up the bum. Why did they do it? Why did this dully charming man, who was already working absurdly to support two children, who got up at six each day to commute to town and was sometimes not home till nine, then go inanely on and sire a third? It must be instinct, nothing rational could explain it — instinct or inattention or else what Edie called poly-filla-progenitiveness: having more children to stop up the gaps

232

in a marriage. I was at the age when I couldn't ignore it; my straight friends married and bred, sometimes remarried and bred again, or just bred regardless. I saw them losing the gift of speech, so used to being interrupted by the demands of the young that they began to interrupt themselves, or to prefer the kind of fretful drivel they had become accustomed to. I saw the huge, humiliating vehicles these studs of the GTi were forced to buy: like streamlined dormobiles, with tiers of baby seats and stacks of the grey plastic crap which seemed inseparable from modern infancy. I saw their doped surrender to domestic muddle, not enough letters on the fridge door to spell anything properly, the chairs covered in yoghurt.

'This is all very sad,' said Willie, with a stern smile. Neither of us knew yet just how seriously the other was taking it, whether we would shortly be telling slightly derisory stories in an air of accomplished melancholy or if one of us would be comforting the other as he sobbed out his bitter regrets and griefs. The thought of a scene of unguarded emotion with Willie, whatever its cause, had a certain appeal.

'I wondered if Mirabelle might be here,' I said.

'No, she's been wonderful with the baby, much more than with the other two' – as if that was the only reason for her coming round.

'Here's a good long life to Ralphie number two,' I said, chinning my glass. 'A new Dawn, you might say.' Perhaps there were unhappy implications to this.

'He was the first of our schoolfriends to go – that's why I chose his name.' This wasn't true, or it depended what you meant by friends; our old boys' magazine now had two epochs to its obituary page – the steady professional deaths of the prewar generations, and the cluster of pinched-off careers, nothing much to say about them yet, dead at twenty-four or twenty-nine, or thirty-three, no causes given, where before it had been climbing accidents.

'It was a very sweet idea. I'm so confused by the shock of this death, having started in a way to prepare for a different one. But if he'd gone as it were knowingly, he'd have been very touched at what you've done. He rather loved you, you know.'

'Well, I rather loved him,' said Willie smugly. 'In my way – of course, not like you did.' I looked at him with a sceptical little smile, so that he went on, 'Even I could see that he was jolly handsome.'

Well, yes, he was quite handsome – dark curls, blue eyes – but that wasn't the point of Dawn, it wasn't why men wanted him. Willie reminded me of people without a sense of humour, who laugh at the wrong moment, or for too long. There was always something lacking in those men who had never had a queer phase as boys, it showed in a certain dryness of imagination, a bland tolerance uncoloured by any suppression of their own, a blindness to the spectrum's violet end.

'I was trying to tell Alison about you two at school, and how scandalous you were. She wasn't very impressed. She said she thought that was what all public schoolboys did – you know she can be a bit left-wing.'

'We're all a bit left-wing, dear.'

'Mmm.'

'I hope she doesn't think you ever carried on like that. She must know you were the great untouchable.'

Willie looked into his glass and shook the ice around in it. 'I didn't really want to be untouchable, you know. But I just wasn't into it. I tried quite hard sometimes; everyone would be mooning about one of the new boys – don't you think he's a perfect orchid, isn't he just like a dark little kitten – and I'd search my heart, but all I could ever see was a rather anxious little chap who'd had his cricket-bat stolen, or whatever.'

'You are aware that virtually the entire school had a crush on you?'

'Well, I don't know about that. It could be quite lonely at times, and I felt a bit of a stick-in-the-mud. In the dorm I pulled the sheets over my head or pretended to sleep if ever naked figures went scampering past. I did feel I was missing out.'

'I don't think you missed out on much. I don't remember much of all that. They might have wanted to do things, but you know they were all too bourgeois and inhibited. I used to long to be at some great ancient school, with a real rigour of vice.'

'Well, you and Ralphie did okay.'

'That wasn't vice, darling, it was love.'

I saw Willie's almost instant mastering of the surprise of

234

being called darling, watched him as he sprawled a fraction more unguardedly on the sofa, as if to deny the intrusive intimacy of my tone and absorb the jolt of grief that must account for it. Perhaps at that moment I saw how isolated I felt in losing Dawn, though he hadn't been mine for . . . sixteen years.

'It's brought so much back,' I said. I went on about that summer, the horrible empty weeks which had just begun to haunt me with their apparent denial of what had come before and of the promise they had seemed to give of what was to follow. I jumped and told him about how good at drawing Dawn was: there was something sexily luxurious about the patient sittings, when the boy who had had me for real an hour before would perch across the room and stroke my outline on to paper, and I felt as if it was me who was drawing him, studying his absorbing gaze, his tongue on his lip where mine liked to be, or wetting his thumb to blur the charcoal with it.

'Were you ever caught?'

'I don't think we ever actually were. There were several occasions of absolutely split-second escapes, you know, when you leap into a deeply studious pose with your pubes trapped in your zip. Everyone knew we did it a lot, of course, and mocked at us out of envy, but though that wasn't a secret, the sex itself was, somehow. But it's like that, isn't it, it's amazing what you can manage, what you can fit in in the unsuspected intervals of the day.'

'I think I must have been a great innocent at school,' said Willie, with a certain self-satisfaction.

'We went out at night a lot of course. We used to meet up by the river.' For an instant only I seemed to smell the damp mud and half-see the river moving in the dark, conspiratorial or perhaps indifferent. 'You remember those trees down behind the CCF sheds. I don't know what kind they were, their crowns were much paler than the rest, they seemed to gleam in the dark.' The dense twiggy mass around the trunk, like some involuntary eruption of secondary life, the leaves dusty and sticky, dropping on to the verandah of the army hut, which by a trick of memory appeared with taped-over windows, as if in wartime. The leaves would be falling even now, the life of the

235

school must still be going blindly on: perhaps kids were huddling at this moment in the smokers' riverside bivouac beyond, or snogging intently in the dubbin-scented hut, unbuttoning each other in the glow of SM McGregor's breathy gas-fire. This was an aspect of the corps that Willie, who had been big in the army cadets, was unaware of; and maybe the hut seemed a glamorous rendezvous to me because I had opted out, and spent those long parade-ground afternoons in the alternative vacancy, the smoky idleness, of 'community service'.

'Do you like being out at night?' I asked, not because I wanted to know, but so as to license what I wanted to say about myself.

'I haven't really done it much. Except you know ... in the car.'

'It may be too late for you now. You need to do it when you're a lad and you feel like part of a secret society, and an old, country thing, standing still and seeing night-sighted animals busying about.'

'Not being night-sighted oneself . . .'

'After a while you are. I can't remember the individual nights, isn't it awful, that whole phase of my life has somehow rendered down to a few scenes – being out under the trees, lying in each other's arms looking at the stars, our naked legs in night breezes and moonlight, seeing a fox trotting round and round on the path by the gym, trying to levitate on the cricket pitch: you remember the levitation craze, I think I did actually levitate . . . and of course all the things we did to each other, well, it was levitation in a way, I don't need to tell you what love's like, but perhaps that's why it's all a mood or just an impression of blackness. I was too pressed up against him to see.'

'You seem to have seen a lot,' said Willie kindly, perhaps touched by my moist-eyed, slightly fanatical manner. 'Um, have another drink,' and he leant across with the bottle and I let him pour as if unaware that I had to say when. The lovely confidence of that tarnished gold liquid in my grasp, the sense of being provided for, of knowing one could come through. I plucked off my glasses to rub my eyes and saw the lamp-lit room and my friend's pale face in an intimate crepuscular blur, like a little etching by Edgard Orst. And I felt the spirit of the

236

time that I had summoned up pouring past me like a night-wind through woods around a lonely shack or long-abandoned nissen hut where two boys squat and banter over a ten-minute fire of twigs and rubbish. My heart was thumping with the certainty that when I put my glasses on again Dawn himself would be leaning forward from the sofa, his teenage eyes and mouth unveiled by love.

'Of course, we had to get away from Lawrence Graves.'

'Christ, I'd quite forgotten . . .'

'Old Graves was mortally put out by the whole business. I tried to make him feel wanted, and I used to have Dawn round for Bruckner and Mahler sessions in our study, but Graves got into absolute paroxysms of irritation if we even smiled at each other. He'd be conducting away and though the music was all part of it, Dawn and I could almost forget it was going on somehow, we were so full of our own latest memories and plans, and he would catch us smiling at each other . . . I think he wanted to kind of hijack our affair, take it over or blow it up.'

'He was in love with you himself, presumably.'

'Of course,' I said impatiently, covering the fact that I had never quite realised that. 'Of course. And it's true that Dawn was never exactly brilliant or enthralling company unless you saw the point of him. I remember coming in one day and finding he'd been waiting for me for hours. Graves was sitting cross-legged on the floor in front of him as if he was trying to mesmerise him or get him to reveal some potent but unguessable quality he had. He was really trying to get down there with him. I said later how poetic a picture it had been – poetic was one of our permitted terms of acclaim – and he turned quite nasty. "Poetic!" he said. "He talked prose to me all afternoon!"'

Willie didn't smile. 'I feel rather sorry for Graves, being left all alone at nights, being told to turn his music down by Head of House W. Turlough, whilst his best friend, actually probably his only friend, was running round naked on the cricket pitch with someone who was clearly more attractive than he was. If I'd realised at the time I'd have been nicer to him.' I gave a humorous snarl at this attempt at a joke. 'What became of Graves, by the way?'

'I wonder.' The last time I'd seen him was vividly clear to me, shocking and secret. Or maybe it didn't matter. Willie ought to know these things. We were both men of the world, of different but adjacent worlds; and we were about the same age now, though Willie seemed to me to have entered the placid, incurious middle phase, the semi-sedation of hetero expectations, whilst I was still running loose, swerving and tripping through the romantic undergrowth outside. He must be thirty-five, I was thirty-three, would be thirty-four in the week after Christmas; but as always I felt that my age was only a term of convenience, an average age, and that one moment I was donnish and past it and the next a bewildered youngster scarcely out of school. I took my glasses off again to spare his embarrassment.

'Do you know about Mr Croy's?' I said.

'No, is it a prep-school?'

'Not exactly.' I gazed at the overlapping aureoles the lamps cast across the ceiling, and saw again the astounding scenes in that house. It was years after school, it was after Cambridge, in my own brief spell as a schoolmaster, on a rainy half-holiday, when I made one of my irregular, urgent visits, and found Graves there, with a crew-cut and ear-rings, and the young assistant from Levertons flushed and greedily at work on him, ribbons of saliva down his chin.

'Well, the thing about it is . . .' I said.

'What is it, sweetheart?' Willie asked quietly. I smirked at the new endearment.

'You see . . .'

'Can't you sleep?'

I looked across with a frown and blush of my own. A little blonde ghost had appeared at the sofa's end, and Willie's strong arm opened towards it and brought it noiselessly into his embrace.

'Sit with us for a while.' I pushed my glasses on again and saw the child wriggle and shake her head and hide her face in her father's shirt-front. He rocked her for a bit, resting his chin abstractedly on her curly crown and gazing at the wall. 'Sorry, Edward, do go on,' he said, snugly, as if he were rocking himself to sleep. 'She'll drop off in a minute or two.'

'Oh, it doesn't matter.' He didn't protest, he seemed to find

238

security in the reawakened claims of fatherly duty. I knew he'd prefer it if I went.

Before long the child was asleep, or had wandered at least into the dream thickets on the path towards . . . I hunched forward and made half-pissed conventional noises about her beauty and temperament.

When he came down again I was waiting in the hall.

'How's that drink?' he said.

'I've finished it.'

'Gosh.'

'I'll get back to my mother's.'

He stood in his socks in the doorway whilst I turned on the step and looked up at slow-moving cloud and three or four stars.

'See you tomorrow,' I said. 'I've got to read, god knows how I'll manage.'

'You'll do it beautifully. Do you want a taxi?'

'I'll walk a bit and perhaps get the little bus if it comes.'

'I haven't asked you anything about Belgium and your job and . . . I don't even know why you went.'

I grinned at him. 'Oh, the usual mixture of panic and caprice – 'I couldn't explain to him why this was a place to get out of. I stepped forward with a shiver and slipped my arms round him and hugged him and after a second or two he gave me a comforting rough rub between the shoulderblades. I kissed him on the cheek and then pushily kissed his mouth, until he shook his head away.

'I can't,' he said, 'I'm sorry. I mean I'm so sorry about everything.'

I waited at the bus-stop at the end of Willie's silent road, wishing I had never come, and thinking about him with a sullen charge of sexual violence. The night was damp and autumnal, the suburban birch and willow leaves came flitting down on to the tarmac, gathered in puddles or were swept about by the breeze in little dying sallies. I stood reading a notice about August Bank Holiday excursions to Brighton, Eastbourne and Dover. At the top a red bus surged forward in steeply exaggerated perspective and a cheery driver raised his cap – oh, the blind future tense of old announcements! How

wrong it was to disclaim our adolescence, to wince at its gau-
cheries and ignorance, when we would be lucky to recapture its
first-hand vividness and certainty. I read the schedule with a
quickly gratified eye for misprints, then scuffed around, uncertain whether to start walking. It was the odd economics of
time, the way waste demanded more waste, like cruising a boy
on the street or just waiting for someone, anyone, up on the
common on a summer night, not knowing if further waiting
was merely adding to the tally of lost time or if it was the essential prelude to a pleasure that would be all the greater for the
falterings of hope that came before it.

At Stonewell each year we had a field-day when the boys
were divided into squads and despatched on surreal errands to
test their initiative: bring back a letter signed by a bishop, or
souvenirs from six Cinque Ports, present a baby to a master in
disguise on Beachy Head. A kind of home-sickness coloured the
early phase of the day. Hitch-hiking was forbidden, and whilst
a few such as Dawn slipped away by bike, the rest of us
amassed in sprawling bands at bus-stops and the local station,
as if reluctant to separate, hoping feebly to tag along with our
rivals, or to absorb the good luck, the slightly manic confidence
of the two or three who were already making with maps,
cameras and phone-calls to high-placed relations. But when we
were an hour or two away from school, forlornly tramping up
to the gates of top-security dockyards or trespassing through
woodland in search of sham ruins, anxiety gave way to a guilty
suspicion that none of it mattered, a muddled sense of futile
freedom.

The days always took place in a perspective of failure, we
never expected to get an interview with a submarine captain,
and we were often stranded as evening fell at some inconvenient
spot requiring to be rescued by the harassed masters in their
station-wagons. Getting home turned out to be the real test of
initiative, and we failed it. We waited at a shelterless bus-stop
just like this, as the rain came on, playing basic games of chance
with tossed coins. I remembered that once I was with a couple
of others, including the palely introverted German boy Peter
Rott (Tommy as he was known) who grew his nails into buckled claws and disguised the length of his hair by not rinsing out

240

the shampoo: as the rain fell on his matted pine-scented head he began to bubble gently, and suds ran down his face like sleepy tears.

My father didn't have a few more months, he had just over a year; he died in that month of shadowed insouciance that precedes the arrival of the A-level results. I was relieved that it wasn't in term, that I hadn't been called out of school to be told, that it hadn't messed up my exams; but later on I mildly regretted the loss of the acclaim and respect that should have been due to me. By the following term, when I abruptly began to grieve, it no longer merited my schoolfriends' puzzled consideration.

His ashes were strewn on the common, because he had loved it, but the idea seemed so gruesome to me that I stayed alone in the house while my mother and Charlie and my Uncle Wilfred set off up the hill, uncertain whether they were a procession or if they should go a bit faster, like a family out for a walk. They had chosen an ordinary workday morning, quite early, when no one much would be around to wonder what they were doing, or have to avert their eyes in sudden understanding and dismay. I hadn't wanted to see the urn – more like my mother's rosewood sewing-box than the samovar I had imagined – and found it hard to accept that my father, the same size, more or less, as I was when he died, could have been reduced to this neatly portable and disposable quantity.

I sat in a kind of frozen observance of my own in the sitting-room, with the silent monument of the piano, the massed records and the unsinging sheet-music – my mother had left a Bach aria open on the music-stand. From beyond, Sir Thomas Beecham peered out over his signature with a look of testy merriment that I thought inappropriate. I thought how much people know when they die: that canterbury full of music, not just known but gone into in some adult never-satisfied way that I couldn't understand. I had always been too easy and ignorant a judge, and said it was lovely the first time, and also the second quite different time, and soon lost patience as he kept working it towards some future state I couldn't envisage and which now would never be.

His going was so slow, and so unprecedented in my experience, that I found it hard to bear in mind or even to believe in. He was quieter than usual, hating to make a fuss, but sometimes coldly demanding. He was glad that I was getting on with things, racing out after minimal bursts of revision to meet my friend on the common, showing the stifled high spirits of a boy with a secret happiness; his occasional words of reproach rankled with me for days, since I knew I was spending less of my time with him than before; an unadmitted fear of illness kept me away. 'Let's have some music tonight,' he would say, and catch my hesitation, my momentary reordering of my plans.

A large oval mirror hung by two chains above our fireplace. There was something aloof about it – it was never one of those mirrors that embrace a room and give it back to itself with a hint of strangeness and enhanced worth. Though I had become rather vain of late and conceited about my inky quiff, I tended not to consult it; but when we had a record on and I was sprawled on the sofa opposite, my eyes would dwell on the slipped horizon of the wall behind me reflected in its high ellipse – a sun-yellow wall like an empty beach reaching up to the sky of shadowed white ceiling, a birdless distance that took on splendour or desolation according to the music and the varying light of the months.

It was about that time that music, which had always been around me, and was identified, through the scent of polish in the sitting-room, with the very air I breathed, gained a new and independent grip on me; I suppose it was love that made me see a Mozart concerto or a lyrical and exultant Schumann symphony not simply as a wonder in itself but as a kind of explanation of life. Like love it seemed to admit me to a new dimension of luminous purpose: music raised my expectations to an ideal level that other friends found comic or unbelievable if they weren't initiates themselves. At school we were played some bits of Janáček, which were the most convulsively life-like music I had ever heard. I gathered up the scraps of Supraphon record-sleeve information, cryptically condensed and obscured by translation, that were all that could be found out by an

English boy, and was amazed by the lateness of his flowering and the fact that this bristling old gent should be the one to confirm everything I felt at seventeen about life and sex and being out at night with winds and stars.

And what were my father's thoughts as he sat limply in his armchair, head back, eyes on a different distance, later on sometimes slipping into noiseless defenceless sleep? He was only fifty-five, only lately robbed by chemicals of the thick black hair we had always had in common; he hadn't reached his late phase yet. He started singing as a young man in the Navy: I imagined his mess-mates gathered round him or lying solemn in their bunks as he crooned some old salt-water ballad and their ship slid on through the moonlit toy sea of a British war-film. He must imagine those days too, I thought, rather than look forward to the final sudden crisis; but I knew he would never say. There was a beautiful accidental integrity about the galaxy of thoughts inside that listening head. Almost everything he knew and felt had never been spoken, never sung, never known to another soul.

The ritual events of the summer unfolded, both more intense and more trivial than usual. The May Day bank holiday fair came to the sloping football-pitch by the Flats, and gave me its annual, slightly threatening surprise as I strolled over the common on Friday after school and saw the caravans and dogs among the new greenery below and heard the mingled roar of generators and jangle of carousel-music. I saw Dawn there later in the company of three of his sporting friends from Drake, leaving a fortune-teller's booth with grinning faces, leaning superbly in at a shooting gallery, then wandering on, the others lighting up, watching shaken kids unloading from an aerial whirligig, Dawn secretly following the acrobatics of a teenage fair-boy swinging from pole to pole on a kind of switchback roundabout. I half-hid from them, paralysed with possessiveness, and dully tensed against the sarcasms that would break out when Dawn and I came together. We had a rather unhappy notoriety by then – ours wasn't a classic prefect-fag tendresse: our terms were worryingly for real, they sounded a deeper note than was tolerated in their lumbering, not unloving, locker-room camp.

Then it was Wimbledon again, watched in illicit paragraphs of two or three hours amid the final exam preparations, sometimes with Ogg's *Seventeenth-Century Europe* numbly open on my knee. Mirabelle was in electrifying form in an early women's heat I saw and seemed to call 'Fault' obliviously at every first service. One of the men players from Eastern Europe evidently had an enormous penis, which I never heard the commentators refer to. I imagined Mirabelle would have some tales to tell about him.

I loved the dream acoustics of Wimbledon, the curtains drawn but the windows open behind them, occasional noises of traffic, distant shouts from the sunny common or close-up chatter of people walking past, louder and more unguarded than we were, as if they had leant right in to the lulled half-light of the room to say 'Yeah, well see what she says' or 'No you fucking don't!'; then, recessed within this, the hushed, attentive sound-world of the court, whose irregular pock-pocks and applause and torpid rallies of commentary themselves gave way from time to time to a further unseen dimension, disconnected applause from another court, the sonic wallow of a plane distancing in slow gusts above, that a minute or two later would pass high over our house as well and drown out the television as it passed. The whole experience was one of oddly compelling languor, an English limbo of light and shade, near and far, subtly muddled and displaced. My father seemed satisfied with it, as if his family could share for a while his own powerless and agitated calm.

There was to be no holiday, of course, for the second year running, and I felt ashamed by this further evidence of the decline of the Manners family. The previous Christmas I had secured a distracted agreement that Dawn could come to Kinchin Cove with us and looked forward to it blindly in the teeth of all the warning signs. My mother rather liked Dawn, who helped with the washing-up, shared in her gentle mockery of my sixth-form posiness, and had a reliable second-row-forward straightness about him; she couldn't make out why we were such inseparable friends, and there was something sweet about her frequently exaggerating his good points, as if these must explain it: 'Ralph's got *bottom*,' she said to me one Sunday

244

morning over pastry-dough and apple-peel. But by the early summer, brittle and hollow-eyed with her own anxieties, she had forgotten her promise. I made a scene about it, half-aware how I was disgracing myself, arguing really I suppose against something else.

I told Dawn it was off and took him some photographs of the cottage from an earlier summer, the beach and rocks just below, the shallow river that ran out over the sand, the loafing figures of Charlie and his genuinely unsuitable friend Gary Quine, who got wrecked in the Wreckers, called my parents by their Christian names and gave me, when I was twelve, my first awed lesson in the use of a rubber johnny. Dawn wasn't much bothered about the place I loved and wanted to bring him to as a new brother, who could teach me to dive. He slipped an arm round my neck, gave me a long hard-working kiss and said why didn't we go off together, camping – we could go to France. He'd already opted out of his own family's trip to Spain. I knew with a sudden grave certainty far bleaker than that of my father's death that I would never go to Kinchin Cove again.

We went to look at tents, quite unaware of their cost and complexity and scaling our plans down from 'The Sultan' through 'The Marquess' and 'The Cavalier' until we ended up with a titchy dun-coloured thing called 'The Pilgrim'. 'I think you'll be rather on top of each other in this one,' said the sales assistant.

The plan that we have a trial night on the common came from my Uncle Wilfred, who had supervised innumerable camps for the de Souzay Trust and stressed the importance for both of us of knowing how to *pitch* and *strike*. It was a wildly exciting idea, clouded at first by the fear that he was going to come up and instruct us himself. But no. He would be sitting with my mother, as he did increasingly in my father's last months; she was the only woman-friend Wilfred had and the evenings, kindly meant, were a strain for both of them. 'Your uncle's more of a man's man' was all my mother ever said about him. Cues for anecdotes about their shared childhood produced only grouchy vaguenesses; when she was fourteen he had gone to war and in a sense the rest of his life had taken place under military camouflage; all we saw was an impatient self-discipline

245

and a sardonic tendency that never quite rose to humour and was especially disconcerting in these visits intended to comfort and distract. At the time I knew nothing of his constant sexual appetite, and it is possible she didn't either: like so many siblings they had nothing useful in common and their attempts at sharing things were marked by childish awkwardness and dogged cross-purposes.

Wilfred checked the kit for us. 'Done it a thousand times with the Susies,' he said, peering shrewdly at Dawn, who was bending to unbuckle his rucksack and looking somewhat resentful of the old boy's drill. I thought he might be critical of The Pilgrim: he declared it ambiguously to be 'a tight little tent'. 'Having a cook-up?' he said. I told him we were just taking scotch eggs and a bar of chocolate, which he clearly thought feeble to the point of effeminacy, but my mother snapped that there was nothing else. I ran upstairs to say goodbye to my father, who was lying on his bed fully clothed. I asked him how he was feeling and he said, 'Not very good, old boy', which was the most he ever did say, and left me habitually at a loss how to answer him. On the turn of the stairs coming down I heard my mother saying hurriedly to Wilfred, '. . . a week or two, perhaps, they say, probably no more' – so that I went into shocked slow-motion, my hand to my mouth, and after ten seconds jogged down in a forced briskness of concealment.

We hiked up the familiar paths, Dawn deliberately testing my loyalties with a good imitation of my uncle. Mimicry, like drawing, was one of his gifts, and both were literal and so at times unsettling. I responded with cowardly jabs and pinches, knowing that he would get me back later with some stifling, bare-breasted wrestling hold. It was still quite early and we wandered across the network of summer paths scuffed and scrawled through the dry grass; we didn't want to pitch our tent in the dark but felt self-conscious about doing so whilst walkers and lyrical late kite-fliers were still about. Probably the best place would be on the far side, the way Dawn came from home, where there would be shelter by the copse-like remains of ancient hedgerows. We circled back to the pond and sat on the bench, eating our scotch eggs and watching anglers packing up their gear. The boys among them trudged away with their rods

and folding chairs like little old men. Behind them the silhouettes of pines and poplars were reflected and the sunset
opened canyons of pink and ultramarine in the pond's muddy
depths.

'Better look out for the folding star,' I said.

'What is this folding star?' said Dawn, with the annoyance of
hearing me keep saying it and having pretended before that he
understood it.

'Don't you know your Milton?' I said pityingly. 'The star
that bids the shepherd fold? As when the folding star arising
shows His paly circlet? . . . Dear me.' I put an arm round his
muscly shoulders and squeezed. 'It's when you know you've got
to put the sheep all safely in the fold.' He shrugged himself free.

'What about putting the boys all safely in their tent?' he said.

'Yeah.' I couldn't actually see the star in question but maybe
it was best to set about it. I was always spoiling things with my
quotations – he saw them as a kind of sarcasm against himself.

The Pilgrim took about five minutes to put up. Dawn dived
into it as if scoring a try and when I looked in through the flap
he seemed to take up all the space. I felt he'd laid a claim to it
that I would never be able to challenge. I slid in alongside him,
in the mackintosh-scented gloom, shocked by the lumps in the
ground. 'It's a good job we like each other,' I said, slipping a
hand between his legs and stroking his balls through the soft
cotton of his tracksuit bottoms.

'Just think. Nice. Antibes. Juan-les-Pins' – each name said
with savoured French Oral vowels.

'Mm.'

He rolled on to me with a fierce grin that faded into a stare,
lips parted, holding his breath then sighing it out suddenly over
my face with a hint of sausage-meat and hard-boiled egg. He
was working his stiff cock against my thigh. I ran my hands
over his lightly sweating back and down under the elastic to the
damp cleft of his arse – he curved his spine and my middle
finger just reached, and drew a gasp from him as it touched his
tender muscle. An outlying root of the ancient hedgerow
pressed harder and harder into my back as if to register a
serious objection.

247

I struggled out from under him and he took it as a turn in the sex-tussle till I said, 'I'm just going outside for a minute.'

I peed into the bushes and then strolled a short way across the hillside. In the late dusk the blanched, feathery heath-grasses looked almost luminous against the darkness of the woods. I sat on a round tump, it might have been a tiny tumulus, and looked out at thin cloud and distant lights. I'd never been this far this late, hearing only the rumour of cars on the London road, the patter of leaves like rain that slackens and stops. Tonight was like being given the keys to a bridal suite: we had come up here with an unwitting blessing. My lover and I. I wrapped the word around me like a stole. The wonder of having a lover – I saw us for an exhilarating moment from outside, the amazing thing we had done. Other boys at school had girlfriends, of course, and left you in no doubt about what they did with them; but what tawdry affairs those were – you saw them hanging around the shops at Saturday lunchtime, in a stumbling embrace as if each had to drag the other along. And how confident and independent we were, how we'd struck home to the real thing.

I looked back at the tent, dimly illuminated from within by a torch, and the shadow-play of Dawn on all fours inside, getting it ready for the night. I fell into an awful blank puzzlement at times about why it had to be *him*; and panic at the thought of hitch-hiking alone with him to Juan-les-Pins – so at his mercy, in those dusty roadside waits, the duty to keep up our spirits, my condescension and his touchiness. It might be very nice to be doing it with another boy, like Turlough or Hall; but they, of course, had shown no interest in seducing me. I saw myself deliberately breaking, no, twisting, my ankle, very badly, just outside Calais and having to come home.

A man was standing about thirty yards away, staring at the tent. I thought he hadn't yet seen me, despite the little eminence I was on: the khaki glow of the canvas and the bobbing rump-shaped shadows thrown across it from inside held his attention entirely. He stepped forward cautiously, stopped – turned his head to catch any sound. I was fascinated by his thinking himself the observer, unguessed in the dark; and chilled by the freedom it gave him, the unhindered time he had to spy on us or to do us worse harm. He saw me, seemed to ponder for a while what to do, then started slowly in my direction. I thought it would be absurd to move away, but stood up, as if I had been spotted in a game of hide and seek, and waited with my heart thumping in my chest. I thought he might be a kind of night-ranger who could tell us to move on, frighteningly without a uniform, so that we wouldn't know whether to obey him or not.

He stopped again a few feet away, slightly stooping forward to mime his curiosity. 'Hi,' he said, tentatively. A loud owl-call came from the wood, and then another, further off. I couldn't tell if they were real or people signalling – I knew real ones always sounded like imitations. He turned his head towards them and the faint cloud-gleam showed steel-rimmed spec-tacles, a white square face with swept-back dark hair. 'Someone's making a night of it,' he said. The voice was troub-lingly cultured, with a hint of drink-blur – he wasn't aware of the long pause that followed as I worked out how I could escape him in the dark. I'd played and stood about all over here, but the dimensions and positions were vague at this moment. 'Looks rather tempting, don't you think?'

He felt slowly, amusedly, in his breast pockets, and brought out cigarettes and a lighter. 'Do you smoke?'

'No' – it was a little anxious cough. 'No,' I said again.

When the lighter flared I saw him lit up for several seconds; black leather jacket, grey jeans a bit tight around the midriff, the ghoulish chiaroscuro of the face above the flustered flame, wishful dark eyes lifting to make out what they could of me. The image floated on the moment's blackness that followed, suspended in the dry warmth of French tobacco smoke.

'How old are you?' he asked.

'Eighteen,' I said, adding on a year as if I had been challenged in a pub. And then, with a tenuous politeness I thought would protect me, 'How old are you?'

'Thirty.' He exhaled ponderingly. 'Three.'

Even more than I'd expected. I felt it like a sinister disgrace, being out in the night with this person, the menacing vagueness of his intentions, the seedy self-confidence of the queers out in their secret element. I'd better walk off quietly towards the tent.

'Why don't you come over here?' he said, with a new intimacy and tenseness. He swung his cigarette arm out in a casual shrug of possibility, but stayed where he was, as though not to waste the effort if I wasn't interested. 'Well – suit yourself. I'd like it, if you'd like it.' I couldn't associate the voice with anything to do with desire. It was like being propositioned by an announcer on Radio 3.

'No, thank you,' I muttered offendedly. And then to my great surprise: 'My father's very ill, actually.'

He took this in with another glowing pull on his Gitane. 'Shit.'

'He's only got a couple of weeks left to live,' I explained carefully, though it was myself I was explaining to.

He threw his cigarette away into the dry grass and I watched anxiously in case a fire began to crackle round it – there hadn't been rain for over a month. I wanted to criticise him bitterly for that. 'Hey, hey, hey,' he whispered heedlessly as he came up close. My face was stiff, I wasn't actually crying, just breathing out through my mouth in brusque sighs. When he put an arm around me I was hugged into leather and smoke and beer – it was horrible but remotely consoling, the firm clutch of another world that could take me if I let it. He stood and rocked me as if I *were* crying – I felt pinched and self-conscious not being able to, the vessel of tears sealed up tight inside. I slid my arm woodenly across the stranger's back. I thought, if my father could see me now . . .

'Edward, Edward?' – a low querying call. Dawn's unmistakable form, the swish of the grasses in his hesitant approach. The stranger smudged a kiss by my ear at the moment I broke away.

'No . . . no . . .' I was saying, almost under my breath, as I hit at his arm and half-stumbled in my desire to get free.

'Edward . . .?' both of them said.

Dawn was triggered into the sudden belligerence I found both unnecessary and exciting. 'Fuck off,' he said to the man, with a short, spittly chuckle.

'Okay, okay,' backing off a pace or two. 'The kid's upset, okay?' A wariness to his tone, as though he'd heard this before.

He began to walk away and called back, 'He just wants looking after.'

'Fucking queers,' said Dawn with another incredulous laugh. And then peevishly to me, 'He can fucking look after himself.'

I couldn't answer that. I felt lost and utterly unknown. 'It doesn't matter,' I said. 'He didn't do anything.' I turned back towards the tent. If only we were in our respective homes, if we'd just put the tent up one morning in the garden to see how it was done. I hated the tent, and the hours to come, with Dawn squashing me and nowhere to escape to but the night and its predators. I wouldn't say anything about it now, but I felt I could reasonably get up at first light, under the pretext of writing a poem.

When I looked back I could just make out Dawn running very fast across the slope, the retreating stranger peeping round at the last moment as he brought him down with a quick easy tackle, got up and jogged back. Beyond them both, on the crest of the hill, figures were moving among the trees.

I hadn't been in All Saints for years and had forgotten what a reassuringly unsacred building it was; the old village church had been replaced in the late eighteenth century by a broad stuccoed box with an organ gallery and white box pews and a huge east window of clear glass, with trees and the vicar's upstairs windows visible as one sat and listened to him or thought about lunch. Only the old grey west tower had been kept from the earlier building, and that was under wraps again, being gently cleaned by weeks of running water. I arrived early and found the vicar negotiating with the masons about sheltering the mourners from the incessant cold downward flow. Then we went inside and pulled the chains that kindled primitive overhead heaters: I paced around through their warping blast, getting the feel of the place, more distracted by nerves than grief. I remembered the nausea that preceded class when I was a schoolteacher; even a personal tutorial could approach with a certain chill tread. 'Oh darling!' I gasped, and loitered, fiddling with a pew-door's loose brass catch, lost in a gripping day-dream of love for Luc.

'Everything all right?' murmured the vicar, resting a hand on my shoulder and swishing his alien skirts against my legs.

It was wonderful who came – our old friends, school contemporaries I hadn't seen for a decade, unfamiliar queens from London in oddly cut, somehow cheerful suits, antiques young men and other frauds, a tall deaf man whom nobody knew, who was Colin Maylord's father, a lad fresh off a motor-bike (oh Ralphie!) climbing in leathers and pony-tail into a pew beside startled country aunts and uncles, Gerald and Anne de Souzay, grandly self-effacing, with Edie's unhappy young brother Pip. I went to greet them, like an usher at a wedding, wondering if perhaps Edie wasn't coming. I was apprehensive about seeing her, after what she had been through, and about seeing her grieving, which I knew might be more harrowing than the grief I felt myself. But she had stopped outside to talk to Danny and Simon, and came in just behind them looking pale and composed, with the ghostly beauty people sometimes have when they are ill. She wore a magnificent black hat, with a tumbled pomp of sooty plumes about the brim. We embraced but said nothing, and she slipped in beside her immaculate mother.

I took a place at a pew's end and waited through that grim interval before the entry of the family and the bearers with their shocking burden of proof. The organist was wittering on through his formless and infinitely extendable introit, music that had never been written down, mere sour doodlings to fill the time, varied now and then by a yawning change of registration like a false alert. The occasional chink of a chisel or half-sung call came from the workmen outside. A sliver of a last night's dream came back to me and melted away as I tried to grasp it. Matt in the bar teasing me and mocking me with the story of how he'd seduced Luc the afternoon I'd left town – how easy it had been for him, the boy almost bawling for it, four, five times, how he was having him again tonight ... I started thinking forward impatiently to my return flight tomorrow, wishing away the unrepeatable hours.

A prospect of the backs of heads, the part of yourself you

didn't know about, which always came as a surprise in a clothes-shop or a barber's glancing hand-mirror, the part so trustingly turned to a lover. There were heads here I'd sat behind in school: Tony Barnett who used to stow his hair into his turned-up collar with the aid of grease and paper-clips, a big director of commercials these days with a shiny bald patch like a tonsure; Hilary Smythe (poor fellow), teenage cottager you saw hanging on the railings by the traffic lights in town, along with the drunks in torn tweed jackets, looking drably smart now, with a grey moustache; beside him that broad-necked figure like a boisterous but not ill-natured dog, actually called Boxer, captain of rugby, mopping at his eyes with a red hand-kerchief; in front of him the forgotten Sindon twins, Doug and Greg, or was it Greg and Doug, completely unchanged, brilliant swimmers interested in nothing else – I suddenly remembered their address, like a far-off holiday, and their bathroom with its smell of chlorine and drying towels – they were here in padded silvery suits; I wanted to lick the identical blond ferns in the hollows of their necks.

I couldn't listen to much of the service before I was on; we sang a hymn with the wrong tune, so that nobody did more than mumble till the last verse. I tried to sing, but was voiceless with tears, glancing forward to the awful box, which held what was left of my friend for the little while before we burnt him again. I kept trying to name people, not to fidget as the time raced closer. Suddenly the vicar announced my reading, before the Gospel, much earlier than I expected. I looked stupidly about, hoping that no one might have noticed. The audience settled back, some blowing their noses. There was a thin wail from Dawn's mother in the front row, I knew how she must long for it to be over, but must want it done properly. So I went up and read.

One morn I miss'd him on the custom'd hill,
    Along the heath, and near his fav'rite tree;
Another came; nor yet beside the rill,
    Nor up the lawn, nor at the wood was he;

The next with dirges due in sad array

> Slow through the church-way path we saw him
>   borne . . .

My father brought me through it, reminded me how to clear my head and strike out with that impalpable falsity that actors need. As I looked down through the grey November light at wretched faces, I remembered him describing an audience and its expectations, the control of yourself you needed to control them. They wanted something from me that it was surprisingly in my power to give. 'Speak out,' he said. It was rather like on certain still nights, I had never told anyone, but I felt him stooping out of the dark continuum he was banished to and pressing about me with advice too stern to be strictly followed.

Back in my seat I was quietly elated, almost expecting congratulations, and took a moment or two to adjust to the heavy-heartedness around me. I'd shared a sympathetic smile with one of Dawn's sisters – all three were in the front row with their parents, two of them married to men who sat between them with the diplomatic dry-eyed look of outsiders. It was odd the role these women played in my sense of Dawn, odd that in my keenest memory of him I was absent and they were there – their family holiday, when he was just sixteen.

It is some banal Mediterranean resort, the sand shuffled and rubbishy at the end of the day, the sea still and salivary, the four children tearing about, Ralph muscly in tight little trunks, his shoulders pink from the sun, lightly terrorising the girls, whom he keeps on kissing and pinching, picking up and throwing into the water. He is full of unfocused energy which finds issue all day long in teasing and chasing, broken by spells of lordly basking, when they rub creams into him and, hoping for a truce, bring him drinks. He is all potential. His sturdy little cock gets hard as he nestles in the sand, and he likes to surprise the girls with the jut of it; they are censorious about it, as they are about his four chest hairs, and as he is about their breasts. What a busty little group they are. The day cools and the girls trail in while he has a last swim – a long fast lap of crawl. Then I see him wait out there, treading slowly, breathing sharply, looking back at the land where the first lights have appeared. He kicks

254

his legs apart and feels the cool water touch his grateful sphincter. No one ever knew, no one ever will know, so I have him thinking of me, back at Rough Common, thinking of him, waiting for him, reaching down, as I imagine him doing, to feel the quick undertow of possibility.

The cars bearing the family nudged their stately way out across the abashed, resentful traffic for the drive northwards to the crematorium. The rest of us gathered loosely on the gravel, I ran over to Edie and we clutched each other in a brief agony of sobbing and stifled shouts. The de Souzays were to give a reception later and she said to come with them now. I clambered into the back of their long senatorial Daimler and into the hushed, complex atmosphere of this other family. We crept forward giving sympathetic smirks to the people who hardly heard the car. Gerald lowered the window and called out, 'Come to us at one, you know where it is', though the Sindon boys looked a bit at a loss. The lad with the motor-bike seemed to have made friends. Others straggled along the road into the centre of town, advised of the fire and mulled wine at the George IV. Out ahead of them was a brisk stooped figure in a dark grey coat and trilby, flicking his walking-stick forward at each stride.

'Can we fit him in?' murmured Anne, and her husband slowed as she lowered her window in turn. 'Can't we give you a lift, Perry?' she called out. But he kept on walking, merely raising his hat and hooting back, 'I'm fine, thank you!'

'See you later, then.'

'He's nearly ninety, you know,' she said as we moved on. 'How very sweet of him to have turned out.'

I glanced back at him, wondering if he'd remembered our meeting as he heard me read, now that I was fatter and older and never wrote poems. He still looked about him in the same way, as if anticipating greetings, still had that air of redundant youthfulness. There was something moving and irrelevant in his having come, as though Georgian England must be represented at these end-of-century exequies.

Later, much later. Five and twenty to midnight the greeny-white figures dimly showed. The day doused in drink and almost out. I rambled home from someone's house, alone but charged up by intense communings with virtual strangers, the compulsive unity that follows a funeral and its unambiguous end. The night was damp and still, the street-lamps hazed among the nearly bare trees, a moment I recognised when no one was about except barmen from pubs walking their Alsatians, taxis bringing passengers from the last train and leaving their perfume of burnt fuel.

I turned into Fore Street and saw an unusual phenomenon: across the far end a great roll of pearly fog that gave the lamps at the common's edge the air of a promenade at a melancholy lakeside resort. Fog had become so rare in my adult years that I looked on it as something miraculous, lucent but opaque, unaccountable in where it lay. I walked towards it slowly, down the middle of the road, and when I got to the low fence, stepped over and into its drizzly embrace.

To my slight surprise, it was almost dark inside the fog, but I soon hit the path, and the land was so familiar . . . I turned up my coat collar and found it misted with little drops. I was exhausted but hated the idea of going back to my room with my thoughts. The path steepened, and then suddenly the fog ended. I came up out of it into a different night of glittering air and a strong enough moon to throw long shadows in front of trees and bushes. I loped on up to the top with a shiver of exhilaration.

The fog circled the hill, and lay thick away to the east — the Flats were submerged, beyond them only the leafless crowns of the tallest trees showed vaguely in its surface. To the south other hills rose out of the pale floe like inaccessible friends, who none the less shared the sense of occasion, the hour or two of local sublimity. I pictured the silent foreign streets I was going back to, under the same moonlight. It came to me that it must be tomorrow — no, later today — that Helene was to be married. Surely she couldn't sleep. I wandered along the ridge almost expecting to be able to see the city's towers.

When I got to the bench I found I wasn't alone. It gave me a moment's gooseflesh, as if the person sitting there had abruptly materialised. I wondered if I'd been talking to myself aloud. He turned his head a fraction, but not so as to look right at me, and the moon glinted on round glasses. He was a black kid – by the generous extension I gave to that term year by year – perhaps in his early twenties; he was perched on the bench's back with his feet on the seat; I made out a woolly hat rolled down and a puffy waistcoat over other dark clothes. We stayed as we were for a while, sharing the unusual view and its mood of stillness and oblivion.

'Amazing night, isn't it?' I said lightly, just for form.

'Yeah,' he said; and hopped down from the bench as though about to clear off, because I'd spoilt it for him. 'Nippy.'

Was it? I'd drunk too much to notice – but, yes, our breath made smoke. He'd probably been up here for ages, too; thinking something through. It took me a while to realise he was holding out a hand towards me.

'Feel that,' he said indignantly.

I clutched it, it was cold and felt chapped; held it for a queer moment longer, only now seeing the point, and he squeezed my fingers back. He let out a sigh and pulled himself towards me in a kind of dance-step, and then we were hugging – he smelt nice, some ordinary girl's fragrance. We kissed sulkily, with a minor clash of spectacles.

I decided I was into this, and fumbled around his waist; his intake of breath as my own wintry hands touched his skin. The bubbled waistcoat made him look bigger than he was, but he had a round, hairyish backside and when I groped through the tangle of undone shirt-front and lolling belt-buckle I felt the start of something beautiful in his rough crotch-hair and had to tug it out, thickening and obstructing itself, from its prison down a tight jean-leg. I could barely make it out in the night be-tween us, while he pressed against me, rubbing at my fly, kissing me with surprising fervour all over my face, his tongue slipping over my glasses and smearing the lenses. He was all stoked up, in a way I couldn't quite match but marvelled at, and at the chance that brought me here on this November night, which was otherwise a cold prospect for both of us.

257

3

A Merry
Goose Hunt

15

Cherif had grown a moustache. It was thick, not quite as broad as his mouth, and gave him a pugnacious expression; the appealing curl of his upper lip was disguised. I hesitated before taking a seat by him at the bar. 'You probably don't recognise me,' he said.

I rested a hand for a second on his cool leather shoulder. 'I recognise all the rest of you.'

'That's good.' In fact there was shyness behind the bristles. 'I thought you must be dead or something. I've been in here the last three nights.'

'Not me, someone else: I've been home for a funeral.'

He turned his glass around on its mat. 'I thought you might be at that men's sauna, I went there.'

I knew about the place, I pictured it in a deeper shadowy circle of the city's sex-life. 'No, I never go there. Any good?'

A shrug. 'One or two guys . . . I didn't really do anything.'

I noticed I was pleased he hadn't. 'I don't have the figure for sauna sprawling any more.'

He kept frowning at his drink and said, 'You look really thin' – with a hint of criticism, an implied allusion to the wasting of unappeased love? I ordered a beer for myself, and added one on for him.

'So where have *you* been?' I said.

He leaned towards me and pushed his hand through my hair and stayed stroking the smooth little knoll behind my ear with a gentle thumb. I thought he'd probably had a few – it was the mid-evening lull already. I'd come in straight from the airport, a bit queasy from turbulence and a string of miniature malts and the mad cabaret of the Kentair stewards.

'Nowhere,' he said. And I thought maybe that was enough curiosity shown.

261

He called something to the barman, who was slow to respond, and gave the impression Cherif was not his favourite
customer as he handed over a newspaper that had been stowed
behind the till. It was the *Flemish Post*, a few days old, folded,
slightly browned already, with the brittle texture of newsprint
that has got damp and been dried out. Cherif set it in front of
me, pointed to a short article, and then watched me as I read it.
I knew his grasp of the language was poor and he seemed to
take the piece in again by following my reactions to it.

'Hm,' I said, pushing the paper back towards him.

'We had the police in here talking to everybody.'

'Oh.' I looked towards the article again. It said how the body
of a young man had been found in the sea-canal; Pieter who-
was-it . . .

'It's Rose,' said Cherif, 'the one you called Rose.' A moment
of uncomfortable recall – his big twitching fist with the girl's
name pricked in blue across the knuckles, his pin-point pupils
and nervy patter and crude attempt to hustle that older man.
The barman came past and took the paper away again.

'I threw him out,' he said. 'Dangerous sort. Drugs. A week or
two back. Not queer of course,' he explained. 'Either a waste of
time or it means trouble.' He turned with a single firm shake of
the head.

'So what have they found out?' I asked Cherif.

'I don't know.' Well of course he wouldn't, but I'd hoped for
a little more. 'He was mad, perhaps.'

'He talked a lot of sense to me.' But Cherif was melancholy
about it. 'You didn't know him, did you?'

'I met him in here, that's all. You sound like a policeman.'

'Sorry, darling.' I drank, and looked down the half-empty
room. It was a doldrums hour, the juke-box silent, the TV hec-
tic but noiseless, one or two bores in uncontested command. I
stroked the back of his hand.

'No, it is a horrible thing, someone just being taken out, so to
speak.' I had my own grief and was alternately resentful and
full of sympathetic intuitions.

'It doesn't matter,' he said.

But he came back to it later, as we lay in the dark: the jingling
of bed-springs was over, I was just asleep, looking for my bunk

262

in the workers' hostel Cherif was staying in, such a confusion of doors and unlit stairways ... Something about 'Rose', out in the cold canal, I think he only called up the image and let it palely float, nothing more to say about it – a kind of dread, though, underneath.

Then I lay awake in my turn, as his breathing slowed, his mouth squashed open against me, the tiny stirring of his moustache hairs on my shoulder. It seemed to have been dumbly agreed that we were back together again. I even believed it myself when we got to my room and we were at each other, just like the first day we met. He said he hadn't come for a fortnight, he'd never gone so long, his cock stood up like a soldier, he wanted me to wank him off so he could admire the sight of such plumes of sperm. 'I was saving it for you,' he said, and my heart sank, though I pretended to be flattered. Then afterwards each of us took the other and I was utterly enclosed in his unguarded fucker's tenderness – I mean lover's tenderness, I knew he loved me in each strong inward push, his face bobbed down to mine in a cross-eyed blur of passion; he couldn't sense the little clench of denial amid my own shudders and grunts.

It was cold by the morning, at least outside the gathered fug of the duvet. I jumped straight into jeans, two vests and my thickest sweater, and he was shivering as he wiped a hole in the window and peered across the misty garden to the dark mass of the school. I felt rather guilty and hugged him from behind and looked out over his shoulder; but there were no ancient rites today, just steam blowing from the kitchen vents and a dull glow of stained glass. It fed a fantasy of power, being fully clothed and holding a naked man in my arms.

'What are your plans?' he said mock-formally when he was dressing. It was a notion of his that I always had plans, and that making them constituted one of my main satisfactions; and I was starting to realise that any plans I announced to him were a defence against his own vagueness and that he knew this, and knew that my days in reality were as plotless and inevitable as his own.

'My first plan,' I said, 'is to take you out for some breakfast. You worked hard last night, young man, you deserve it.'

'And your second plan?' he said, hopping towards me as he

tugged on stiffish old socks, contriving to stumble and pull us both back on to the bed.

'My second plan is to pack you on to a tram, bus or other public conveyance and get you off to your place of work.'

He was putting a line of kisses up the side of my neck, pushing me gently backwards, till he lay half-covering me. 'And your third plan, Mr Manners?' There was a hint of aggression in this game, which seemed like a distant parody of 'witty' sex-talk in an old film-comedy.

'Well, after that I've got to, er, I've got to do some teaching.'

He lay very still, and I could feel his heart beating indignantly.

'Are you teaching Luc?'

I pushed myself free of him and sat up. 'For god's sake don't go on about that,' I said. 'That's all over long ago. I can't think what I ever saw in the little shit.' I walked out into the main room, improvising as I went; I didn't want to watch his re-actions. 'He's so ... so arrogant, and lazy, he's impossible to teach. He's got a girlfriend. I mean ... He's not attractive, his mouth is horrible, as everyone says, it's virtually deformed...' My flesh was prickling and I had tears in my eyes from the confusion of play-acting and heresy. I kept myself hunched away when Cherif padded after me and hugged me from behind in his turn.

When I swung into Long Street I nearly tripped on a busy little terrier that yapped in alarm and scampered aside. I looked up and there was the bearded figure of Old Gus. He came on with his glaring swagger, his stick slicing as if at grass-stalks. I stepped aside myself, and as I was just by him he halted and said amiably, 'Could you spare me a few francs?'

I pretended for a moment not to have heard, but then in an old muddle of principle and superstition dug my hand into my pocket and brought out all my change, quite a bit, a couple of quid, started to pick among it and then just gave it all to him. I felt an immediate certainty of worth, of providence's palm being greased and of a prompt reward, an hour of new sweetness with Luc.

Old Gus pocketed the money, and stared at me with his withering eye. 'Bastard!' he barked, with hatred and ferocity, smacked his stick against the pavement, turned on his heel and stamped off.

I stood there grinning out of sheer alarm and an odd sense of shame, and then went slowly on towards the house. I peered about defiantly, but I felt my surroundings had instinctively sided with Old Gus. The austere façades were clouded for me by this brief injustice; their vigilant high windows looked on an offender, someone who brought no credit to them. I answered them back, but for a moment I hated the street and the long perspective of failure to which it had condemned me. I stopped to collect myself and spurred myself on with the beautiful new idea of an outing. I would borrow Matt's jeep for a day, pick up Luc quite early, showered, talced, full of curiosity and a sense of privilege, and drive out to some historic town for lunch, a walk, both of us admitting boredom in the brown old museum, conversation freed of the inhibitions of the Altidores' dining-room and their starchy ancestors. To be out in the storm-crossed countryside together, both rising to the occasion with new charm and candour! And then – best leave it there. I sprang up the steps and pressed the bell with a zing that felt slightly manic.

His mother opened the door, clasping a knitted orange shawl round her throat and almost over her mouth. 'Quick, quick,' she said. 'We've all got colds.'

'What, all two of you?'

'I got it from going out in the rain, and now he seems to have got it from me.'

You stupid old nit, I thought, just don't *go out* in the rain. I thought of him almost like Dawn in his latter days, he must be kept from the least infection. 'I'm so sorry.'

'You may prefer to cancel your lesson.'

'No, no,' I said with a hasty cough, a covert self-inspection as to whether I didn't myself have a slight sniffle.

She shooed me into the dining-room, still with the shawl swept across her face. She was very pathetic in it, like an elderly actress playing a veiled houri. Then she flitted off, leaving me with my darling's forebears. There were those I saw each time, who hung facing me and behind Luc, and whose features I tried absently to map on to his in a kind of genetic photofit; and the others, behind where I sat, whom I looked at for a moment now. There was the interesting Guillaume, with a thin grey book in his hands, but a dull picture. Why didn't he get our mutual friend Orst to paint him rather than this conventional journeyman, whose muddy signature was already obscured by candle-smoke? And balancing him, his wife Anona, the Princess Cirieno, no less, a fine-featured woman with sexy eyes but equally subdued to the sobriety of her new family. And after them, nobody; it was as though they had hidden their faces.

'Are you going to be painted?' I asked as I heard Luc come in.

'Not like that,' he said. 'And not like this.' I turned and saw what he meant.

'Oh,' I mildly protested. And really his invalidish look touched me in a new way. He was pale, sore-eyed, bothered by his cold but perhaps finding something luxurious in his achy passivity, in the enormous woolly, chequered neckscarf and baggy old corduroys he was slumming in; he was more glamorous for looking shitty, like Garbo playing a tramp. His hair was dark and greasy and stood in thick furrows when he ran his hand through it.

'Don't come near me,' he said humourlessly as he pulled out a chair at the far end of the table from where I had left my music-case.

'All right,' I agreed with a pained laugh.

'So what does your L stand for?' he said, with a nod at the gilt-stamped initials on the black leather.

'It's not my L,' I said. 'It was my father's bag for his music, I think I told you he was a singer. I've just brought it back with me from England.' My mother had suggested, with some emotion, that I might like to use it. 'Edward Lewis Manners. ELM, a kind of tree we don't have any more in England, thanks to some beetles from Holland.'

'So you don't have a middle name?'

'Yes, I do actually.'

There was a pause. 'Is it a secret?'

'Yes. No, don't be silly. It's, it's Tarquin, in fact. I always think it sounds like a horse,' I added hysterically.

'I'm quite pleased I don't have a middle name,' said Luc.

Mrs Altidore tumbled in with my coffee and a lemony drink for her son. He hunched over it sniffing, cross and negative.

'LA stands for Los Angeles,' he said.

'It also stands for Library Association.' I knew everything it stood for, not all of it repeatable to LA himself.

'I'd like to go to Los Angeles.'

'I don't think you'd like it when you got there,' I warned him, 'it's extremely violent and the air's poisonous.'

'It's also a long way away.'

'I'm not sure that's necessarily in its favour.'

'Oh, I think it is,' he said, nodding and staring past me out of the window. I undid my case in the chilly silence that followed. He'd exposed me to his anger before, and it scared me, mortified me, even though I knew I was not its object, merely the listener who was there when it chanced to be expressed. There was something mad and unsocialised in it. 'Let's not talk about the William Wordsworth today,' he said, as I opened the book.

'Okay.'

'I'm not ready to talk about it yet.' So he hadn't looked at it, I thought. 'I'm not quite well, you know, we can just talk.'

'Okay.' Sure, whatever you like. I started looking for an uncontentious subject, as he sniffed the vapour from his mug; but I was clueless with unhappiness.

'So you have had to go back to England?'

'I'm afraid so.'

'Then you prefer it here?'

'I suppose I must do,' I said, thinking how I had been sick to return, and how odd these personal questions were from him, who had never shown so much curiosity before. But he turned aside again to a bleak comment of his own.

'I would prefer to be there. I am looking forward to going to the University of Dorset, if I can get permission.'

'I'm sure you will do very well. I'll be able to come and visit you and take you for drives to Maiden Castle and Cerne Abbas,' I said, recouping something of my earlier exeat fantasy, and only then seeing the Freudian gaffe of my choice.

'Cerne Abbas is the man with the giant prick?'

'That's right,' I said briskly, through a broiling blush, 'it's a late Roman chalk figure, probably of Hercules . . .'

'I'd like to see that,' he said firmly, though the implication was that he could do so under his own steam. The sad ghost of the couple of Dorset visits I'd made when Dawn was there drifted like rain across my image of vast grassy hillsides. It was obscurely moving, like a dream sighting of a lost friend, that Luc was set on going there too. Then I remembered the wind-swept walkways of the campus and the lethal loose cladding and the sticky carpet of the students' bar.

'The friend whose funeral I've just been to was at Dorset, that's why I know about it.' For once I regretted the invitation to intimacy; he looked at me levelly, in a way that slightly frightened me – boys don't want death around, spoiling every-thing, they haven't felt it if they're lucky, like Luc. Or perhaps his stare was one of capable sympathy, narrowed and hooded by his cold.

'I'm sorry,' he said flatly. 'Why did he die? Or she . . .'

'He. He was killed in a car-crash. It was very sad. He was very ill anyway, he had AIDS; but he probably had a few more months to live.' A snatch of the funeral's heightened sorrow made me turn my head aside.

When I glanced up again Luc seemed shaken himself. He had the hunch of new responsibility that team-mates have when the ambulance trundles from the pitch and they jog back to their positions, one man down, amid instinctive brief applause. Something had touched him. He started talking about car-accidents. He said you never had accidents if you thought you might have one, because it was the essence of the accident to be a surprise. I said you could drive down the wrong side of a motorway and be pretty sure of causing an accident, but he maintained that it wouldn't be an accident for you, because you did it on purpose – though of course it would be for the totally unsuspecting persons that you drove straight into. He seemed to feel fairly confident that this sophistical state of readiness would protect him on the roads, and I couldn't quite get him to see through it. And in a way I agreed – rather as one imagines terrible losses, as I sometimes, with prickling scalp and hot tears, imagined his death or disappearance, as a charm against its happening. I said, 'I hope you're right', and even so was filled with a superstitious fear of one or other of us being squashed by a lorry the next time we ventured out.

One of us will go first, I thought later, as I sat in the Cassette waiting for Cherif to turn up, drinking keenly to heal over the morning and the gape of the quickly darkening afternoon. A year from now I won't be here and nor will he. I was by the window for a change, looking out through its brown wrinkled glass at the wonky street – it was hard to tell who figures were as they loomed and flowed under the stained street-lamps. A raw air from the sea filled the squares and alleys this evening, as it did the phantasmal night-scape of the coast and Channel and boats wrecked on the Dorset rock-stacks that was all I could see of the future. Well, let him go. I'd backed out of the house after twenty minutes, with minimal politeness, pleading his ill health as if it were mine. I didn't even go to the bathroom.

Cherif came in about five and I was lifted by his reckless grin and ignorant confidence. We kissed and his jerkin was cold and slippery. When he came back from the loo I watched him approaching down the length of the bar – his cock looked lovely and lively the way he had it, middle and leg inclined to leg, I thought, transporting him for a second to the alien field of cricket. He sat down as it nudged into a major hard-on – a fact not wasted on the bar's arch-bore Harold, whose window franchise we had strayed into. He leant between us in a jet of pipe-smoke and said, 'You're very lucky to have this young man, you know' – a remark which seemed both insulting and in some ways unquestionably true.

'Did your lesson go well?' asked Cherif, almost with a note of mature concern for his trampled rival.

'He was ill,' I said, 'terrible cold, we didn't have the lesson.'

'Oh. So what did you do all day?'

Cruel question. 'Well, I had Marcel Echevin in the afternoon. We did cloze tests. It was fun,' I said bleakly.

'What's that?'

'It's when you miss out words from a passage and he has to provide them to show he's understood it.'

Cherif looked alarmed by this. He ran his hand up my thigh,

and gave me a fluttered kiss as if to blink away all this stuff he didn't know or care about anyway. I went on, 'I might say, "Cherif Bakhtar comes from Paris – he is a ____." And he will say . . .'

'"He is a very sexy man".'

'No. "A Parisian" is what he will say. It has to *follow* from what I said; actually that does kind of follow, I agree.'

'And I will say, "Mr Manners comes from England", and he will say "He is a very, very sexy man".'

I suppose there was a sort of wretched charm in this squashed joke. 'I don't think he would say that, you know. He's in love with a beautiful girl called Sibylle. Unfortunately for him Sibylle is the girlfriend of Luc.' I ran the name in quietly as a test for both of us – he gave a sweet cooing laugh he had, whilst I heard a drumming protest from my heart at the syllable, and the pain of his coldness, and the force of this supposition about the girl. Otherwise – I went on to myself, while Cherif had started talking again – why did he pretend she was not at St Ernest all those futile weeks ago? Hadn't he told me, even earlier still, that she was his closest friend, and set my prospects sickeningly askew? Why did nothing lead anywhere but to the stale air of this bar and the blond shallows of the glass?

'. . . and it was really cold,' Cherif was saying, 'and it started to rain, and I didn't have anything.'

He slumped into an indefinably fictional posture – I'd seen it before, where he acted out his own neediness, made a quite possibly unconscious bid for sympathy.

'You ought to have a proper coat,' I said – like my firmly benevolent mother again. 'That skimpy little jacket's useless.' I was kind of fond of it, a street-market bargain of years back, fashionable only in a time-locked Third World way, the gingery surface coming off in patches, like cracked veneer.

He shrugged. 'Okay, but I haven't got the money.'

'Don't be ridiculous. You must earn good money, doing all that heavy work, whatever it is.'

'You don't understand,' he said. 'I have my mother and four sisters in St-Denis and I send it all to them.' He made a new gesture he had at his disposal, parting his moustache with thumb and forefinger and sweeping his palm across his mouth

270

in a way suggestive of secrecy or an only partial truth. It may sound odd but I liked the hint of pretence, it was a relief from his coltish open-heartedness, even if I was the one to be exploited.

'All right, I'll get you a coat,' I said, knocking back the rest of my drink and handing him the empty glass.

Alejo's shop was still open, though you wouldn't have known it from the shady discretion of the front, which gave it the air of a sex-shop or a turf-accountant. Cherif followed me hesitantly into the spotlit hallway, puzzled as I had been by the chic absence of stock. One could have, it seemed, a hanky, or a rubberised vest, or a single green shoe. Alejo himself was loitering at the counter, languidly folding a shirt. He looked captivating in racing silks and olive velvet breeches.

'Hola, Alejo!' I called out gittishly, but it was enough to make him look and remember me.

'Hello,' he said, trotting forwards and kissing me Spanish-style on both cheeks.

'This is my friend Cherif, he's feeling the cold, he wants an overcoat.' They shook hands, and Alejo walked round him a couple of times appreciatively before leading him through the mirror that was a swing-door into the busy grotto of the shop. I followed on, warmed by my new role as patron, but also reaching down for a certain prudence, like a parent at a school outfitters. Through the speakers came Doris Day singing 'Buttons and Bows'.

'Rudi, can you go on the till,' he said to a little blond in braces; 'I'll look after this one.' Rudi whispered something and glanced across the room as he went out. 'Trouble in number three,' Alejo explained cryptically, and ran straight on with 'Your friend is *fabulous*.'

'Do you like him?' I said, looking at Cherif as he walked along and shyly felt the sleeves of a rack of coats; maybe we could come to an arrangement.

'Where did you find him? Are there any more?'

271

'There must be some fairly similar. In the Town Museum, actually, looking at a picture of Heaven and Hell.'

'Well, I know which one you got!' I stroked my chin consideringly. 'After the coat I'm going to interest him in some other things.' And he sprang off to guide him, a hand confidentially round his upper arm, almost resting his cheek on his shoulder.

I wandered about for a minute, idly flicking through the clothes on the rails. There were a lot of idiosyncratic items of a kind you'd never wear but that a colour-blind trendster might carry off at a party or club; there was plenty of leather, with weirder cuts and zips than my own dear old jacket; and there was a strong vein of Englishry, Tattersall checks and thunder-and-lightning tweeds. I tried one of the jackets on but it made me feel like Jimmy Edwards. A third assistant, who was very nervous but had learnt the basic cant of salesmanship and stuck to it through thick and thin, kept telling me it really suited me.

I put it back on the rail and in the mirror beside me was my rival. I looked down quickly and then slyly peeped and saw that his smile extended beyond his own admiration of the black denim jacket he was trying and called ironically for my opinion of it too. 'Hello there,' he said. 'We keep on meeting.'

I turned and gave him a black stare that I couldn't keep from weakening into residual good manners. 'Yes, don't we just.'

'You remember I ran into you twice. You're English, aren't you? You're usually with that tall, fair Belgian boy. Amazing-looking kid.' I felt sick of being complimented on the beauty of my companions. 'I can't remember what his name is.' He turned sideways to check the cut of the jacket and show me his compact backside – perfectly acceptable in itself but irrevocably horrible by dint of being his.

'Hans,' I said. He raised his chin and frowned in the mirror as if to say he didn't for a moment believe me.

'We really ought to have a drink some time,' he said, with the same menacing naturalness. 'You know, two Brits abroad, mutual interests . . .'

'I'm afraid I don't drink,' I said, probably with a trace of beer on my breath. Probably he'd seen me in the bar when I was far gone.

'Amazing shop this, isn't it? It's like a fairy grotto.' He looked at me archly. 'What do you do, actually?'

'I'm a writer.' I turned to see how my friends were getting on.

'I don't do much at the moment,' he said. 'Well, I work out.' He smiled and peeled off the jacket. I thought for a disgusting moment he was going to start working out right there. He pulled a bill-fold from his shirt-pocket and handed me a card. 'If you change your mind,' he explained confidently. I shook my head but he held it out till I took it, with invisible fumigation tongs, and walked off down the shop with it. To my confusion it didn't say 'I am a noxious berk' but 'Rodney Young – Researcher'.

Cherif had picked a rather New Look full-skirted brown coat with wide shoulders and a tie-belt. It was going to cost me a lot but I was determined to go through with it, without quite understanding why. I supposed it was a substitute for the love I couldn't return, or what's called throwing money at a problem and is always held not to work. He turned up the collar and stepped back to the mirror, to catch the surprise of his metamorphosis. And it was a different Cherif, bourgeois, self-conscious. It seemed to imply that further changes would have to be made: those old jeans, those dusty boots, that cap. Alejo's ideas were even more radical.

'What about some new undies, to go with it?'

'I can't afford anything else, I'm afraid.'

Cherif came and hugged me and I sniffed in the expensive and assuaging wool smell. 'Thank you, my friend,' he said. It struck me that it wasn't a practical coat for going to the docks. I supposed he'd carry on wearing his old what was it?, *bolero*?, to work and the coat would at once be elevated to luxury evening wear. The whole exercise was a useless indulgence.

Alejo bobbed back with some slithery packets of underpants. 'You can have one of these with the compliments of the house,' he said quickly – obviously an offer to be kept from the management and the one or two other customers moodily riffling the shirt-shelves.

'Which would you like, darling?'

'He'd better try them on,' said Alejo demurely.

273

Cherif was helped from his coat and sent into a curtained cubicle, wondering if he was being made a fool of.

Alejo drew me aside. 'Whatever did you do to my poor cousin from Bilbao?' he said.

'Oh dear . . .' I laughed guiltily. 'Agustino. Well, I think I . . .' I didn't quite know what I'd done, of course. 'What did he say?'

'He was too shocked to say anything,' said Alejo solemnly.

'I certainly didn't do what I wanted to,' I said. 'I guess I just fell madly in love with him for two or three hours.'

'He breaks everyone's heart,' Alejo confirmed. 'And you know he is still a *virgen* – his parents are very strict and religious. All my queer friends are crazy about him, they keep sending him flowers and asking him to imaginary parties.'

'I haven't seen him around lately, you know he sometimes stays next door to me.'

'Oh, he's moved from there! He couldn't stay next to you!' I was aghast. 'Only joking' – he laid a hand on mine – 'he has a room of his own, I'll tell you where.'

'There's not much point, is there?'

'None at all,' he said complacently.

'You're clearly a very attractive family,' I pressed on.

'Come with me,' he said, and led me through a door into the shop's back room – bare bulbs, a sink, a white work-table, clothes pinned and chalked for alteration. I wondered if I was about to go down on him. 'Look at this,' he said.

Mounted on a ledge at the side was a small black-and-white TV set, a security monitor for the shop. It showed the central area in an odd convex perspective, a customer passing beneath looming with enormous cranium and dwindling curved body ending in tiny shoes. It made me instantly suspicious, the distortion seemed to challenge you to notice the thief's shifty recce or his smooth concealment of some small pricey item. The lack of sound enhanced the sense of stealth.

Alejo turned a knob and the scene changed to the front vestibule, if anything even more sinister for its emptiness. In the bottom corner little Rudi was lolling at the desk, staring at nothing, unaware he was being spied on. He looked at his watch.

'Now let's see what's up in number three,' said Alejo and

switched again. We had a steep-down view on to the row of changing-cubicles. 'It's amazing what you catch on this camera – I don't mean sex, just the things people do.' I knew uneasily that he must be right – those crises of contemplation, envisaging the changed future some garment seems for a moment to guarantee. Over to the left the naked upper part of my rival could be seen, pale and powerful, clouding his underarms with talc.

'What the hell's he doing?' I demanded.

'You have to do that for the rubber vests, you know, or you never get them off.' Alejo kept watching professionally, like a policeman waiting for a hesitation to turn into a crime. 'We've had a lot of trouble with him.'

'I'm not surprised.'

'He's weird, he keeps trying things on but he never buys.'

'Why don't you ban him?' I said, though my indignation was sapped by the view of the cubicle immediately below. It was clear that Cherif could not be less interested in the chi-chi underwear he was being tricked into trying; he hadn't even opened the packets. I was pleased and somewhat possessive. My friend was simply sitting on the narrow bench and turning a piece of paper over in his hands. Then I knew, despite the plunging perspective, that the paper was a letter I had written to him, in our very first week, full of unguarded declarations, and marked by me in various shamefully personal ways. The two of us frowned into the little screen as he tilted his head back and ran the letter contentedly under his nose.

16

Later that week we put the triptych together. Paul was jumpy and hard to please, and when he asked me to do things for him I got in the way. The facilities of the Museum were so cramped, he needed to close the first-floor gallery to assemble his new acquisition, and brusquely dismissed a polite young student who was already in it copying, as well as the woman who came in to do the typing. On the threshold of his fulfilment we all seemed potential obstacles, who needed to be thrust unsentimentally aside.

We were waiting for an overnight courier from Munich, bringing the central section, the townscape. I knew these were special art-transport experts, but I couldn't banish the image of a lad on a mud-streaked motorcycle, with the canvas strapped on the back. At the same time the loaned wing from Switzerland was being flown to our little airport, the whole thing being destined to converge in a nerve-racking climax just before lunch. As Helene was abroad on her honeymoon I opted to get out of the way and sat at the front desk, with my chair tipped back against the dim warmth of a radiator.

I was reading the text of an article Orst had contributed to *The Studio* about his childhood summers in the Ardennes. He described the days of preparation, the tremors of anticipation that ran through their well-ordered household as the morning of departure approached. Then it was the train to Brussels, the 'stupendous and terrifying impression' of the capital after the empty thoroughfares and grass-grown quays from which they had come; a second train to Namur, and after a long wait, 'when it seemed that for all our efforts we might never arrive', on to St Hilaire, where the great towers of the basilica, glimpsed from a distance through the forest as we approached, gave the first assurances that our pilgrimage was ending and that we should shortly be traversing the blessed domain of Givrecourt. On descending from the train we were welcomed by my grandfather's coachman and conveyed to the house in a great black carriage which quite resembled, to the imagination of my sister and me, a stage-coach of the last century, sent to bear us off into the regions of romance.

The manor of Givrecourt is a low old house, from the time of Charles V, with tall old trees about it, a mighty barn and stables and a hamlet of ancient cottages. It lies in a safe declivity among the pine woods and oak forests, the bleak sandy heaths and upland bogs of that high country so astonishing to a child reared on the level Flemish plain, with only the theatre of the skies and the plains of the sea itself for contrast. In Flanders, for those with an eye for landscape, there is extent without contour; a design ruled by the single and inflexible horizontal, which cuts the picture in two and advances indefinitely before and all around, and is not without its force and grandeur. But here the straight line was everywhere turned awry – in the quaint old work in stone and plaster and the time-worn floors of the manor-house itself, in the gnarled and ancient giants of the Forest of St Hilaire, whose boughs dropped wearily to earth and then rose up again in fantastic forms, in the rocky outcrops above, which reared against the sunset like wind-bitten visages of heathen gods.

I have been at Givrecourt since then in other seasons: when the woods were full of snow, or in the autumn twilight – loveliest and most tragic of times. Among the pictures I have lately exhibited in London were a number of studies of a pond there among the pines, done on a spring morning or in the winter dusk; as well as others of the village people as the evening finds them, the forester in the lane, the gamekeeper ready with his bag and gun. They were said by some to lack the merits that they discerned in my work before, and by some to show a wish on my part to leave behind the legendary subjects that are for several of us the highest calling. But to me they are merely further expressions of an idea that lies beyond legend, and to which legend offers the most inexhaustible and luminous forms. I mean of course the little door each picture opens upon mystery, upon the unknown and the unknowable. To the admirer of my mysteries, the silent pond and lanes of Givrecourt may serve as thresholds to the ineffable as surely as my Medusa and my Percival. And if it be objected that my gamekeeper and my sacristan have voices of their own and call out to us in tones that break that subtle harmony, I can say only that they are also the voices of my childhood, and that the imponderable harmonies of childhood linger beneath all that I attempt to do.

The article was dated October 1898. I knew that a year later he would have met Jane Byron, and that she would be dead.

The three pieces of 'Autrefois' didn't fit. Paul had leant them against the wall, side by side, like some classic puzzle, simple in its elements but requiring genius IQ to solve. The left-hand part was the one the Museum had already, the candle-lit image of the woman whose face was seen only in the mirror. It appeared on postcards and posters and I thought of it as an icon in itself. It had its original frame of dull gilt wood. The right-hand wing, the seascape, had been reframed and stood several inches higher, its intense dusk colours heightened by a broad surround of silvery pearwood. The larger middle panel, the deserted town, which had undergone so many vicissitudes, should have had a huge recessed frame, into which the hinged wings could be folded, and a broad plinth. Paul showed me the murky old studio photograph, in which the triptych could be made out, its doors open as if on an altar, and for the first time I caught the shock of its arrangement, the figure of the virgin displaced from the centre, the gothic townscape, such as often clustered behind a Flemish nativity, unpeopled and sepulchral, and where at the edge the donors might have knelt only the grey sea and violet sky.

'I'll have to get Mr Pauwels in,' said Paul, 'our historical framemaker. The right panel has obviously been cleaned quite recently, only last week by the look of it, whereas the dentist's part is relatively filthy and more damaged than I realised when I saw it before. Of course the light was very bad . . .' He appeared both thrilled and forlorn about the work, and inspected it with extraordinary technical thoroughness. I wondered what it was he read in it inch by inch.

'When do you think it was painted?' I asked.

He stood up and steadied himself with a hand on my shoulder, as though momentarily dizzy. 'That's a very good question.' We contemplated the slightly pathetic reunion of the three canvases, which now seemed to me like long-separated friends who no longer have much to say to each other. 'And one that you should be able to start answering by now,' he said, giving me a tutorly shake.

'I'm afraid I've only been looking for spelling mistakes,' I said.

'Well, there's a kind of spelling mistake in this.' I scanned the pictures again, knowing I wouldn't find it, and gave a shrug.

'I suppose the seascape is quite different stylistically.'

'It is indeed. One can be pretty sure that it was painted at least ten years after the other panels, possibly as late as 1932. His sight was deteriorating steadily then, and he only painted from memory. You can see how broad the handling is, and the composition is of the simplest. I mean, I think it's a very beautiful picture, and a very moving one – his later works sometimes have that kind of force.'

'Helene was telling me about the white pictures,' I said, not without a certain nervousness. I saw his twinge of weary annoyance.

'Yes, I'm afraid that's all a lot of nonsense,' he said, as though determined to be reasonable. 'I refuse to show them as finished works – they're only prepared canvases in many cases. Helene, bless her, was very taken in by a young art-historian from Paris who worked here for a while and started giving them titles like "Dans la Neige". The fact is, Orst couldn't see. As you must have realised he was riddled with syphilis, he tried bravely to keep on painting, almost as a kind of optical experiment, while the fog closed in. If they do have any interest then it's purely medical.'

279

'I see. I'd no idea – that he had syphilis.'

'He could still paint, with vision, as it were, up until about '33. The other two panels can be dated much earlier, as they're both copied from known photographs. As for the syphilis, yes, of course.'

'I suppose I should have worked it out,' I said uncertainly. 'I don't think you mention it in the guide, do you?'

'I've never laboured the point. I mean, it's known, obviously. I'm afraid I'm of the school that rather disapproves of publicising artists' private lives,' he said, with an unhappy stiffness that was quite at odds with his normal shy cleverness.

'I'm not sure.'

'You forget that I knew him; and – I'm sorry, I don't know why I'm lecturing you. It's simply a matter I have strong views on.'

I spread my hands to deny any wish to contradict him; though it was surprising to learn that the monkish Orst, the exquisite recluse, had been the victim of this quaint, almost romantic, sexual disease. I thought Paul could tell from my expression that I was going to want to know more.

'It's ironic of course', he went on, 'that he could never see very well anyway – at least from about Marcel's age onwards.'

'Really. Well, I've noticed the thickness of his glasses. But his work is usually so incredibly fine.'

'Close up he was all right, his sight was superhuman, but anything more than a few feet away gave him increasing trouble. He was just very myopic, as so many artists of all kinds are.' Paul squinted sympathetically at the pictures against the wall, and I felt as if my own short sight had been flatteringly vindicated and explained. 'I remember he said to me when he was completely blind how strange it was that into his fifties he had had an eye like a microscope.'

'So what about the portraits, and the landscapes even?'

'Oh, they were all done from photographs. Of course he gave up portraiture after about 1900 anyway. The later landscapes, all the Givrecourt pictures, were simply based on earlier pictures, with brilliantly imagined or remembered changes of light. They used to create the impression, in the galleries, that he went there year after year, but actually, no. Not after the turn of the century and all that change in his own life. Well, you can see he didn't need to. And he couldn't. The old house there was sold to finance the Villa Hermès.'

'It's strange, I was just reading his piece about Givrecourt this morning, and thinking about what lay ahead for him.' I was never quite sure if Paul grasped the full extent of my innocence about his man. 'So did he not travel at all?'

'Hardly at all. He still went occasionally to London. Once or twice to northern Germany and Jutland. There was a brief trip to Italy, but he didn't like the abruptness of the southern sunsets, and never went back there. In general he followed Rembrandt's advice, that artists shouldn't travel. What is rather revealing – I can't remember if it's in what you were reading, but he tells how as a boy at Givrecourt he was set to study and copy his grandfather's collection of English watercolours, and how he was painting Suffolk scenes and the Lake District indoors before he was allowed to go and paint the forest just outside.'

'I used to think how odd it was that he photographed Jane so much, but perhaps it wasn't after all, if he needed the photos to paint from.' It seemed an explanation of something I knew I had never liked about him, the work prolific but not abundant, the passion chilled and codified, almost menacing.

'I often ponder it,' said Paul, and drifted across the room as if lured by another image of her there with an orange lily beside her, and an amulet in her open palm. I was very touched, even so, by the way his subject absorbed him, and made him seem both formidable and childlike, as if each judgement were somehow referred back to their long-ago meetings and whatever had communicated itself then. 'It seems to me one of the deep coincidences of art,' he said, 'that he should have amassed all that material with no awareness of how fate would require him to use it.'

'I was wondering if the photographs still exist.'

'Oh yes – well, a large number of them. His sister kept everything, religiously. She wasn't a scholar, by any means, but she did have a high sense of what posterity would demand of her, she wasn't like those famous obstructing widows who make scholars' lives a misery. She passed everything on to the

Museum – even things that must have shocked or disturbed her.'

I noted this impassively and asked another question: 'But you say the seascape wouldn't be based on a photograph or earlier picture?'

Paul paced back. 'As it happens, there *are* much earlier sketches for it. And it is also the subject of one of his blackest lithographs. But the forms are so simple it hardly required any model. With the woman, we have a photograph of 1899 as the *terminus post quem*; with the city picture we have a photograph – in an English volume on *Historic Flanders* published in 1911, on which it is modelled directly. There are complications, which I won't go into at the moment. For the seascape I offer a date on strong stylistic grounds – it comes from a different phase of his career, though I'm sure it won't have escaped you that it is in fact the emotional fulcrum of the whole work.'

'There's a sort of movement outwards,' I hazarded. 'From the interior, to the city, to the open sea. It's like a kind of ... spiritual journey?'

Paul didn't look especially impressed with this. 'I'm not sure that's quite how it works,' he said.

Cherif was lying on the bed, smoking a joint and blowing the smoke over his nodding cock. The rackety little blow-heater gusted the air round and round in a stuffy indoor anticyclone.

'This is all very North African, dear,' I said; 'but I don't actually approve of smoking in the bedroom.' I was banging about, clearing the place up, powered by a few dull resentments. 'Lovely in a brothel in Tangier, I'm sure, but here ...'

'Don't you want some?' he said.

I had started to sort a ruck of clothes into piles before a visit to the launderette, Cherif's thick socks and nylon underpants and cheese-cloth shirts, Luc's bits and pieces that it was a shame in a way to wash, my coloured shirts with fraying collars. I went over and took a quick crackling drag. It gave me the usual giddiness and distant aphrodisiac buzz – I'd never really seen the point. The hot air from the blower went wolfing up the back of my legs, I thought my trousers might get scorched; and he was warm too when I bent down to him and kissed him as I let out the smoke. He was a wonderful kisser and left me each morning with my lips tender and glowing, as if they'd been lip-glossed. And now there was the moustache and its softly scratchy exercises.

He pushed his hand through my hair. 'I love you,' he said, quietly sing-song, a routine reminder.

'Mmm.'

'Don't go out now.'

'I've got to, I'm afraid. Actually, I think my trousers have caught fire.'

He lifted my glasses off, as if to make it impossible for me to leave, and put them on himself, saying now he would have 'Edward's view of the world'. I left him wincing and recoiling at the steep-down sharpness of things, and stepped into the other room, hesitant, with an outstretched hand, not noticing what I was doing. I opened the cupboard to get my leather jacket; it hung there obscurely beside Cherif's vulgar coat, which still gave off the expensive new smell of opera cloakrooms. My life seemed to be one of understandings based on sex and mis-understandings based on love.

Out in the street, shouldering my bulky hold-all, unshaven, whistling that trite song that was played over and over in the Cassette, the song the man had whistled on my neck the day I arrived, 'See Me Tonight' – 'seamy tonight' I thought each time – I came round a corner and saw Paul leaving an old house across the way. Again, the fleeting impulse to go on as if I hadn't seen him: I was too scruffy, too seamy, really. 'I say,' he called out.

'Good morning, Paul.'

'You look as if you're eloping.'

'Only as far as the washerama, I'm afraid.'

'I've just been to see Pauwels about the frame. He's got to get the right gilt to match. I've given him the photograph to go on for the design.'

'Oh good.' It was almost as if my approval were being sought.

'Where is the laundry thing by the way?'

283

I gestured generally towards the area of the shopping streets. 'Isn't it rather a bore?'

'It's not especially fascinating.' Though there had been some nice working lads there last time, folding up old-fashioned winter drawers.

'If you don't mind the walk, you could do it at our house. Lilli's always got the machine going.'

'It's sweet of you. But there's such a lot,' I said, stooping and shrugging under the burden. 'It's not all mine,' I warned candidly.

'And there's something I want to show you too,' he said.

We walked on in silence for a while, adjusting to being outdoors together for the first time. I felt more observant, filled with a slightly precious regard for my surroundings, as though Paul owned the place and were graciously making it available.

'I was quite wrong the other day,' he said, clearly himself unmindful of the splendour of the main square. 'I'm sorry. I could see you thinking something wasn't right.'

'Was I? I'm sure there's no need to apologise.'

'There is because I was being inconsistent. You asked me about the white pictures and I got snappy about sex and said that artists' private lives didn't matter or should be kept secret and then I started testing you with questions which are actually all to do with the artist's private life.'

'I think I thought,' I said carefully, 'that you felt a special respect for this artist, because of having known him.'

'Well, that's perfectly true,' he said, 'though not exactly the point.' He looked at me shrewdly. 'I'm quite a reluctant curator, you know' – almost with the implication I had somewhere claimed the opposite. 'I certainly never planned to end up back here, where I'd begun. As I think I told you, my original field of interest was the seventeenth century; I spent a year at the Courtauld in London, with your famous Sir Anthony Blunt! Then I came back and taught in Amsterdam, and so on and so forth, I won't bore you.' He was nervous these past few days, and I often found him, despite all my sympathetic politeness, my genuine delight in being with him, at least a step ahead of me, or to the side. I caught his arm to stop him as the tram came silently across our path.

284

'I'm not at all clear how the Museum came about,' I admitted; 'I ought to be by now.'

'Well, that is perhaps where the problem lies, the problem of my talking nonsense. The point is if you have been spending years with Van Eyck and so on, and then with Rembrandt and even Rubens, and you have your own passion for Delacroix, or Manet, or Picasso, then Edgard Orst does not seem after all to be an artist of, shall we say, world standing. Then his sister is dying and she asks me to help her set up a trust, to make a permanent museum of his works; she says it was his wish and she thinks I would be the right person to run this museum, which is to be in the family house – where she, incidentally, continued to live, unmarried, to the end. That, very briefly, is the story of how this place pulled me back. And also perhaps explains a little of why I felt the need to protect him. Now if he were a Delacroix I don't suppose I'd worry.'

It couldn't be the whole story. I said, 'Nowadays people are more interested if they know, say, that an artist had syphilis.'

'And even more so, don't you think, if that artist had the image of being austerely celibate? For years the pious people here saw him as a model of devotion, the scandal of his affair with Jane was completely forgotten, they knew nothing about it, they thought of him as a kind of hermit, like St Anthony or something. And like St Anthony he had his temptations.'

In the kitchen Lilli (could I call her that?) was chopping vegetables at the table, whilst Marcel sat opposite, picking bits and being indulgently ticked off. I thought how innocent he was and how Lilli and he carried on like a parody of a mother and child. I wondered what form his passion for Sibylle took, what images enshrined it in his mind. He gave me a friendly greeting, as though I wasn't his teacher any more – an uncle, perhaps. He'd got used to having me around; it showed in his work, which was lazier but better. And as for me, I was charmed to be in their warm kitchen, stuffing my washing hurriedly into their capable machine, accepting an offer of coffee, all ready to be absorbed into these simple Saturday rhythms.

'Will you be working on the picture?' Lilli asked.

I hadn't planned to do anything of the kind – but if Paul

wanted me to ... It would be a few more hours away from Cherif.

'I'm going to take Edward for a walk,' he said. 'There are some things I want to show him, my dear Lilli.' And she smiled warily.

We followed the curve of the streets at the town's edge. Paul had put on a dark hat, which gave him an adventurous look, almost a kind of glamour, with his mild pale dome eclipsed, and a subtle air of self-mockery too. I realised he was excited. 'I don't have your splendid raven locks,' he said. I strode alongside in the mood of suppressed annoyance that precedes being given a surprise.

'That's the old Altidore house, by the way,' he said, as we passed a long building with an arched entrance and tall gables of cut brick. It had the plaque of the regional water-board beside the door, and office lighting glowed inside the warped old windows; but high up there were gothic As in the brickwork. I tried not to show how immoderately interested in it I was.

'When did they sell it?' It was a sudden troubling possibility that Luc had spent his early childhood there. But in fact his gambling grandfather had made the move to Long Street before the war. The Germans had used the house as a local headquarters, Paul said, and the fifteenth-century woodwork had been wantonly damaged before their departure. It was the first time I had heard him refer to the Occupation that must have hatched his own adolescence so darkly.

A nice crew-cut soldier with the bulk of a body-builder came slowly striding towards us — as often happened in these empty streets I saw him some way off: there was time for interest and self-consciousness to quicken or be mastered as you approached each other, strangers crossed with a heightened sense of promise. He was wearing camouflage gear over a roll-necked jersey, the dappled trousers tucked into socks and boots — he looked fit, supple and compact. Charmingly he wore tortoise-shell glasses.

Paul was talking about something and I found myself laughing exaggeratedly so as to make an impression of happy

286

indifference on the young man; at the same time the laugh was a mask behind which I looked at him all the more keenly. I wasn't listening to what Paul was saying and didn't know if he had registered my lapse of attention: he tended to busy on, caught up in the oblique runs of his own thoughts. But he looked across with a moment's surprise as the man drew level with a questioning smile and I let out a bold little 'Hi!' My heart sped up for a while, I even fell a pace or two behind and glanced back at him moving away. It wasn't often you saw a soldier by himself. He was a natural buttocky type, like the young Dawn, though what cut into me was the glint of intelligence, the hint of witty *sous-entendu* his glasses lent his square, inexperienced face. And maybe we did make an enigmatic couple, me stubbly and leather-jacketed and fucked-looking, Paul, in his oddly vented paletot and broad-brimmed trilby seeming perhaps a little fruity and mysterious, like one of those flamboyant but watchful dons who recruit discreetly for the intelligence services. When I caught him up again he stared at me for a second, and I thought his large pale eyes had never been more subtly comprehending. I felt he must know about Luc and everything, but simply, kindly held back from touching on a situation which he could only see as futile and perhaps improper. He wasn't a drunk or a gossip. I knew he cared about me. He must have read my smothered hints, my trembling unconcern at every mention of Luc and his ancient family. I looked away into the arched stillness under a bridge that the road rose and swung to cross. Almost a circle, arch and reflection crossed by the water's wintry line. I was working with nothing, I had nothing on Luc, nothing of him that mattered, nothing from him. It came over me with a certain desolate formal perfection and for the first time.

'Have you been to St Vaast?' said Paul.

I told him I had passed it on the evening I arrived in town, roaming about . . . 'It was locked,' I said, 'I couldn't get in. It looked rather melancholy, I think.'

'I'm afraid it is. This little parish is a very poor one. The people still use the church, but they've never had the money to do it up. It had that rather wonderful porch tacked on in the seventeenth century. Since then it's been more or less left alone.'

We turned a corner and there it was, at the end of the street. It gave me a shock: not only its nightmarish appearance – the bleak, battlemented tower so out of scale with the low old cottages around it, the derelict theatricality of the porch, with its barley-sugar columns and shit-crusted ledges – but also the shot of pure recall, my first hours here, full of forced excitement and independence, fighting back home-sickness.

'The area's suffered a lot in the past ten years. There used to be several factories across the canal but they've all been closed down.'

'And I believe there was a hotel?' I said – half-expecting to be told there wasn't.

'The old Pilgrimage and Commercial? Quite right. You have picked up an amazing knowledge of the town.' I thought how lamentably wide of the mark that was. Anything I knew had been absorbed unconsciously on my wishful loopings through certain quarters; I'd been incurious about every history but one.

When we entered the church Paul swept off his hat and at the first pew-end dipped to one knee, his coat fanned for a second behind him on the stones. I was surprised, and the way he rose and hurried me on suggested it was mere habit, a conciliatory gesture to the believers kneeling here and there in prayer. In front of them, and at several side-altars, pyramids of patchy candle-light lit up the insensible faces of saints and Virgins. Beyond that there was only an impression of decrepitude and Romanesque gloom.

I followed Paul as he wandered down a narrow aisle, almost blocked with the black wardrobes of confessionals. Perhaps we should just pop into one of those and get it over with. Then he turned back, he seemed uncertain himself, hesitated with a hand on my shoulder, looked guardedly across the scattering of kneeling figures. 'Let's stay a moment,' he muttered, and slipped into a pew. I followed him again and sat by him waiting. There was a sombre echo. It was as if a coffin might any moment be brought in.

Sometimes a careworn old woman entered, or another ended her prayers and shuffled out; sometimes a shuffling old man, a widower among all these widows who presumably believed in miracles and hell. The church was lively, in its destitute way,

288

compared with the emptiness of the streets outside. Perhaps that was itself the secret, the place where the pious gathered as they approached the end, though no one saw them come here. It occurred to me as a vague possibility that it might be something to do with Paul's wife, whom he never spoke of and whom I knew about only from the tragic anecdote I'd bullied from Marcel. There was a snapshot of her in an ivory frame on the desk in Paul's office, a sensible boyish blonde among Orst's menacing red-heads. To marry at last at fifty and then lose your wife, to find the long decades of bachelordom creep up again like some funereal Daimler that matched your pace, its leathery solitude always in waiting, patient of the brief postponement . . .

'This is probably a complete waste of time,' Paul whispered. 'I can't quite think why I bothered dragging you out here.'

'I remember Orst used the tower of this church in the picture for the story of the False Chaplain,' I said, like a doggy student.

'Yes. He used to come here, you're quite right.'

There was a pause. 'It's not easy to imagine why,' I said.

'It had one attraction.'

'Well, it *is* a church.'

'He wasn't a religious man. Well, he observed religion, in the sense of looking at it very much with an eye to its forms and legends, and he was moved by the primitive faith of his country and obviously the idea of mystery; but he wasn't properly a religious *observer*. He liked to watch people at prayer, but didn't pray himself – or so he claimed.'

'I think you're suggesting there was a particular person who prayed here that he liked to watch.'

Paul looked a little embarrassed that I had got the point; I couldn't help feeling he could have just told me – back home in the warm, proposing a pre-lunch gin as he opened the burgundy to breathe . . . Or would it have been quite the same? I glanced away, to shawled figures, lost profiles, lips moving almost silently, as if in troubled sleep, the bleak old building given depth and tenderness by the multiple soft pulses of the candlelight. And here Edgard Orst would sit or kneel among the poor, his fastidious mouth closed, his eyes behind his powerful spectacles drifting always to the same unwitting worshipper.

'They seem all to be old people here,' I said quietly – some perhaps were only Paul's age, though so much more bent and buffeted.

'She was a young woman of the parish – only twenty-five or so when Orst first met her. I believe she had lost her fiancé in the Great War. She took in washing, like so many of the women round here. I can still remember the long drying-racks along the canal-side, and the tunnels and alleyways of sheets you could get lost in if you were a child.'

'So they had an affair?'

'Well, it must be said she didn't only take in washing.'

'I see.'

'She had always had something of a reputation, though it's not clear to me that Orst ever knew that.'

'He became her – client, do you call it?'

'He saw her one day coming from the market-place. She got on to a tram, and he immediately followed her. The thing was that she looked uncannily like Jane Byron; rather statuesque, with of course the amazing red hair – orangé was his word, I think quite literal.'

'He surely didn't tell you about all this.'

'No, no. Mad though he often was he was never indiscreet. But much later on he told his sister, and he started to keep a journal, just under the force of the new emotion, which no one but she and I have ever read.'

'You are incredibly protective,' I said rudely, with a short laugh, in unchecked exasperation; he paled, looked aside as if others might have heard the accusation, but didn't retaliate. In fact, no one seemed to care that we were talking. 'Go back to the tram,' I said softly.

Paul paused a moment longer. 'He followed her on the tram, and followed her when she got off. He felt he was seeing an apparition, as if the image he had been painting over and over for the past twenty years had suddenly come to life – come *back* to life, as it were. He noted which house she turned into, wrote it in his pocketbook, then wandered on bemusedly and got lost. He didn't know this part of town, despite having lived here all his life. He had to get right back to the other side, to the new suburbs where the Villa Hermès so incongruously was.

'Like many rather severe people he was actually quite shy.

You know he spent the years of the Great War in England' – again, I just smiled and shook my head – 'and he had cut himself off so much at the Villa, and in effect denied the present so successfully, that he didn't know how to go about meeting an ordinary girl again.'

'But he must have been much older,' I objected. 'Surely too old, too self-conscious, if he didn't know what sort of woman she was, to go chasing after her.'

'He was in his mid-fifties, that's all.' Paul did look rather piqued at this. 'Besides he was infatuated, so age was hardly a consideration he would let stand in his way.' And he gave me a complex little smile that referred perhaps to me, perhaps to his own past, I couldn't tell.

'So he came to the church.'

'He came many times before he spoke to her; he hired a fiacre every Sunday morning to bring him and take him back. He could really hardly believe his eyes, he longed to be with her, but dreaded meeting her and being disabused.'

'Was she really so similar?'

'It's rather touching, at first he thought identical, but myopically he couldn't be sure – the whole impression, the slow but electrifying movement, what he called Jane's Lady Macbeth quality, seemed to be perfectly reproduced. It was only when he had, well, picked her up, and taken her for a drive that he conceded the single difference – in place of Jane's virtually colourless eyes, hers were what he called chrysanthemum brown – a tarnished gold colour.'

'Presumably he got her to go with him without too much difficulty.'

'Of course. I think she virtually leapt into the cab. But then to him that only confirmed the sense of reincarnation, of a destined meeting. And she was no fool, she went along with it; she must have had a bit of the actress in her too, although she didn't have anything of the real Jane's artistic background or family connections. She was just a woman of the people. There is an awful kind of unintended humour in his diary if you know what she was and what he thought about her. He simply believed what he so very much wanted to believe.'

291

'He can't really have believed there was any connection between the two women, surely?'

Paul looked mildly around the church. 'Belief's a funny thing,' he said. 'It's the little obstacles to belief that spur one to make the leap of faith.'

When we were outside again, he had the air of someone who has dragged you to see a cult movie at a remote suburban cinema and suspects that it wasn't an unqualified success. 'That was very fascinating,' I said.

'I'd hoped to show you something else; but we can't wait all day. It's simply that this church is still used by the prostitutes. I'd hoped some painted ladies might be praying to St Vaast.'

'I think I've got a much better picture of what happened without seeing the real thing.' Though it was true I didn't quite feel the thrill or shock of it as Paul clearly hoped. My own obsessions made it hard for me to grant the force of someone else's – and besides it was long ago and part of the never fully plausible world of heterosexual feeling. I started trying to convert it into my own terms; if I had met someone physically identical to Luc would he have done just as well as the object of my wild longings – which flooded into my throat for a second and pricked my eyes as we turned a corner into the cold wind.

'You say that I'm secretive,' he said, in a tone that admitted the charge but showed his pride had in fact been scratched by my remark of a few minutes before. 'But I've always been prepared to tell, if I could first find the right person. That's why I'm so glad you've got the point: I very much want you to get the point, since you're helping me so much to get all this done.'

I shoved my hands into my pockets and nursed this to me in a silence I hoped he didn't feel was negative. I wondered if I *had* got the point. I had the sense that my importance, my helpfulness, were being flatteringly exaggerated. Proof-reading, fact-checking, were necessary of course; but they could be done just as well by somebody else, better perhaps by somebody who didn't share my groping remoteness from the subject. At the same time I was warmed and bucked up by the confidence Paul put in me, the tone of urgency I had sometimes heard before and the implication that I could meet the crisis, even if I didn't

quite know yet what it was. It was as though he saw some virtue in me that I had lost sight of myself, or never believed myself
to have possessed.

Towards the end of lunch I pressed him further about the
war. I'd had two or three, perhaps four, glasses of wine, he'd
drunk more than usual himself and seemed cautiously to be
celebrating. He was giving a comic account of some French art
critics and their notions about Orst. I got a very clear impression of their style and their theoretical obtuseness, and also
of the disquiet beneath Paul's mockery. Lilli listened to everything he said with her usual, rather stolid, attentiveness,
sometimes repeating a phrase when he fell silent as though to
memorise it or to help me to. I said simply, 'Tell me about your
visits to Orst' – and saw her gaze settle on his down-turned
face.

After a while he said, 'I only hesitate because it's hard to
know where to begin.' He smiled at me distantly, but seemed
reluctant to meet Lilli's eye. Marcel, opposite me, bundled up
his napkin and pushed back his chair – I saw he waited for Lilli's nod before he got down. Then she too stood up and reached
for our plates and asked us about coffee. Paul watched her go
out with the kind of exasperated tenderness I remembered noticing sometimes between my mother and father.

'I wish I'd seen the Villa Hermès,' I said, unsure if he was
going to tell me about it or not.

'I'd like to have seen it in its early days,' Paul agreed
promptly. 'Yes.'

'Do you mean it had fallen into disrepair when you knew it?'

He fiddled with some breadcrumbs on the tablecloth. 'The
thing is, I never did know it. Orst had moved out years before
that brief period when I used to go and see him. It was let to an
English artist up until the war, and then stood empty. I knew it
as a landmark, of course, if I went to visit schoolfriends on that
side of town.' I had been hurriedly revising the scenario I had
been loosely carrying, of young Paul's visits there and the
aesthete blind in his own treasure-house. 'No, the only time I
entered the Villa was in the period before its demolition in the
early sixties, when several of us tried to save it and there was a

293

petition signed by, well, by almost nobody really. The Symbolists were still seen as a bit of a sick joke then. Even the children
of Symbolist painters were teased about it, as if they had con-
victs or madmen for fathers. Things which would fetch a
fortune today were being sold for their frames.'

For a moment I found myself regretting those missed
chances; I wasn't someone who would ever own anything. 'But
he was still a well-known figure when you met him?'

'Honestly, no,' Paul admitted. 'He was remembered in the
town, but rather as someone from long ago. His great London
days were forty or fifty years before – when he was your age,
more or less. He was a blind, half-paralysed, half-mad old man,
who might as well have been dead for all anyone cared. I was
quite frightened of him, and of course determined to prove I
wasn't. If I say so myself, I was very tolerant of him, and came
to be fond of him. I used to do a few chores in the house, read to
him, listen to him muttering and raving about the past, and the
beautiful woman who'd ruined his life and brought him to this
state – I didn't understand it all, but I gained a sense of his own
mythology, you might say. I knew my way around a place I'd
never been. And he could still be quite lucid about the world:
"You be my eyes," he used to say. "Tell me what you saw in the
street, what was the sky like, what colour were the clouds?"
Often, of course, I had no idea, and he would shake his blind
head and pretend to be angry. And really he did teach me to see
for myself: I did start to take notice. I remember starting to im-
itate his expressions of aesthetic pleasure – a rather feminine
and troubling language for a fifteen-year-old boy, this *charmant*
and *exquis* and *ravissant*, all in French, which was the language
of his kind.' I nodded slowly with recognition – how music had
demanded something similar, like the language of endearments
which I never voiced except inside my head. 'Well, it was a lesson in real life, and I discovered I needed it, I wanted to come
back for more. He was my best teacher, not the brave monks
who actually taught us and looked after us through those terrible years . . .'

I felt great wide-eyed questions welling up, about what it had
been like; and then shamefaced doubts about what could toler-
ably be asked by someone who knew nothing about it, who had

never known anything like it. 'Your parents weren't worried about your spending so much time with him?' was all I prudishly came up with.

'No, no. It was they who arranged for me to go.' I thought Paul was cross with me for a moment, then saw that perhaps it was only with himself. 'Put simply: when Orst became too infirm to stay at the Villa he had moved back to his sister's house – now, as you know, our Museum. I'm not sure when he contracted the pox. You probably know there was a great spread of it during the war – it may have been soon after he returned from England, in 1919. I suspect the tertiary stage was very delayed, and when it came it was clearly very prolonged. Anyway, Delphine took him in: she was very tough and capable and ... unsentimental. That would have been in about 1930. She looked after him with her old servant, who was married to the cook – dear old people. The paintings and most of the contents of the Villa were brought over and stored, a lot of them in this house that we're in now, which had been left to Delphine and which stood unused for years. It was she who made the little passageway that you go through from our sitting-room to my office.'

'Oh!' I said, with slightly more wonder than I could account for.

'And there he stayed, painting until he could see no more and taking a long time to die.' This was what Helene had hinted at on our evening walk – it seemed the embodiment of something I had always felt about the old town, and found shadowed forth in many of Orst's eerie lithographs, a sense of dying life, life hidden, haunted and winter-slow. 'The trouble came with the new war. Edgard and Delphine's mother had been Jewish – oh, quite assimilated, but Jewish. Obviously, they must have watched the deepening of race-hatred among the Belgian fascists with alarm; but when the Germans made their move, it was all so incredibly quick and so feebly resisted, they had to make a plan. She fled to England again, at really the last possible moment – it was almost Dunkirk. She stayed with friends until the end of '44, in Chislehurst – they were old patrons of Edgard's.'

'Chislehurst!' This trivial detail surprised me much more

than the lightning progress of the German army. She could have known Aunt Tina. I remembered Orst's love of the *legendary* sentiment in English art.

'Of course there was no way Edgard could be rushed out of the country, so they did the simplest thing, by pretending he no longer existed – which to all intents and purposes and in most people's minds was the case anyway. The cook and her husband stayed on and looked after him, and if asked they would say that he was either dead or in England too.'

'He lived a kind of ghost existence, a premature ghost.'

'Indeed so. At first, the measures weren't quite as drastic as had been feared. I think initially the Jews had to wear a yellow Star of David – I remember those in the street; but not for long: the next thing was they weren't allowed to leave their houses. The final stage, of course, was the order that they must go off to work elsewhere, which many thousands of them, with no freedom or civil rights, did without any great reluctance. Or they had persuaded themselves that the summons to the train-station offered them a positive chance of a better life, rather than . . . what it did.' And I shared Paul's evident reluctance to name their destination: I felt it on the pulses, hearing his bleak summary of the facts. 'On one occasion, quite late on, the house was searched – I believe in a routine way. Orst was wheeled and bumped through the secret passage into the other house and no one suspected anything.'

And there he left it hanging. I wanted to help him on towards the story's wretched climax, though my sense of it as an adventure had withered. I looked round and saw Lilli in the doorway.

'Ah,' said Paul, both relieved and confused. 'Why don't we go through?'

I cleared a space on my side of the desk and sat there as if about to be served a second meal. I pictured Cherif back at my room, gaping with boredom, stirred slowly into resentment and jealous fantasy. I hadn't actually said I'd be back for lunch. Paul came in with a large old box-file and set it in front of me – I felt I'd rather jumped the gun, he still had this stage of my education to lead me through.

The file contained all that survived of the painter's photo-graphs of Jane Byron. They were creased and curled and compressed and when I lifted the restraining spring they rose with a ghostly tremor to the brim of the box.

I was looking at a large-faced woman wrapped and scarfed like a desert-dweller in a length of dark material, her pale, heavy features set off in half-profile by the silky cowl. Her skin was rough and pouchy, there was a pitiless quality to the photo, heightened by its metallic register, which rose out of black through obscure leaden greys to glaring blurred highlights. In the next picture her hair was down, she was gazing up from within it, in pained adoration, her long, powerful hands twist-ing a lily. In the next she lay on a kind of day-bed, her hair dragged backwards, eyes staring at nothing. It was the first one I recognised as the basis of a painting – the Ophelia that hung upstairs – and it gave me, across nearly a century, a quick shud-der to see her acting out that particular death.

Paul stayed in the room, abruptly taking down books and putting them back, not hovering exactly, but there to watch my progress, commenting occasionally, as I picked another photo from the box, on the picture it had become. 'That of course is "Le Collier de Médailles",' he said when I paused on a staring full face, chin pushed up by an elaborate heavy collar of what?, Roman medals, the impressive white slope of the bosom wrapped in a sheet – it was sexy and monumental at once. And then, at a very shadowy little study, a reverie, the eyes averted, a pale gloved arm gleaming against darkness – 'Ah, that's a lost picture, it disappeared in the war, it was called "La Musique" or "Palestrina" – oddly enough, I only know the painting itself from a photograph.'

Many of them were torn at the edges, or showed the little tooth-marks of pegs or rusty pin-holes. On several a white crayon had added its own emphases or drawn a detail out of darkness, like a picture touched up and sharpened in an old magazine. On one or two there were smears of paint, lemon or violet thumbprints that were disconcerting evidence of the man himself, who took care never to be seen at work. Sometimes there were splashes of that intense blue he used, which Paul said was the costly blue of a Bellini Madonna but given a further resonance – the Symbolists' *infinite azure*.

Almost at the bottom of the box was the photograph that Orst had based the famous triptych wing on, where Jane was seen at the mirror, seen *in* the mirror, hidden from us by the shimmering high-necked cope figured with lilies. The photo was brighter than the painting, but it seemed to me just as accomplished, with the sheen of the fabric disappearing into folds of shadow, and the sources of light subtly diffused. In a way I liked it more than the finished work, I liked it before it had been coloured in, while you could still see details in the background – a littered desk, a doorway with a tacked-up curtain – that Orst would blur and dissimulate into shadowy panels and dim thresholds.

Sometimes Jane smiled, was required to smile, either distantly, at some soft recollection, or close up, with a kind of lustful fixity that I registered with a shock through the momentary delay, the fluted dusk, of a veil. Paul helped me with reproductions of paintings, and I looked at them with a dwindling sense of amazement, side by side with their originals. They had the unintended effect of making the paintings seem predictable and the photographs more and more mysterious. Or perhaps they were just two different kinds of mystery, one deliberate, the artist making things vague and portentous, and the other to do with two lovers in a Brussels studio and the things they did for each other on certain mornings, the posing and play-acting given solemnity by the long exposures, the need for unblinking stillness. There was even a touch of irritation in one or two of the expressions, the mood of some protracted rehearsal, a sense that they had been at this long enough. I found myself imagining the face cracking, the hand dropping the golden bowl, a casting-off of wraps, a move to coffee and cigarettes in the next room, the intimate accommodations of an affair in a bachelor apartment.

And there was a further minor mystery, to do with famous beauties, beauty as it seemed to have been judged in the days before cinema and running water: sallow skin, broody jaws, great hanks of greasy dark hair, a greasy sheen too to collars and lapels and sweated-in satin, but no faltering of confidence in front of the camera, no suspicion that they might not appeal to the fastidious viewer a century ahead. Jane wasn't as grim as some I had looked at bemusedly, but she was big and middle-aged close to as she might not have been in the magic of stage-lights, and was never to be in the necromancy of Orst's art. Perhaps her skin was spoilt by corrosive paints, it was only natural that he should give her this radical, classicising face-lift; I wasn't sure I could say so to Paul, but I liked her best as she came solid and unembarrassed before the camera, when she was only acting. I liked a sexy sense of latent power she had, a cleverness in those large eyes, so colourless they seemed faintly fiendish and barely changed between photo and painting, pupils of grey ice. I knew nothing about her, but I felt she could make her own way, she wasn't just the silent screen of the artist's fantasy – or at least, wasn't meant to be, wouldn't have been if she'd lived.

I laid the pictures carefully back in the box-file and looked up at Paul, who swept it away like an attentive waiter. 'That was very . . .' I said, able after a few seconds to produce only a rather special smile, which he seemed to find adjective enough.

'I knew you'd be fascinated,' he said quietly. 'I think we should have a few of them in the catalogue, don't you?'

'But obviously.' It had become our catalogue only in the past week or so, and he appeared to welcome the uninformed certainty with which I saw some matters he had fretted over for years. 'Besides they are themselves art-works by Orst,' I pronounced. 'We – you might even put them all in.'

'It's not usual,' he said crisply, crossing to the print-cabinet, and stooping to tug out one of the wide shallow drawers. 'But see what you think later' – in a teasing tone; was I drunk?

He came back with a big square folder, and handed it to me carefully. 'A la nuit tombante' was written on it in an old-fashioned hand – not Paul's pretty writing, some earlier guardian, perhaps the high-minded Delphine . . . 'I just want you to see this,' he said. I opened it with a little mime of curiosity, as if it were a present.

An expanse of creamy-white, a sheet that was more like a wall, with a small square aperture at the centre – through which you looked at a dark sea and a sky that rose from a rim of light into deepening greys. The image was only four or five inches high, but intensified by a heavy black frame that gave one the impression of looking out from a high-up window in a thick-walled castle – for some reason I thought of Elsinore. At the same time I knew it was the lithograph to which Orst had returned in the simple late panel of the triptych, though there he had dispensed with the heavy masonry of the surround. It had a certain power, the lonely sea and the sky, though I felt it took enigma to the verge of emptiness.

Underneath, though, was another sheet – an earlier state, Paul said, that showed what the black margins hid, like worn old details boarded up against the salt air: the white balustrade of a balcony below, tall windows at either side folded steeply back, in the left one the letters DROME reversed, running downwards and very faint. The sky was lighter and crossed with high striations of cloud and in its depths I thought I saw (what may only have been a hesitation of the pencil) a pale speck of the folding star – well, you didn't fold at sea, but it gave me a disconsolate shiver.

'Presumably Hippo and not Aero,' I said, envisaging the white cliff of sea-front hotels, it might be Eastbourne, and then seeing of course where it was, the whole thing shifting into a deeper perspective, a hotel at Ostend – 'Cold as the wind without an end'.

'Eh? Oh, you're very clever.' Paul smiled. 'But not quite clever enough!' I frowned and he stooped beside me; I was in his breath as he looked very closely at the picture. 'You have to think what hotel our friend would be likely to choose for a romantic escape with his lover. And right next to the Kursaal, too, for Jane, who loved to gamble.'

'I've never been to Ostend, where I assume it is, except getting off the ferry to come here.' I was trying to think what other sorts of drome there were. A velodrome? The Belgians were keen cyclists. Or perhaps it was the beginning of the word. 'The Dromedary Hotel?' was my unconfident attempt.

Paul stood back. 'No matter. It was the Hotel Andromeda. It really doesn't matter, though it was a favourite legend of his.'

'Did he see himself as rescuing Jane from something? I suppose her jealous husband . . .'

'It's possible. Actually, I don't think it was the rescue side that interested him, he was much keener on the idea of the chained-up woman. He had a bronze Andromeda at the Villa – school of de Vries, a beautiful thing, but with a very long and heavy chain that hung down the pedestal in a loop.'

'Anyway', I said after a moment, 'he certainly didn't rescue her on the most important occasion.'

'He couldn't swim,' said Paul abstractedly, still pondering the images he must have seen so many times, as if there were more of these secrets in them if you only knew how to look. 'He stood at the window in the late afternoon and watched her go out till he lost sight of her. She swam right out, as she often did – she was a strong swimmer. He never saw her come back. He sat in the room and sketched the window and the view, almost as a kind of reflex: he liked to be busy with his work all the time. He made this simple empty drawing – evening was coming on – he followed the hour and darkened it into his favourite twilight. Later he went down to the beach to look for her. I've always had a very clear idea of the scene, the dandyish young man in his owl's glasses, rambling back and forth on the sand in the thickening gloom, trying to make out faces, putting questions to strangers: that awful fear that makes you an idiot. At last he told the police, but it was dark by then, and there was nothing they could do; and besides, who knew which way she had gone? Perhaps further out a current would take her. They alerted the coastguards at Middelkerke and De Haan. She was quite a well-known figure, so the news travelled fast in other directions. Apparently they had registered at the hotel under false names, but Edgard forgot in the turmoil of the moment. He seems to have been briefly deranged by anxiety – he went out quite late to the Kursaal, believing that he would meet her there. Then he made a scene. He was still so young, remember, he was only thirty-four, and he thought he had lost his great love – well, he had. I must say he seems a touching figure to me – self-absorbed, of course, not particularly humorous, but slightly comic even so, and, you know, vulnerable.'

We were both resting our eyes on the framed photo above the bookshelves, which dated, I believe, from 1910, when he looked a good deal older than forty-five. His proud turn of the head, I

301

realised, had put me a bit against him ever since I had seen it on my first visit here. But then who could ever tell what their next decade held? 'When did they find her?' I asked.

Paul carefully returned the prints to the drawer. 'They didn't,' he said.

I was impressed by this, as I always was by the idea of a total disappearance, the vertigo of it, and the way it none the less left room for wasting hope. And again I was full of questions, and objections too, that I hesitated to put. Had she killed herself, did no one see her from a boat or ferry, might it have been a planned escape, involving another man, a change of identity, flight to another continent. I needed the photos back to look for further signs.

'The husband was questioned, of course,' Paul said. 'He was in Deauville, which seemed vaguely suspicious. But I believe he had a perfectly good alibi. And Edgard himself virtually ruled out suicide – there was no note or explanation, and he knew her moods.' I watched Paul unlock a drawer on his side of the desk, with an apprehensive frown. 'I think it did all give him a feeling of life being unaccountable, of not having much idea about what even those closest to him were thinking and going through. As well as being a dreadful shock, of course. But when he'd settled down and kept on coming back to her over and over again I assume it was his way of asking those simple questions, the how and where and why.'

'And not coming up with the answers.'

'Well, he never came up with answers. It was fortunate', said Paul with a giggle, 'that he had always made something of a point of that.'

He was holding a battered manilla envelope to his chest – the next part of the demonstration. I remembered Helene's account of after-hours tours of the Museum, the child's sense of privilege almost regardless of what she was being shown. 'I'll leave you with these a moment', he said, 'whilst I go and er . . .'

When Paul had hurried off through the wall I got up and stretched at the window – just at the moment a few drops striped it. I looked lazily out, as I had often done before, at the inscrutable houses opposite, seen clearly now that the trees were bare. The houses Orst had looked at as a boy, that his sister had seen each day throughout those later years. It was possible to believe, in the yawning after-lunch stillness, that the same people lived there still, a minimal ghost existence of creaking boards and early dusks, looking out from time to time at our dark gables through the rain. I thought of my own view of the old doctor's house, with its shuttered upper floor, its air of professional secrecy, the occasional faint escape of an hour's silver chime. Then a window flew open, and a man in a cap dropped a sack of rubbish into the street.

I shook the contents of the envelope on to the table, and quickly spread them out. It was photographs again, and bits of photographs – of women, I thought at first, but then saw that it was just one woman, who like Jane was put through a number of hoops. There were the same veiled close-ups, the hieratic poses, the flaked-out half-lit reveries. The pictures were smaller, printed I supposed in Orst's own dark-room, 'the dark crucible of his art' as his impressionable English visitor had called it. Unlike the others, though, they included a lot of nudes, or near-nudes, the long hair hanging in falls that hid, or nearly hid, the woman's outward-turning breasts. Sometimes she looked back over her shoulder in affected surprise, sometimes she reclined on a sofa in short black stockings, or with the black feathers of a fan clustered between her legs. She was a handsome girl, young, unembarrassed; she looked cynical but dependable. I was very slow to realise that this was the second Jane, the laundry-woman who was the actress's reincarnation.

There was a general likeness, though in monochrome the overwhelming feature, the torch of her hair, could have been any middling colour. She was pale and strong-jawed and big without being fat. She could certainly have been a relation of Jane, a younger sister, with a similar humour and nerve. I tried to forget she was a prostitute, and had presumably been paid for these sessions in the studio, but the impression of detachment and compliance couldn't be dispelled. She met the camera's stare very levelly: she still had life and self-esteem, but her bright eyes, in the middle range of the sepia, had nothing of Jane's disconcerting power, the impression she gave of seeing through time and experimenting with dangerous drugs. The new girl could never have been the Kundry of 'Jadis Hérodias, quoi encore?' In one picture she stood with her arms full of the dusky bundle of her hair, though at first glance I mistook it for a cat.

There was another small envelope among the photographs, on which the word 'Private' had provocatively been written. I opened it circumspectly, the old gum still dully tacky, and slid out yet another set of photos, that made me wince and hesitate. I knew for a moment or two what 'Private' meant – desires expressed without the filter of art, glum shaming needs . . . I made my interest scientific, dimly thinking what a prig I was when it came to women and the indignities men demanded of them. It figured that the downside of Orst's mysticism should be something coarse and exacting. The young Jane – I didn't know what to call her – had a wary look now: she was a professional, she would have upped the fee, but she was not an actress like her predecessor. There was a sense, that was perhaps the cruel erotic pivot of the pictures, that though she was a working woman she was a good Catholic too, who believed in eternal fire and wondered, as she took the lash or pissed herself for Orst's camera, if that might land her there.

There were only half a dozen of them. In the first, she stood with one foot on a table, one on a chair, looking back over her shoulder (he seemed to like that startled supplicating glance), two fingers spreading her cunt from behind. There was a glistening detail to it that was far beyond the things I had puzzled out long ago from Charlie's under-mattress stash of *Escort*s and *Parade*s. Then I noticed indignantly that she was wearing the collar of medals: her dead original's magnificent choker was part of the apparatus of bondage. In the next she lay sprawled on the carpet, fettered to what?, the camera-tripod?, with Andromeda's chain. In another she was bending over and I saw with a little protesting 'Oh . . .' the black boss of a turd lodged patiently in the tight opening of her arse. I put them back thinking, 'Well, after all, these aren't the worst things' – they wouldn't quite go in, there was something in the envelope that stopped them. I funnelled it and tapped out on to the table a sprig of orange hair tied with a thread, a tiny crinkly switch. Somehow one knew it had not been taken from the head.

304

Cherif was crouching barefoot in the armchair, with his overcoat on, drawn tent-like round his knees.

'Baby, you're not even dressed,' I said.

'I've been waiting for you, so that we can go out and get lunch.'

'Half past five's a bit late for lunch,' I said. 'Look, I've got all the washing done, and free! Washed, dried *and ironed*.' I unzipped the bag and tilted it towards him: buttoned shirts, folded pants, rolled socks all neatly compacted. I recalled Lilli Vivier's slightly flushed and compromised look as she gave it back to me. Had there been something shameful? I lifted out a shirt of Cherif's that had PARIS written all over it, and was presumably not intended for Parisians themselves. Did Lilli think that was mine? I supposed after the Orst tie débâcle anything was possible. I handed it to him and he took it with a moment's admiration, then scrumpled it up and hurled it into the corner.

'Oh.'

'Edward . . .'

'You prefer them unironed. I'll remember that in future.'

He looked at me miserably, and I felt my face tighten under his reproach. 'Why do you keep going away from your Cherif?'

It was a courtly phrase of his – I thought I heard it plaintively rehearsed all afternoon.

'I never said I'd be back for lunch,' I brought out. 'I had a great many things to do.'

He jumped up and came over to stare at the washing. 'I suppose did Luc's mother do this for you.'

'Is that what it is?' I said, with a little fake anger. 'I've already told you Luc's over, I'm over Luc.' What was it they said about love being proved by its constant renewal? I swallowed desolately at the sudden thought of him. 'No, it was Marcel's father's housekeeper who did it for me – for us. I've been at the Museum. You know I have a lot of work to do there.' I knew too that Cherif never asked about that inaccessible realm, which wounded him by absorbing me so much. I reached into his open coat and stroked his stomach. 'You must have other things to do,' I said. 'I can't spend every moment with you – much as I'd like to' (words hardly voiced). I saw a string of obvious questions coming, the painful catechism of reassurance

– we had been through it several times this week, with tears on one occasion and his insistence I was the first person he had really loved. I couldn't bear it – either for itself, or for its perverse requirement that I keep swearing to something I was more and more keen not to mention at all. 'Do you want a drink?' I said, and set about unpacking the laundry into the cupboards.

'We haven't got any,' he muttered. 'I'd have drunk it if we had.'

I reached to the back of the sock shelf and brought out a hidden quarter of brandy. 'There you are.'

He grabbed it and huddled back in the chair, taking nips from the bottle as if he'd just been rescued. It wasn't as if I'd been with another man, or only with dear old Paul, I didn't see why I should have to cajole him back into humour, but his suspicion stuck to me and wakened some vaguer guilt. Still, it seemed I was off the hook. When the questions started they were lugubriously tarty.

'Edward?'

'Mm.'

'Do you think I'm too fat?'

'I don't mind how fat you are. Let me have men about me that are fat. Anyway, I can hardly talk.' I went over to the window and looked into the murk below – a gleam on the canal from a light on the bridge, the school weekend-dark.

'Edward?'

'I am the only person here . . .'

'I know, but, Edward? What do you think of my *tuyau d'incendie*?' (his own vainglorious euphemism).

'I think it's, um, admirable.' I badly wanted to be somewhere else. It would have been a relief to see Matt, to spend a night or two in illusionless infidelity, but there had been no sign of him since my return from England. I wondered how Luc was spending his evening. I realised that since our aborted lesson, the lesson of the cold, I had unconsciously swung round to my old view that Luc and Sibylle were, well, lovers. Perhaps I was just rationalising my sense of rejection – though it wasn't honestly as decisive, as dramatically cogent as rejection: it was the awareness, late in the day, that I had made no impression, that I simply didn't figure with him, that I hadn't yet even become a thing to reject.

'You should see my brother,' Cherif was saying; 'he's got a much bigger one.'

'Really, darling, I'm quite satisfied with yours. Anyway you haven't got a brother. You've got four sisters, remember? You send them all your money.' It was the old evasive Cherif for a second or two, sexily unreliable, the one I had dumbly exchanged for the plaintive lover, the dopy stay-at-home . . .

'Just because I haven't told you about my brother, Ahmed, before doesn't mean he doesn't exist,' he said, with a certain self-satisfaction. 'He is in Rotterdam. I was staying with him when I was there, after you sent me away.'

This was just about possible, I supposed. As for sending him away – there was nothing I could do about the stories he told himself.

I even went to the Museum on Sunday, not sure I'd be welcome, though there was always work to do. Paul had given me a paper he had written years before on Orst and his English contacts, that might somehow be condensed or reworked for the catalogue – he was vague about it, and seemed to want my advice. I couldn't help worrying, as I walked through the town amid the perfunctory tolling of bells, familiar coded calls to a dozen congregations, whether I was the right person to give such advice, when my only qualifications were literary and when Paul's style was so cautious, so lacking in the scurrying charm of his talk, so unable, as a matter of principle, to take the vulgar advantage of his material that might have made for more than scholarly interest. In the past twenty-four hours his fastidiousness had come to seem more nervously defensive, and so, of course, more revealing, though I couldn't tell yet what it revealed.

Yet clearly something was about to happen. If he suspected that the time had come to tell all about his painter, then I could easily support him in that view. Nowadays the sexual details seemed often to be the whole point of a biography, with the implication that they had been for the subject as well. Paul's book would be arid and out-of-date without them, but with them it

307

could be a small sensation, and with no loss of scholarly standing. In fact, since the details were not just details, since he was dealing with a whole career lived in the baleful light of a sexual idea, scholarship really demanded that everything be told . . . This was the sort of argument I was going to have to put to him, that I felt him equipping me and tentatively exhorting me to put.

I didn't quite see the importance of it – I tried to do justice to Paul's sense of a moral conundrum whilst wondering who in the busy outside world gave a fuck about Edgard Orst anyway. Who were the Orst admirers? I imagined them like the fans of some eccentric minor composer, the Delius-nuts who turned out when my father did *A Mass of Life* at the Fairfield Hall – snuff-stained old sex-maniacs who sat conducting in their laps and collected bulging leather shopping-bags from the cloakroom afterwards. You couldn't tell from the rare bewintered visitors to the Museum, but the Orstians must be a similarly dodgy lot, joss-scented fantasists, nineties queens in velvet – perhaps still flared – suits. It was fairly clear to me that Paul himself wasn't one of them. He had admitted yesterday that Orst was something of a come-down after Rembrandt, that brilliant though he could be he lacked the range and sympathy of a major artist, that his was a 'world of impossibilities'. But that only seemed to make his personal loyalty firmer. I thought about what he'd said of their meetings, though in retrospect his words seemed cautious and inconclusive: Orst and his last days remained as yet in the deep shadow of his reticence. I felt sure some primary promise had been made to the blind old man by this clever teenager who came to talk to him or (as Helene had evoked it for me) to go through the print-drawers describing the pictures. Paul had come back to him decades later without much enthusiasm, but it may have seemed like destiny. There was a deep slow tempo to it, the half-hidden line of another life, that demanded respect and acceptance, and could never be changed.

On reflection I saw that yesterday's lesson had been as much about the pleasure of having a pupil as about Orst's techniques and preoccupations. It wasn't that Paul was lonely exactly, but that the painter's secrets were offered, very deftly and instructively, as symbolic of secrets – or not even secrets, discomforts – of his own. There was a sense, as he locked the nude pictures back in the drawer, that something else had been revealed; and he gave me an optimistic smile. I was surprised, slow-witted, had the feeling of some benign plan unfolding in which I played a useful part without knowing quite what it was – the younger person who mysteriously performs what an older one despairs of. Not that I minded – I enjoyed being distracted by the Orst world and its nice problems, it had become a wonderful shadowy refuge from my own. I stepped into the Museum's inner glass lobby with an expectation of comfort and bookish peace.

Behind the table, with the postcards and cash-box, sat, not the pleasant student of the past few days but the repellently spruce figure of ... I found I'd completely suppressed his name, for some reason Rex Stout came to mind, in the second or two that I stopped dead, wishing it wasn't true.

'Hul-*lo*,' he said. I gave a bitter little grunt, and he said, 'I suppose I should have known you'd be an art-buff.'

Even in that moment I found myself recalling my spluttering efforts to convey to Edie the intensity of his awfulness, his pseudish self-confidence, his active vanity, his thick-skinned suggestive matiness, his, his ... and seeing all over again how I had failed. 'I'm not an art-buff,' I said in an icy mutter; and went on towards the stairs.

'Even so, it's fifty francs to go in.'

I was just by the desk and looking down at his work, densely written pages of notes that he was going through with a yellow highlighter. It was A levels looming, a hopeless pretence of system ...

'I work here.' (By which I clearly meant, I work here, arsehole.)

Any sense of a gaffe was lost in his satisfied twinkle as he absorbed this fact. Ronald something – 'researcher'. It must be paranoia but I couldn't help feeling that one of the things he was researching was me – not of course for myself but as a figure in the life of a certain tall lean blond young man ... 'I wasn't told about anyone working here.' I shrugged. 'You mean you're one of the guards?'

'I work with the Director – I'm his assistant.'

I saw him glimpse the opportunity of delaying me and asking me further questions. 'And you say you're not an art-buff!' I sighed sharply. 'You've never told me your name, incidentally.'

Was there any way I could refuse it? I could use a false name, I could be Casey Hopper again for a minute ... 'Manners,' I said sternly, pleased as I had sometimes been before that it meant something and could sound like a reproof.

'Well, Manners,' he said, 'I hope this means we may see more of each other.' He took up his highlighting pen and settled forward again with a queeny wobble of the head, as if to imply I had discomposed him unnecessarily. As I started up the stairs he said, without looking round, 'The Director's not here today, by the way. As I'm sure you know.'

The office wasn't locked, thank god, and I closed the door behind me as if I had just escaped from something vile in a dream. I was telling myself already that it was absurd to have such a phobia of a person – it was the kind of loathing that could creep into your empty corners, a neurotic preoccupation. I switched on the lamp and sat down and stared across at the place where normally Paul would be sitting. I was remonstrating with him silently, how could he have taken on Ronald Strong, how come he had never mentioned him to me? I felt as if I were the Director of the Museum and Paul had gone over my head in some important decision. I took out 'Orst and his English Contacts' again and stared at a paragraph of it for five minutes.

The truth was I felt a real anxiety about being in the place by myself – not a day I normally came in, Paul 'away' but perhaps about to return, no arrangement having been made. And it wasn't as if this was an ordinary office, it was almost part of his house, he might come through the little passage in his dressing-gown, in unsuspecting possession of his morning, to find me there: not exactly an intruder, so surprise and displeasure would be mastered but revealed in later mortifying hints. I'd got the terms of our friendship wrong, it seemed, perhaps it would be better if I didn't come in any more. As it happened, another young Englishman, Rex Stout, was interested in Orst, really very keen, he could be a great help, a trained researcher ... I got up and looked out of the window. Of course I had no intention, no desire, to go through Paul's desk, but I began to feel a queer conviction of petty criminality. I left everything just as I'd found it, and went out very quietly on to the stairs.

The door of the first-floor gallery was closed, but not locked, and I slipped in. A table had been set up where work on the triptych could take place, and some temporary rearrangements had been made. The pictures themselves were still there, the two new parts hooked up in an approximate line with the 'Mirror' picture. I stood and tried to focus my attention on them. It was the middle panel that we had not covered in our little seminar – taken straight from a photograph, Paul had said, but was the subject of special importance? An empty street, a bridge, a gothic oriel, a density of old roofs beyond, the tower of St John's evidently, with the black flecks of the jackdaws circling; it was the odd quarter-hour of evening when you find you can't see properly any longer, the details fog, you strain to read grey against charcoal. Or maybe it was just the dirt, which from the side you saw on the surface – it might have been swabbed with muddy water. Maybe it was a bright spring morning, waiting to dazzle, full of things to be done, unaware of the tragedy welling at the day's end.

I looked at the familiar panel of Jane. Real shadow here, it was a dream of beauty, glimmering silk, folded angels, troughs of velvety dusk. Then I pictured her splayed successor, the plunge from reverence to cruelty. I assumed that, after once being robbed of what he loved, Orst had needed to chain his girl down (Marthe she was called), to insist on his power while he could, with a kind of futile force – it was like watching the anger of bereavement hugely delayed. I met the face in the dark oval of the mirror, and caught my breath as much at my own stupidity as at the halting gaze of chrysanthemum eyes.

311

17

A suntanned blond dawdled past, looking down at me coyly, noncommittally, seeing if the memory hook caught in the murky pond. 'Hi,' I said.

'Oh hi!' He dropped on to the banquette beside me. I felt him briefly adjusting to the gloom that I gave off and my lowered stare across a clutter of empty glasses. 'How are you?' he said brightly.

'How are you, Ty? You're looking very brown.'

'Mm – I've been in London.'

'Oh . . .' (And what sort of name was Ty, anyway? It sounded like an actor in one of Matt's films. 'And then at last Casey submits to Ty's throbbing fuck-pole . . .' And there *it* still evidently, self-importantly, was.) 'How is the old dump?'

I saw him wince to have the city of his dreams mocked. I knew to him it was size and grandeur and fashion-shoots and nights at Heaven; it wasn't crap and decay, the maze trodden by the wispy-bearded youngsters who slept in doorways when you glamorously left Heaven at two or three. 'Oh, it was *great*. I did a lot of work, you know, modelling? Everything from anoraks right down to jockey-shorts!'

'And who was all this for?'

'That was for C & A,' he said negligently. 'Soon I shall be on all the bus-stops.'

'And do you show off your dick in the C & A brushed-cotton slacks?'

'No, you are not allowed to,' he giggled. 'They make you put it out of the way.' So living models had to aspire, as one had sometimes surmised, to the generalised sexlessness of the old chocolate mannequins. He took the opportunity to change gear, I remembered it all now, up to the sing-song fifth of his fantasies and achievements, he set the cruise control button, he might go on for hours. 'I met this really sexy man in the Bloomsbury area, he is in the fashion business – well, he makes window displays, you know, they call them charm pads, and – '

'*Charm pads!*'

'Yes, you know, charm pads for the jewellery and rings. What you call the charms. Well, he is an older man, but still very sporting and fit. He has a huge apartment with the most fantastic curtains . . .'

What was an older man, I wondered? I was looking at Ty close to, and in a better light than when we had first met: he might be my age or more, to judge from the little creases around his eyes when he beamed at his own anecdotes, though in composure, and in a general innocent vanity, he was amazingly fresh and young. I began to admit to myself how like Luc he was, the high cheek-bones, the rather small, guarded, grey eyes, the thick fair hair. I hadn't realised before – of course, I hadn't even met Luc yet that night at the Bar Biff: I was looking at anyone in that first week as though they might be my friend and my future. I wondered if Ty had been an abortive first attempt, a dry-run, at Luc, who was made to the same formula, but was the real brute thing.

'. . . anyway, *he* said, "Why don't you come to my house, which is in the country, because we have a lot of things in common to discuss, and maybe, who knows, we can work something out." So I said – '

'I know,' I broke in, 'why don't you get me a drink. I find it hard to concentrate without one, somehow. Also, I'm fucking miserable, fed up.'

'Oh . . . what is the matter?' He looked round as if the explanation might be to hand. 'Are you by yourself here tonight?'

'I was,' I said rudely. 'I'm waiting for someone. Well, Cherif, you remember him.'

'Oh him,' said Ty condescendingly. 'He's a stupid young man.'

'He's living with me at the moment,' I said, not exactly to contradict him. And then in a few sentences I told him how I was despairing in love, trapped in my own home by a boy who was in love with me, and now my place of work had been infiltrated by someone I hated. I doubt I would have poured it all out so succinctly and bitterly to anyone capable of responding, but to formulate it to Ty was a distinct lonely relief. All I kept back was the repeating shock of Dawn's being dead, my own regret at his not having said goodbye, the guilty certainty that anything I did was something he couldn't do.

His reply was blithe but still surprising. 'Well, I know what you are like. You must tell your love to the boy, otherwise you will never have peace with yourself, and try to find out the good side of the Rex Stout person, which there must be, and say to someone who has just come into the bar that he must go and live somewhere else and go to hell too.'

'Thank you,' I said, as he got up and finger-waved goodbye. I wondered what had happened at the man's house in the country. Perhaps he ran a moral self-help centre. I heard Cherif give his mocking hoot at Ty as they passed behind me.

'Baby, why do you call Ty Mouchoir?' I asked him, when he'd settled and fussed over me enough. He grinned and pointed between his legs.

'Because it is not real. Just a rolled-up hanky.'

'Don't be ridiculous.'

He shook his head with a little moue of incontrovertibility. 'I know,' he said, clearly not wanting to offend me with the details of proof. Actually, I thought the story might help to pass the coming hours. I longed for Edie and wished she would come back again, with her gift for sharing and judging my feelings at the same time. She didn't know how many imagined dialogues she took part in, how often her friend addressed his silent pleas and exclamations to her. Still, soon I would be beyond caring, the wave of drink would rise and after a pretence of doggy-paddle I would embrace Cherif and go under.

We sat in silence for a while in one of the side bays, like a couple of forgetful old drunks in the Golden Calf, who had known each other all their lives. When I looked up and across I saw the darker far reaches of the bar, towards the lavs. There was a group of men there who only appeared on Sunday nights, heavily leathered, cropped, studded and tattooed, quiet amongst themselves, like steady-nerved conspirators, holding each other's eyes as they contemplated whatever it was they were about to do. I suspected it would be something demanding and uncomfortable but I envied them − they gave off, in their sexed and sombre way, the certainty that it was what they wanted. Then I heard Luc saying, in his Ealing Films toff accent, 'Well, what's it to be?'

For a second I thought the question was addressed to me. I started and then sat very still. A girl's voice replied, 'How frightfully kind!' and a rowdy young man said, 'Simply splendid!' I reddened at this English mockery, turned, mad and frowning, to face it, but in fact the high varnished back of the stall cut them off from view: they couldn't have known I was there. My heart was pounding with danger and opportunity − the Three right here in the Cassette, joking in spiffing English that no one younger than Perry Dawlish used, though they still clearly thought it was spot-on. I felt crowded and troubled. Why were they here? They were the world beyond, the bar was where you came for refuge and solace from them. I hushed Cherif to hear them better as they dropped into Flemish. It was possible they had just blindly and high-spiritedly stepped in for a beer, or they might think it coolly affirmative to drink in a more or less gay bar; what I dreaded was the note of mockery flaring up again, the trouble there sometimes was with the trash. I would have to join them, of course; I was destined to go through that little purgatory.

'Cherif, darling, I'm sorry I shushed you then, I was just thinking, which you know I find hard enough.' I was rather feline in my pissed decoying movement, my nest-plunder obliquely in view.

'Sometimes I don't understand what you are thinking about,' he said serenely, even proudly. I looked down and smiled.

'Well, I'll tell you. If you promise not to be upset.' He was silent, as though considering his rights. So I went into a long spiel, full of lulling reasonableness, about how I wasn't used to spending so much time with someone else, the years that had passed since I'd had an affair like this, how my sex-life had pretty well petered out before I came to this country; how of course it was all amazing and wonderful, but how I was still

315

naturally a rather solitary person, and also, as he knew, trying to be a writer, and messing round with a few ideas ... The thing was that just now and again I would need a bit of time to myself. I'd like to go back by myself tonight, and could he go out to the hostel?

As a lie, this one had the merit of being almost entirely true, but Cherif didn't see the charm of it. His head jerked back as if from a blast of heat, his jaw rounded biliously. The whole clumsy plan depended on the fact that he had never seen Luc and his friends, and on the last bus out leaving surely any moment ... I was prepared for a sulk but hoped to avoid a row. I pressed on him with a sort of blind volition, at the same time struggling to appear honest, weary, calmly elevated, the saint sighing for his cave and his lion. After a fashion it worked. I sucked the sting out of it, made the little passionate avowals that came automatically to me now, adding in a bit of reproachful cant about maturity and trust, and by the time it was over he had to sprint to the Grote Markt. I was amazed at myself – I had been watching my own performance as if I were Luc, say, craning over the back of the booth.

I went for a pee and then waited, as if soliciting, just inside the door. The Durex machine was beside me, I bought a packet of three for something to do; then I washed my hands with anxious thoroughness and checked myself in the mirror under the illusionless strip-light. I was terrified. Someone murmured something to me – I stared blankly at him in the mirror and he shrugged and went away. There I was again, but now entirely by myself in that further observable world; I leaned forwards as I might have to study a portrait that was brilliantly but ambiguously painted. What was it that made the subject tick? It was hard to tell. I stooped closer, in a kind of vertigo of detachment. I saw that the lenses of my glasses were covered in dust – smoke particles, stuff out of the air, tiny flakings of skin and scalp.

Luc had his back to me, as I came along the bar, and I took him in for the first time, relaxed, holding forth, speaking a bit loud perhaps to show he was at ease among the heedful queens. He was wearing the exact clothes of the morning I fell in love with him, the suede jerkin, the white jeans slightly

316

bagged and tucked up his arse as he lolled with ankles crossed, the nerdy discord of the trainers. I thought how I never knew just what size and shape he was – it must be because I worked on him so much in my dreams that I always found him different, always frightening and always remotely banal.

He was saying, 'He rewrote the whole thing, though, that was the point – he didn't just cut bits out and add bits on. The 1850 text is usually much better written than 1805, more concise and vivid and I think even witty.' I saw Patrick's stance of tolerant boredom, as at something that might be useful to him at some stage, and his slow double-take on me waiting at Luc's shoulder. I gave a little smirk made up of such warring elements, pleasure at Luc's plonkingly retailing what I had said to him in the fragment of our lesson, regret that he wasn't passing on my feelings in *favour* of the 1805 *Prelude* and its youthful life (the pain of only half-remembered words), paranoid suspicions again that I was somehow being mocked, even a hint of a mime of rueful, clumsy love; and love itself: not the cool blue pilot-light but the rumble and flare as the clock came on . . . I began to feel hot in the face, my mouth and neck were hot, my balls ached helplessly.

I touched Luc's upper arm just as Patrick said a neutral hello and I embraced them all with an eager beaming 'Hi!', like a popular young schoolmaster. Luc was startled, embarrassed to have been caught talking Wordsworth, but as usual when we met in the outside world excited and, well, charming. We shook hands, both comforted by each other's confusion, blushing and grinning, almost jeering, like old friends who can't at first think what to say.

'How's your cold?' was the best I could do.

'Oh, it's gone away,' he said, with a lyrical gesture as if lifting a veil from his face, though there was still a wisp of hoarseness to his words.

A silence fell in our group, and I wondered if they could hear my heart pumping. Perhaps they were waiting for me to move on or out, they didn't know I'd come to stay; or maybe they knew all about me and my pathetic unwelcome passion. I looked up shyly at Sibylle, who was herself looking humorously at Luc; then glanced at Patrick – but he immediately flicked to Sibylle. Then, 'This is my friend Patrick,' said Luc. I nodded and smiled. I hadn't seen him since the morning I found him in Luc's bedroom; I still didn't know what damage I'd done. 'And this is my friend Sibylle, Sibylle de Taeye' – with a hint of his own pride in a distinguished name. 'And this is my friend Edward Manners.' The rhythm of the scene demanded that he call me his friend, but still it made me very happy.

We simmered in our introduced state for a moment, as if each pondering afresh the bracing mystery of our being who we were. I longed to be who I was, to be natural and funny, but I knew I was doomed to be someone else by the violence of my needs and the enigmatic little circuits of the Three. They'd only been talking about Wordsworth, but they gave me the feeling I'd broken dampeningly into some far more intimate and sophisticated transaction. They may have been bored, but they were bored in their own satisfactory and really rather amusing way. I found my hand was oddly empty and pushed myself among them to the bar. I heard myself booming, 'Well, what's it to be?'

First of all I talked to Sibylle – I was suddenly too upset to manage Luc under the scrutiny of his best friends. I half-turned my back on him, though I kept picking up his chat with Patrick through the thin medium of our own conversation. I thought if I was very charming and could somehow imply a closer knowledge of Luc than I had then she might let some commonplace thunderbolt drop – 'When Luc and I get married', something like that. She had great composure, as of a child brought up to talk well to strangers, and keep cool under the pressure of extravagance or bad behaviour. Her face was round and calm, a convent-girl's face, lightly made up to suggest other attainments. She was wearing white jeans, in ominous twinship with Luc, and a shirt open over boyish white collar-bones and buttoned firmly between unboyish breasts; there were old, elderly pearls at each ear. I wanted to find her naive or even brittly snobbish in the English way, and was rather daunted by her poise and openness as she assessed my career and aptitudes.

'You also teach my friend Marcel, don't you?' she said.

'Oh yes, I do.' I was tracking a story of Luc's about a holiday in Italy ... Padua ... Galileo ... the anatomy theatre ... How formal he was with them tonight. I wanted to shout 'At ease', to drag him back to the beach, kids sparring in the sand ... 'Yes, he's, he's a nice lad. Of course he's had a difficult time.'

'He's very frightened of you,' she said, in a way which showed conclusively that she wasn't. But I respected fright this evening, I knew the warping pressure and panic that another person's presence could cause.

'He has no need to be,' I said. 'In fact I don't think he can be any more – we've become great friends.' I pictured him at home, pottering with the pastry scraps, always reaching back for childish solace, just the opposite of these three, drinking beers in a gay bar.

'He tells me you've been doing work for his father.'

'Yes, that's right.'

'. . . incredibly handsome Italian men . . .' Patrick was saying.

'I always think he's rather a pathetic figure.'

'How come?' I said, with a cross little laugh.

'Oh, having lost his wife in that bizarre way. Marcel and I talk about it a lot. We think he hasn't had the heart for anything since.'

'He's extremely fond of his son,' I said warmly, wondering if even so I did justice to his devotion.

Sibylle shook her glossy bob and leaned back on the bar. I thought I didn't really like her confidence. She said, 'My father says he'll never finish this famous catalogue. He says that Paul Echevin used to be a first-class scholar when he works on Rembrandt, but for some reason he gave it all up to work on Orst, since when he's written no more than a couple of articles. My father thinks he's lost hope.'

'I can't tell you how wrong you are,' I said. I'd had this before, from Helene. I was sick of the conspiracy against my friend. 'For a start he works on the catalogue every day. I've never seen such a hard worker. He's a real scholar, you know, he wants to get things right. It will be finished by next spring.

And he's written far more than a couple of articles, I can assure you.' (I certainly recalled seeing three.)

But she stuck by her high-up father's opinion, even if she distanced herself from it in some canny way. Patrick was giving Luc an update on St Narcissus gossip, tales of nicknamed masters, football news, told in his sturdy bollocksy voice but full of the shiver and gloom of winter school. Luc laughed and I felt his exclusion from it all, a hint that he would rather not hear about it.

'And how do you find my lovely Luc to teach?' Sibylle asked loudly, to be heard and perhaps break up our pairing and its faint antagonism.

I swivelled round to take him in, my heart punching with foreboding, and gave a sickly smile, while Luc himself turned with a cough and showed an interest in the bunched leather-queens. I saw one of them catch his eye and smile, and he swung back with a blush. 'Oh, your, your Luc is a joy to teach,' I said. 'If he's not in a bad mood.'

He put an affectionate hand on my shoulder, but it made me jump, and then curve apologetically against him, bungling his easy gesture. 'Last time I was in a very bad mood, and poor Edward just had to turn on his heels,' he explained, and gave my arm a squeeze that wiped out all the pain of the last week. I felt my throat streaming, pulsing like a dove's with unspoken 'I love you's', I wanted to kiss him all over his face and burble them into his flushed ears.

'He's been in a silly mood for several days,' said Patrick, and Sibylle shot him a frowning glance, and Luc narrowed his eyes at him. I still had no idea of Patrick's role or influence; he might have been the jester, the outsider, or he might have been their leader, if they admitted one. A silence extended and I soaked up how healthy and sexy he was, in a heavy jersey over a blue shirt that hung out over frayed old jeans. I thought, if the queens in here knew what he had between his legs . . . I was basking for a second or two in the simple randy thrill of being with a truly huge-cocked kid. 'So you like Luc, do you?' he said. I couldn't tell if he was needling me or hoping to get a good price for him.

A moment came when Sibylle refused a further drink, slid

from her bar-stool and quietly stated that it was time to go. 'Some of us have got school in the morning,' she said. Patrick seemed happy for me to buy him drinks all night, but let himself be persuaded. So it was over already – it hadn't lasted an hour. I saw my futile excitements, as though through glass or as the sceptical barman must have seen them, setting up round after round for me, the boys getting noisy, heartbreak waiting – and what else could I have expected? I began to think wistfully of Cherif.

Then Luc said, 'I'll stay for a bit longer.'

Sibylle peered around, assessing the imprudence of this decision. 'Okay,' she said, with an upward flick of the eyebrows. Patrick had sauntered hunkily to the lit console of the juke-box, and we all watched as he thumbed in a coin and deliberated over the corny menu of titles. I couldn't think of anything to say, I didn't dare look at Luc. Then a button was pressed and after several seconds a distantly familiar intro came at us from all sides. It was one of those rhetorical songs you heard in a late-night minicab, 'I want to be where love is', drunk yourself, and the requests read out – Darren, don't keep breaking my heart ... I need you but I need time – as you accelerate through the glittering streets.

Luc kissed Sibylle on both cheeks. 'Be good,' she said, 'sois sage.' And Patrick rolled up with a grin and barged him and kissed him on the mouth. I thought, Ah, you do that, do you? – or was it just young sportsmen's faggoty closeness, their high butch pained regard for each other and themselves? It wasn't the treatment I was going to get – I gave a little absolving wave, but he grabbed my hand in mid-air and shook it: it was a bit like jiving. 'We'd better leave them to it,' said Sibylle. Patrick turned at the door and grinned again; I wondered if I was the subject of some broad joke – but then if I was, Luc must be too. All that mattered was that he wanted to stay for a quarter-hour more, even if only to grouse about his troubles away from his smothering critical friends.

It had been a terrible time. I had watched myself trying different gambits, donnish to start with, pursuing the matter of the 1850 *Prelude*, then holding forth about Milton, Schubert, F. R. Leavis etc etc and clearly being the greatest bore on earth; then I smoked a cigarette (which they hated) and swore a lot (which seemed to displease them too); then gave them maximum charm, which they resented as a puzzling form of satire. At one point I was even nodding about to a song on the juke-box, but Sibylle stilled me with a glance. I was young and lively and clever, I told myself as I blundered like some awful Ronald Strong figure from rebuff to tacit rebuff. And then Luc wanted to stay.

There was a lovely sense of cleared space, of spreading calm, like sunlight out to sea, in the gold and copper cabin of the bar, as we drew two stools closer and settled ourselves knee to knee and the song wailed grandly on and then faded out.

'Oh dear, Edward, I'm sorry about that. But I'm very glad you were there!'

I was astonished. I was gesturing for a drink with one hand, not wanting to miss a moment, a single muscular movement of his face. When he smiled there was a fleck of spinach above a tooth at the side and I hungered to suck it away. 'What are you sorry about, and why are you glad? I was going to say sorry for barging in on your drink.'

'No, no.' He sighed and looked down. 'We've all been, you know, arguing. Sibylle and Patrick are my dear friends but this is the first time we have been together all week. We went out for our dinner, and it was terrible, and then we had to have a drink, to show we didn't just want to go home, though I think we all did!'

'Oh. What were you arguing about?' I was looking at his down-turned head, but also at the veins standing out on his long hands loosely cupped between his thighs; I didn't care what they'd been arguing about, I felt a ridiculous contentment at having him to myself, amazement that we hadn't done this long before.

'It's very difficult to explain, I feel very embarrassed.' He took a slurp from his fresh drink. 'Well, it's, of course, all to do with love.'

'Mmm.'

'And as we all know by now, the course of true love never did run straight.'

'Exactly.'

'You're much older than me, maybe you can tell me what to do,' he said. I studied my thumbs responsibly, wounded, honoured, and when I looked up he was smiling, not quite at me but over my shoulder. 'Hi,' he said. There was a quick bloom of scented body-lotion, a hand squeezing the back of my neck. Matt was back.

He ducked vaguely for a kiss and his gelled hair was cold on my cheek. 'Hi,' he said quietly, nodding slyly at Luc. 'I didn't know I'd see you two in here.'

'Well, here we are,' I said, with a self-satisfaction that made Matt smile. 'As it happens, we were just having a terrifically private talk.'

'Oh, it's not important –' said Luc, who was gazing happily at Matt as if he were his special hero. And he did look glamorous, in his crook's suit and cashmere overcoat, and with his sapphire stud.

'No problem. I'll see you soon,' he said, moving on down the bar, patting Luc on the shoulder as he went, as though he were a promising pupil of his, not mine. I followed him with my eyes and he turned smiling and made a fisting gesture – I shook my head slightly to say it was not alas like that. He started talking to one of the leather-men. As far as I could see he had something for him in his pocket.

'I think that guy Matt must be gay,' said Luc.

'You're absolutely right,' I sighed, as though reluctantly admitting to some long-held secret. And I sensed further questions coming, the boy must be a bit drunk, but still he held back at the edge of this new terrain. I felt that for once I had aroused his curiosity: he was about to be interested in me and my friends. I glanced sideways across low tables where men were gossiping, some with their arms round each other, or snogging in the shadows. How was Luc with all this? A qualm of propriety came and went. They must be sick with envy seeing me with him, my face lit up by his aureole of young heat. 'Let's get back to solving your problems,' I said, so pleased to be invited in that I ignored how those problems might tangle with my own.

I saw the pain alter his face, saw him weigh the difficulty of

323

telling against the relief of it. He gazed at me abstractedly. Was I his buddy or his moral tutor? 'I think maybe you won't know what I'm talking about,' he said. 'You're a very sensible, correct-minded kind of person. I think you are always in control of your own feelings, and maybe you don't have all so strong feelings about other people.'

'Try me.'

'It's that very bad thing, where you are in love with somebody and think about them all the time but they are also your dear friend and you see them all the time too. But they are not in love with you. And every time you see them you feel more in love.'

'That is a bad sort of situation.'

'Sometimes I wanted to tell you in the lesson, but it is better to talk about books and current affairs.'

'Is that why you were so keen to go to Los Angeles in our last session? Well, you had a cold too.'

He slapped his hand on the counter. 'I had a cold because I was out all night, standing in the rain under a certain person's window like a bloody idiot.'

'Your mother said you got it from her.' It was too touching to think of him – the romantic semaphore of young love, the old courtly gestures, dreading to bring things to the point. I pictured us backing into each other, like rival serenaders in a comic opera.

'My mother's like that, she always takes the blame.' He smiled at me steadily: he seemed to find comfort in me. And my eyes were revelling gently over him. 'The thing is, Edward, I fear I must certainly go to the gentlemen's.'

I hadn't a clue what he was talking about – it must be something like the dogs, or the wall. But he stood up and looked about and I understood and told him. I watched him wandering to the far end of the room, pushing his hair back, sweetly self-conscious under twenty pairs of eyes. I was blasted with lust. I thought why don't you just go on me, hose me down, unbutton my fly, slip your dick in and piss my pants ... why *don't* you? I saw a voracious dark kid I had come across before get up and follow him in. I wondered what Luc would think

324

when he heard the clink of his foreskin-rings against the urinal's china cup.

I caught the barman's eye and ordered another drink. I seemed to be virtually sober, I was drinking without noticing at least, it was rather like those trick-glasses where you tilt them to your lips and the liquid disappears. Did the boy want one too, he asked, perhaps impressed after all that I'd fought off the minders and rescued the star. I said yes, they were only light little beers, it would keep him a few moments longer before he shook hands and left for home.

Matt came up and said quickly, 'I don't know what you've done to Cherif. He's over at my place. I found him standing at the bus-stop crying like a baby.'

'Oh fuck, thank you, it's just . . . as you can see . . .'

'No thanks required. I think he's hot, as you may remember.'

'Yeah, he's not so delectable when he's all snotty-nosed. But have him, do what you want with him!'

'He's in a serious way about you, you know.' I grimaced impatiently. 'Anyway, we'll compare notes tomorrow night.' And he gave his casual stare, with its usual assurance that the world of fantasy need not stay fantasy for long.

I watched Luc's return, he was utterly beautiful, but I didn't feel annihilated by his beauty: he was coming to me, smiling from a distance like a friend who seeks you out where traders gather, on the Caspian shore – I had segued into a forgotten line of Violet Rivière's, from *Poets of Our Time*. He hopped on to the stool with a clear sense of reaching home in a risky game of touch. At the same moment a startling black object obtruded between us and was clonked on to the bar.

'Hello, dear,' said Gerard in his weary, what-a-fascinating-life-I-lead way. 'I haven't seen you for ages.'

'No, actually I'm just . . .'

'Do you want a drink?' It was rare for him to offer – I assumed he'd seen my full glass. Where Matt's haunting scent had been there was the smell of someone busy all day in baggy woollies and a hopeless sort of anorak. I was bewildered to think how I'd wanted to sleep with him. 'The animals are going very well,' he said.

'Oh good, look actually you're just really sort of crushing in between me and my friend's knees here. We're having a rather important conversation.'

Gerard stood back and looked at Luc with the brief cynical calculation I remembered before when he asked about other people's sex-lives. It struck me he probably didn't have one of his own.

'Okay, this is Luc, this is Gerard.' I noticed Luc took his cue from me, and merely nodded. And then, my incurable weak politeness: 'Gerard plays in the Ghezellen van der whatsit. They're all going to dress up as animals.'

'Oh!' I watched him ponder this, then reach out and touch the bombard case. 'And what is this, please?'

'It's his bombard. Now if you don't mind . . .' But Gerard was already pushing back the clasps and revealing the instrument, broken in three and secure in its velveteen hollows. 'Splendid, thanks very much,' I said.

Luc was perversely intrigued. 'Is it a kind of oboe?'

'Yes, it's actually a bass shawm, which is an early kind of oboe. It's modelled on a fifteenth-century one which you can see in the Town Museum.'

'So you had it made.'

'That's right.' Luc dawdled his fingers along the thick dark stem, around the flared bell and over the set of reeds, which were long and curved and bleached like an old pipe. 'You look as if you enjoy instruments,' said Gerard fatuously.

'I used to play the oboe,' said Luc. 'In the school orchestra. But I gave it up.'

'I can't *bear* it when people give up instruments,' I muttered, mortified that he had never told me. 'I mean what's the fucking point of learning them, it's all such a *waste*.'

Poor Luc was quite abashed at this and mumbled sorry: since he wasn't *at* school any more . . . Gerard seemed to sense some advantage and pressed on with an account of the Happy Entry of Philip the Good in 1440. I had a nightmarish feeling that he was going to deliver the whole lecture on ceremonial antiphons that I had had a couple of months before. But Luc broke in childishly with 'Does it make a lot of noise?'

'As a matter of fact', said Gerard, 'it's the loudest instrument there has ever been. It used to be used for raising alarms.' He gave his hooting laugh, took out two of the sections and looked mischievously around the bar.

'I absolutely forbid you to play that thing in here,' I said. And fortunately the juke-box was activated at that moment, the Beach Boys came spinning through, and Gerard having got his drink and said how Luc was welcome to try his bombard some time, moved off. I thought I'd rather hurt him with my brusqueness.

I heaved a big sigh and Luc started working on his backlog of drinks. 'So,' I said, resuming a conversation that he seemed quite prepared to let drop, 'do you still want to leave the country?' It was mad of me to persist, I was grasping for evidence that could only upset me, but to be in his confidence was itself like love and I was thirsty for more.

'Well, of course, I still do want to go to Dorset. But not maybe so far as LA! It would be nice not to be always in this town, where I have lived all my life and where my family have lived since the thirteenth century – but – ' There was bragging in his complaint, and I felt the crisis was probably over. 'You know how it is, sometimes, things get worse and worse, and then you attain a point when you think, I just want to get out of here and start all over again from scratch bottom.'

I laughed and puzzled him for a second. 'I do know what you mean. Maybe that's why I'm here and not in England.'

He raised his eyebrows and leant forward as if this was especially astonishing, but in fact he was indicating someone hovering behind me, as the hand of another farcical interruption landed firmly on my shoulder.

'So we meet again.'

The wrong-note matiness of Ronald Strong – it grated on Luc as well, I was glad to see. I turned and smiled at him for five seconds, then said quietly, 'Piss off.'

He pushed against me, grinning. You'd think I'd just offered him a drink. He nodded at Luc and rocked up and down on the balls of his feet as if warming up for one of his famous work-outs. 'My name's Rodney, by the way,' he said. But Luc, firm, a little frightened by my reaction, glanced away.

'Well, catch you both later,' said Rodney, slapping me on

the shoulder again and moving confidently off. I saw someone eye him up.

Luc swallowed the rest of his beer, and put down the glass with a hesitation that disguised a tremble. 'It's impossible to talk in here', he said, adding, 'where you seem to know every-body.'

'I'm sorry, darling, we'll talk another time.' My god, I'd called him darling. I pressed on, 'Actually, I was going to sug-gest we might go out for a drive to some nice old place one day – you could show me some of your country.'

'Instead of a lesson?'

'If you like.' I put some detail on it. 'Matt's got a sort of jeep, we could go in that.'

'Will Matt be coming with us?'

'Oh no, I don't think so.'

'Oh.' Then, 'Yes, that would be lovely' – and he gave me a smile that had me gasping and gripping the bar.

Luc's zip had snagged on a fold of the lining. He tugged the toggle up and down, but it was jammed. 'What a bloody thing!' he nattered.

I wanted to help but held myself back. I was afraid to be too close to him now, out in the street; I was getting ready to say goodnight, nervous as hell, wondering if I could kiss him, star-ing up at the clouded night. Quarter to something chimed from the Belfry's chilling height. It would be like being up there, when he'd gone – the giddy darkness, my pounding heart.

'Edward, can you help me?'

'It should be quite simple,' I said briskly – crossly he may have thought. He lifted his arms in surrender and I gripped the little tab and yanked it. It gave by one tooth, and was more firmly stuck than before. 'I can't quite see,' I said, 'come under this lamp. Now . . .' We were leaning together to work out the problem, his hair fell forward into my face. 'Get your head out of the light' – and he looked aside like someone squeamish about an injection. I grabbed the bottom of the jacket, where the zip was correctly engaged, and tugged it down as I tried to move the zip up: my hand was against his belt, I even brushed the winking tab of his other zip. 'It'll have to go down,' I said, peering into the dim scent of lad and leather, the soft world of quilted jacket linings and hearts beating under wool and silk. The knuckles of my other hand rubbed his stomach, I felt the little dip of his navel through his shirt. He apologised with a giggle that showed it was not a heaven and hell of love and lust for him, and peered down again with a beery breath across my mouth as I concentrated with tongue on lip. But I had coaxed the zip down, one notch, two, three, then it ran like a ladder.

'So which way are you going?' I said.

He pulled the zip up to the top with a shiver and a grin of new confidence. 'Oh, I don't know' – looking to left and right. 'I don't want to go home too much.'

'It is quite late, and you've got a lesson in the morning.'

He put his head on one side, with what I realised was a rather drunk bit of foolery. 'But it's only with you,' he cooed. I didn't know whether to feel slighted or favoured.

'Your mother will want us both there at ten.' I found myself obscurely reassured by her presence and requirements. I felt the seconds thudding past. There was only the remote noise of the bar across the street, and the occasional taxi speeding perfect strangers from place to place.

'For some considerable time I have wanted to see your place of residence.'

He didn't know what he was doing to me. I said, 'My dear Luc, you really mustn't model your speech on that of our new prime minister.' And he went into a wince-making spiel of what-whats and tally-hos and jolly good shows.

When we came to a wide bridge he jumped on to the wall, and walked hastily along its coping, arms stretched for balance. I'd seen younger kids doing it before, here and there, and wondered if I would jump into the icy water to save them if they slipped. The wall was broad enough, but I heard the scrape of his jeans as he set one foot directly in front of the other. How strong and beautiful his white legs were in the glare of an old rococo lamp with wrought-iron shells and other reminders of the not-so-distant sea. I didn't know, but I thought he'd probably never 'taken someone home', the walk wasn't crowded for him with curious precedents, it wasn't the mock pick-up it was for me. I leant at the bridge's apex; there was a hint of mist on the still canal. Then he came trotting back and steadied himself for an instant with a hand on the top of my head.

I was mentally searching my room, noticing things as a newcomer might. It was bleak and barely furnished – a loft, a fashionable space, Luc might think, and feel at home there, unaware of his own clothes lying newly laundered in the cupboards. I felt secure about that, I kept all the Luciana tidied away from Cherif – in fact the past two weeks had turned me into a humourless char, putting everything straight at once where Cherif had made himself at home. I wondered if the room was going to smell.

When we approached the house Luc fell back, as though having second thoughts, or thrown into a reverie by the sight of the white façade. I opened the wicket and looked round and after a moment he jogged up to me with a smile that seemed to deny his hesitation. 'What a quite obscure place, Edward,' he exclaimed. There was something camp, mischievous, about him that I hadn't heard before; I hurried through into the yard with my face fixed and tormented. Of course he'd been drinking. It occurred to me he might be deliberately teasing me and tempting me into some bungled assault – I wasn't sure I could carry on being pally like this any longer, without at last defying the force around him, like some enchantment in *The Magic Flute*, that froze my intentions in mid-air and padlocked my tongue. 'Is *that* where you live?' he said, looking up at the square of the Spanish girls' window. I caught a strand of music and laughter.

He sprang lightly up the stairs behind me and stood with his hands in his jerkin pockets as I groped for the key. I was distinctly paranoid, I thought there was something quite *plain clothes* about him, almost leaning on me, sceptical, observant. Then I remembered he was only a teenager, and that he never noticed the same things as I did, certainly never noticed *me*. I flicked on the light and bustled obstructively round the room – just checking.

Luc ambled over to the window and peered into the dark; the room itself seemed to pass him by. I didn't know what to say, my mouth was dry, my mind milling and jamming as if I had to deliver an important speech without notes. I watched him covertly, thinking he could see my reflection in the glass. But he pressed his hands around his face: his eyes were working on something farther off. 'It's my old school,' he said, in a tone of puzzled recall. 'Did you know you could see St Narcissus from here, Edward?'

'Of course. I'm always being interrupted by the bells and boys pissing out of the window.'

'Oh, you have to do that,' he said abstractedly, straining to make out the dark gables against the sky. 'That used to be my classroom. That big window on the second floor.'

But I stayed where I was, in the middle of the room, my hand in my pocket holding my cock, looking at his backside and his broad hunched shoulders. I was haunted by potential moves tonight – it was like trustless stoned nights at Cambridge, when I never knew if I'd just said something or was still planning to say it. I saw a phantom me, in the jerky, melting moves of a time-lapse film, going over to him, slipping an arm round his shoulder, hugging him and kissing him. I saw him turning with a raised hand, it could have been to hit or to . . . caress.

'You know, I'm trying to work this out. I've looked at this house, well, quite often. I never saw anything, and I used to wonder to myself what it was. You must imagine, in a very boring lesson. Of course, not like nowadays!' He turned with a grin. 'It's all so long ago.'

'Now, do you want some coffee?' I said. It was the thing you were always asked back for at university, if not for a smoke. I'd spent a hundred long nights on the edge of sleep, worried and exhausted by coffee. 'Or a drink?' I thought he probably shouldn't have any more.

'Oh, drink, drink, drink,' he said, swinging back towards me, knowingly reckless. He picked up Cherif's cap from the table and perched it on his blond stack, a bit at a loss without a mirror. 'Not exactly one,' he tooted.

'Nor one.' I went for the secret brandy, and was quite relieved to see most of it had gone. I was full of troubling punctilio, I thought I might be struck off for getting a pupil

331

drunk. I remembered why Luc was here and not in the darkened school across the canal: the night on the ship, whisky and
cards and who knew what else – we'd never talked about it. It
came up in my dreams, a low scene lit like a Caravaggio by a
single bolt of life-changing light. And did they fuck you? I
needed the brandy. I was queasy from the sea-heave of lust.

I busied myself self-consciously with the tumblers, switched
on the blow-heater – not that I felt cold. Luc dropped into the
big armchair and sprawled, pulling the printed cotton throw
off the bursting plush of the back and tipping Cherif's cap forward over his eyes. For the first time since St Ernest I had a
sense of his balls, held and slumped astride the seam of his
jeans. I saw my phantom self kneeling and licking at the
stretched cloth till it was soaked.

'Who was that very boring and awful old guy at the bar?' he
said, taking an eager drink, his eyes rounding at the burn of it.

'Which particular boring and awful ... as we left, you
mean?' It had been Harold, pushing in critically amid spouts of
pipe-smoke, seeing me snatching this delicious kid away when
only the other day he had been envying me Cherif. I settled on
the desk-chair opposite and started to tell Luc his story; it presented itself as a subject. Harold lived with Andy, a Filipino
boy, a boy in his early forties, that is, whom you hardly ever
saw. It was a sad affair – Harold had rescued him from service
in Brussels, where he worked without a visa for a sadistic businessman. He was trapped all day in a big apartment-block
with alarms. The only times he went out were to drive the
businessman in his Mercedes, sometimes to pick him up late at
night, when the businessman would abuse him or be sick in the
car. He forced himself on Andy and made him cry and spanked
him for hours until he bled.

I thought, why am I telling Luc this? But I'd never seen him
pay such attention. Forget Wordsworth and the stolen boat.
He swallowed more brandy. I went on to how Harold used to
work in security on the building; he used to see Andy in the
underground car-park vacking the sick out of the Merc. He
took a shine to him. After a while Andy confided in him, and
somehow they started to have an affair – they used the flat, it
was all very easy. Harold was by all accounts a monstrous

332

bore even then, but his kindness was a new thing for little Andy. Then one day the businessman found them together. It turned out he'd known about it for a long time. According to Harold he'd been videoing them at it for months. But he'd started to get jealous. He immediately arranged for Harold to be moved elsewhere, but that very night Harold and Andy eloped.

'My god!' laughed Luc, with the rough cold-end catch in his voice.

'The awful thing is that the whole situation has kind of re-produced itself. Andy stays at home while Harold goes out and smokes his pipe and eyes up young men. He says it's because Andy's still afraid to be caught, that the businessman is still after him. But that was years ago. I gather the truth is that Andy's kept home by force, he has to do the housework in the nude, he's actually tied up naked while Harold's out and about. But he's still devoted to Harold because he rescued him, and looks after him.' I was inventing rather freely in the latter part of this.

'Maybe it's time someone rescued him again,' said Luc care-lessly.

'I don't think it's very likely.' I remembered the one time I'd seen him – sallow and queeny, with a wandering rear-end. 'Harold's at that time of life when he's terrified of not being young – he hasn't noticed young people don't have cravats or tuck their shirts into their underpants, he's always very pushy about not being pushed out.'

Luc was quite amused by this, he liked to show himself un-shocked, and not being young was a lifetime away. He smiled self-confidently, sexily from under Cherif's tweedy peak. I blinked away the hint of parody. I thought I'd give him a minute or two and then firmly throw him out, with a quick cheek-kiss at the top of the stairs. Then I'd go into the bed-room and in some way break down. Already I felt an agony of regret rising inside me.

'I'm afraid it's gentlemen's again,' he said, groping for the floor with his drink and surging out of the chair. I showed him where and he went in and slammed the door as if I might want to help. I came back into the room so as not to torture myself with hearing.

When he reappeared he had the stricken jokey look of some-one battling with tension or the unsaid. He didn't meet my eye. I thought of the unfinished confessions of earlier, and how I didn't want to know more. He threw off the cap with a breathy laugh, wandered to where I was standing and put his arms round me in a loose hug.

'Bye, my dear,' I said. It was a lovely gesture, but I almost wished he hadn't. My head in the crook of his arm, his head on my shoulder, face hidden from me. I raised a hand and ran it lightly, sorrowfully over his suede back. He seemed to want to draw it out, there was a charge of emotion I hadn't allowed for. I felt him press himself against me, nuzzle his chin more snugly at my collar in a final clinch, let out a mumbled sigh. I supposed he must know everything, it was his clumsy way of saying sorry, a rugger-faggoty brush-off from which I would have to break free any second. I felt his lips pressing, lifting, pressing on my neck.

I tried to say 'Luc', it was just a swallow, a bubble. There was a shriek of laughter through the wall, a spasm of gabbling, the knock of some dropped object shaking the floor.

'What was that?' whispered Luc, chuckling, not nervous, standing back, but still holding me, putting both arms more comfortably round my neck, as I stood there, clutching him feebly, with little terrified sighs. He leant his forehead against mine, he was open-mouthed, too close to see. Slowly I shifted, power ran back into my arms – it was as if something had come into the room or something had gone out. We started to kiss.

Luc was asleep. I lay propped up beside him, thinking of later days in our affair, unguessed afternoons of sex, drives beside long canals, his cock curving out of his fly in the car, high-summer lulls when we lay like soldiers under Flanders willows and poplars, shirts off, watching clouds drift in the canal, his crude, obsessive demands.

I tiptoed out for a drink of water and came back gulping from the glass like a child. I thought he might have vanished, it seemed foolish to let him out of my sight; but there he was, a goldish blur. I half-stumbled on his clothes, and crouched to rifle them – but what did they matter when the boy himself was here? I found every fear answered and calmed by that luminous fact. He was lying in my bed, naked, sleeping – flat out. It was a triumph. Tears slipped down my face, I didn't really know why – it felt like gratitude, but also they were the tears that register some deep displacement, a bereavement sending up its sudden choking wave. It struck me I must be mourning everything that came before – it was the desolate undertow of success.

When we had started to kiss it was what I wanted, he was warm and strong, our cocks, lying opposite ways in our jeans, rubbed and jolted off each other, we were going to fuck, but for a long while I just held him there in a hard, shocked grip. His tongue pushed into my mouth but I blocked it with my own: I felt my tongue was the tip of some passionate organ that was rooted deep inside me, so densely coiled, so fiercely self-involved, so hardened to its own darkness and starvation that it reacted with a spasm of bewilderment to the free gift of what it craved. He lifted off my glasses and looked at me as if he found me drolly beautiful. I brushed and moulded his face and neck with incredulous fingers, kissed his eyelids, his long nose, the soft burden of his upper lip. He was squeezing my cock already and still I thought I would be mad to let this happen. I thought once I started I would stifle him, frighten him with my dreadful unconditional needs. He would break away with a sickened laugh.

I was reckoning without his own madness. Of course it wasn't just mischief, he wasn't trying to trap me: he wanted fun, experience, anything wild – either you did it with him or you didn't. Somewhere out there was the person he loved, a boy or a girl, but for now he was making do; I felt I was getting the benefit of some stored-up passion intended for someone else, but brimming and spilling; and maybe he liked the switch of power in seducing an older man. It struck me it might even be a kink of his, that he'd done it before – there was the dream I'd had about him and Matt ... I started pulling off his clothes in a turmoil of jealousy and pride.

Luc naked – apart from his white briefs. His hard cock had a vein in it so thick that it showed in contour through the stretched cotton. I turned him round in my hands, kissed the back of his neck, stood away from him a moment as I undid my cuffs, glancing down at his legs, where the summer tan-lines still palely showed. I thought, I mustn't say I love you, though they were the only words I had in my head. He looked back, swung slowly round, swallowing, wondering; there was a mastered shyness in his face, his movements had the seduc-tive blur of drink, the sureness heightened by delay. He took my cock in his hand for a stroke or two, then hugged me again – I was kissing him adoringly, gasping a bit crazily as I worked at his mouth, confusing him; calming him too with my hands across his back, tranced arcs falling gently to his waistband – my fingers slid firmly under and he caught his breath as I fur-rowed through. He curled against me, then started pushing at his pants to get them down.

Luc's cock – with that fat little rope of blue-grey vein that ran out along its broad back and then curved capriciously under, the tight foreskin, still with a tang of moisture under it – I kissed it and licked his blond-wisped balls just briefly, in acknowledgement, whilst his hands went softly through my hair. I stumbled him back a couple of times till he bumped the chair, he didn't quite know what was going on – he raised his foot on to the arm and I slid beneath and twisted round with my face in his arse. It was bolder and more beautiful than I ex-pected, the flare of it as he leant forward to play clumsily with my cock. I stroked his pucker with a knuckle, longing to lick – I breathed on it, sort of whistled as if cooling something. It had a pretty, spoilt expression, a puzzled pout. I kissed all around it, decoyed my tongue all down his raised thigh, came back and tried it with a licked thumb. There was a kind of pride in him as well as me; he would take whatever I gave him. I felt for a second or two the strict obligations of the teacher's role, then doubted, as my thumb slipped in to the first, then the second knuckle, whilst he complained and jacked his cock fiercely in his hand, if he had anything left to learn.

336

I fucked him across the armchair, his feet over his shoulders; I had to see his face and read what I was doing in his winces and gasps, his violent blush as I forced my cock in, the quick confusion of welcome and repulsion. I'd used up all the lube Cherif had left in the jar, but I saw tears slide from the corners of his eyes, his upper lip curled back in a gesture like anguish or goaded aggression. His hand flickered up against my chest to stay me or slow me. I was mad with love; and only half-aware, as the rhythm of the fuck took hold, of a deaf desire to hurt him, to watch a punishment inflicted and pay him back for what he'd done to me, the expense and humiliations of so many weeks. I saw the pleasure start up inside for him, as if he didn't expect it, his cock grew hard again in two seconds, his mouth slackened, but I made him flinch with steeper little thrusts.

I was up on the chair, fucking him like a squaddy doing push-ups, ten, twenty, fifty ... I had a dim sense of protest, postponed as if he wasn't quite sure, he was folded in two, powerless, the breath was pushed out of him, there was just the slicked and rubbered pumping of my cock in his arse, his little stoppered farts. His chest, his face, were smeared with sweat, but it was mine: the water poured off me like a boxer, my soaked hair fell forward and stung my eyes.

And already it was about to end. I pushed myself back on to my feet, I came out of him for a moment and tugged him back by his haunches, his arsehole glittered and twitched and I thrust straight in, then held it gently, barely moving in the gulping shivery limbo just before the end. I had a high starlit sense of it as the best moment of my life. I stroked the inside of his thighs, stooped forward to lick and breathe the faint rubbery smell of his feet; took his cock out of his fist and worked it unyieldingly for him. I saw his balls clutch up, he said 'No, No' and rode on to me as his thrown line of sperm soared into my face, my hair, and again, and then again. So I pushed over the edge myself – I made a grieving moan at the bitterness of it, craving the blessing of his gaze, though his eyes were oddly veiled, fluttering and colourless like some Orst temptress's.

Luc was perfectly friendly in bed, though he smiled more to

reassure himself than to charm me. I was given the feeling I'd slightly overstepped the mark. I was sweet to him, our heads together on the pillow, though I tried not to crowd him and torment him. I laid an arm carelessly over his warm stomach. I wanted to hold him, he was everything to me. His eyes were closed, but he would never sleep when his heart was speeding so.

'Are you all right, darling?'

'Mmm.' Another slow smile, a pat on my protecting arm.

'It's a jolly good job you came into the bar this evening.' A pause, in which he sighed and swallowed. 'I mean, it's not as if you often do.'

'No.' It struck me that if I hadn't been there he could have ended up with someone else; perhaps on other nights he had – it made me feel sick.

'Had you ever been in the Cassette before?'

'We had a bet,' he said, with a smirk. So it was just a dare, I thought there'd been a certain bravado to him ... 'About whether you'd be in there.'

'Oh ...' I couldn't tell if that made me a fool or a dangerous dark horse. 'And who thought I would be?'

'They did. I thought you might be, but I didn't know. I said not. I thought I'd won, because I didn't see you in there, but then you came up to talk to us.' Did it quite figure? I caught their cryptic exchange of looks again, saw the thread of mockery glint again in the story of the evening. Still, he had stayed for me, and I had triumphed. I had obliterated Patrick and Sibylle. 'They think you've got a crunch on me,' he said.

'And why would they think that?' I asked lightly and then wished I hadn't.

But he was too clever to answer, or too kind. He turned towards me, saw my confusion and kissed me on the cheek. Well – even if he was of their opinion, it clearly didn't trouble him. Even, I thought, if he's just using me, slumming it with me here, it's happiness, it's a fucking miracle. I ran my hand over him and between his legs. He was hard again, and so was I. I half-rolled on to him and he lounged round me like a cat, drawing up a leg, a heel that rubbed along my thigh and rested roughly and electrifyingly in the crack of my arse. I thought

338

'scratch bottom' and smiled at him and to myself but I didn't explain; it felt both a comfort and a sadness to live so much more than him in the world of metaphors and puns. He gently pushed me off, saying 'Not now', though he left an arm limply over me, our calves were crossed. I wondered if he felt the transgressive thrill of a man's hairy legs against his own.

While he slept I kept watch over him – a smooth shoulder, the little pool of the clavicle, his neck, his extraordinary face, his hair muddled and pushed back. His lips were parted and dry, and I felt anxiously that I should wet them from a flask or with a soaked rag. It seemed mad to have him here and not be making love to him over and over, but I was consecrated to his repose: my mood became oddly chivalric. I remembered the old Altidorean legend – not as far as I knew espoused by Luc – which made him a direct descendant of the Virgin Mary, admittedly in her later, post-virginal phase. I'd known from early on that he had something unearthly about him – it was all more than likely. I lay back dazzled by his mere companion-ship, the trust he put in me to see him through the night. I thought of Ty's little agenda: get rid of Cherif – for the moment that seemed to be done, my thoughts didn't even track him as far as Matt's and whatever they were doing there; find the best in Rex Stout – I perhaps hadn't followed that to the letter, I'd been a lout; tell Luc you love him, or you will never have peace with yourself. So I said it into the air, not loud enough to wake him – I hardly heard it myself over the blow-heater's rattle and rumble next door, that might have been a ferry's trembling engines, heard from a cabin on a night cross-ing.

I dreamt I had met a young man by the seaside. We went for long, energetic, rather tense walks, away from the sea and through a derelict industrial estate. I was very keen on him; he had curly dark hair and blue eyes and was astonishingly strong. He ripped a steel door off a windowless, bunker-like building, just to show me what he could do. I was exhilarated. I was too shy to ask, but I hoped he would do other such tricks. We sat down on a dusty doorstep, there was no one around, and he tugged his shirt off to show me his chest muscles and his biceps. I was calling him Luc, though I was almost certain that wasn't his name, and he took a slow, calculating moment or two to react to it. 'Yes, I'm Luc,' he said; 'of course I am.' And he lobbed a breeze-block through a window across the street as though to prove it.

Luc stirred against me – the shattered glass's rhythmic tinkling was St Narcissus striking three. He sighed and burbled but seemed not to wake, or if he did he pretended sleep. I eased on to an elbow and studied his face. I could just make out, under the veined and silvery eyelids, the rapid oscillations of the eyes that mean dreaming, or in a waking person the secretive reflex when a wish is glimpsed and then denied. I wondered what townscape he was rambling through and who he fell in with in that luminous world of his own invention, that no one but him would ever see and that he himself would prodigally forget.

18

'I'm afraid he's not back yet. But come in.'

'Oh.' I was a few minutes late myself, delayed perhaps by unease about this meeting as much as by tiredness and a light
hangover and the magnificent shock of last night. It made me
feel like a kid again, going to call on Dawn's parents, when the
outrageous fact of what we did together seemed to bulge
upwards like some monstrous erection under the tea-table –
one saw the cups begin to tilt . . . I was imagining the weeks to
come, the shabby little subterfuges Luc and I would be put to. I
thought he'd probably be better at it than me: it was part of his
daily reckonings with his mother, whereas I flinched guiltily
from cheating her.

I followed her into the kitchen. 'Where has he gone?' I asked.
I'd wanted him to be there as I arrived, very much.

'He stayed overnight with the Dhondts, their boy Patrick is a
great friend of Luc's from school.' A capable subterfuge
already.

'Oh yes, I've met him. I ran into them at the Town Baths one
morning.'

'It was a rare chance, then. Luc normally hates swimming.
He doesn't like anything where you have to take your clothes
off. He was so tall as a little boy, and ashamed of being skinny.'

'I hadn't thought of him as being skinny,' I said, as if willing
to entertain the idea, still feeling his warm dips and curves in
my palms. It was clear to me the whole preoccupation with fat-
ness and weight was the mother's not the son's.

'I'm making some coffee, just as usual,' she said. Then, 'So
are you pleased with his progress?'

'Oh, he's terribly good,' I said. 'I'm sure he's right just to concentrate on the Dorset English exam – I know you were worried
about it, but I can promise you he'll do well. He's going to do

his first big essay for me this week, on Wordsworth and child-hood.' I beheld its careful pages already, and myself correcting them firmly, reluctantly.

'He's so wild sometimes.' She had her lost look. 'He's crazy keen to get away from here. And I suppose I must . . . help him to escape! Of course I love the old town. You know his family have lived here since the twelfth century?'

'I knew they went back quite some way.'

'I wish he showed more interest in the church. I don't think young Patrick Dhondt is a very good influence, he's quite a rough noisy boy with a terrifying little car which I'm always afraid he will crash and kill them both. Luc seems to be devoted to him. I think it must be a sort of hero-worship, you must have come across it. He spends as much time with Patrick Dhondt as possible.'

'I see.'

'Of course the father, Roger Dhondt, is a famous ornithologist. But he's always stalking about with his binoculars. I don't think he's got much time for anything that can be seen with the naked eye.'

I laughed and saw how it warmed her on this dark November morning to call up her worries. It seemed I might be able to help by keeping Luc out of Patrick's clutches. 'I'll do what I can,' I said.

She put me in the dining-room, just as usual, and I sat and stared at 'Tintern Abbey'. Luc was always punctual, so this seemed a kind of test. He'd left me in the cold of the dawn, nervy and hurried, a bit embarrassed, with a tense smile as he slipped out of my arms, and something about getting back while his mother was at early mass. But maybe he hadn't been home. He was doing something that was painfully hidden from me. And then his timing must have gone wrong, there having been no rehearsal. He would come in panting, with a light, un-elaborated excuse, grinning at me as he entered the room, calling back reassuringly to his mother. I sipped the coffee, my hand shaking. It dropped into my mind that he was avoiding me.

'It's very odd,' said Mrs Altidore, popping in five minutes later. 'I've just telephoned Céleste Dhondt, she's French and always quite rude. She says Luc didn't stay there last night. She says Patrick got home very late by himself, she thinks about one o'clock. This morning he said Luc had made other plans.'

'How curious . . .' My pulse was thudding in my neck.

'You see what I mean, he's so *wild*. It truly frightens me at times, Mr Manners. I don't want to drag out his whole history in front of you, I've always wanted you to see him at his very clever and gifted best, but I think you will know anyway that there have been *catastrophes* before.'

'I'm sure he'll be fine. There's no reason to think anything . . . untoward has happened to him.'

She wandered over to the window – I saw for the first time a haunting fore-echo of the son's lazy stride in her gangling actions. My mind was slamming round the maze of alibis and explanations. I found myself impotently concentrating on the fact that Patrick hadn't got home till one o'clock.

'The awful business of the boy last month, found in the sea-canal,' she said. It seemed cruel not to tell her the happier truth about her son. I dismissed her fears quite brusquely, burdened by the familiar glimpse I'd had of a mother's forebodings, a video nasty of the threatening world.

'He was a drug-addict and a, a gigolo,' I said, and saw that I'd only conjured up two further dangers and brought them dripping into her house.

I went out to find her a few minutes later. I felt sure Luc must have gone to my rooms, this once, through some simple mis-understanding, a glitch in our polyglot pillow-talk. I wandered softly along the passage to the kitchen and came to a halt when I saw her through the open door. She was half turned away from me, standing by the stove, eyes fixed, I thought, on the teeming emptiness under the table. Behind her hung copper pans, far more than could ever be used at one time, and in front of her were spread potatoes, curly red cabbage, fretty French parsley, a lemon, a mortar, a bottle of oil and a huge mauve, bearded, festive fish.

I scuttled across town through a vapoury drizzle, running for a few yards and then dropping back into a winded walk; I was muttering with anxiety, Luc fouling up on this morning when everything needed to run sleekly and deceptively. I sensed it as a protest or a tease, it seemed to register in my body, the dull ache in my thighs and back after the rigours of that particular exercise. My yearning for his lean, fit body became a flustered envy of it, a hopeless need simply to be seventeen, to be half my age, at the wondering outset . . .

Cherif was sitting at the top of the stairs like love locked out, or as if he'd come himself for a lesson. 'Are you ready for me?' he said.

'Baby, shouldn't you be at work?'

He looked at me indulgently. 'I've got to get my clothes first. I can't go in my best coat.'

I unlocked the door with the fear that last night had been a hallucination, and that normality had come back, noiseless and solid. But then I saw how he went through the room, only half-disguising his suspicions; and I must admit I had cleaned up as if after a crime. There was sick worry and accusation in his face and way of speaking, inexpertly and bravely and cloyingly covered up. When I explained about Luc going missing he brightened and mimicked frowning concern.

So we went hunting for him together. Cherif was to be my partner on this one, he didn't want this drama between me and Luc ranging round town unchecked; and I let him come because I had no idea where to look and didn't expect to be successful. It was like a task set in a dream, you went busily around, you were pointlessly systematic, your eye searched through shop-windows and cruised the crowd till you felt giddy, as if you were trying to count them. You saw a blond boy and ran to the street corner, caught up with him, as you might have wanted to anyway, and felt licensed to scrutinise him and turn him down. Cherif was useless, never having seen Luc: it was a charade for him in his high-collared coat like an old film gumshoe, more watchful for me than for the kid. He cursed him a lot, and criticised him as a truant and a trouble-maker.

We checked out one or two cafés and bars, though it seemed likely to me Luc would be at a friend's house, or else just walking in one of the tree-lined streets at the town's edge. As the morning lengthened he became more poignant – suffering and confused after our night together, needing confidence and love.

I contrived to come past the Cassette, and ran in for a pee, drifting back by the deserted tables and booths, the bare bar-stools where we'd sat. It didn't seem impossible he'd be there, waiting for me, as if he had a bet on it.

In the main shopping-streets the hateful advance parties of Christmas were out, wiring up tinny speakers from shop-front to shop-front: mechanical music was heard in the distance, even worse than the carillons, with none of their lofty resonance. I thought hysterically how I would have to go back to England and leave all this behind, give up the search with the boy still unfound. And a winter of Cherif's bickering and disappointment. The rain spotted and blurred my glasses. I said, 'I'd better get over to Luc's mother – he may have turned up.'

When we came out into the Grote Markt the low cloud seemed to buckle and bruise above the gilded gables, the belfry-top was lost, there was a sense of steeply heightened concentration. The rain was suddenly audible and swelled in a few seconds to a steady fizzing racket on the stones; it came down on us and up at us, intent and oblivious at once – I turned up my jacket collar and started to run and Cherif was splashing along beside me, shouting and laughing. There was nowhere in particular to hide: it was like being caught on a shingle beach or even out at sea. I took off my glasses and ran with them clutched in my pocket. It was a chaos of jumping, vague forms and watery obliteration – I headed for Long Street, drenched and gasping, ready to surrender: on top of all the anxieties it was oddly hilarious. I ran up to the steps and slammed the bell with my palm, and Cherif, dripping but protected by his coat, came after me and was swearing rowdily when Luc's mother opened the door.

We stood panting and bedraggled in the hall, like two truants ourselves, with nothing to say. Mrs Altidore was clearly alarmed by the sight of Cherif, in his filthy boots, ambling round the room as she spoke to me. The whole day was so odd it hardly surprised me to see him in this least likely place, with the water still sparkling in his curly hair, looking critically at the hangings.

'He's left town,' she said. 'I'm sure he has.' I longed to say no, he's here, he was with me all night – it was all a bother, with my

345

clothes wet and clinging and cold, though I was hot from running and red-faced in the dark old mirror opposite. She groped in the pockets of the purple knitted house-coat she had on, and brought out a letter. 'This has just come. It's from Luc's friend Arnold, who is a very responsible young man. He's like an older brother to Luc. He's brilliant. He's at the university of Leuven.'

'Yes, Luc's told me . . .'

'He says . . . "I thought I should tell you that I have had a long letter from Luc . . . much of it is very personal but he does say how much he wants to leave home . . . you probably know he has been very upset lately, affairs of the heart have not turned out well for him . . . I have tried to calm him down but I thought you should be prepared for him to do something unexpected, as he has before."' She held the letter out to me with the stare of someone demanding help. I read it quickly and resentfully, as evidence of an older intimacy, a more disinterested care. My hair dripped on to it and made the inky tendrils float.

'I don't know,' I said. It was priggish, wasn't it, and sneaky? But then Arnold didn't know about me, about us. Nobody did.

'I want you to find him,' she said in her cracked, imperious way.

'Well, of course I'd love to, but I've just been searching . . .'

'I think I know where he's gone. There's no point in my following him, alas – it wouldn't help. It's not easy for a mother to look after a seventeen-year-old boy alone. He misses his father, it's quite natural.'

'You think he's gone to his father, gone to Brussels?' I was alarmed that he might blurt out about last night.

She chewed her cheek. 'Can you drive?'

'Yes . . .'

'Then take my car; I'm sure you should go straight after him. He trusts you and likes you and you're . . . disinterested – you could get him back before he does anything stupid.'

I saw myself boarding a ship in disguise and infiltrating a tense strip-poker game deep below decks. It was going to be a test of initiative, like one of our mad field-days at school. It still seemed to me somehow beside the point, but I began to catch the mother's agitation, her dread not only of where he was going but of having driven him out. 'I don't want him falling

346

into rough hands,' she said, glancing narrowly at Cherif as if he were himself a manifestation, a messenger, of the underworld (long ignored, long suspected and feared) that was waiting to receive her son.

'I'll do whatever you like,' I said. 'But first I really must change, I'm soaked to the skin.' It was clear she hadn't noticed this till now.

She tugged open drawers, and chopped through the clustered hangers on the cupboard rail. I wasn't sure if she was looking for old things that didn't matter or for something good enough and suitable. She didn't know the leather me, only the sports-coat and tie me. She laid out a couple of shirts. 'A vest?' I nodded. 'Underpants? Well, you can help yourself' – thank you, I will. 'But can you get into his trousers?' I said I'd try them and see.

'The two of you are the same height, but you of course are much fatter.' She lifted out some dreary flannels which none the less had a beauty when you imagined them ironised by Luc's long legs.

I couldn't really start changing till she'd left; I squatted to un-tie a shoe, and she watched me interestedly, as if to say it was years since she'd seen a man undress even so much as that. 'I'll give you the keys to the car,' she said, 'and to the Pavillon de l'Aurore.'

'Thanks very much,' I said, thinking of it still as a treat, whose magic might be broken if I protested or asked questions. For the past twelve hours or more life was living itself with a logic and fluency of its own, everyone else was in a state of crisis, but I had become calm, I knew it couldn't be resisted.

When she had gone I pushed the door quietly to and dragged off my wet clothes. I still had the sensation of being chilled and hot at once, like a neo-classical description of passion. A pile of heavy unlovely garments grew in the middle of the floor, as if placed by an orderly suicide. I stood in my damp jockey-shorts and slowly dried myself with Luc's face-towel; then wandered about, looking at his pictures, the muddle on his desk. I read some notes on a pad – 'W. born at Cockermouth(!)', 'Fostered alike by *beauty* and by *fear*', various other quotations and 'Ask

Edward about' followed by nothing. Well, I'd certainly have told him if I could.

The framed school photo was four years old – one might have expected Luc to be cross-legged at the front, with the cups, but because of his height he was standing with boys who were evidently older – he looked vulnerable among them, his smile anxious and pre-sexual beside their thinly nonconformist grins and sneers. There were some beauties at St Narcissus, those Benelux blonds – and there, at the headmaster's feet, was a dark Puck, round-faced young Patrick, holding a polished heraldic shield between his knees and leering as though to say, if you could see what's behind *this* . . .

I thought of the day I'd found Patrick in this room – sprawled just there, scuffed school shoes on Mrs Altidore's richly worked bedspread. And the first visit – my secret excitement, the yearning I'd stifled under a kind of snootiness, it seemed to me now, as of someone only just out of his own Airfix-trophied den. And this third visit, how young it all still looked, and how unguarded, and hence reproachful.

The flannels were too tight to get the zip up; I flicked through the other trousers and found a baggy old pair that looked possible, made of thick navy drill with carpenter's pockets, faintly musty from a season's neglect, with chalky lines at the knees from the oxidised hanger. On me they weren't so baggy after all, but they could just be buttoned unflatteringly at the waist. I drew on Luc's socks, I went to the mirror and buttoned his shirt over his cotton vest, I climbed into his russet sweater – all these things mothered and fabric-conditioned and freshly stored. I looked at myself with eerie satisfaction.

The light wasn't good, the rain still thrashed into the street below, and I stepped forward to see myself in the mirror, the flushed impersonator. There were long gold strands in the teeth of Luc's comb, which must have come out as I drew it through my rain-sleeked hair and stayed there, like the first fine threads of age among the black. His clothes hugged me tightly, exactingly, like sports gear; I felt the little heart-weight of dread that preceded sports at school, looking out down the relentless track. And yet it didn't seem to matter – I stroked my thighs and somehow they were his, this was what it felt like to have a

348

medallist's legs, to carry the tape with you and have it flutter down about your waist as you reined and jogged loosely on. The churches were striking noon, but in the glass it was dusk. I hovered and peered and glowed there, his inhabitant.

Then I saw I had accepted his mother's intuition – I wasn't expecting him to come springing up the stairs and catch me in his things. I saw my own face sicken in the mirror. Each second that I gave up to becoming him only took him further from me. I pictured him hurtling away through the rain, faster than any runner, in a car hidden from pursuers by a twirling wall of spray, or in a train that seemed to cross in seconds from one side of this little country to the other. And why stop there? He disappeared into France, or Holland, or Germany, he was among the youthful detritus of Paris or Hamburg. And then the questions were asked. Patrick and Sibylle said how they'd left him in my care, a red-eyed slanderous snapshot, like that of Rose, was passed around the bar. No one from among the stooped churchgoers and cleaners of the winter daybreak came forward to remember him in the street, after he left me. I was the last person to have seen him alive.

There was a knock and his mother came straight in. I saw her troubled for a moment by my rueful grimace. 'I've just had a phone-call', she said, 'from Kristien de Taeye, the wife of the Minister of Culture.' And already it had happened. I felt the accusing finger quiver and jab and fence me back – the finger was an épée – shielding my face into the corner of the room.

'Oh yes,' I said, feigning a search for a shoe.

'Her daughter Sibylle is a very close friend of my Luc. Apparently she was with him last night. Up to a certain point.'

'Aha.'

'Well, she's gone too.'

The car was a laurel-green Renault saloon, about ten years old but with surprisingly little on the clock. Inside there was an oppressive smell of polish and plastic, it was a bit like sick, sour and sweet, or like cod-liver oil and malt. In spite of the rain I opened my window for air – the drops zipped past me on to the crocheted seat-shawls and strewn cushions of the rear window.

So the Three had finally declared themselves. Their egg had

rocked and cracked and out from its opaque wreckage had scuttled the blanched baby basilisk Luc and Sibylle. My mouth was open in a rictus of contempt, loss, jealousy, guilt – to run so quickly, and with her . . . How had they arranged it? Why had they even bothered? I grew claws and wings, I was a monster of gross, intolerable demands. He couldn't face me, after what had happened. And here I was coming after him with a roar. I stamped wretchedly on the accelerator, and after a moment's uncertainty the car thrust forward with a power it seemed almost to have forgotten. We thrummed over the cobbles of the Street of Disappointments with a new speed and a new compression of misery.

There was something about Cherif's coat, as he sat beside me, that only darkened the mood. It had got a soaking, of course, its first, and even within the sour-sweet stuffiness of the car it gave off a melancholy smell of its own, of wet wool, doggy and defenceless – a smell of defeat. I knew that it had lost its sheeny down, its expensive freshness, and that it would never be new again.

I wondered why he didn't take it off. He had sat hunched in it in the Altidores' hall for quarter of an hour whilst I changed and talked. I came downstairs patting the pockets of Luc's best sports-jacket, the one I had sometimes envied him, fine grey tweed with a wide yellow square in it, and there Cherif stubbornly was, unattuned, unamenable, like a foreman summoned to the mill-owner's house. In the car he said nothing, but I knew he was glancing at me as I drove, and at the little buffetings my face was taking from the feelings I was sparring with. I winced and ducked at the wheel and knocked my glasses as I knuckled away furious tears. I couldn't take him with me on this journey, or pretend a merely tutelary interest in Luc when I was gasping already with anger and anxiety. I would have to tell him he couldn't come. Then he said, 'Let me out of the car.'

There was a van on my tail in the lashing rain, I couldn't instantly stop, but he was in a passion of his own. 'Let me out,' he said again, with a frightening edge.

'I can't,' I shouted. 'Just fuck off a minute Cherif, Christ I've got enough to think about without you freaking out, you stupid cunt.' But something had cracked in him, he was beating on my arm so it was hard to steer; I squinted in the mirror through the already misting rear window, and for a second at him, bare-toothed. I indicated right and craned forward through the murk for somewhere to pull in, and Cherif, who had never driven in his life, snatched at the hand-brake – the car swerved out for a second at the rear, and the van blasted its horn and swerved too, it was going too fast; in the wing-mirror its headlights flashed as it loomed within an inch of the wing and then hurtled past, a hand like a conductor's, brutal, damning, out of the window.

'I was about to stop,' I said quietly, when I'd come to a halt. 'You could have written off Mrs Altidore's car within two minutes of leaving her house.' I felt in fact that I had somehow escaped from a run of bad luck. I had caught a mirror before it shattered or avoided seeing the new moon through glass. I could speak for some time in this prudential vein, in the hushed control I placed on my fright, denying the childish wound of being accused, however justly. But he was fumbling with the seat-belt, prodding and tugging at the simple catch, which at last came free. It was an old belt that didn't retract and he flung it with a clatter against the tin and plastic of the door. He jumped out of the car and stood for a moment gazing away, as if trying to choose the perfect phrase with which to go: I waited for one of his broody poetic claims, while the rain streaked down around him and over the inside of the open door. But he merely pulled the belt of the coat free and then shrugged the heavy garment off. He bundled it loosely, tumblingly, and with-out looking tossed it in at me like something common and contemptible. Then he turned back down the street, leaving the door standing out like a broken wing. I leant over and pulled it to and then sat and watched him quickly dwindle in the rain-bubbled side-mirror, with an involuntary catch of pleasure at his big handsome backside – he was terribly sexy to me for a moment.

I stayed and calmed myself. I was going to the Museum, to warn Paul I was leaving town, but I couldn't turn up like this. I groped for a handkerchief, and of course it was Luc's, not alto-gether clean, with a trouser-pocket staleness, gummed up with snot which clung in the creases in hard translucent grains, like rice: I placed one on my tongue, half-expecting it to liquefy as in some miracle with a saint's salved fluids. The jacket was a lovely one, a somewhat conventional garment, with its Scotland-Piccadilly-Brussels pedigree, for a teenage runaway – but that was just Luc's ambiguity. It suited me more than his other things, and gave me that stamp of square-shouldered smartness I could never fully attain myself. I had seen his mother's hesitation as I lifted it down on its hanger, like something I couldn't afford. 'Yes, take it,' she said – I was only borrowing it, but I could tell it helped her to let it go, it confirmed how she was rising to the challenge. She seemed almost enthusiastic when she saw the clumsy simulacrum of her son that had assembled itself in her own house.

In the breast-pocket was a *carnet* of tram-tickets, half of them already punched with the dates and times of errands across town – remote evidence of . . . something; a pair of rosy ticket-stubs from the Memling Cinema that spoke of a shared two hours of darkness with . . . someone; and a folded strip of paper with St Alban Street 73 written on it, which was my address. I had no idea how he knew it, or why it was there; it seemed vaguely incriminating, so I tore it up, and then struggled with the question of where to put the scraps, when I was in his clothes and in his mother's car.

19

On standard speed the wipers made an indolent, halting trawl of the windscreen, but on full speed they flicked from side to side so fast you felt the mechanism was about to snap. Marcel told me about the wipers on a friend's father's BMW, apparently adjustable to anything from lento to prestissimo at the touch of a finger, and with varying degrees of intermission. He was interested in cars, but only so far at the level of fixtures; he played determinedly with the cigarette-lighter and had quickly assessed the austere alternatives of the heating-system. We travelled in a roar of boosted warmth, peering out under misted arcs at the flowing stampede of cloud.

The idea that Luc and Sibylle were somewhere ahead of us and would wait to be found lost all sense in the midday darkness, streaked with cars' lights, in the drowned anonymity of the road. Oh, I wanted to get to him first, to find out what story he was telling, to do a deal with him – but if he had been at the station early he could be hundreds of miles away by now. His mother thought not; she said it was another of his moody crises, which could be drastic in effect but were local in physical range. I gripped the wheel, ignobly anxious for myself but also with a larger, dimmer wish that he shouldn't fuck up his young life.

Marcel was restless, eager, whisked away from his lessons on a quest for his beautiful and scandalous senior. He was pink-faced at the privilege of it and chattered solemnly until my nervous silence, my curt demands for help with road-signs and turnings, affected him too, rather as a parent's misery seeps into a child and subdues it. I heard the drag of his breathing amid the heater's bluster, and then the breathy squawk of his inhaler. When I remembered I gave him a little side smile and saw him sigh with sudden reassurance. I knew that under all our tension and ignorance we were both excited by our own activity, and admired ourselves, swept forward through the murk by the exhilarating imperatives of a crisis.

It was a little crisis for him as well, of course. He had stood by with an ironic mime as I told his father that Luc had run away again – his gestures were still the moue and wiggle of the head of Lilli Vivier, his protecting friend, maybe even of his remembered mother. When I said that Sibylle had gone too I had quite forgotten for a second how Marcel worshipped her. I saw him caught by a real discovered feeling of his own – he stepped forward. Then Paul had calmly proposed that Marcel come with me and made the condition that we speak only in English – it was to be a lesson of a kind. Marcel hesitated – he wasn't quite sure of the momentum of the thing; and again I saw his father rather clownishly encourage him, rather bruisingly exaggerate and publicise his blushing little *tendresse*. I put a hand on the kid's shoulder out of generalised sympathy. It was true he was a friend of Sibylle's: he knew far more of her than I did. I thought Sibylle herself probably didn't know, or at least kindly overlooked, the full extent of his feelings, however vague and ideal they may have been. As I glanced across at him in the car I wondered if it was my own failure of imagination – there was no reason he shouldn't be just as filthy-minded as I had been at sixteen. For a mad moment I thought I should tell him what Luc and I had done last night; but the moment passed and left me more wretched than before.

'I expect they'll have to tell the police,' Marcel said.

'Ooh, let's hope we can get to them first,' I said; though I saw he thought the police would be best, both at finding them and at somehow punishing Luc. 'It's a bit early for that. As a matter of fact I know Sibylle's father wants this kept very quiet – it could be embarrassing for him, and Luc's father too, of course.' I'd stood by as Mrs Altidore rang both these figures, and watched her persuade them of her exciting and ridiculous plan. De Taeye had been called out of an important meeting and had evidently spoken under some constraint; he had jumped at the idea of my going to sort things out. I heard her give me an incredible reference, a summing-up not exactly of insights, but of a high regard she'd never hinted at to me in person; and Martin Altidore too

354

had been right behind me: I picked up from his wife's reactions his opening tone of shifty exasperation and then his relief, almost a shout when she proposed me as an envoy. As before I thought, I don't know what I'm doing, or why these people trust me so much. Their expectations crowded on to me and became a reason in themselves.

'Were the police involved the last time?' I said.

He had the story all ready. 'Yes, they brought him back to school in the first lesson.'

'But he hadn't actually done anything wrong?'

'Drink. Drugs. Smoking. Theft. Trespassing. Swearing at a policeman.'

'You're supposed to be talking English,' I said, to hide the shock this incident still caused me. I didn't want him to find the words to go on about it. The imagined scene was too tender and painful, too much my own dark possession. 'I have the idea you didn't like Luc very much.'

He was silent, turned to gaze through his smeared side-window at the hidden farms. 'He set fire to my hair,' he said at last.

'Oh my god.'

'Altidore and Dhondt. Dhondt was worse, but Altidore always did what he said. They set fire to my cape and gave me an asthma attack.'

It was a wonder he wasn't done for arson as well. 'But that's terrible,' I said; I was cross and disappointed and very slightly excited.

'Yes, it is. I had to go to hospital as you know. Altidore had already had his warning before he ran away.'

'But you think it was . . . Dhondt who was really behind it.' I was lost in this horrible vision of Luc as a coward and a bully. It must have been Dhondt with his dreadful gorged cudgel who had driven him on.

'Turn left, turn left!' shouted Marcel, as if I were stupid beyond redemption.

We came to a nondescript town – it didn't even have a name: the sign lay in the verge beside a lorry's water-logged tyre-ruts. Marcel announced that he was hungry, and I wished he hadn't

355

come with me: I saw my quest hindered by his needs and robbed of its proper comfortless urgency.

We sat in an empty café and looked out over the empty square. Marcel ate a cheeseburger greedily – he laid claim to his food as though his fat had its independent demands; but it delayed and solaced him too. I half watched him, half kept an eye on the war-memorial and the passers-by in the precipitate dusk. Then the rain ceased – there was a brief brightening, hurried glimpses of light above the housetops, yellow cloud-grottoes from which winged faces might momentarily tumble above a holy victory or a martyrdom. The pavement dazzled. I smiled at Marcel and his clown's mouth of ketchup. The truth was I didn't know how to talk to him – I only had the stock resources of the language lesson, the useful topics, the factitious interest. I got out my cigarettes and then thought smoke might upset him. 'I'm just going outside,' I said.

I strolled across the square, jittery but slow. I was trying to picture a meeting with Luc – they were hitching and ran up to the car with a grateful look, not a great car but still, Luc saw it was his mother and swerved away, while Sibylle tugged open the door and saw with horror it was me. Luc and I not knowing if we were friends or enemies, friends or lovers. Or we met at the coast, and for a long time said nothing at all. I lost my feeble advantage, I didn't know how to talk him down off the high ledge of his decision.

The memorial was a little crag in itself, with a hundred names still sharp in the granite of the base. Up above stood a bronze soldier, handsome, downcast, with a virtuoso moustache, not quite attractive to me, but solid with pathos. He was broad and steady, and confident of effect. I took him in with a shock – the rain-shiny helmet and cape, the out-of-doors certainty of him after the arcane fictions of Orst.

I was watching the Mini for a second or two before the thump of recognition – its provoking mauve, the unforgotten number-plate. It trundled toy-like across the square, the driver's visor down against the sun and the lights still on from the rain. I saw the mission helplessly complicated by Patrick, coming after the others to persuade and alter and exercise whatever his uncertain power was. And then it made my job more lonely and

356

absurd. Already I was embarrassed to be seen, so quick off the mark, there ahead of him, panting after Luc, he would think. I turned away from the approaching car.

But when it came past it wasn't Patrick but Sibylle at the wheel, frowning forward – though in the moment she was alongside her eyes flicked to me (a figure she knew, in clothes she remembered), held me and then denied me, though a little swerve of the car betrayed the effort of self-control, and I saw her in silhouette shift her head to follow me in the mirror. So Luc was here or close by, there was a twist of relief that it was almost over already . . .

I ran towards the café, gesturing through the window at Marcel. I'd seen which road Sibylle had taken out of the square, but by the time we were back in the car and after her there was no one to be seen ahead. The street curved and wandered for a few hundred yards, until it reached a T-junction. We both of us peered to left and right and Marcel gave a shrug and dropped his hands, as if to say he had never rated our chances. I went right, with what may have seemed like decisiveness. 'Keep your eyes open,' I said. Rain slapped across the windscreen, like water tipped down from an awning after a storm.

If I had chosen left it might all have been over sooner. It wasn't till twenty minutes later that I spotted the parked car, semi-concealed in the forecourt of a building – tall, grey, pebble-dashed, metal-shuttered, a newish apartment block on the rubbishy edge of town. I left the Renault in the road, and sprinted with Luc's jacket pulled above my ears. I thought my fate today was to be drenched over and over – I saw a succession of changes into strangers' clothes. Beside the front door was a panel of lit buttons, and I read the names twice, first as gibberish, then slowly, as if each of them did indeed distantly ring a bell.

'We're waiting opposite the house.'

'I see. Thank you.'

'I suppose we'll just have to wait until one of them comes out.'

'I wish I knew who they were with – I don't know anyone who lives there. They must be friends of Sibylle's.'

'Or Patrick's, perhaps.' I heard Mrs Altidore's sigh. 'Of course I don't know that Patrick is actually here. I've only seen his car.'

'That car!'

'But if they're all here, then it looks less serious – it's just some silly prank.'

'I've had Kristien de Taeye on the phone for an hour at least. She blames it all on Luc.'

I twisted round with the receiver under my chin, but I couldn't see as far as the house from the bar's back corner. I'd taken the precaution of having a small beer pulled. It was waiting, out of reach, chilled and golden on the dark oak counter. 'I'm running out of change,' I said. 'I'll ring you again.'

'Yes, please.' I was improvising my new confidential role, *in loco parentis* – I felt the sharp tug of her dependence on me, Luc at the centre of all our needs.

'Or maybe I'll just turn up with him' – I almost said 'bound and gagged'. I rang off and downed the beer in two swallows, like a reward for being prompt and considerate. Outside it was already dark and it seemed like a freak of virtue to leave without setting up a few beers more. But I did.

It wasn't easy to keep watch, with the dark and the rain and the pearling of our own heat and breath on the car windows. I felt rather fatuous – I hadn't found the tempo of it yet, I expected something to happen straight away and sat forward, staring vaguely. When it rained, the view was rapidly obliterated; the dark bulk of the building, with the glare of the lobby and one or two chinks of shuttered light above, was puddled and smeared by the water on our windscreen, streaming in its own multiple faint refractions of the street-lamps. Then I would start the engine and swill the rain off with a couple of sweeps of the wipers. Everything took on a new clarity – it was like putting on my glasses and catching the world as it came to attention, legible and commonplace. Then the corner of a window wobbled and ran, the concrete canopy of the porch twitched and melted.

Marcel was easily bored and easily scared, but he took to the long tedium of the stake-out better than I did. He said it reminded him of a scene in a film where Eddie Murphy was being watched in a hotel by two incompetent cops in a car; he had it on video and gave me verbatim, twice, the sequence where Murphy, who in fact has come and gone as he pleases, surprises his guards with a tray of coffee and rolls. I winced to think how far away the morning was. I failed to rise to his little performance, too taken up with my own memories of waiting and watching, the involuntary predator.

'I'm sorry about Luc bullying you,' I said, almost taking responsibility for him, swallowing at the memory of his softly interrogative kisses, seeing in the blurred glass a weird and displaced image of his naked body rinsed with my sweat.

'It doesn't matter,' Marcel said, sounding weary of indignities. 'I don't suppose he could help it.'

I gave a snuffly little laugh. 'Well, anyone can *help* bullying, surely?'

Marcel nodded from side to side, as if weighing up long experience. An approaching car washed us with light, like a couple in front of a television, then left us in shadow. 'He was, you know, very mad. A lot of people at school were not friends of his. Then Dr Boesmans used to come and see him.'

'Oh yes. You mean my landlord in St Alban Street?' Marcel nodded. 'And what did Dr Boesmans say?'

'I don't know. It's confidential. He used to see some of the boys in the sick-room after school – if they had problems . . .' – and he tapped his temple with his forefinger.

'You mean he's a psychiatrist. I thought he was just . . . an ordinary doctor.'

'He's a very famous psychiatrist,' Marcel said quietly.

I felt a futile retrospective tenderness for Luc, having his boyhood troubles sorted out by this famous old man. And then I saw, with a bleak little sinking of the heart, what the scrap of paper in his pocket had been. It wasn't my address he was remembering, but Dr Boesmans'. It was just the sort of thing his mother would keep from me: she must have sent him to him again. That was why he had faltered for a moment when he saw where I lived, the escapade was shadowed for him by meetings of another kind.

'How do you know this?' I said.

He rubbed his side-window and peered out. His answer was

reluctant. 'Sibylle told me.' Well, she would know. 'But she says Luc's mother is mad herself, and so does my father.'

'She's not mad,' I said sternly, 'she's just very unhappy, and anxious about bringing up her son by herself now Luc's father's run away.'

'His father is a mauvais sujet,' said Marcel.

'I suppose that's what Sibylle says too,' and I laughed.

He didn't deny it. I thought of Maurice that evening at dinner at Paul's, the sense he had given that Luc was as mauvais a sujet as his father. It seemed the masters and the boys mistrusted him, shunned him, for being a bit mental.

Later on it cleared and there were stars. It felt like midnight but it was only 8.30. Cars came and went from the forecourt opposite, my heart raced whenever figures appeared in the glass hallway or we heard the dim boom of the heavily sprung front door. I felt our secrecy leach from us as the roadway dried; people walked past and noticed that our head-rest silhouettes shielded two real watchful heads. Luc might already have glanced down from an unlit window and seen his mother's car and wondered what posse had come to claim him back. I was full of envy of the town and its ordinary evening. An Alsatian came alongside, followed by a man in a leather jacket: they crossed in front of the car, went past the flats and slipped through a gap in the fence, the man swinging the leather-handled chain suggestively/threateningly. The dog barked as it ran off over the dark waste ground.

It was Marcel's idea that we take it in turns to watch while the other slept, with him to sleep first. He bared his wrist and swivelled and counter-rotated various rings of his shockproof chronometer: they seemed to indicate that it was time to eat, so I sent him off with a few francs and he came back with a card-board tray of chips, some coffee biscuits and a sickening lilac pop. There was an intent little feast in the car while I smoked a cigarette outside and wandered to the wasteland for a pee, thinking my way casually but grossly through a fantasy about the man with the dog.

It was getting cold so we plundered and distributed the rugs and cushions; Marcel lifted a lever and pressed back in his seat till it was fully reclined. For the first time I felt a kind of comfort in having him there: I thought he didn't know what was going on, his attention faltered; but he'd be useful with Sibylle – I'd have to make use of him if the moment came. His breathing slowed as he slept and sounded like widely spaced snorts of vexation.

A sort of eternity opened up, like double physics on a school-day afternoon, the palate dry, the hands smelling of rubber and copper . . . My head lolled in yawn after yawn. Events were dull and rhythmless – a cat's finical patience along the forecourt's low wall, the passing of long-distance lorries, tared and flagged, that shook the car with their bluster. I tried to remember the whole of poems I'd once learned by heart, to keep awake, but memory was tarnished, words were spotted over, image blurred into image and poet into poet. When they faltered I left them and went drowsily towards the mirage they had conjured up, of summer dusks, funny old anecdotes, old embarrassments that still made me burn, boys' cocks and kisses under elms that had died with my boyhood's end. And then the poems had their various occasions and points of view, which like the advice of well-meaning friends seemed hardly to take the measure of my own mood and problems. It was all so far from last night. I lived back through that with thumping heart and closed eyes. 'This man is quickened so with grief, He wanders god-like or like thief, Upstairs and down – round and round – something like that – below, above, Without relief seeking lost love.' God-like or like thief: I saw what it meant for the first time in the twenty years I'd known the poem. But then *lost* love . . . Had I lost it? Had I ever had it? Or hadn't I cleverly maximised the trouble by losing something that had never been mine? I looked at the ugly shuttered building with a moan of pure need – and a wild, small-hours certainty of being punished and forbidden.

> I went down by the waters, and a bird
> Sang with your voice in all the unknown tones
> Of all that self of you I have not heard,
> So that my being felt you to the bones.

When Marcel's alarm went off I woke with the same metallic fear and sense of being far from home. He roused himself so slowly that it seemed pointless to expect him to sit alertly until 6 o'clock. Still, he snapped his seat upright and sat pawing his head, as if expecting to play his part. Perhaps he wouldn't feel as lonely and foolish as me. I settled back, pulling the musty multi-coloured crochet of the shawls around me, already fetishising them as remote kin of Luc's own bedspread, familiar, unnoticed trappings that he sprawled and stirred amongst, thinking of elsewhere.

I dreamt we were at Mr Croy's. Luc was lying naked on the table, surrounded by five or six men, some in naval uniform, a couple in cheap suits with their huge cocks jutting sideways and already seeping into the taut cloth. I was somehow amongst them but also outside and above their casually concentrated circle, as if I were writing the story of the dream and setting them in motion. I seemed to catch and share the haunting, forgotten dynamic of group sex, jealous and democratic at once. And Luc was ready for the ritual, lifting his head slightly, moistening his dry upper lip with a nervous tongue-tip. But to my bafflement all the men did was inspect him, closely but politely, as if they might have him but hadn't decided, and didn't want to mark him and be obliged to pay. Or almost like doctors, whose interest was scientific and excited by other invisible symptoms. I saw them push his legs apart, run their hands lightly, testingly up and down his thighs, and over his chest and stomach. One of them weighed his balls noncommittally in the palm of his hand, while another slipped back his foreskin and pinched open the little goldfish mouth of his swollen cock-head. They turned him over and one of them pressed his cheeks apart while the rest appraised his other hidden orifice; I saw it clench and gape with anticipation and delay.

I was in the bathroom, confused by the back corridors of Mr Croy's, the pantries and stairways overhung by dripping cisterns. I knew I wanted to get back to the main room – I had left it with the repressed anxiety with which one leaves luggage briefly unattended or asks a stranger to keep one's place in a long and hungry queue. I trotted round in confusion, sometimes hearing a shout or a slap from behind locked doors, through walls. I caught just a glimpse of Mr Croy himself, in a curtained back parlour – gross, brilliantined, with a gin and tonic, listening to 'Beggars in Spats'. A sense of misery and wasted money began to weigh in my chest.

When I got back to the room, they were fucking Luc one after the other, the inside of his thighs was slimed with sperm and spit. A line had formed, and when one had finished he pulled out and stumbled back to the end of the queue, briefly stroked and kissed by his friends as he passed them. I kept trying to join the queue – I explained to them that Luc was my lover, and made extravagant claims about his Wordsworth essay, but they thought that was a bit of a joke and pushed me away. Each time I came back they repulsed me more roughly, till I was thrown to the floor, and then kicked at as I crawled back, gazing up at their sweating naked buttocks and slicked cocks, not hearing their whispered jokes as they jostled and practice-fucked each other and edged forward towards the splayed, stoned, leering boy. 'But why?' I kept pleading, sobbing. 'He's *mine*, I'm sharing him with *you*, because I want you to be my friends.' But they sneered and punched me and told me to piss off.

I woke shaken and convinced. I lay there panting, almost grateful to find myself in a cold, smelly car in the bleak twilight of a foreign roadside. I stretched and looked at my watch's faint hands: 5.45 – it made me groan for my big high bed. Above me rose the back of Marcel's seat, and his head hung sideways as he slept, never quite rolling off the edge and waking him. I sat up, hardly surprised, sorry for the kid. Each forceful breath of his misted the windscreen in a circle that shrank and cleared before the next one fleetingly condensed there.

I slid out and went gaping and stamping down the road. The dream-mood still muddled me and startled me with scree-rattles of panic and pique. Croy's venetian-blinded bathroom, and the men cleaning up as if after cricket or squash, with occasional comically ordinary remarks – 'That was a good one this evening', 'Yes, he's shaping very well' . . . Of course I knew those days would never come again, it was only in dreams of one kind or another that the party went on – I didn't need so brutal a reminder. It had the vividness of waking experience, and seemed available to memory with none of the usual fade. Beside it, all around it, my real situation, wandering before dawn on the out-skirts of a Flemish town, seemed relatively dreamlike, implausible, only to be accounted for by the subtlest symbolic analysis. An old man with a knapsack came past and greeted me humorously and I answered him with tremendous gusto – the day's first phlegmy utterance mad with unadjusted warmth. I strolled across the forecourt of the flats and looked again, more at leisure, at the names on the bells. This time they all seemed brightly familiar, but only because I had looked at them before. I frowned back from the porch to see if Marcel's alarm had rung yet: I wouldn't tease him, I supposed he would absorb the lapse into his general resignation, his history of witnessed failures . . . I came down the steps with a lurch when I saw the Mini had gone. I ran to the empty space and stared at where an irised patch of oil glinted freshly in a pale oblong of tarmac.

We had Luc's mother's hand-drawn map and went at a crawl along country lanes, like a couple invited to a party in a remote farmhouse. The distances were meticulously given but hard to judge on the ground: I slowed and craned out through the grey dawn light at several gateways. I was furious to have lost the youngsters and was coldly forgiving to Marcel; at the same time I felt the irrational high spirits that come with a brief reprieve, a beating held off. 'That's it,' said Marcel, with odd optimism.

It was a gate into a wood. I pulled over on to the grassy half-circle in front of it and sat looking for a minute – it was clear no one had been here, at least not by car. A heavy chain lay slumped round the central uprights, but when I got out I found that it wasn't locked. In the middle of each gate a roundel like a battered hubcap was fixed to the flaking wrought iron and on it I could just make out in rust-blurred relief the monogram TA. Oh, they left their mark on things. I peered through into a pine avenue, where it was still dark.

We agreed that they weren't here, but both pandered to the other's half-hidden desire to see the place. Mrs Altidore had had it in mind from the start – Luc had talked of it so much of late, she said; he had got out the original plans and a book in which the architect had bound water-colour imaginings of the décor. There had been something of an argument because Luc

364

wanted to ask his father to do it up and his mother had been against encouraging him in any more extravagance. I uncoiled the chain and bumped and shouldered the gates back. Then I brought the car in, gingerly, along the track, brushed and knocked about the roof and windows by the crowding lower branches. On either side of our headlights the plantation stretched away in exaggerated darkness. I thought Luc would have needed to be quite brave to come here alone.

We came out into a wide tussocky field, the drive remembered and rutted by farm machinery, and juddered over a dully chiming cattle-grid. In front there was a high silhouette, a bulk of grey, that I steered towards, the car's underside slithering over long grass. Then there was a paved court stacked with farmer's hurdles and fuel-drums and a mossy, moping statue peering down: it could have been anyone, a shepherd, a prophet, even Aurora herself. Beyond it a few steps rose to a padlocked steel door. This was better, it was adventure in a recognisable form – we clambered out and sniffed the air.

On the far side of the little château stretched a ravaged lawn, marked out by the bloated thriving forms of what must once have been pyramids of yew. From the slippery elevation of the terrace I could see a pond, a lake, beyond it, choked with reeds and fallen branches. The light rose steadily, there were bars of orange above the tops of the firs, a blackbird started up, clear and unconcerned. It was just the time to see the place, not the kind of dawn Luc's grandfather had named the house for or would ever have witnessed there, cold skies above a drenched wilderness; though there were hints of classic pleasures, a cloud on the lake just big enough to clothe a god in a fresco stooping on a sex-quest. I'd lost Marcel; I wandered down towards the water, reluctantly moved by the relics of all this fake galanterie, my mind vaguely in summer, though a cold gust insisted it was December and made me twitch up Luc's jacket-collar. I turned back and saw the tiny top windows of the tower colour in the early sun, as though lanterns burnt in them.

The main part of the Pavillon de l'Aurore was a French-looking villa with long windows boarded up and stucco that gaped here and there on to cheap red brick. One end of it had sunk and opened a wandering crack in the upstairs wall; above it the roof was hidden under a canopy of rusting corrugated iron that the wind had loosened and buckled – from time to time it gave a squawk.

Marcel was quite excited. 'I think he could be here,' he said. He'd been exploring the garages and the kitchen-yard – apparently a window had been forced, but he wouldn't be able to get through it without a leg-up and a push from me. He took me round to show me and I peered in at a derelict pantry, the door at the back half-open on to pale gloom. Well, it could have been Luc, but I played down the likelihood. 'Thieves always break in at the remotest part of a house,' I said, alarmed for a moment that Marcel might dare me to go in. I poked at the mossy sill as if I knew what to look for. 'It's probably not that recent.' He leant in and called 'Luc', then jumped back when there was a distant scuffling and the creak of a pigeon's wings.

I laughed nervously and Marcel gripped my arm. 'I do have the keys to the front door,' I said, and he gazed at me as if I might unlock his first grown-up experience; he was shrinking from it already. I thought how later I would tell Luc about this – then remembered that he might actually be here, might have heard the car ticking over and taken it for steady rain on the laurels, might have heard our voices beyond shuttered windows, might be roused from shivering runaway sleep by the key in the lock and the scrape of the heavy door.

The air inside seemed to wake reluctantly, to turn and eddy in the light and draught after years of accumulated stillness. Dust climbed and spun on the edge of the bright threshold; the hall smelt musty but obscurely alive, as if animals tunnelled and marked their territories in it. I groped and found a stiff old metal light-switch and forced it till it gave out a dead click.

Marcel said there was a torch in the car and ran out to get it whilst I stepped timidly into the near-darkness, following the wall around with a squeamish hand. I came to an opening, the moulded edge of an archway, and registered as a blind person might an impending change of scale; I slid my feet forward over the gritty flags, thinking there might be a step; when I coughed the echo climbed and dropped through a hidden vastness, like a chapel. Too scared to go on, I slunk back into what seemed the dazzle of the hall, the spotlight of the winter morning through

366

the open door, along which Marcel stepped like a comedian. 'Come on, there's nothing to be scared of,' I said – then he switched on his own strong beam.

Away to the right a succession of rooms opened out. We went through them as if Marcel were my guide to an ancient tomb, I was itching to seize the lamp off him. He played it about solemnly but without interest over bare walls, high coved ceilings, the battened-up embrasures of the windows. The place had been abandoned but wasn't quite empty – in one room there was a trio of gilt ballroom chairs, in another the bench-seat of an old car where vagrants might have drunk and slept. High up on the walls ran the brass rods for hanging tapestries, bare plaster below them never meant to be seen. The torch came back and steadied on scrawled lettering: KRIS and a spouting cock and balls.

The final room was the grandest and most ruinous. Here the floor had dropped, and with it a pair of pillars which leaned apart, showing iron spindles which ran up through their wooden cores. It was all trumpery, up to the café-rococo of the ceiling, where a naked woman hovered in the blue. Perhaps she really was Aurora, faded and leprous, with a chalky beard where the plaster was rifted with damp. One eye was lost, the other large and inviting. The chains of a massive lamp descended from her feet – it hung in a dangerous canopy above the great slate slab of a billiard-table. Marcel was astonished by the table – the vanished baize, the few rotted strings of the pockets; he pushed the tabs back and forth on the scoreboard's rusty rails.

'We'd better look out the back,' I said, and he swallowed with fright and swung the light about again, over the pillars and the sylph of the cold ceiling. Since I was in charge I was resolute – it happened like that; and he came along trustingly. I was talking to Paul in my head and didn't get the feeling he minded what we were doing. It wasn't like the time I had followed Matt into the Rostands', though that distant episode seemed to haunt this one, rather as one place in a dream becomes another.

We had nothing to fear beyond birds and rats along the kitchen corridor. In a dank larder the shelves of a dresser were piled with straw and shit like some old *colombier*; the boards had been ripped from the windows, brambles quested in. The kitchen range held a nest that took me back for a second to the drawings of a childhood nature-book – auburn fieldmice perched on ears of wheat. There were bottles and cans and cigarette-butts of temporary residents, as there must once have been cases of champagne empties and the ash of gaming parties that went on till dawn. KRIS was commemorated here too, with the same phallic totem; I wondered if he was the object of fantasy or the boastful vandal-artist himself. We went down a passage where the paint on the wainscot had shrunk and cracked like the glaze on an old dinner-service: at the end a door with a splintered upper panel swung open on to a descending stair and a shallow cellar full of water.

We came back through a side-door into the entrance-hall. It was time for the echoing room – I knew what it must be, the rotunda of the tower. I took charge of the torch at last – just borrowed it a moment and swivelled the beam up the dark walls. The stairs rose from here and were glimpsed again higher up, pausing at an opening with a balcony. The light swept over a cupola and down, and there on the other side the faces were waiting.

The artist had painted another balcony for them, cunningly shadowed, and the revellers lounged along it, some gazing upwards, as it might be at stars or fireworks, others leaning on the rail to peer down at new arrivals, whose imagined lanterns charmed and dazzled them. Some of the men had high white collars, buttonholes, cigarettes, the blank sheen of a monocle – supercilious but impassive under the torch's challenge. The women had fans and mantillas or cloaks and tricorn hats; one raised a gloved arm and opened her mouth to sing. Two or three children were dressed as playing-cards, like the gardeners in *Alice in Wonderland*, and pointed gleefully through the wrought-iron banisters.

Theo Altidore stood in the middle, hand on hip, turbaned and robed in red, a scimitar in his belt. I couldn't tell if his rajah's moustaches were real or part of the costume. He was stout and high-coloured, with the irritable glare of the determined pleasure-seeker, handsome, young still, but already the man he would become. The brilliant picture, untouched by smoke or rain, could only show, like the Pavillon itself, how far he had wandered from Guillaume's austere refinement. He reminded me of bankers at Glyndebourne pretending to be aesthetes (betrayed by drink) or *Tatler* spreads on charity balls – the Duke of Somewhere, a frightful old monster, got up as a sheik or an Indian prince, never anything less than his own status. And it was notable how Theo had chosen the glamour of another empire than the one that was to ruin him. I could see why he'd frightened little Luc with his sword and his stare and his party of idlers.

But then the whole place spoke of adult pleasures and delusions – it was mad to think that Luc would ever have wanted to come here. His mother and I revealed some romantic failing of our own, poetic suppositions that had nothing to do with the boy's troubles and discoveries, the hidden upheavals of love. I was such a bad teacher. I stood for a while at the open front door, feeling tired and dirty. It wasn't just that I hadn't found Luc there in person. He wasn't there in other ways I'd hoped for: I'd dreamt of the house as a means of possessing him, of entering his past at a deep and early level, but the jumpy ten minutes inside gave me nothing but a lonely shell. I started to snivel pathetically and turned away in case Marcel should see me. Then I heard the dull report of a car on the cattle-grid.

The mauve Mini was coming over the field, bouncing and struggling on the rutted track. That terrifying little car. I waited for it shiftily, trying to make out if it contained one, two, or even three people – perhaps they'd all come to tell me the game was over, they would get out and lean on the open car door and marvel at my folly. It buzzed on to the mossy flagstones and stopped dead in front of the statue. There was only Sibylle inside – she sat for a while glaring out. It was clear to me she'd been sent by Luc to deliver some ultimatum and was working herself up to it and concentrating her anger at me and my blind interventions. Then she spotted Marcel, who was standing away to my right, frowning, head on one side in one of his gawky 'grown-up' attitudes.

She got out and hurried over to him, kissed him on both cheeks. 'Mm, you need to shave,' she said. Marcel giggled and fell silent; they stood blinking at one another, as if each trying to formulate an explanation of how they came to be here.

'There's an amazing billiard-table inside,' said Marcel.

'Is there?' She smiled encouragingly and sauntered towards me, unnervingly calm, like a trained nurse approaching a violent patient. I came down the steps apologetically. Then we too looked at each other.

'That's a very nice jacket,' she said. I nodded and rubbed the cloth of the lapel between forefinger and thumb. 'I hope it kept you warm out in the car all night.'

'Yes, thank you' – foolish, not wanting to add being cold to my other weaknesses.

'Yes, it is a warm one, isn't it? I've worn it myself a few times, when Luc thought I might be getting chilly – it was like an overcoat on me.' I saw her shrugging it on, his arm brusquely round her shoulder to shiver her. She looked down, piqued, as if she thought I too might offer it up. His other clothes went without comment, they were perhaps anonymous enough not to speak clearly of their owner. And that of course was all I longed to do, to speak of him but not to give him away, not to seem to share him with her, to be proud in defeat. I started obliquely:

'You must have left very early.'

But she was on her own fuse. She looked at me blankly. 'You'll never have him,' she said.

'Then you don't know . . .' I didn't say that, but a kind of stifled smugness like heartburn must have crossed my features and shielded me from her brutality. 'All I want to have', I said, 'is the chance to talk to him and help him if I can. His mother's dreadfully worried, she wants – well, she wants to do what's best for him.'

She gaped at me as if I were a total idiot: I had never imagined such disrespect, but I was too raw for the usual prickle and bluster at the outrages of the young. 'His mother.'

'So why don't you just tell me where he is? No one's trying to come between you. He thinks of me as a friend.'

'How on earth would you know what he thinks. You haven't got a clue what goes on inside his head. He thinks of me as his best friend.'

'Yes,' I said disarmingly, 'he told me he did.'

She wandered off in a circle, hands in pockets, pink-cheeked with anger and cold. Marcel leant against the Renault and scuffed the ground – he hadn't known what a terror she was.

'So where is he?' I said.

'He's not in the house,' she replied, slyly neutral.

'I know that.'

She paused and scanned the decrepit elevation. 'I'd wondered too.'

I glinted at her as if detecting a trick. 'You're not going to pretend you don't know where he is, it's too tedious.'

'I haven't any idea,' she said *sotto voce*.

'But you've run away together.' She raised an eyebrow. 'Or do you mean he's run away from you as well?'

'We didn't run away together,' she said after a moment. 'He ran away, as you call it, and phoned me to tell me. I asked him to meet me at a friend's apartment, not to do anything stupid or get arrested. I borrowed our friend Patrick's car and went there. That was where you spent last night. At 3 o'clock this morning he rang again and said he couldn't come to meet me. He was – on the coast. I drove off to another rendezvous and waited there, for hours, but he didn't turn up. He wasn't trying to trick me, I think he just couldn't manage it.' I had to stop myself grinning as I heard her tight-lipped itinerary of failure. 'I thought he might have come here.'

'There's no one here,' I said, more gently.

'Then I don't know where he is,' she threw off, and hit her fist against the top of her thigh and crumpled into tears.

She'd taken on such power as my rival that it was perplexing, somehow shaming, to see her tremble and cry. But it was Marcel's moment. She turned away from me with a wail as someone utterly unfitted to comfort her, and hid her sobbing face in her young friend's arms. He patted her back and nestled his chin into her hair like a boy getting his first slow dance, anxious, radiant.

I backed off, happy to be an adult, far from wanting to intrude. My thoughts were all on Luc and our meeting at the coast – I thought we could take up where we'd left off, I was catching my breath imagining it. What an unexpected sight the two of them were, hugging under the weedy stone giant, like a gorgonised reveller, and beyond them the brown and damson of the winter woods.

After a minute or two in the car Marcel began to sing, without realising, it seemed, looking out of the window, gently nodding his head. It was 'See Me Tonight', but done in a light boy-baritone that made the song freshly amorous. I came in on the second chorus – it was stuck in my brain and had only to be activated, as if by a hypnotist's codeword. We went on for a while in hesitant boisterous unison, both of us high on relief and altered prospects. There wasn't much to 'See Me Tonight' and after a couple of high-spirited run-throughs we petered out. Marcel looked quite surprised that it had happened. 'Do you know, um, "Heartbreak Hotel"?' he said; and I started it off. We swooshed along the empty road, bawling, 'I'm all so lonely, baby, so sad and lonely, baby' like schoolboys on a coach-trip.

Apparently his mother used to start sing-songs in the car and his father and he had sometimes remembered the practice since – they sang the same old Flemish folksongs as they had ten years and more ago. With us it had been hymns, all the way to Cornwall in the Humber's leathery heat, my father putting them deliberately to the wrong tune. I always chose grand Chestertonian ones, 'Take not thy thunder from us', 'Smite us and save us all', whilst Charlie reluctantly nominated the Geography Hymn. Sometimes we boosted the sunshine mood with 'Summer Holiday' or 'The sun has got his hat on' – a phrase that always troubled me with its counter-suggestion of cloud. Most difficult and lesson-like were rounds, in which you couldn't merge in the general din but came in alone and on time, although Charlie dragged and forgot and sang flat. 'White sand and grey sand. White sand and grey sand. Who'll buy my white sand? Who'll buy my grey sand?' The words were always drivel but you had to pipe them out and hold your own amongst the unfriendly circling of the others.

The hotel was stifling and deserted, but the sea had a grim beauty, seen from the window, while the hard valanced beds seemed to promise a cloudy luxury. I lay down while Marcel was in the bathroom, hearing only the hiss of the shower and the creak of the pipes. It was a lull in the chase, like one of the puzzling calm intermittences in love itself. I was still unused to hotels, I wanted to stay here for days, for months, perhaps, forgotten by the staff – they would wake us in spring with coffee, and newspapers like April Fool editions, full of just-possible absurdities.

I dreamt that Gordon Bottomley was staying at the same hotel. I was filled with emotion, and took Luc to see him in his room. The poet was vigorous and well-preserved, and busily at work on a verse play which he had started in the 1930s and which was now over a thousand pages long. He threw open a wicker hamper in which the curling bundles of manuscript were carried from place to place. He said how much this work had cost him, what he had given up, of ordinary pleasures and griefs, in order to find time to get it right. I spoke to him about a poem of his that my father had sung in a setting by Finzi, but when he asked me what it was called my mind went blank: I said I thought it was called 'Mud' and he said 'Oh yes', though neither of us was convinced. Luc was polite but indifferent and after a while drifted off into the adjacent room – I saw him through the open door, masturbating calmly and talking to someone else out of view.

Marcel and I patrolled separately through the day, among the beach shelters, the steamed-up cafés, the meagre amusements of the resort. Sometimes my beat would cross his and I would buy him a snack, some local speciality – a helping of chips or a hake sandwich. His attitude had improved dramatically. He might genuinely have come here for a holiday. Mrs Altidore had backed our hotel booking with her Mastercard and the cashier advanced us a clip of thousand-franc notes. Marcel spent much of his time in a cacophonous games arcade, claiming that Luc would be drawn to it. I watched him as he went on further chases, through landscapes that opened up at sick-making speed, violet, rose, lime-green, where loss was met by derisive klaxons and victory by urgent trills. Other, rougher boys began to cluster behind him, sullenly impressed by his nerve and his quick hand. It wasn't Luc's sort of place at all. I saw him kicking along the beach, sunk beautifully in himself, hurling bits of driftwood back, watching the waves' sloping approach – like something felt *along* the heart . . .

The storm had thrown up sand on the esplanade and caked the seaward windows of hotels with salt. Miniature reparations were being made with brooms and ladders. Something in the mood of leisured routine, the morning vacancy of hotels, snagged me with longing. I drifted to the station, asking 'Why?' and 'Where?' again and again – it was like some endless *Lied* my father might have sung, 'Warum?', 'Wohin?', the conventional stanzas shifted into breathtaking depth by the modulations between them. And the station too, with its tiny repertoire of arrivals and departures, was the threshold of everywhere else – Luc himself was perhaps already miles beyond the shining vanishing-point of the rails.

Even so I was on edge for him. I sat and smoked in a bleak public garden sheltered from the wind but in sound of the sea; the flower-beds were stripped out for winter, puddles shivered on the concrete paths. No one whatever came into it, which seemed to make it apt and ready for our reunion. There was a yelp from behind me and the slap of feet. I thought, this is it, and turned with a smile I knew would be half a grimace of doubt and fright. A thickset blond was jogging up and for a fraction of a second I tried to commute him into Luc, I wondered what he had done to himself. He glanced back at me as he passed, big features abstracted by the rhythms of running and music: I could hear the tinny racket from his headphones. He ran on round the garden's perimeter, then stopped and rocked on the spot, bending from the waist and doing exercises surely more eye-catching than useful. But what did I know?

He was a type I often liked, a stone or more over-weight: I guessed his backside looked like mine would have done in tight, sweat-darkened cycling-shorts – he made the whole idea of *me* by implication rather sexy. He also wore a zipped-up tracksuit top and the stacked rubber running-shoes which since my night with Luc exercised a confusing appeal. His calves were hairy and I thought his arse might be too if I got to lick the thick buried cord behind his balls and stab my tongue a little way into his muscly hole. My fantasy flowed out and caressed him –

374

I felt light-headed with fatigue and with relief at having some-one other than Luc in my sights; for a minute or more I was absorbed in this solid substitute, and when he turned to face me, twisting, bobbing, high-stepping like a horse, I carried on looking at him with what must have been an oddly simple ex-pression of welcome. He loped back round towards me, his cock and balls compact but emphatic; I was making the best of his rather loose mouth, the coarse hair squashed under the alice-band of his personal stereo. He nodded vaguely, but I saw it was only to the thrust of the music – it seemed he hardly took me in as he thumped past. I turned with a snigger of regret, torn already between dispraising him and a spurt of envy for the runners' world that I had always loved but never entered.

At dinner we had the restaurant almost to ourselves. Marcel drank a glass of wine and chatted about the day's excitements, how he thought he'd seen Luc several times but in the end it was always another 'funny-looking' boy. The months he had spent playing video games in the sanatorium had paid off magnifi-cently this afternoon – he'd emerged as a kind of champion in the amusements arcade: it was altogether one of the best days he'd had for years. But soon my lack of attention made him fall quiet; he looked at me with his head on one side and made sweet little attempts to jolly me along, but I was sinking fast into incommunicable gloom – the first bottle was already empty. He was still aglow with his new role as Sibylle's esquire, sent on to the coast whilst she retreated home. I glanced in a tall mirror and saw us as a headwaiter might, as a boy with an uncle, a godfather perhaps, a bachelor evidently, who lacked an easy way with youngsters, and disheartened the lad when he was meant to be giving him a treat. The age-gap seemed to widen between us; he gripped his cutlery like a child, and piled in the good, overdressed food as if determined to get value from that at least, whilst I was too racked by other hungers to want to eat. Sometimes he pointed his knife at something and I told him what it was called in English, and he repeated the word with a nod. Dismal canned music played, the short tape slurring from incessant repetition, fragments of Mozart and Tchaikovsky swung and sugared – I saw the morning studio, the shirt-sleeved sessioneers, the villainous arranger, the mockery of everything I held dear.

At another table was a respectable couple with a clever-looking boy in glasses. I knew the constraints between them at a glance, and picked up some of the exeat talk, the mother's resentful account of things at home, the son's attempts to convey the excitements of study in which the parents had no interest. A reading-list was gone into in some detail; one gathered this week he was doing *The Republic* – 'by Plato'.

I found myself enlisting their support. 'Isn't this music awful?' I called across. They didn't at first get my meaning, and when they did it was clear that the parents, if they'd noticed it at all, were quite grateful for its faceless protection, whilst the boy allied himself with me: 'Terrible, terrible', and then seemed to regret the momentary hysteria of his tone.

At a further table two old ladies had noticed the unusual break-out of conversation between strangers and I took their anxious gaze for support of my cause. I gestured to a waiter but just at the moment that he slipped away into the kitchen. I realised I was terribly angry, shaking with a sense of injustice that had glimpsed an outlet. Marcel kept his eyes on his plate, but could hardly swallow for embarrassment and horror at finding out for sure that he was sharing a room with a madman. As I turned round I kicked him under the table and he gave a yelp that accelerated the frenzy. 'Excuse me!' I called to another waiter, whose back was to me, already laying the tables with sugar and jams for breakfast, when doubtless, if nothing was done, the same tape would be inanely spooling. It had just begun its second circuit of the evening, a hellish perpetual loop. He looked round and I saw that he was the jogger from the gardens.

My fury halted and trod air for a moment – I saw it like a freeze-framed cloud-mass on the TV weather, dragging northwards over Europe with a payload for London by morning . . . The boy didn't know what tenderness of mine he'd awakened. He came over promptly, very sleeked now, like a peasant in church, his bow-tie crooked, still holding the half-formed lily of a napkin in large hands. He stood by me and I absurdly savoured having him at my command; my look was knowing, but drew no sign of recognition from him. 'Sir?' (Or was there a hint of irony there, at the drunkish foreigner who travelled with a schoolboy: his disdain for the celebrated Flemish fare, his scruffy, slept-in clothes?)

I smiled. 'I wonder if you could kindly turn the music off?'

He didn't sense the danger in my courtesy, though the request itself clearly struck him as malign and uncultured, quite possibly a threat to the principles of the hotel and the probity of the management. 'I'm sorry, sir, the music plays in all the public rooms.'

'I'm aware of that. What I'm suggesting is that it should stop doing so. It's absolutely *unbearable* to anyone who cares about music in the slightest.' And there my voice had jumped and the storm-cloud twitched nearer. I looked across at the scholarship boy for support, but found him studiously involved with his chocolate gâteau. His parents though were alert, and indignant on behalf of the waiter, whom I felt, in the social contraction of those few seconds, taking strength from their ignorance. Then I heard a new tune vilely segued into, all the brighter in the new silence of the restaurant. It took me two or three insensing seconds to realise what it was.

'Do you know what this music is?' I barked. 'Madam?' The mother quivered and flushed and firmed up her chin, and the father, not easily nettled, I suspected, but trapped on an old-fashioned point of honour, exclaimed, 'Really, young man . . .'

'I'll tell you then. It's an aria by Mozart, from *The Magic Flute*, "Dies Bildnis ist bezaubernd schön", in fact.' I sat with pounding pulse through the next few bars, crooningly underpinned by Hawaiian guitars, prinked with a cocktail-lounge piano, fouled by slurs of blue, and felt that I might well have proved my case. The whole lost day had been haunted by my father – I heard his clear tenor on a childhood morning, in the old Dent translation that seemed gracefully to describe the song itself, 'O loveliness beyond compare'.

I looked up at the waiter, who was nodding as I had seen him nod earlier to his Walkman, and who gave a shrug as though politicly conceding that this classical stuff wasn't too bad, if you actually listened to it; while the mother said, 'We've always loved Mozart.'

Nothing I said in the next two minutes was brilliant or even persuasive, but it came torrentially, from I don't know where. I was only faintly conscious of my small audience, of other staff coming in from the kitchen and standing with cloths in their hands, and of their swings of feeling between hurt and anger and cynical appeasement. I had ruined their evening with my bad language and my fist banging the table, but perhaps I had made it too: they would never forget the man who went mad and raved against the music that no one else had minded, and against them too and the poor young waiter who seemed to draw from him a special wildness of reproach, like an unfaithful husband.

Afterwards I couldn't remember my words, only the sensation of having spoken, of voicing opinions I never knew I had, of the routed resort to fundamentals. I didn't manage a peroration. I faltered on my high phrase about 'the mockery of everything I hold dear' – one hand gripping the waiter's reluctant but dutiful wrist, the other tugged at dumbly across the table by Marcel, in pity or fear or the shadow of an earlier day, when his mother had made such a scene in a public place. Then I was free, I strode out as if my tears, after this, would be somehow a disgrace, and hurried into the Gents; though even there, in the deadlit gloom, the vandalised music was faintly relayed.

I went out later and walked in the damp, buffeting air to the end of the town. The night was cloudy, the sea invisible save when it thumped like a distant bomb-blast on the sea-wall below and sent up drenching spouts into the lamplight of the promenade. There was no one about but me, dulled to the cold by cognac but lucid and suggestible. I thought of the place in summer, jostling with randy youngsters, indistinguishable shrieks from the water's edge: but for once I was content for all that to be in the past. I was applying myself to the subtler connoisseurship of the out-of-season, days without warmth and nights without encounters, empty pleasure-grounds and the violence of the tides.

I turned along a short pier and propped myself for a while above the pounding, self-rebuffing blackness. The unseen water's ejaculations awed me: I felt barely connected to the town's ghost façade or the land that lay beyond it. I pictured the dark ploughed distances there, farms and villages secured against the torrents of wind and rain, a blurred lamp swinging. Then there were towns with wind-rocked belfries, the street where I lived. The light in the yard would be throwing its pale stripe across my ceiling. With time the eye would grow accustomed to the shadow and make out the solemn bulk of table and chairs. How spectral the abandoned room was, no rhythmic gasping would ruffle the Spanish girls tonight.

I remembered clearly something Paul had said about Orst's prints, how they were the mirror of a northern world, silent, wintry, interior, remote from the outdoor brilliance of the south. They were *adressés aux esprits de silence*, discreet signals between one solitude and another; their sombre vaguenesses and mystic gleams were images too of the world of their collectors, the inward vigil they kept before the precious sheets, their trembling attunement to the indefinable. So that Orst's tenacious remembrance of Jane was an ideal form of the collectors' passion: he flattered their archaic yearnings and enrolled them among the rich in spirit, scorners of the vulgar modern world and what he termed its *demolishing wealth*.

I felt the poetry of the thing tonight, perched above the breakers and the dim phosphorescence of the returning foam. I knew nothing about this country, to me it was a dream-Belgium, it was Allemonde, a kingdom of ruins and vanished pleasures, miracles and martyrdoms, corners where the light never shone. Not many would recognise it, but some would. I seemed to have lost Luc in it. It was his wildness that had brought me to him and now it had taken him away. I studied my situation with a certain aesthetic amazement.

20

Helene was back from her honeymoon in Rome and Naples, and radiating a new self-esteem; it showed in the lethargy of her movements, the unembarrassed glow that came to her cheeks, her evident sense of returning to a quaint little world whose rules she observed with a new irony. I asked her what was it like, and though her answer was restricted to days among the ruins of the Forum or Pompeii it was clear that the real wonders had taken place, and kept on taking place, in the up-to-date privacy of the hotel.

'Paul's found a funny box,' she said, and her chuckle, too, came with more confidence of there being something to chuckle about. I was sceptical, of course, but still I envied her; I kissed her on the cheek to associate myself with luck and happiness.

The box didn't look funny, as it stood on the floor by Paul's desk. It was tuck-box sized, with the lid flung back because the restraining leather strap had perished. He had taken a piece of coloured glass from it and was rubbing it gently in his handkerchief. I came round and craned over. 'You'll be interested in this, dear,' he said, as if I'd been Marcel, and held up a ruby-coloured lozenge, with a clasp at the top.

'It looks like a bit off a chandelier,' I said.

'Mm. I think it probably was.' He laid it on his blotter beside another identical piece. 'There. The price of a virtuous woman is far above rubies.'

'I'm sure.' I looked into the jumble of the box, neck-chains, costume jewellery, remnants of peacock-patterned silk.

'Kundry's ear-rings,' said Paul. 'You'll find some other familiar things in there.' And he nodded to show that I could have the treat of looking. I squatted and rummaged disparagingly, as I might have done at a fleamarket. There were cheap brooches with rusted hasps, a crystal ball, a moulting fur cap ('Le toquet

380

de vair'!), the beaded blue veil of 'L'Infini', that tore as I lifted it, a slender wand with a bird on top – I knew it from Orst's 'Osiris', though not how the resting hawk was an infant's wooden toy. It was real junk that would never have passed muster at one of Theo's fancy-dress balls. At the bottom lay the collar of medals, that heavy treasure that had held up the chins of both the Janes in their different poses, the antique profiles blurred by time and the inscriptions rubbed down to vestigial runes.

I lifted it out with a sceptical smile, but surprised at how much it weighed: the medallions were thick, and the setting too was of some dull metal, inlaid with flat pink stones. It slumped round my two hands as I held it up to Paul; it would have pinched the women's white necks with its embossed edges and hidden hinges. He took it from me in a priestly way and stood it on the desk, saying quietly, 'Now that is old, at least the medals . . .' They still showed emperors' curtailed names, garlanded pillars, chariot-wheels – a miniature clamour, a very distant triumph. I wasn't sure if the collar was beautiful or hideous, poignant or shocking: like an Orst painting it was somehow all these things at once. It was a fetish that had become a relic, and engaged both of us perhaps with a mixture of respect and distaste. I leant forward to turn it round and pretended not to notice Paul's quick covered yawn.

It was Lilli's day off. Marcel had been in bed with a stifling cold since our return from the coast, so Paul and I had a bowl of soup at the desk. Paul carried on reading a journal beside him; sometimes he set down his spoon with a frown and scribbled something in the margin. He seemed very dissatisfied with much that he read.

I fancied a bit more of a break than this – if it hadn't been for the freezing mist, I'd have gone for a walk and a cigarette and probably a drink and an abrupt surrender to the bitter vacancy that our lamplight feebly held off. I scraped up the last of the soup with a childish racket and started a conversation more determinedly than I need have done.

'Where is it Lilli goes when she's not here?'

Paul dabbed at his lips with his napkin. 'Didn't I tell you? She goes to her sister-in-law's farm.'

'Oh yes. Where is that?'

He waved a hand abstractedly. 'It's . . . the other side of Roeselare. It takes a while on the bus.'

I found I liked it better when she wasn't around. There was something uncommunicative about her, and so in a way repressive. Everyone who knew her said how marvellous she was; I said the same if the occasion arose, but in fact I hadn't quite seen where her gift lay.

'I do think she's wonderful,' I said.

'Oh, I'm glad. You couldn't not like her,' said Paul – and added, 'I was afraid she might be a little severe with you. I wasn't sure how she'd take to having another member of the family to look after.' I smiled and looked down, pleased but also dimly suspicious of the process of mutual courtesy I had activated.

'How did she come to you?' After all, she wasn't strictly a member of the family herself. Then I saw that I had entered a room whose door I had always tiptoed past before – nothing to do with Lilli, but with Paul's wife, whose death had offered Lilli her role.

Paul wiped his bowl with a piece of bread and took his time to answer. 'When Marcel's mother died, he was only six, he needed someone to look after him.' It was a scenario from which he had interestingly omitted himself. He looked at me with a hint of a challenge – defused a moment later by his mock-pedantic tone: '"Ah yes," you will say, "but how was it that the person chosen to look after him was Lilli Vivier?"' I nodded, and then shrugged to say I didn't really need to know. 'Well, there are two answers to that question. The short-term answer is that she had lost her husband less than a year before, she didn't want to carry on working on a farm, she had been . . . rather unwell herself. When Marcel's mother died, she wrote to me. We met, and came to our present arrangement.' He pushed back his chair and turned it so as to look out at the chilly suspension of the fog. 'There is a long-term answer too, if you want to hear it.'

If I did, it was only as a distraction, or for the sake of talk, or to avoid thinking fruitlessly about another question which so far had no kind of answer at all. 'If you want to tell me.'

'I can tell you today. I wouldn't want to if she was actually here.' He raised the palm of his hand towards me in a gesture of deference and restraint. 'It goes back to the war again.'

'Well, I would be interested in that.' I recalled how Lilli had stiffened and left the room when I had finally asked about Paul's war-time visits to Orst. 'I feel very ashamed at how little I know about it; I've never quite taken it in.' In Belgium I had barely heard the epoch mentioned, unless under the pressure of questioning, or when Helene had given me her vaguely sensational impressions of Orst's death.

'Well, you know something about the Occupation. It's honestly not at all easy for me to convey what it was like, although I grew up in it: there were years of it, it just went on and on. It was very frightening, and humiliating, and drab, with rations, and that awful hunger you have as a growing boy. But it could be exciting too, at times, if you were young and had a lively imagination. The town was full of soldiers, the Germans and of course our own Nazi militia, it was military rule – which had perhaps a certain glamour: no one ever says that, of course, it sounds frivolous in the larger context of what was going on, but my schoolfriends and I had thrilling times deceiving the soldiers, who were often very stupid and very bored themselves. We took a lot of dares, and became great heroes in our own eyes. Probably we were stupid ourselves, I know sometimes we were. My father had a constant phrase, "It isn't a game, it isn't a game!"'

'What did your father do?'

'He was an outfitter, in that splendid English word. He supplied all the schools, jerseys and jackets and corduroy short trousers. And he was quite right, of course; all the time we boys had other people's lives in our hands, particularly later on.'

'Did he supply St Narcissus?'

'Yes, he did – though in the war they had to make do with plain serge suits, which everybody else was rather glad about. In fact I believe the gold thread was all commandeered for military uniforms.'

Poor dimmed Narcissi! 'And you lived above the shop?'

'Yes – in St Thomas Street. I was there all the time until I went away to university. It was a nice old place, but odd having the shop downstairs – I remember playing behind the counter after hours, and a sense of being privileged but also being left behind.' Which chimed distantly with Paul's situation now, at the Museum. He clasped his hands in front of him and studied his thumbs. 'Various odd things happened in the shop,' he said. 'I didn't know for a long time why it was that people called late in the evening and used to talk with my father in the stock-room. They would come in during the day, as well, men and women, and in the school holidays when I used to work in the shop sweeping up and opening the door. I noticed how they would often ask for something rather unusual, some purple ribbon, and be shown through to the back, whilst I would be told to go out on errands. They used to leave with brown paper parcels which I thought would have held really a very large amount of purple ribbon. I did once try asking about it and my father took me aside very solemnly and said I must never mention it again. And of course that it wasn't a game.'

I pictured the future Rembrandt scholar running errands through the town and leaping to the shop door when its bell tinkled for a new customer – and with something of his present dignity already. 'What did you think they were doing?'

Paul smiled wistfully. 'I mustn't exaggerate my innocence. You probably know about the Rexists, who were the French-speaking fascists in this country, and of course there were various Flemish groups of Nazi sympathisers. I think I just absorbed my parents' contempt for them, as a child does – though the picture wasn't entirely clear: several people on my mother's side of the family welcomed the idea of our becoming part of a vast new Germany. It's too complicated to explain. Anyway, I don't need to explain. Many of the Nazis went straight into the local militia the Germans raised. I remember a boy called Frank, who'd been an assistant at our shop and played with me when I was little, coming in one day in uniform and shouting "Heil Hitler" when I opened the door.' Paul muttered the infamous salute in a half-suppressed belch. 'Also, how the demand for purple ribbon dried up abruptly after that. So I had some idea what might be going on. School was full of gossip and rumour, of course, and I learned about all sorts of things there that were never mentioned at home – often, it must be admitted, because they were completely untrue. My recollection is that you never knew if you could trust somebody.' I looked at him steadily, with a renewed sense of how much he wanted to trust me; but he avoided my eye, his gaze wandered nervily in the gloomy oblong of the window.

'One day at breakfast my father told me we were having some other children to stay. A boy of about my age, about fifteen, which I wasn't altogether pleased about, and a rather younger girl. I was told I had to look after them, as they had left their families and would be very lonely and unsure of things. The boy would be coming to school with me and I remember being very anxious about having to introduce a stranger to my own rather exclusive little group. I clung to the thin excuse that he was apparently a cousin, though one so infinitely distant that I had never heard of him before. But I needn't have worried: he turned out to be very bright indeed and had read more books and seen more American films than anyone I'd met. He was actually a great asset and if anything enhanced my standing with my friends, by association, as it were. He had to share my bedroom, and he talked all night – all about books: I know it sounds unlikely.'

'Oh, not to me,' I said quietly; and he smiled.

'The girl, I can tell you, was a very different matter. She seemed utterly lost, a little dark-haired thing, sunk in herself; at night we used to hear her crying in her room and my mother going in to comfort her. I'm afraid I probably neglected her, I left her to do tasks in the kitchen, where she seemed happiest. She gave the impression of living in another world. Of course she was terribly homesick, and she had the curious habit of not answering to her name, until the second or third time you called her, which was unsettling to my new-found self-importance.'

'What was she called?'

'She was called after St Augustine's mother: Monica. But as you will have guessed that was not her real name. I'm amazed now to think how long it took me to realise that we were sheltering two Jewish children, and how confidently the boy disguised the fact. Actually he was full of confidence; in some odd way he was able to block out what was going on by concentrating intensely on his school work and living so much in books. I think he'd read all the Waverley Novels except one, which had been stolen from the library. But . . . Monica somehow knew from the start that she had lost everything. She was so quiet because she was in constant fear of giving herself away. They had false papers, false ration-books, and school uniforms run up by my father – that was what the visitors were always taking away, of course, children's clothes with the forged papers hidden in their linings. It turned out that my parents were part of an underground network that helped thousands of Jewish children to disappear, or change identity, when their parents gave them up.'

'Or they'd have been deported . . .'

'Exactly. It makes me shiver after fifty years. And they didn't all get away with it – children don't have that much discipline, they can't remain in the land of pretence for ever. The monks and the other masters of the various schools were playing with high explosives. They risked their lives to save the children, but the children actually had the masters' lives in their hands as well. If a hidden Jewish child was found in school by the Gestapo, neither the child nor the master who was deemed responsible was ever seen again. Personally I wouldn't want to place so much trust in a frightened or bereaved teenager – but what could they do when it was their only chance?'

'I'm afraid you're going to say something about Monica and the boy.'

'No, they were among the lucky ones.' He gave me a surprisingly bright grin. 'Our little threesome became quite close, in time. They stayed on with us until after the war, until we knew for certain that their parents had been . . . exterminated. We became inseparable, in that way that teenagers do – with a secret language, each of us half in love with the others, and full of rivalry too, which sometimes burst out in dreadful rows. Those were the occasions when I first heard my own faults described without mercy. Of course our all being under the same roof made it very intense and inescapable. There being three of us gave us a sense of mysterious power, to

386

ourselves and to outsiders. It also made it hard to do anything independently, or in a couple without the third. I don't know if you've experienced anything similar.'

I rocked my head and raised my eyebrows to say, 'Have I ever.'

'You've guessed the point of the story, I'm sure' – and for once I thought I had.

'Well, Monica I suppose must have been Lilli.'

Paul gave a sighing smile, and looked down, so that I wondered for a moment if I was wrong. He said, 'I won't pretend I wasn't fairly anxious when she came back. We'd lost touch after I'd gone to England. She went back to the country, and married very soon. It was natural, she wanted her new life. But within a few days we'd each remembered how the other ticked; we were both somewhat raw from our bereavements, we had disagreements, just as we always had. To be honest, it has often been very difficult for us. The most important thing was that Marcel got on so well with her. I could see he was a way for her to come to terms with the city again, at least as far as it was possible for her to. They took each other for long walks, which must have brought back terrible thoughts for her, the whole mood of those years, and the subterfuge that had allowed her to survive when all her family had been annihilated. She used to come back in with Marcel, exhausted, gripping his hand tight – obviously he didn't realise what he meant to her. She never said so to me, indeed she's never spoken of it at all, but I'm sure he helped her to see things through his eyes – I mean, with a certain freshness, and optimism. He seemed to forget his own woes, too, when he had her to protect him.'

I thought, why did no one tell me? I might never have found out. I scurried back over various semi-drunken mealtimes, thinking I might have said something awful. 'And what happened to the boy?'

Paul looked at me kindly, uncertainly. I saw he was still thinking of Marcel. Then, 'Oh, the boy. Well, we remained great friends, we went to university together. If I tell you he became a schoolteacher,' said Paul, with a slight amused hesitation, 'I will probably have told you enough.'

In fact it took me a few seconds of clumsy verification. I said nothing, but smiled and nodded slowly to acknowledge my surprise and then my lack of any reason to be surprised. So the two former orphans both looked after children – well, that seemed right, it was the form some unalterable need had taken. I heard the familiar crack of a board, and half-turned to see that Helene was standing in the doorway that gave on to the stairs. Her hand was on the door-knob and she leaned into the room as though waiting for a sign that she was not disturbing us. I wondered how long she had been standing and listening. Paul must have seen her; that hint of amusement perhaps came from having her there at the dénouement of her father's story.

She went round the desk, behind Paul's chair, and leant forward to embrace him, her arms crossed loosely under his chin, her cheek pressed to his temple. The gesture seemed full of her fresh adult confidence, though it was also the embrace with which a child cajoles a stern but sentimental old relative. She stayed there, looking up at me with a glow, until Paul patted her hand and she slowly stood back. I shared their quiet pleasure that I was in on the secret; as well as feeling the initiate's disadvantage, the tacit admission of how clueless I had been before.

I got up more suddenly than I'd meant to, and in my customary reflex stared out of the window, at the fog which annihilated the street and at the same time cast a faint illumination.

'I nearly told you before,' Helene said, 'when we went for that walk, do you remember? But you know they never talk about it – Daddy and Lilli don't – and so it never seems quite right for me to either.'

'I'm just so glad they're here at all,' I said after a moment, though with a sense that I shouldn't now pretend to like Maurice more than I did. I saw how the schoolboy role of know-all and competitor had lasted and soured like a tough old jacket. It was hateful of me, but I began to be irritated by the ubiquitous power of the unsaid, and by the generous little enactment of Helene's gratitude, the stooping hug that said for them the crisis was over – not still waiting to happen, somewhere along the invisible roads.

*

'Any news of Luc?' said Matt, in a tone that for the first time admitted tender concern and caught me unawares. My voice cracked under the light pressure of sympathy.

'Nothing,' I said, and walked away from him, my mouth turned down at the corners like a child in the silence before a wail. I stood looking over his twisted bedding, sucking in deep breaths; wondering abstractly who'd been sleeping here. Matt kept away from me, stacked up tapes with the noisy briskness of someone pretending to do housework. After a while I went over to him and gave him a kiss. 'Actually I'm terribly hungry,' I said.

He gave his crooked smile of relief. 'Run out and get some burgers.'

'Okay. I don't have any money.' And I dug with an inverted kind of pride into my jeans pocket and displayed a palmful of coins that would buy nothing, the change one expects a beggar or busker to be grateful for. Matt did something similar, though he brought out a bookie's roll of banknotes with large rudimentary sums jotted on the top one. He pulled a couple of thousands off and tucked them into my waistband, as if I were a stripper; then kissed me again.

When I got back with the warm polystyrene boxes, he was on the phone. 'Yeah . . . that's right . . . the American guy . . . yes, really sexy . . . he's not a jerk . . . oh, a jock . . . yeah, he's a jock all right . . .' He gave me a wink, head cocked to hold the receiver whilst he tipped the packeted condiments out of the bag. 'Okay, here he is . . . Ed, yeah . . . This one's for you,' he said, a finger on the secretary's hold button.

'Who is it?'

'Some guy from Ostend.'

'What's he want?'

'You're an American college-boy, okay, he just needs talking off.' I ducked away puzzled. 'Come on, he's paying good money. His dick's in his hand. Just tell him how sexy you are.' Matt held the receiver out to me, and I gestured wanly at my cheeseburger, already cooling after its journey from the Bishop's Palace. 'Eat while you work,' he said.

I sat down. 'But I'm not American . . .' There was no help for it. 'Hello?' I said in a suspicious growl.

'Oh hi! Is that *Ed*, right?' The man was speaking in a heavy American accent himself, but with homely Flemish vowels.

'Yep.' I settled myself and turned my head so that I couldn't see Matt. The scope for confusion was so great that I found myself taking it quickly and self-mockingly, like something done as a dare. I'd never rung a sex-talk line – I didn't know what the conventions were.

'So, where are you from, Ed?' the man from Ostend asked with patient excitement.

'Oregon,' I said, wondering if it sounded as wrong to him as it did to me. I remembered doing *Our Town* as the school play, only Dawn being able to sustain the accent amid a medley of Yogi Bear and something oddly like Yorkshire.

'Oh great. That's the Rocky Mountains, right?'

'We have the Rockies.' Though doubts immediately formed.

'And lumberjacks, don't tell me, that's really wild.'

'Uh-huh. Though I'm a student, remember.'

'Right! That's very sexy. But you must know one or two lumberjacks?'

'Well, one or two, I guess.' And I heard myself give a guilty laugh, as if I really were confessing to some rough weekends in the Oregon woods. I reached for my burger, and balanced it up in my hand so as not to shed the loose onion-rings and swell of ketchup.

'That's great. So what do you major in?' I'd no idea there was so much background in phone-sex. I heard a little catch in his breath and wondered if that was what he got off on.

'Oh, let's not talk about boring old work!' I said, beginning to feel more at home in my accent, which had swerved irresponsibly southwards and seemed to have settled on hunky Bobby in *Dallas* for its model. There was a pause, in which I could hear faint rustling sounds. I took a bite of tepid beef and bread.

'Well, Ed,' and the voice was slower and more serious. 'Aren't you gonna tell me what you look like, and you know, what you're doing to yourself?'

I chewed frantically. 'Sure, sure. Well, what shall I start with?'

'You're blond, I think your friend said?'

'I'm blond. Very blond as a matter of fact. And I'm pretty

muscular, like, I work out a lot, swim a lot, all that shit.' I seemed to be turning into Rex Stout. 'Yeah, I've got a washboard stomach.'

'A washbore?'

'That's right.'

'Oh . . .'

'Or so the guys all say.'

'Tell me what you weigh, Ed,' he breathed, as though just to hear the figure would be the same as having my real weight on top of him. I knew I couldn't do the conversion from stones to pounds. I supposed 140 pounds must be 10 stone, which was so much lighter than me as to sound almost anorexic.

'One hundred sixty-five pounds,' I said masterfully.

'I think I really like you, Ed.'

'Thanks very much.' I took it as a compliment to me as well as to the person I'd invented, whom I found I'd started to rather fancy too. I wondered who my interlocutor was. I didn't mind this phase of arch foreplay – my innocence of the whole system seemed to make me more genuine. 'What's your name, by the way?'

His breathing was – heavy: it was heavy breathing. I felt it wasn't polite to show that I'd noticed. All the same, I pictured a person, perhaps no older than me, naked on a bed, in subdued light, somehow encumbered with clips and straps and probes, greased and hard but holding off the time-and-money-saving moment. I imagined I too was naked in his scenario. I took another mouthful of burger.

'Have you got a big one, Ed?'

'Mm. Mm.' And when I'd cleared my throat: 'Yeah, it's huge. It's like, a half-pounder.'

'Oh Ed, that's really wild . . . A big, big sausage.'

'Well . . .'

'Do you have it in your hand right now?'

'Yep, I sure do. I can hardly get my hand round it. I'm lifting it up towards my lips . . .'

'Oh, *man*' (though it sounded like oh, *men*).

'It's kind of oozing stuff out of it!'

There was no immediate reply to this, so I carried on eating, faintly troubled by the priapic monster I'd so concisely evoked.

He must have covered the mouthpiece – a residual modesty screened the final moments. Then he said, crouching right at my ear, 'I love you, Ed.' I didn't know if I should respond with something similar; I could only think of 'Well, I'm very fond of you, too', but before I could say anything I heard the clunk of the receiver being dropped and saw it twirl on its flex, knocking a table-leg. Then the line was dead.

'Who was that?' said Matt as I hung up.

'I don't know.' Now it was time to eat, please; and there was a surprising twinge of regret amongst my hunger for my new friend. I wondered if he'd get in touch again.

'You were great,' said Matt, stepping towards me through the clutter of the room.

'It seemed to do the trick.'

'Of course it did.'

'I didn't really say anything, though.'

'Well, that's what the trick is,' said Matt, and gave me a horrible leer.

It seemed Matt was toying with the idea of a phone-sex line. He already had a couple of ansaphones on a separate number with tapes in them of American porn-stars giving true confessions. Occasionally throughout the evening as we sat watching football there would be the clatter of the tape starting, and a real American voice, turned right down low and sounding oddly fake to me, would drawl away, half-obliterated by the chanting in the stands and the raving of the commentators – 'Hi, you've reached Chad Masters, I guess you've seen me around . . . yep, it's one of the biggest . . . oh, boy . . . could you take all of that motherfucker? . . . like I had to every day when I was a kid . . .' It left me shivering and anxious, the night around me, it seemed, threaded like tracer fire by lines of anonymous lust. I squashed up uncomfortably with Matt in his chair and drank bottle after bottle of beer.

Later Matt got out a video; I supposed he was trying to arouse me or distract me. His business was pleasure and people paying for it: he couldn't fathom those darker states of mind that were immune to titillation, or that took it somehow amiss.

392

I groaned and thought I might weep if I had to watch people fucking.

'Let's just go to bed. Can I stay the night?'

'Sure. I think you'll be really interested in this though.'

'I'm not one of your punters, darling.' I was yawning and stumbling round.

Matt pressed the cassette into the machine. 'It's got someone you know in it. Someone who once made a big impression on you.'

'I refuse to think,' I said, my mind none the less thumbing through the torn catalogue of men I'd known or merely seen and felt for. 'Anyway, I don't have friends in that world.' An unsteady card appeared on the screen, and a soundtrack of rock music came through fitfully.

'This is just an amateur thing, made locally, no production values or proper editing – a lot of people like them better, when it's boys they might know in real life, they're getting very popular.' I'd read about something similar at home, where men on a housing estate would gather to watch a video of one of them fucking one of the others' daughters: I felt I was seeing my own fantasies held up to the distorting hetero mirror – how they liked the men beery and unshaven and the girls busty and young. I covered my face with my hands; then, when Matt had wandered to the kitchen, I reached for the remote control and fast-forwarded for ages.

Matt woke me with a shake and I sat up and frowned at a couple of men going at it dementedly, with the noiseless hysteria of an early motion picture. He took the remote, and abruptly slowed the film – I groaned at the artless dawdling of ordinary time, the wanton deferral.

Later there was a horrible bedroom where the light came back off silvery 'abstract' wallpaper, and two skinny boys who couldn't get erections were doggedly sixty-nining. It must actually have been someone's room, of course, probably the director's if you could call him that – he would spend the night there, perhaps alone, after he had paid the boys their drug-money, less than they needed – the room glinted with bad faith. I said, 'This is the worst thing I've ever seen.' Above the bed a

393

female saint, perhaps the Virgin herself, turned saucer eyes heavenwards. I pretended to sleep, and then slept.

Later still – a minute later? twenty minutes? – there was a young man lying face down on the bed, naked and pale, but bigger and stronger than most of the movie's phantom crew. His legs were apart and you saw the dusk of hair on his balls; his face was buried in the pillows. The camera prowled down on him as a fly settled and walked about on his white arse. It flew off when the camera panned away to show the door half-open and behind it a man standing – fortyish, bearded, over-weight in a T-shirt. His jeans were round his knees – he was already wanking as he spied on the boy; he seemed genuinely into it, it was a new note in the film, something voluntary and felt and so in a way more difficult to watch.

'That's the guy who made the video,' said Matt.

The boy was standing with his back to us, we saw him only from the shoulders down, whilst a pair of hairy hands mauled and probed his backside. Like everything in the film it went on for ever – you felt you could have flown to Athens or read *The Spoils of Poynton* in the time it took to change to something new. I was bewildered to think anyone could watch this for pleasure, it seemed to mock any thought of sexual happiness. Then at last we were round the front, where the man was kneeling, the boy's limp cock in his mouth. He went at it and went at it; sometimes he took it in his hand and pistoned it into a semb-lance of life, but then it died again. We never saw the young man's face, only the strong, lean body; but he began to generate a vague sense of apology, his hands reluctantly caressed his fel-lator's thinning scalp, and lingered there long enough for us to see the skull charm of a ring that bit into his finger and the tat-tooed letters R, O, S, E.

At the end the older man shot off up Rose's leg and you saw the milky drops hang and trickle among the thick hairs of his calf. Rose himself didn't come, and the camera drifted off in a cliché pan to distance that went out of the open window. It was night now, and for a few seconds we saw from above the shadow and flare of a city, the walkway lights of high-rise hous-ing echoed further off by the ribbons of light on ships in dock, and between them a network of streets, pulsating and nameless.

I felt the greatest reluctance to take my clothes off and hurried into bed in shirt and trousers. I pulled the blankets around me and when Matt got in, shivering and excited, I hugged him like an old wrestler, so that he could hardly breathe. By the time he had started snoring I was boiling hot and had to get out of bed to strip. I stood there wretchedly, eyes half-closed with fatigue, unbuttoning my shirt. As I fumbled with my jeans there was a clatter that made me jump and fall over, and a voice close behind me, intimate and unwelcome. 'Hi, you've reached Chad Masters, I guess you've seen me around . . .'

I strolled across the empty arena of the Grote Markt and stood to admire, or at least acknowledge, its weathered self-acclaim. I felt alone, like a survivor in a city visited by a curse – and nervous about how long I could hope to carry on myself, pitted and limping as I was. I turned up the collar of Cherif's coat and raised my head to scan the belfry, which seemed to curve and topple against fast-moving cloud. When I looked down I was giddy almost as if I'd been up there – it was steadying to hear my name called out.

I turned and there was Patrick coming quickly towards me, half-smiling, glancing away. There was something free and yet formal in our coming together at the centre of this great square, and I spread my arms to gesture at the scale of it, though he may have thought that I expected to embrace him. He was vividly conspicuous in a pink skiing-jacket over a green tartan shirt that as usual hung out at the front. I thought how good-looking he was, and then saw the disquiet and resolve of someone who brings bad news.

We shook hands and frowned and stamped as if waiting for others to turn up, the rest of the routed Three perhaps: I saw that Patrick and I only had a friend in common, we weren't friends ourselves.

'Do you want to go for a coffee?' he said.

I had come out in search of breakfast, but any appetite I had was obliterated by worry. We moved off towards an old café on the far side of the square, a place I thought might be too smart and hushed, but I lacked the will to suggest an alternative. 'Have you heard from Luc?' I said lightly.

'Not for a week,' he said, almost as though he didn't know anything had happened.

'Ah. I thought you might have done.'

'No, I haven't seen or heard from him since that night we all met in . . . the bar. I think you're the last person to have actually seen him.'

I knew I was in very deep. I wondered at moments if I had murdered Luc and then wiped all memory of it – he was crouched rigid in one of my big cupboards, and the Spanish girls were picking up the smell. 'Your friend Sibylle has spoken to him since, of course.'

Patrick shot me a glance that was oddly mournful. 'Well, she may have done,' he said, pushing open the door and giving me a shiver as we stepped into the warm. I sat down wondering why I went through life not knowing anything, never any the wiser; I seemed to be my pupils' pupil.

'You mean she was lying?'

Patrick flung himself down opposite, his chair at an angle – his arm sweeping the table. 'No, I wouldn't say that.' He seemed to me reserved and proud and a little solemn with those early emotional upheavals adults are accused of not under-standing. 'She makes up shit,' he said, like the bully he once was, and with the same hidden doubt.

I thought of her snooty theories about my friends – but wasn't a certain premature decidedness allowed among the young? It was how they charmed and achieved – I was suddenly on her side. 'Why would she make up that? I mean she bor-rowed your car, I think I'm right in saying, and drove all over the place on the strength of that phone-call – he told her to meet him at . . .wherever it was.'

'No, you're probably right . . .' The waitress came and he left me to order; I was aware of him watching me. 'I don't know what you know about Luc,' he said afterwards.

'Um . . .'

'Sibylle is madly in love with him,' he shied away. 'That is why she can become very rude – she always looks so cool, and

396

so bloody beautiful, you don't realise she is very worried under-neath and says things she doesn't mean. She's trying to keep hold of him and keep him away from everyone else.' He looked at me with the large brown eyes of an extrovert boy who is learning about the heart; I thought he would always be un-afraid of its demons and would get what he wanted. 'She thinks of you as a great threat.'

For a moment or two I believed I wasn't reddening. 'I'm just his teacher,' I said, scratching my head in a spasm and feeling more generally compromised, as though Patrick had implied some sordid leering motive in my merely being with him now. I twisted and shrugged out of the hot coat. 'Luc's not in love with me, for heaven's sake.' I hadn't put it quite so cleanly before, even to myself.

'It might be better if he was,' Patrick said, masking the riskiness of the words with a prudential frown.

We were silent for a minute or more, gazing towards the counter as if we were thinking about nothing in particular. I couldn't tell yet what hostility the boy felt for me and began to suppose he didn't know either, and expected no more than the gloomy comfort of a chat. 'Can't Luc sort of make a go of it with Sibylle?' I deviously put out.

Patrick grunted mirthlessly. 'I'm sure he'd like to' – and held back, I felt, from saying more, as the milky coffees arrived. Then, 'No, they're very old friends.'

I sipped the warm froth with its hot undershock of liquid and was back for a few seconds in the stifling love-culture of the late teens, its thrilling new absolutes, the hormonal frenzy. 'Forgive me if I'm too curious,' I said with a smile. 'I was under the im-pression – you remember one weekend you all three went down to I think it's your parents' house somewhere on the coast?'

Patrick looked at me warily. 'We often do.'

'It was quite recently. Luc told me afterwards it had just been you and him there – then later he let slip that Sibylle was with you too. I assumed he was . . . covering up for having been with her.'

Patrick was slightly impatient of this finical enquiry, I thought, and made no answer for a bit. 'My friend Luc is very loyal,' he said. 'He was covering up, in fact, for Sibylle and me.

We were, we were lovers then; as you say, quite recently. Well, the father of Sibylle is the Minister of Culture, and we cannot have any scandals. He thought Sibylle was staying with ... some other friends.' He picked up and set down his coffee-cup. 'That was the weekend, in fact, when she suddenly decided she was in love with Luc and not with me. I remember I went out with her in a boat we have and she almost – ' he flopped his hand over backwards on the table.

'Capsized it.'

'Capsized. I think she has to fall in love with her boyfriend's best friend. So as to cause the most problems for everybody.' He was shadowed by his experience, but proud of it too, and the licence it appeared to give him for scepticism about girls. I felt tensely light-headed as the twists of this drama, quite separate but bearing so darkly on my own, were recalled.

'She certainly seemed very passionate, and possessive, when we met at dawn in the middle of a field the other day. It was almost like a duel. Of course I had no idea why he'd run off again, he's never told me anything personal. She couldn't help giving me the impression that it was her he'd run away from.'

Patrick gave a nervous flicker of a smile. 'Au contraire,' he said. 'He was running away from me.'

This had the air of a briskly unwilling confession, and I was generous, welcoming, to the surprise it sprang. We had something in common, I could help him after all. 'So you were both after him!' And of course there was nothing surprising in that – it puzzled me that Luc wasn't mobbed through the streets by defenceless admirers.

'Au contraire,' he said again, with a certain satisfaction at the chime and at the polymorphous stamina of the Three. 'He was after me.' I felt I'd have had to be Racine to keep abreast of this convulsive trio, their switches of allegiance that seemed compacted in retrospect into little more than a day.

My heart quickened, absurdly, at the glimpse of a second chance, the beautiful confirmation of how Luc's thoughts turned, the need to get to him now before anyone else did. My mind roamed the map with a new sense of danger and jealousy. The unprecedented guilt of the past week, the fear that it was I who had driven him away, was lost in the deeper draft of these other explanations – went unseen, unguessed. If I had killed him, then it was only in a dream.

'Yes,' he went on, perhaps noticing my queer glow and wanting to distance himself, 'after all these years he has announced that he's in love with me.'

'That doesn't mean he wasn't in love with you all along,' I said, tender of Luc's own feelings in the face of Patrick's touchily butch manner. 'Or ready to be in love with you when the moment came.' At which he looked down and faltered. 'Anyway, you don't love him.'

'Well, of course I *love* him,' Patrick said, with the same secret pride at his recent graduation to the fellowship of high feeling, and a hint of a sulk at the suspicion he might still have something to learn. 'I've known him all my life. He's my clever friend. I am his friend, well, I'm almost his only friend, we were always together at St Narcissus, though other boys didn't like him. And of course we ... did things together ... years ago. And I can't do those things any more – that's all I can say.'

'That's perfectly understandable. In fact it's dreadfully commonplace.'

'I wish I could, you know, make him happy,' he said, both rueful and smug. 'But nothing seems to fit together any more. Our little group of friends has become like a group of enemies!'

I laughed, sympathetically in part. 'The time I saw you together Luc said you'd been arguing.'

'You mean in the bar?'

'Yes. He told me then he was in love and how he caught cold standing under a window, it must have been your window, at night . . .'

'I wouldn't be surprised. That's nothing. I have hundreds of letters, every day more letters. He's gone crazy – as I said, quite suddenly, though you say perhaps it was always there. He says if I would just go to sleep with him once, it would be okay.' I clutched at my throat and looked away. 'I told him there would be no point.' Patrick hunched and drank off his coffee in a few gulps. 'No, I think he had that idea from his friend Arnold.'

'You mean his clever friend?'

'He mentioned him? He is now at university. He was madly in love with Luc for years, and they were quite good friends too, though Arnold was going on like a second mother to him and making him be interested in classical music and reading poetry. Luc was quite flattered by his attention, well, he's quite intelligent, he didn't want to be unkind. But he did make the mistake of . . . making love with Arnold, just once, and as a matter of fact I don't think Arnold has ever got over it.'

'I see.'

Patrick was unbuttoning a shirt-pocket beneath the ski-jacket's whispering cocoon. He fiddled out an envelope, and drew a letter from it, and half unfolded it. 'It's very sweet,' he said, as I stared away from it and then let my eyes flick back in an involuntary attempt to decipher what was visible of Luc's rapid, clumsy hand. Patrick held the letter close to himself and scanned it in a vain and rather tasteless way – I had the feeling he was teasing me with its private and unguarded contents, that he carried it as a sentimental token and liked to let me glimpse, when he turned it over, the wild and old-fashioned endearment with which it began, and which I might hunger for ever to hear from Luc myself. I thought he was going to read a bit out, and then with a shake of the head and a little smile he decided not to. He snapped the letter away and gave me a quick cold stare as if to repudiate any spurious intimacy.

'Anyway, he hasn't written to you since . . . he left.'

'No.'

'And you think he's run away to escape from you, or from his feelings about you?' I pressed this point with something of a policeman's dullness and scepticism.

'I don't know,' said Patrick crossly. And then, 'I don't see how I can be in charge of him. He's done this before.'

'Yes, I know. But that was only for a night.'

'Who told you that? He was away for about three days before the police found him.'

I'd no idea. I said, 'Thousands of young people do leave home, and nobody knows why.' The bewildered parents were filmed in their well-appointed homes, numbly repeating how happy everything had been. They always seemed to me to offer proof of the stark unknowability of others, of a lurking violence, touched off by some invisible pressure into damage

400

and self-destruction; it was what love sought to tame, and lived in half-excited fear of.

'I just wondered', said Patrick, 'what happened that night, after we left you in the bar.' I saw how subtly and yet un-forgivingly he had brought the little interview round.

'Well, nothing much that I can remember,' I said, almost lan-guidly. 'Luc did say how unhappy he was, but never quite told me why. We chatted with other friends of mine.' I remembered the little stings of his pillow-talk – the bet the three youngsters had had about me, Sibylle's jealous intuition of my feelings. And yet she had left me with him. But then Luc himself had deplored the strained talk of that evening – the eerie politesse that masked the break-up of the Three, and acknowledged it. I went on carefully: 'I said Luc must get home to bed, as we had a lesson first thing in the morning.'

'Yeah, yeah,' Patrick broke in.

I wondered what he knew. I found I was longing for his confi-dence: I wanted to step in and take the place of the absent friends, soothe the unacknowledged bereavements of his awk-ward time of life. I thought how pained and creepy I might seem to him – both predatory and vicarious. 'I wish I could have helped him more,' I said.

But he was reasonable: 'You did what you could. You've been all around the place on that merry goose hunt!' He slapped the table to mark his pleasure in knowing this imaginary idiom, and frowned in slightly forced exasperation. 'He's a bloody nuisance!' he said, and ran on quickly, 'Do you think he might be dead?'

I hushed the idea away, and as I did so saw Orst's simple panel of the beach and the sea and the dusk sky.

21

I waited for Paul in the portraits room. The women and children there were strangers to me still, waiting themselves, it seemed, pink-cheeked from the outside world, in the vestibule of the dark laboratory. I had hardly been to see them since that first half-conscious visit, stumbling from the early shock of Luc. They were the beginning of the tour, spirits of the happy region the painter had left behind. They looked out, from their background of indecipherable old tapestry, like figures from a sunlit ante-bellum, suspecting nothing. The children especially, girl-cousins and long-legged boys, were stirring and faunal, for all their blue-ribboned hats and courtly knee-breeches. Orst captured their restlessness, the brevity of the repose he had exacted from them, penned in a deep corner of the sofa, or in a fur-edged coat and hat as if just returned from a winter walk alive with new knowledge, hands behind back pressing the door to, the attention barely held. He discovered the girl in his mother, also, though the swept-back hair was grey, the skin silvery-soft above the high white collar. Her eyes were cast down Memling-like on an open book, her cheek flushed as if by a first compliment.

Paul came in with his briefcase and trilby. We were going up to Brussels together, where we would see an Orst sculpture that was due to be auctioned, and I would go on to a chat with Martin Altidore that filled me with apprehension laced with furtive eagerness. Paul handed me the catalogue with the place marked, and I looked at the photo of the naked plaster torso, disingenuously called 'Printemps', and the high-class patter beneath, 'une de ses très rares œuvres plastiques'. I went out to the car wondering if I could possibly have converted the estimate rightly.

For a minute or so I found something inexplicably comic in

the sight of Paul at the wheel of his desirable little Alfa Giulietta
– upright and circumspect, as though he still remembered his
lessons. I'm afraid it communicated itself in some way and
sharpened his edginess. I did what I could, admired the car,
then talked blandly about the town in the winter morning light
– though once we were free of the outskirts I saw how little I
missed it, what a ghost city it was, now Luc had gone. I felt a
dread of living on there without him, the pointless months, the
paralysis of ingrown failure.

'No news of the Altidore boy?' said Paul, out of some subtle
and forgiving sympathy.

I turned my head and watched the slow wheeling-past of the
farmlands, each shed and bungalow and leafless poplar bald
and staring with his absence. 'Nothing at all.'

I was aware of Paul watching me for a moment. 'You're very
in love with him, aren't you?'

Poplars, a windmill, a level-crossing. 'Yes – yes, I am.'

A slowing, waiting, then overtaking. 'I'm so sorry – sorry,
that is, that you must be going through hell.'

Paul was unembarrassed by my crying, or sensed the gleam of
relief through its drizzle, the snivelling smile that welcomed
comfort. 'It must have been . . . obvious!'

'Oh, not at all. Or hardly. I think in retrospect perhaps I
wondered, or had little glimpses that I failed to make anything
of at the time.'

'Quite often I thought you'd seen.'

'It was Lilli who told me. You know, you left some of the
boy's clothes mixed up with your wash. It was only then I
realised that you were having an affair.'

'Ah . . .'

'Don't worry, she won't tell anyone. I assume it is a secret.'

'Um – I don't think his mother would be very pleased.'

'One can imagine the effect on her needlework,' said Paul
quietly, not sure if a joke was allowed. I gave a grateful low guf-
faw.

We drove on in silence, an expectant silence, whilst I
wondered if I dared say more. I fingered the catch of the glove-
box abstractedly.

'Rodney told me he'd seen you together in a bar,' said Paul,

403

so that I thought he had just been softening me up before the serious trouble could begin.

'I was very rude to him. I suppose he's been what he'd call researching me, has he? He probably thinks I've bumped Luc off. I'm sorry, but he's a nightmare – Rodney.'

'I suppose he's not perhaps very . . .' mumbled Paul, trying to adjust to what was clearly an unexpected view of his new employee. 'Anyway, that isn't the point – he just appeared very concerned about the boy's whereabouts. He was asking Marcel all about your expedition.'

I thought, I'm too upset already to have to think about Rodney Young. 'I can't explain,' I snapped. 'He's just my *bête noire*.' Paul made a 'Sorry I mentioned it' face, and went on at once:

'I'm not criticising you, my dear Edward. I don't know if what you've done is right or not. Some would say that you are in a position of trust in the Altidore household, as you are in ours, and that such a trust hardly envisages your starting an affair with your pupil.'

I muttered my fatalistic tag, 'It happens, it happens.' It would have been too feebly extenuating, too woundingly true, to have said that it was the boy who had seduced me.

'Of course it happens. I know it happens. Really what I want to say is that it does not alter or diminish my trust in you at all.' The curiously formal language with which Paul entered this new phase of candour.

'Thank you.' I glanced at him and saw that he was stiff with nerves; I began some further socially graceful acknowledgement, but he cut across it with the already prepared continuation of his speech, perhaps with a tiny stutter of delay –

'No, it's all quite fascinating to me. May I – there's something I'd rather like to tell you.'

We were nearing another small city, large signs gathered to explain the inescapable choices we had to make. I gazed out across fields, depots, the sun-reflecting car-parks of factories, to the cluster of gothic towers like a bungled version of our own. I felt a certain reluctance to listen to Paul. My mind was running on ahead to the meeting with Martin, which I imagined would

404

test me a good deal more thoroughly than this one with Paul. I thought Paul could be using this hour to rehearse me, as if for a viva after a wobbly exam. I didn't want the journey to be over too soon, but at the same time I fidgeted to be out of the car. I suspected what he was going to say would be one of those admissions the teller considers to be 'oddly similar' to your own and which, offered as proof of sympathy, serve only to rob your predicament of its force and singularity.

As if I hadn't heard him, I said, 'I'm terribly worried about seeing Martin Altidore.'

I felt him flinch from my rebuff – for a second I recalled the atmosphere of scenes in the car, the two parties strapped in their positions, glaring forwards. But when he spoke it was in a tone of negotiation: 'I can see it's difficult'; and after a moment he reached out and patted me on the arm just as I moved it. 'Are you thinking of coming clean?'

'No. Not unless it's clear that he knows – if Luc's said something, or . . . I don't think anybody need know apart from me and him – and you. To be honest, I'm pretty certain his running off has nothing to do with him and me being . . .' (I couldn't quite pronounce Paul's happy version of events). 'It's to do with other things. I don't want to muddy the water by appearing to incriminate myself.'

'Altidore could hardly object,' said Paul, 'after everything he's done. You know, the poor mother must be sick of being run away from. But I think you're quite right. You're being truthful to yourself, and that needn't call for exhaustive or unnecessary truthfulness to others.' There was a long pause in which I ran mistrustfully over this welcome advice. 'I've never told anyone about my first affair, because it would have caused distress and served no purpose – it would have been . . gratuitously honest.' His discomfort was palpable, his determination dried his mouth and gave an odd new depth to his voice. I was being callous: he had planned to be listened to; but even so I wanted to let him off the hook, spare him these abrupt breaths and incessant mirror-checkings. Perhaps he could tell me about it on a later day, when we weren't so busy, weren't riding steadily above the speed-limit. 'I do think that, don't you? One mustn't mistake brutality for honesty, as so many young people do nowadays, or impertinence for wit, incidentally! Oh, in my case it was a summer's passion, when I was seventeen too, as it happens – with an older man.' So there he went with the oddly similar – and brought out lightly after nearly half a century, in a tone not practised but certainly rehearsed, it caught my sympathy. I could see what it had cost him, though not yet why.

If I still failed to encourage him it was because I didn't want to seem crudely eager for the details – I didn't quite know in what terms to express an interest. I assumed an indefinably sham expression of sober receptiveness. 'Tell me about it if you're sure you want to,' I said. He nodded irritably, but then waited, as though struck unexpectedly by the margin of doubt my words allowed for. Or perhaps the rehearsed words had died on him, or turned into nonsense with time. My head was a little on one side, I was focusing on his predicament, which seemed to grow and become more inexpressible as a full minute passed, and then another. The tension became rather sickly and embarrassing then, and I couldn't look at him. I found myself shifting and gazing out of the side-window while my own briefly arrested spools of anxiety and regret started up again. I made some trivial remark, but he didn't reply, only held up his hand in that gesture of his that called for patience and consideration. We raced on for maybe a quarter of an hour, switching rather madly from lane to lane, Paul hunched forward as if the road demanded all his attention. I thought, if he's waited fifty years, what's fifteen minutes? But Brussels was already beginning to rise around us and inflict its own further squeeze of anxiety.

Paul said, 'Do you know where I mean by the Hermitage?'

'Yes, I do,' I said, with a relieved smile that he turned for a second to see, and thought perhaps was satirical.

'Oh, I daresay it's very routine to you. I believe it's very busy, what's the word, very *cruisy* these days.'

'It's not part of my routine. I've been there once and got completely lost and freezing cold and had . . .' – well, I mustn't mistake brutality for honesty. 'I had a hopeless time. I've sometimes thought of going back in the daylight, just to look at the trees, but I've never quite got round to it.'

'It is a lovely park. There's only a fragment of the Hermitage itself left, very badly restored' – his confidence quickened with that professional phrase – 'but fine avenues and a canal, and the remains of a round garden with a basin that is fed by a natural spring, and alcoves of yew – it's like a three-dimensional Fragonard.'

'Yes, I think I saw all of that on my, probably rather drunken, peregrinations.'

'I just heard someone mention it at school,' said Paul, with a swift compression of time that it took me a moment to catch up with. 'I pretended to take no notice, but like a lot of the boys I was fairly preoccupied with all that. This boy said that someone in the town, a shopkeeper who was very obliging to the Germans, was always going there in the evening. He went on with quite a detailed account, until he started to get funny looks – you know, it seemed he knew too much.' He gave me a quick smile that was all at odds with the expression of his eyes. 'Anyway, the idea took hold with me. I became somewhat obsessed with the Hermitage, though I knew I would never dare ask about it directly; I used to provoke other people into mentioning it, and then make a great thing about how I'd never want to go *there*. Which, of course, is what I finally did, one Saturday evening in early May of 1944; and not before establishing elaborate alibis to Maurice and Lilli and stuffing my head with excuses in case I should meet anyone I knew. As I told you before, we all found we were quite brave in the war, but I had only been brave up to then in obvious common causes – never for myself. I was almost running up to complete strangers to explain what I was pretending to be doing.'

I laughed and thought of running out late to Dawn, under the wood's edge; I felt a certain delicacy, as if the tables were turned, and held back from contributing my own oddly similar anecdotes in support of what he said. I thought I'd quite like to see photographs of him at that age. There was something of the same self-conscious bravery in him now.

'Well, I won't spin it out, but I crept round, and the trees were all coming into leaf – you couldn't see far through the wood, and I couldn't in fact see anybody at all. I wondered what I would do if I did meet someone, and exactly how it was that whatever they did was done. If ever I go back there – oh, with Lilli and Marcel, on a Sunday morning! – I hear the wind in the trees and that reminds me in an instant of what it was like, alone, entering an empty avenue. The light was beginning to go, and so, I thought, must I; I knew that after dark was more likely to be the time, but I started to think none the less that my inadvertent school informant was wrong about the place. Then I saw a man stride across the glade straight in front of me – a young man, I would think now, probably about twenty-five, but old to a boy of course.' I sighed resentfully, and remembered my own provoking faux-pas about Paul's age, out at St Vaast. 'He caught sight of me and without slowing up called out a greeting, and went on into the trees.

'I wasn't sure quite what had happened. I stood there for some time weighing up things like what time it was against the obvious fact that he appealed to me, even if he wasn't my absolute ideal; which in turn was balanced by the likelihood that he was only out for a walk – a workman from town perhaps. But in *that* case there could certainly be no harm in following him.

'So I did take the path under the trees, and there, just a few paces on, the man had stopped – he was half-hidden by a great beech-trunk he was leaning behind. And so – one thing happened; and then another thing . . .'

I felt slightly cheated by this brisk curtailment, as though the dusk and the foliage hid these happenings from me – but perhaps glad, too, that Paul hadn't forced himself to say. I merely hummed approval.

'Well, they were the first shocks of sexual reality for me – a man's large hands, a man's rough chin and cheeks, as well as all the rest. I was not a little confused, my dear Edward, and terribly aware of doing wrong. But I found I was excited by the risk. And then afterwards what inflamed me, as much as the guy's big prick and everything, was his gentleness, like being cradled and protected by some great giant. I'm sure in memory I've exaggerated that difference – I must have been fully grown myself; but Willem was a big man. I'm sure there was that class thing, too, which you're supposed to have so much worse than us – the place and the event conspired to make me think of him as a, what's the word, a woodlander.'

I felt it flourish, from deep nostalgic roots, and cast a

dappled shadow across glass and concrete, slow-moving Africans outside discount stores, scaffolders high up. The whole recollection was beautiful, affirmative – it was hard to see why Paul had left it lying so long in the briars and the loam. 'So you saw him again.'

'I probably would have wanted to, because of course I was a young romantic and to me ten minutes with a handsome stranger was clearly the same as true love, and besides it had the romantic complexities of danger, and sin, as I suppose I thought of it then. I can see now that it also conformed to the sense one had in those years that everything important was secret, and so anything secret must surely be important.'

'It wasn't a game.'

'Actually, it was he who asked to see me again. I didn't realise at the time, because to me *he* was marvellous, but he must have thought himself pretty lucky to get a fresh and well, quite nice-looking seventeen-year-old, don't you think? Anyway, it seemed that we had fallen in love.' I was silent, rather shaken. Paul went on quickly, 'This probably sounds foolish to you – all I can say is it was wildly unusual then.'

'Not at all,' I said warmly, to allay the recurrent note of un-certainty, as though he felt he couldn't measure up to some fast and cynical standard he imagined me to hold. I couldn't say without condescension how touched I was by his doubting, pedantic candour.

We mounted the pavement and swung into the low mouth of a buried car-park. At each turn of the hairpin descent the Alfa's tyres squealed. It wasn't until the fourth or fifth level that spaces showed – Paul backed into a bay and stilled the engine and we sat looking out into the shadowy coffered perspective, shuttered concrete, stripes of yellow light, the weight of silent floors above.

'Well, we kept seeing each other, Willem and I. I managed it because I had to. Often I used my visits to poor old Edgard Orst as a cover – I went to him for ten minutes in the afternoon and left the old fellow babbling and confused to cycle out to the Hermitage. We didn't think we dared meet elsewhere – in fact it was the perfect place. He came from a village a mile or two out, and lived with his old father. I outwitted everybody, at the same

409

time being barely able to believe they couldn't tell something was up. It went on for a couple of months – of heaven and madness. We didn't at first, but later we did . . . everything with each other. Our meetings themselves were always terribly brief – I think we can hardly have talked.'

I realised I was flinching with envy from Paul's account. I thought of my own two months of paralysed trepidation with Luc, nothing in them beyond talk, and the pointless wondering, now, if I should have moved at once, leaned very early on into his milky coffee breath . . .

'Then one day I was walking to school with Maurice. We were crossing the Grote Markt, making our usual jokes about the soldiers – just to ourselves; there was a group of them quite near, the local militia, and I knew already, just because I loved him and would have known the shape of him among a hundred strangers, that one of them was Willem. He had his back to me, he was talking with his fellows, smoking – how stupid they were, Maurice and I agreed, and how little time they had left, now that the Allies had landed in France and would be here within weeks. We had an image of huge, blond, actually rather Aryan-looking Americans sweeping into town on tanks, mowing down the Fascists at the same time as they gathered us up to ride with them above the crowd. That was my image, anyway. I think I rather hoped for a, well, a special relationship with one of the Liberators. And now I was plunged into confusion – I don't know, my guilt was suddenly ten times deeper, it was proved, it was in uniform; but at the same time there was a defiant thrill, as if I was a kind of double agent myself; and then there was the thought that this great big *boy* really, who was moved by strong passions of his own and was rather daring, a bit of an original, was about to be swept away by the good Americans and Canadians – I wanted to hold their advance back, perhaps the Germans would rally. Then a moment later I knew again that I was hopelessly wrong.'

Paul's knuckles were white on the wheel, he was staring narrowly forwards like someone driving too fast through fog, weighing urgency against prudence. 'Did he see you then?'

'I didn't think he had. I was completely distracted that day; and I couldn't sleep at all that night. Whenever I hear the phrase

410

"a sleepless night" it is that one that comes back to me, which lasted for ever, though it was a short summer night, with Maurice across the room, who was in far greater danger than me, sleeping peacefully. I went through every possibility and in the end I decided I would have to give Willem up. But I decided that I had to try one desperate measure, and ask him to renounce the Fascists before it was too late. I thought maybe I could save his life. I spent many hours running through the words I would say and bringing all the arguments of love to bear. My wildest plan was to persuade him to become an informer, I thought I could introduce him to my father, with his contacts in the underground, although I knew that would be to risk the lives of hundreds of other people. I felt the most dreadful weight on my heart, that I had to make such decisions and know such things when I was so young. I suppose the truth was I had to grow up over night, and I rightly doubted whether I was able to.

'The next evening I cycled out to the Hermitage, but he didn't come. I waited at our usual place till it was almost dark – I remember there were noises of other people moving about, I was afraid I would be found.' Paul spread his fingers as if to conjure up the woodland maze in front of us, with all its blind options. 'I was acting with a strong, if very romantic, sense of honour. My mind then, as I've said, was full of chivalrous imaginings, though now they carried a darker burden.

'I think it must have been a couple of days later that I went round to see Orst in the afternoon, after school. All I really recall of it is a scene of curtained gloom, rather as if he'd disappeared into one of his own prints, if you can imagine – so little light that the colour was closed out of things. The old housekeeper said he was much worse, the doctor who came to him secretly had warned them he probably didn't have long. I wasn't sure why they'd plunged him into semi-darkness, since the light meant nothing to him. I suppose it was a symbolic or superstitious gesture. It was frightening in a way, but I think I was too preoccupied with my other fears to care, and anyway prided myself on the secret access I had to him and on my good-heartedness in coming at all. Nothing he said made sense, except perhaps a suggestion that I was beginning to neglect him,

411

which I tried to brush away as just another of his paranoid delusions. He was full of plans around then for a holiday at the seaside – I think they were mainly what he talked about, what's the phrase, "among the deepening shades".

'When I came out of the house Willem and another soldier were standing just across the street. I was an accomplished pretender by then, but I know I jumped guiltily, or looked astonished enough for the other soldier to call me over. He made me show my papers, asked me whose house I had just come from, and what I was doing. I said I'd been visiting the old cook and housekeeper, whom I helped with various things. We looked back at that very big house, and I was glad of the curtains and shuttered upper windows. I didn't dare catch Willem's eye, whilst he said that the house had already been searched, and that the degenerates had fled, and that it was in the care of a couple who came of good Flemish stock – which seemed a lot for him to know about it. The mass deportations of the Jews were going on all that summer – by then they thought they'd pretty well got them all, so I suppose they attached more glory to finding any who were left; in fact there were thousands hidden, but they were getting nervous about ... the end. I got on my bicycle, and as I moved away Willem called out "A nice evening for a ride", and then I looked back and saw him smiling, and the other fellow frowning suspiciously still.

'So I took that as a sign and went out later to our meeting-place. He was there waiting, but in uniform. "You know now," he said, and looked rather ashamed as I undid the jacket and took it off him, horrible brown stuff. I thought I couldn't do anything with him, but then I found I could, just as usual. After we had ... made love, he tried to make me put his jacket on, he wanted me to be a little soldier, he said. I did put on the jacket and sat there in the undergrowth with the prickly cloth against my skin and talked and talked to him. I remember the surprise and novelty of that for us both. But not what I said. The truth is I went through it so many thousands of times afterwards, slowly pressing it into a new and less accusing shape, rather as a carpenter or boatmaker steams and twists the wood into the curve he needs. I won't pretend now to know what reasoning I

412

used or what evidence I produced. I know most of what I remember is what I made up later, to my own advantage.'

'Well, you were only trying to help.' I felt my nerves about Luc's father focusing on Paul's predicament – I was trying to justify myself as well with this bland remark.

'The next morning I woke up knowing I had done something terrible. I slipped out very early and cycled round to Orst's place as fast as possible: I had to warn them that the house was being watched. When I turned the corner – into *our* street – I saw a van parked, a group of people outside the front door, soldiers, a tall Gestapo officer who was well known in the town, the *Gruppenleiter*, as well as various neighbours. It was most imprudent of me, but I couldn't keep back – I should have turned away at once, my father had drummed into me how I must never involve myself unnecessarily. I came up to the edge of the group, and just then the dear old couple were brought out and pushed into the van. They didn't see me, but the image of their silent terror makes me ache to this day. There was a long pause, a stoical illusionless pause on the part of the neighbours; though they were curious too, there was a miserable sense of occasion, that something so hidden was about to be brought to light. When Orst came out, they all crossed themselves, Willem was pushing him in his wheelchair, though he was dead, and bounced and lolled as the wheels went over the cobbles. His face was bloodless and his eyes wide open: he seemed to stare angrily, his mouth was open in a sneer. There was a smell, and the women lifted their aprons to their faces. It was grotesque, but the faith of the bystanders was equal to the challenge – it was quietly stated among them who he was, tears were shed, prayers were muttered, the spectacle was taken in without flinching.

'Then the soldiers hoisted the body, the painter, up into the van in his chair, and he stayed for a moment, before the doors were slammed, as if he was sitting in judgement, it was pointless my hiding in the crowd, he could see me now though he never had before. I was in that mad shocked state when your head is full of rhetorical voices: he seemed to be bitterly asking me, as he always used to, what it was I had seen in the street, what colour the clouds were now. Then he was gone – they were all gone. Later the bodies of the servants could be claimed for burial. Orst as you know has no tomb.'

No tomb. How often I had failed to register the negative evidence, the white canvas, the invisible wingbeat that flutters the page. 'But what had happened?'

'That, my dearest Edward, I do not know.' And he glanced at me keenly for a second, as though I might at last be able to tell him. 'Willem must have known. I watched him standing by the van, and I remember thinking how well I knew him, physically. I saw through his dreadful uniform. I knew just how his shoulders moved, and how the hairs grew on his chest and at the bottom of his back, and between his legs. I knew where his appendix scar was, and the rings of his vaccination on the upper arm. I knew what he could do with those big limbs in his other life, his love life. In spite of disaster all that still seemed a triumph. You'll think I'm mad. He could have walked over then and arrested me; he saw me weeping in the crowd and maybe didn't know it was not for Orst but for him. He gave me a look, but he didn't betray me.'

'But he already had betrayed you!'

'Well, I don't think he betrayed me to anything like the same degree as I betrayed Edgard Orst, and the blameless people who protected him.'

'And you can't be sure you were responsible – the house was being watched, you don't know how he died . . .'

'But how does one know what one is responsible for? It seems to me a youngster cannot know. He picks up an older person's life and then – he is distracted, self-absorbed, over-zealous, or perhaps quite unreflecting, he's no idea what he's doing – lets it drop.'

For all the humiliations Paul was owning up to, I felt again his subtle grasp on life, the quick intelligence that was impotent against his own problems, which it could only watch and bemoan. And then the confession itself was so hopelessly belated, kept back, by some begrudging mechanism, until the secret it enshrined had spread and shadowed his existence almost to the end. I felt properly sorry for him, but was aware too that the long perspective of his revelations made him faintly unattractive to me. I sighed and shook my head and wondered if there was some way in which I could politely dissociate our two predicaments. 'Now let's go and see this sculpture of his,' he said.

We waited in silence for the lift to rattle down. I knew I was failing to make the capable response, and sensed his disconcertment – it was tinged with a panic that he overrode with a fresh avowal: 'I can't quite explain how it is that you've helped me so much with all this, but you have – oh, you've helped in a dozen ways with the proofs and your patient work, but that's not quite it.' He hesitated. 'I've sometimes felt like protracting the catalogue even longer, just to keep you busy and looking after me, to keep us looking after each other.' There was a ping! and the doors slid open on to an aroma of cigar-smoke, like the still fresh trace of a wanted man. We stood inside, the doors closed, and after a second or two of ascent Paul kissed me on the cheek and flung his arms around me, banging his briefcase against the small of my back. I stared over his shoulder at my reflection in the lift's steely wall.

I found 'Printemps' quite sinister, a little smaller than life-size, with a steady grey eye and a torrent of red hair. The right breast was shiny and worn, as if often rubbed, like the burnished toe of a saint, by day-dreaming devotees. The figure ended at the knee and stood on a dulled and chipped gilt plinth. It gave a troubling sense of merely suspended animation, as though waiting to catch the viewer off-guard. I felt there should be a slot in the base for a coin that would set the head nodding, the eyes rolling, the lower lip and chin dropping and snapping shut; perhaps it would utter a slow, repeating laugh; then it would freeze again, just as it was, with the mockery and promise of its stare and its smile.

22

It was party time again for the Spanish girls: their voices cut like buzz-saws through the background of guitar-music and chatter. Christmas, of course. And what a lot of friends they had. I looked down into the utter stillness of the back garden, the bare trees, the canal, the rotted water-door of the darkened school. It was only three but the light was going, I couldn't quite find the little statue under the apple-boughs: it pleased me that I'd never been down there and didn't know what it was. Relentless flamenco chords, and the proud rapping on the box of the guitar taken up, stamped out hilariously on the bare floor and sending its tremor through the ancient joists. I felt neglected but at the same time sniffily anti-social, as I sometimes had in childhood, when Charlie's parties had no role for me. I pictured the goings-on like the fake head-tossings and eye-flashings of a sixties 'Latin American Fiesta' LP sleeve.

There was a knock at the door.

This was something so unusual that it seemed to bring my whole life before my mind's eye. What I dreaded was Cherif's return, some maudlin rapprochement or pretence that nothing serious had gone wrong. Or it could be poor troubled Paul, I supposed, in search of the solace I alone seemed able to offer him. But what if Luc was standing there, fluffily unshaven, greasy-haired, hungry . . .? I crossed the room assuring myself it was only Marcel, who had got the time of a lesson wrong, or forgotten it was the holidays.

Outside, in a vision of unbruised youth and beauty, were Alejo and Agustino. So I had been forgiven? The former, in one of his bright silk waistcoats, like a wicked prefect, kissed me on both cheeks, while his cousin extended a hand stiffly, but with a slight smile: he gave the impression of having been coaxed round and of relying entirely on Alejo as a chaperon. Still, I felt in some way blessed by them, ridiculously moved to find myself in their thoughts.

'Agustino wants to ask you something,' said Alejo. I shrugged and spread my hands to say 'Anything, anything.'

'Both my sisters say, would you like to come to their party.'

'And . . .' prompted Alejo.

'And I invite you too.'

'And so do I.'

'Oh . . . it's terribly sweet of you.'

'It is for Christmas, and also for my sister's, um, onomastic . . . holiday,' said Agustino, glad of this further rationale for their gesture.

'I'm very touched, please thank your sisters, it would have been wonderful to meet them at last, but the truth is I'm tied up with something here.' I was aware of their both looking curiously past me into the grim fug of the room. 'And then any moment I have to go out to meet a friend on the other side of town. But thank you, thank you, my friends.' For a minute I was Scrooge playing Mr Brownlow. 'I hope *you'll* have a very happy time.' I caught on Agustino's incomparable face the glow of a double satisfaction.

I couldn't have borne the party, simple social sweetness was beyond me these days; yet by the time I skulked out through the yard, aware I was noticed from my neighbours' window, a hunched figure in the dusk, I had begun to feel humiliated by their offer, like some difficult old widower invited to share the family turkey. I saw I was shy, too, of dancing with unknown girls.

After the tinny carols in the streets, the automated mania of the shoppers, the limbo of Christmas, garish but dank, it was like reaching home to push open the heavy door of the bar, to hear the spring sweep it shut behind me, to move again in the slowed rotations of this other limbo, in its deep-sea gloom of copper and green.

I was at the bar, settling and ordering, relishing the management's sullen refusal of all festive crap, before I heard a toot of recorders, like a pert echo of long-ago end-of-term concerts. I turned, and there in the corner was a group of hairy mutants, bodies in jeans and sloppy jerseys topped with heads of crumpled felt and black bristle, with holes for eyes, as if a finger had punched through bone. One, with an ambiguous long jaw and flopping ears, gave me a wave, that was followed by muffled giggles from the rest. I nodded back, hoping that would be it. A certain silly terror of masks.

Of course I knew it was Gerard, I knew his wide hips as he came over, and the blond fuzz on the back of his hands. 'I'd forgotten you were a donkey,' I said.

If there was sarcasm in his look it was entirely absorbed by his grotesque proboscis. 'I'm a hare.' He had two mouths: his real mouth and chin were left uncovered beneath the contraption, so that he could play, whereas the mouths of the bear and the monkey more troublingly coincided.

'So when's your concert?'

'It's tonight – aren't you coming? In the old Council Chamber.'

'Of course, I'd love to. Can you still get tickets?'

'Totally sold out.' I winced regretfully. 'But I can probably get you in. Come early' – and he started on an account of how and where. It was obviously Kindness To Me day. I thought back, to rid myself of all this, to when we'd first met, just here – how I wanted to kiss him, how he dodged me but stayed with me, warm and breathy and avoiding. I thought he couldn't kiss anyone as he was.

There was a ghastly moment as the others crowded round, like clumsy chimeras, their own embarrassments hidden under fur and whisker. The bear with the recorder, playing the thing he would normally be goaded to dance to, gave a few further tootlings. I stared them out with an unconvincing grin. Then they shambled away, plucking their heads off like fencers and showing their flushed young faces beneath. The door shut behind them and I turned with an apologetic grimace to the barman, dear little Ivo, who had helped me at moments before, who kept his ears and eyes open – there was a horrifying noise from outside, a cracked re-echoing whoop, and another, and then another. It was like the never-before-heard siren of a sinking ship. Gerard had let loose with his bombard at last.

Ivo made a camp gesture of alarm, and clutched his tea-towel to his heart. A moment later, 'I'm glad they've gone. They got on my nerves!'

'Mine too.' He paused by me, and stared at the counter, as if trying to pick up the thread of an interrupted conversation, then shook his head.

'Staying in town for Christmas?'

'I'm going back home in a couple of days.'

'Back to London, yeah?'

'Well, a bit south of London.'

'Lucky you!' He unbuttoned his shirt-pocket and took out a packet of Marlboro. 'Want one?'

'Thanks a lot.' I offered a light.

'Thanks. No, everyone seems to get out of here as quick as they can. Not that I blame them.'

I didn't know what I thought about that. The place irked me, made me ache with the absence of Luc, each street mocked me, but I dreaded leaving, just for a few days, when he might need me, or might feel the seasonal tug home. 'I was hoping Matt might be here.'

Ivo glanced at the clock. 'It's a bit early for Matt. Or whatever he's called.'

'I suppose you're right.'

'Anyway, he's probably busy.'

I smiled and blew out smoke. I wondered how much he knew about my friend. 'Could well be.' And indeed it was early for anybody: only the solstitial nightfall gave the hour the aura of drinks-time.

'Being *kept* busy, from what I gather.' I didn't quite see this. 'Is he still seeing that boy?'

I thought about it for a moment and a swallow of beer. 'I don't *think* so. Which one do you mean?' I couldn't honestly say I knew or was jealous.

Ivo assumed his scandalous 'discreet' manner. 'I don't know his name, dear. I just watched him pick him up in here one night. Then the next night he was telling me all about it when the kid comes in again. Couldn't get enough, Matt said.' He glanced both ways along the bar. 'He had him *seven times* – and that was just the first night. I was moderately jealous. Not that he was my type – you know, tall, tall schoolboy, blond,

419

mouth like a sponge. Still – only seventeen . . . It must be nice to get something really fresh.'

My hand was still steady, my heart flinty. 'When would this have been?'

'Ooh . . .' he searched with no sense that it mattered: 'Three or four weeks ago? One thing about Matt, he always gets what he wants. Though even he looked a *bit* shagged out. Then the kid kept kissing him, and Matt was groping him between the legs – white jeans, you know – I'm saying I didn't fancy him but come to think of it he was completely gorgeous. I just prefer dark men,' he said, with a bat of the eyelids, and slid off to answer another customer.

I was still perplexingly calm, though I pulled on the cigarette fiercely, and stared at the threadbare pommel of the bar-stool next to me, where he had sat so untouchably that evening. It was the arch ingenuousness of his remark 'That guy Matt must be gay' that came to me first; and then Matt's obscene and encouraging gesture behind the boy's back. I finished my drink quickly but thoughtfully and I was almost at the door when it flung open with consummate timing to admit the busy world of Ronald Strong. I thought for once I would speak to him, my mind was clear and fuelled, I stopped with an ironic glance – but he looked me up and down in an expressionless second and swept past. I went on out with a dull, half-audible 'Fuck you'.

As I walked across town I was shocked but composed, as one is at first after a death one knew was coming. The horrible fact had been with me, known to me all along – it was none the less plausible for having been imparted in a dream.

Out towards Matt's, those wide neglected streets, the houses shaken by lorries, the pavements and windows silted and blinded with dust. I was watching my own purposefulness curiously, wondering when it would falter. Matt cared about nothing, and so was oddly invulnerable – he was the great facilitator, he would say he was 'only getting the kid ready' for me, and perhaps that was true, perhaps he'd set him up to the whole thing. I pondered whether Matt could be involved in his disappearance – I couldn't see the point. I'd thought I was about to break with him for good, to limp away in the laughable shreds of my dignity, but maybe that was pointless too; he liked me but he wouldn't miss me, whereas I was snagged with a sentimental respect for the part he had played in my fiasco. I went on past the end of his road.

I was dawdling alongside parked cars that the street-lamps filled with shadow, though sometimes there was a box or a child's shoe cross-lit all night in the back of a shooting-brake. How sombre and secure those welled interiors looked, with only a pane of glass to keep everything else out. Of course I'd always wanted a car, but never a car that I could afford – I scorned the prospect of days in the drive, daubing at the rust on a Maxi or an 1100. I wanted a Jensen CV8, or a love-hunting Giulietta like Paul's. And here was the Fratry of St Caspianus, half-derelict, still sheltering some unimaginable obscurity of devotion. And then a sound you often heard at Matt's, the two-note blast of a juggernaut's horn, echoing from a narrow street like the Last Trump in an unknown Requiem.

The back of the house was dark, the jeep standing in the yard, loosely swathed in a nylon tarpaulin that rustled and lifted and sank in a stirring of breeze as if someone was there. I let myself in to the glass porch, which still held a dim vegetative smell from the withered azaleas and sprawling rubber-plants, and then into the flat, with its own bouquet of cologne-smothered squalor. So he'd brought Luc here. I lit a cigarette and hung around by the bed, disordering it further with a fastidious toe. For a second or more at a time I let myself imagine them. I seemed to have forgotten that I had slept here since, unknowing, hoping to forget.

The jeep was a raucous starter – and after that it took a while to figure out the lights and the dip-switch. Getting into reverse proved tricky too. But then I was out of the gate, sitting high up, ready for off, hearing in the growl of the exhaust a tremor of that first outing to the sea; I went jerkily round the block, getting used to being in control, quite hoping I'd pass Matt walking home, then relieved I hadn't. I came up to a red light behind a little Fiat with three lads across the back, two more in front, joking and rowdy, off to a good time; my beam stroked the clean backs of their necks. I revved forlornly, and one of them turned, took in the flashy chrome and zipped-up rally

421

lamps, and grinned — while the driver, scenting a challenge, revved as well, and when the light changed shot forward with a squeal. I let them go.

Out of town the night was windy and glossy, the lights of farms and isolated houses burned clear across the fields, or bare treetops dipped and splintered them. For a while the road followed the high embankment of the sea-canal, the water black and barely visible below. There was no shipping in it, only the archaic hulk of a dredger, its platform lit and deserted. I rested my free hand on the seat beside me, as if on the thigh of an invisible passenger. The jeep's hood gibbered at its fastenings.

Luc was waiting at Ostend, staring out to sea through salt-stippled glass. He looked hollow-cheeked, eyes narrowed in hurt and defiance; I felt he had been robbed of his beauty, and that I would hardly have singled him out from the other kids around him. He had become a victim, to be stared at and pitied, to provoke pity for his family and friends — and just at the moment when his future was clearing like hills in the first light, to be ready for him when he woke. I stood in front of him and repeated his name, though I knew he couldn't see me, or recall the night he had taken my life in his arms. He gazed past me, as if in a truer kinship with the shiftless sea. A few late walkers passed us, and saw me vigilant in my huge unhappy overcoat; they didn't know if it was the charts of tides and sunsets I was studying, or the named photos of the disappeared.